Monument Road

A novel by

Charlie Quimby

TORREY HOUSE PRESS, LLC

Salt Lake City • Torrey

This is a work of fiction set in a real place, which means the author has allowed the maps to be wrong on occasion, the characters were granted permission to turn up where they never did in life, and a girl in 1989 may read a poem from the 13th century no matter when it was translated.

First Torrey House Press Edition, November 2013
Copyright © 2013 by Charlie Quimby

"The breeze at dawn" is from *The Essential Rumi*, Copyright 1995 Coleman Barks. Used with permission.

Excerpts from the Hello song are used with permission: *Hello/ Getting Better at Getting Along*, Copyright 1988 Jack Hartmann, MA, BMI

Cover photo: Tim Mulcahy Photography
Author photo: Susan Cushman
Cover and book design by Jeff Fuller, Shelfish • Shelfish.weebly.com

Published by Torrey House Press, LLC
P.O. Box 750196
Torrey, Utah 84775 U.S.A.
www.torreyhouse.com

International Standard Book Number: 978-1-937226-25-1
Library of Congress Control Number: 2013952247

For Susan, my best and closest reader,
and for the readers of ghost maps everywhere.

Monument Road

The breeze at dawn has secrets to tell you.
Don't go back to sleep.

—*Rumi*

A Year of Days

INETTA MADE HIM PROMISE: a year to the day after she passed, he would carry her ashes to the cliff edge at Artists Point. "I want to be good and dry," she said. "Me and Jesus'll be watching, and I want to float for a while."

Leonard Self promised and left his wife to sort out the rest, since some in Shower of Blessings Holiness Temple held that cremation expressed insufficient belief in the Rapture. But her pastor said, "Inetta's passed all the Lord's tests, so I'm sure the Lord can handle hers."

The Lord's tests were the usual trials and tribulations dealt out in mysterious ways, and Inetta had been sorely tried. Cancer that had come on headlong and hungry seemed far too slow near the end and so did the year of days that followed. What was Leonard supposed to do with it? Regroup? Get a new wife? Find Jesus?

Well, that wasn't quite the way it worked out, was it?

He remembered, from the one science class he made it through, that bodies of different weights should fall at the same rate. That was the book science. He was certain that a flake of bone would descend at the same speed as a cinder, but neither, cast into the canyon winds, would fall as fast as a man.

For seventy-some years, he had stayed put here where the Rockies start to give up their grip at the alkaline shore of a sagebrush sea that spills all the way to Oregon. It wasn't like he felt deprived living in one place. In this country, he always said, where you think you are depends on where you look. Now, snaking down Monument Road, he passes through a thousand sheer feet of sandstone and granite where all of earth's time is laid open in vertical autopsy. At the bottom of the switchbacks he crosses the parched outlet of No Thoroughfare Canyon, a sandy tumble of shale, broken granite, basalt, mud rock—the ancient shrapnel of earth's upheavals. Mars overgrown with greasewood. Across the green sliver of valley, the Book Cliffs crumble and spill into dry runnels and drifts. When he worked on one of Donnie Barclay's road crews, he'd had to descend this twisting stretch five or six times a week, and the drive lost its fearful mystery. Monument Road became just one more delay for him and so many of his cash poor neighbors—floor hands, janitors and deliverymen still wanting to call themselves ranchers. But today, he takes it slow, tries to absorb the lesson. Explorers saw this desert as a place of quick passage, retreat or doom. Grand Junction's thin crust of town life was finally established by railroads, ditch lines and the readiness of water to follow industrious men. Now the city sprouts from the dust that turns to gumbo each spring, as if man could override the warning written here in sand and stone.

Rain falls in dark columns that stand miles apart like smoke rising from spring burns. In the sizzling air, these drops of virga will never reach his windshield; his wiper blades tend to dry up before they wear down. With the ground so parched and bare, men can't help but look skyward. It's no wonder, Inetta used to say, God chose the desert to reveal Himself.

Leonard still has the fifty in his wallet, left folded gum-wrapper style the way he received it months ago. He carries it absently like a ticket stub from a past event. The woman meant well with it, and he smiles at the memory of her attempt to wrap him in the arms of poetry. Not a chance. He is past all spending or saving and beyond verses from mystics. He has no desire for a last meal, no need for more gas in the truck, no inclination to mail a last payment to the bill collectors. They'll get theirs soon enough. He imagines some hiker at the bottom of the canyon going through his pockets and finding the fifty. He considers the glum vagrants with the HOMELESS ANYTHING HELPS GOD BLESS signs and wonders if it really would.

Inetta's sketchbook is on the seat, sealed and addressed to her brother, Elliott, the one person on earth sure to appreciate it. Inetta is there, too, in the squat ceramic container she'd picked out herself. A Smith & Wesson .32 police revolver rides in the glove box. He brought it just in case. In case of what? He should have left it behind, but last week's dry run at Artists Point shook him a little. He doesn't need any doubts today. He wants to be clear and true in the long last moment.

Stitches has her head out the window, clabbers of drool swinging from her flews, a plastic bucket of kibble rolling around in the truck bed. When he asked Winnie Bonniver if she would take the dog for a spell, Winnie'd acted a little flustered, cordial and put out all at the same time. Their relationship had always been off kilter, with Winnie always trying to do things for him after Inetta died, and him wanting to be left alone. Winnie's house would have to be the last stop.

Vaughn Hobart's place is near the river, a short turn off Monument Road. Calling it a work in progress would overstate both terms. The front yard is sheathed in plastic with drip system lines laid across it, a litter of dog turds showing

3

how long the project has been suspended. Another sheet of the plastic is anchored on the roof with four bald tires likely salvaged from Vaughn's Mercury, which tilts on blocks in the back shed, a fabrication of corrugated metal, wooden pallets and other salvaged lumber. Vaughn's latest ride, a retired police Crown Vic, over-sprayed white, is nowhere around. The last time Leonard saw it, its dual spotlights dangled from broken mounts and swung on the wires when Vaughn came to a stop.

Stitches seems to be smelling Vaughn's dogs, so Leonard quick-steps to the back of the house, where he can leave the half bottle of Old Crow out of sight from the road. He could have poured it out instead of returning it, but he didn't want Vaughn to overlook the envelope containing his extra set of keys and a signed-over title to the truck.

The post office is next. The long line of patrons inside surprises him. Before he makes it to the counter, he listens to a man tracking down his VA check, two kids applying for passports so they can go on a mission trip, a Mexican wiring money and a woman buying a stack of Express Mail boxes.

"You still sell stamps here?"

Either the clerk doesn't get the joke or he's heard it too often. He picks up Inetta's wrapped sketchbook from the counter, places it on the scale and asks, "When do you want it to get there?"

"Just so it does."

The clerk peers through his glasses at a screen, then over them at Leonard. "Parcel Post, you're looking at another seven dollars and twelve cents to what you've got on there. Express Mail's more but the contents are automatically insured if the value is less than two hundred dollars. What would you say the value is?"

Leonard stares at the clerk. The question has no right

answer. Two pounds and a fraction on the scale, somewhere between worthless and beyond price. The clerk checks the line of customers over Leonard's shoulder. "And however you decide to send this, sir, it needs a return address."

Leonard picks up the package, turns and slides past the counter, through the doors and down the steps. He pauses beside the outdoor collection boxes and hugs the sketchbook once more before slipping it down the chute. Let them mark it insufficient postage. Elliott will note the postmark and pay whatever is due.

Backing out from the curb, he hears a sudden whumping on the side of the pickup. "Is that how you treat your dog, leaving it in a hot truck?" demands a fierce woman, her ponytail shaking behind her ball cap.

"Both windows was down. She's fine." Maybe she's new to town, where trucks have dogs as standard equipment.

"It's sweltering! I've called animal protection."

"'Preciate your concern, but my dog is none of your business."

"No one's entitled to endanger animals! What if you were in an accident? She'd be thrown out on the road! I'll be watching for you!"

He puts up his window and she gives his fender one last thump.

Where do these people come from that think they can just walk up and give strangers grief? Used to be you were left to your affairs. Now these newcomers want to call down the government on you if you don't cover your damn cough. He could have just put Stitches down or left her with Vaughn. Instead, he's endangering himself by taking the dog to Winnie Bonniver's house.

He checks the traffic over his shoulder. In the corner

of the mirror, a wild man glares back at him. Oily clumps of hair point from under his brim, like rainbow trout spilling from a full creel. As he'd emptied the house, he'd also pared his domestic routine. Among its many uses, a man's hat was an efficiency measure, he'd maintained to Inetta, saving on shampoo, combs and unnecessary trips to town. When he lost the argument to *You may not care, but I have to look at you*, Inetta would touch him up with a retired pair of sewing scissors, and when she threatened to fetch the rusty hand shears from the barn, he knew it was about time to seek professional help.

On those occasions he'd pay a visit to Dave Grantham, who would take the crown down short and shave the sides with a straight razor three inches above his ears. Inetta called it *the reverse tree line*. Leonard called it getting his money's worth.

It won't hurt to see Dave before he shows up at Winnie's, he thinks. Dave used to have a shop in the grand old La Court Hotel, where he cut hair for the town's merchants, the occasional traveling salesman and cowboys on the way to their weddings. In those days, a man cut a man's hair. But in the late 1960s, hotels, haircuts and walk-in traffic started to go downhill about the same time. A Holiday Inn opened out by the airport and the La Court closed the next year. Dave moved his pole, his chair and his elk head to North Avenue, but not everyone followed and he gradually spent more time in the chair than standing behind it.

A bell tinkles when the door opens, announcing the obvious to the barber sitting ten feet away.

"S'pose I could bring my dog in? Had a run-in with a pet Nazi and she might be on our trail."

Dave sets aside his book. "Come on in. I always wondered if I'd have the guts to hide someone from the Nazis."

Leonard likes a barber who's quick, who holds up his end of a conversation but doesn't push it. He also likes that Dave still wears a white smock, like a dentist, and pops the cape matador-fashion across the chair to signal that it's ready for him. Dave anoints Leonard's neck with talc before applying the tissue tape and then folds it carefully over the top of the drape to seal out any trimmings. He takes both arms of the chair and points Leonard at the mirror. "The same?"

Leonard watches himself nod, feels the twin discomforts of having his picture taken and seeing the result. His nose, slightly flattened across the bridge where a stallion got the better of a head butt. Left ear jugged, right ear in close. Strong cheekbones which, coupled with a lifetime of squinting in the mountain sun, make his slitted eyes seem cheery or skeptical, depending on what his tight-drawn mouth is doing. Wide paws on the armrests, skin blotched and dry rivered, knuckles like walnuts. His high forehead never got any higher, but over the years, his hair has grayed, coarsened and thinned out a crop circle only visible when Dave holds up the hand mirror in back. When the chair pivots around to face the waiting area, Leonard's relieved to be rid of the sight of himself.

Dave uses a spray bottle and comb to separate Leonard's compacted hair into cuttable strands. Inetta never would have allowed him to get to this state. He could hear her as she escalated her observations from *Maybe you should see a barber, hon,* to *You need a gosh darn haircut.* He does and he doesn't.

In the strip mall location, a narrow slot between a hearing aid store and an insurance agency, the artifacts from Dave's old shop seem like secondhand goods up for sale. The trio of chrome-trimmed chairs might once have seemed reserved for customers awaiting a space flight, but now as the wounded turquoise vinyl weeps cotton wool, they're revealed as remnants from a lost dinette set. The standing metal ashtray with the broad Saturn rim no longer accepts cigarettes and can only serve as a teetering end table. Framed photos of Little League teams portray boys who have long gone bald. The elk head, majestically mounted on the plastered, lobby-high wall at the hotel, merely calls attention to yellowed acoustic tiles and the fluorescent tubes buzzing inches above its rack.

Leonard thinks of all the goods he's loaded into the truck over these months and distributed surreptitiously—clothes to the Catholic Outreach, furniture to the Salvation Army, books and knick-knacks to the Goodwill. The horses, the tack and most of the equipment sold here and there. Tools quietly left behind at a neighbor's. When it came time to clear out the ranch, he still saw life in its residue of spare parts and disused objects. The only way to dispose of even the lowliest article was through a wholesale cleansing that first exhilarated him, then left him with the melancholy of release.

"You ever think of packin' it in?" Leonard asks.

"Where to?" Dave snips as he considers. "What would I do?" He hunts down invisible wisps. "I like to read military history." He finds one. "This barber chair's the best reading chair I own. Lighting's good." He lifts two strands between scissored fingers and compares. "No refrigerator here, so I don't eat too much or start drinking too early..." He cups his hand on Leonard's skull and trims the stray hair that sprouts between his fingers. "People come in, but not too many. Enough to pay the rent. Gives a shape to the day."

But the day had the same shape, like the shape of the haircut: the buzz of the clippers, the swick-swick-swick of the scissors, the slobber of the bristles in the shaving cup, the slap of the razor strop as the lather soaked in, and the faint skritch of the straight razor as it exposed the high ridge of pale, smooth scalp.

Dave completes a final etch around a mole and then circles Leonard back to give his approval.

"Okay," he says, but the barber isn't finished.

Dave points a small scissors tip into his ear and deftly snips away a nest of curled hair, then probes the folds for others. He works around each ear, inside and out. Next, the eyebrows, combing out runaway flares and cutting them flush one at a time. The nose. Snipping the nostrils clear. Tweezing away the hairs that had taken root on the tip.

"This took any longer, you could give away the haircut and charge me for the trim."

"I went on a cruise once where they had this Turkish barber," says Dave, who makes a hobby of getting his hair cut in new places. "He waved this flaming wick around my ears like he was shaking a maraca. Whoom-whoom-whoom. Couldn't feel a thing. Took off all the peach fuzz and the stubble. I suppose if I finished a trim like that, I could charge extra."

"You might even charge admission."

"Want to try it?" Dave asks.

"Not if I'm your first victim."

Dave laughs. "Somebody'll go for it one day, but... Shave?"

"Nope."

"You like to leave half a lip long?" Dave reaches for the magnifying hand mirror, but Leonard's fingers find the missed bristles. With his mirror sent off to Goodwill, he's been shaving by feel for a month. Dave whisks off Leonard's face and the back of his neck, shakes some Lilac Vegetal into his palms and rubs the newly exposed scalp. Then he unpins the tissue, taps Leonard on the shoulder and cracks the cape. "There you go."

Leonard stands up and empties his wallet. He wants to be out the door before Dave gets the fifty unfolded. He's almost made it when he hears the barber say, "Did you mean to give me this?"

"Keep the change—for not settin' me on fire."

"What about this writing on the back?" He holds up the bill scrawled with red ink. "*Don't go back to sleep?*"

"It come that way. You can keep the poem, too."

What women tell each other is one of the great mysteries of life, but most of the time Leonard could live without the knowledge. Winnie Bonniver was one of Inetta's book club friends, so it was possible she knew of his promise about the ashes. Women remember all kinds of things on their own, too—birthdays, anniversaries and operations; insults, disobedience and deaths—so maybe she connected the dates. Whatever, now here he is on her doorstep, hat in hand, dog at his side. If she asks where he's headed, he wants to be honest but he's willing to lie. She'd expect to be invited. Might insist on being there, turn it into a production. Inetta had just asked for him, Artists Point and a little breeze, and that's what she was going to get.

"Len." She says it the way a woman wakes up, looks out the window and says *snow*.

"Brought her food."

"How long'll you be gone?"

He knew she would ask this so he shrugs in the way he practiced and says, "You'll know in a couple a days." And when she looks at him askance, he says, "I promise," which is not the whole truth but pretty damn close.

Winnie says, "Did you plan to be off without any dinner?"

Even though things with the dog are settled, he knows hanging around a bit will be taken as thanks, so he says, "Guess I could have a bite."

Winnie sets down a plate of cold cuts, sliced tomatoes and sweet pickles. Cheese and crackers. Not quite dinner, but it's early. "I still miss her," she says. "Inetta, of all people."

Is he supposed to complete the thought? Maybe he can. But not with the things he heard at Inetta's service. The things they say about everyone. Inetta, of all people, had chosen him, of all people. He was a nonstandard thread tossed in the wrong bin, and somehow he found the right mate. Life didn't get any more miraculous than that.

Winnie clears the plates. She makes a clattering in the kitchen he knows means he's expected to come and ask if he can help.

Instead, he says, "I have to go." Clattering plates and tinkling barber's bells and postal rates and dog-eared Crown Vics are not what he wants hanging on his mind for the drive ahead. And certainly not any expectant dance at Winnie's front door. He didn't think he'd ever encouraged her. In fact, he'd tempered his appreciation of her kindnesses to avoid any misunderstanding. She didn't have a year to waste and she wasted one on him. At least tomorrow, she'd know for sure it was never going to happen.

He really has to go. He's been slowly turning down the lights for a year and he wants to time it right so there'll be just enough left to see some of Inetta's ashes in the air. Well, not ashes. That's not what showed up in the container from the funeral home. Her sediment, soon to wash down from those cliffs like everything else.

Stitches whines and rubs her rump on the floor as he gets ready to leave, but she is an old dog and her distress will subside. Winnie, he couldn't say.

"Take care of yourself," she says.

He looks into her eyes as deep as he can and says, "You,

too." And when she doesn't let go of his elbow, he shakes it loose gently and adds, "We'll just see."

Leonard was hard to read in the best circumstances, Winnie thinks. Reserved, Inetta always said, and once she died he tended even further toward standoffish and gloomy—especially around Winnie. But she's never seen him quite so flat, his eyes barely letting in the light. It has to be a hard day for him what with Inetta's ashes.

She can imagine the effort it took for him to come by. The food didn't seem to perk him up and her hints about going along with him didn't get through. Direct is probably best with Leonard, but the lesson's too late to apply now. He always seems to be misconstruing what she says and does as she keeps a kind eye on him, like Inetta had asked. He's a good man, and she understands what Inetta saw in him, but she likes her town life and isn't interested in adding animal husbandry to her list of commitments.

She finishes washing up and then completes the crossword she set aside when Leonard stopped by. Stitches lies curled and comfortable at her feet. Old dogs, she remembers, settle down better than old men, so she can handle this for a few days, while he works out what he needs to. She goes into the pantry where Leonard set the bucket of kibble and rearranges a few things so she can shove it deeper out of the way. It's far heavier than she expects, and suddenly she knows he isn't planning to come back for the dog.

She walks to the phone and lets her hand rest on the receiver before she's even completed a thought of what to do. What Inetta would want her to do. It's been a long time since she had to tiptoe around a man and read the silences, so maybe she's been slow to see what was going on. Inetta believed a year was enough for him to get going—he'd been straightening up the place in what looked like progress—but what if it wasn't enough time? She could call the police about a suspicion, but what was she suspicious of, exactly? Dog food? And what if they showed up at Artists Point and spoiled everything? She wouldn't want it known she was the one who sicced them. Winnie doesn't want to be the one at all, but Inetta had chosen her, the least churchly of all her friends, as the one to best usher her husband past this day and on with life. At first, it had been harder than she expected, because he didn't want the help, and then it became easy for the same reason. By now she isn't so sure Inetta's faith in her was well placed.

Winnie takes a deep breath and holds her finger on the nine for a long time before she presses it. The ones come quick, as if she were sending Morse code.

Out of sight from Winnie's house, he pulls over next to a little park and shuts off the truck. A playground rocket ship points up to a blue and clear sky. Although he can't see the Monument's red ridge from here, he knows sunset is already falling along its north flank, where the cliffs cast deep afternoon shadows, even on these longest days of the year. It's still a touch too soon to head up. *Time to kill*, he thinks. With no one to tell, Leonard lets the joke sink back where it came from.

Undampened by the truck's diesel rumble, a shrill, unwavering signal courses between his ears. It must always be there underneath the drone of life, transmitting like a radio tuned between the stations. He tries to dial it out, listens to his nostrils whistle as they pick up breaths and put them down again. A fly buzzes and pats the windshield in search of an exit. Cars sweep past, vacuuming up the remaining quiet.

It won't be that long now.

He watches a young woman work a stroller across the park's bumpy grass, with a second child leaning into the handles, helping her push. As they reach the playground, the boy ducks under her arms and runs to the wireframe spaceship, clambers to the top of a silver slide and peers up into the red nose cone, still high above his head. The ladders leading to two upper platforms have been removed for safety. The boy attempts to shinny up the steel skeleton but can gain no purchase on the slender yellow rods. After one last skyward look, he whoops, plunges down the gleaming slide and scuttles around for another circuit. Poised at the top, he cries out, "Watch! Watch, Mom. Watch!" and when the woman does not watch, Leonard sees it is because she is on her cell phone, staring intently in his direction.

He starts up the truck and eases away. This is not how it was supposed to go, him driving aimlessly with a jug of Inetta's ashes, waiting for dusk to fall. Once, he had figured he'd just keep going until he ran out of gas and coasted to a stop. Or he'd drop like Abner did, surprised by a thunderbolt in his brain, and that would be about it. Inetta would be the one to carry on, becoming herself fully as some women seemed to do once they were unharnessed from a man for good. That would have been an amazing thing, but neither he nor anyone else would see it.

He heads past the hospital where the other half of Inetta's paperwork must still be awaiting his reply. *Soon enough they'll have it.* The route down the hill leads to a sprawling feedlot packed with franchises, the West's new brands. He stops for a light and looks up at a grassy knoll that has been spared the bulldozers so far. The sheep that used to graze there are gone, and a dun-colored mare in her powder blue turnout blanket looks to Leonard like the last loaf of bread on the shelf.

Fireworks

"COME ON, LEN, a little fun won't kill ya."

As far as Leonard was concerned, his cousin was the one who'd have the fun up on the stage where he would pump out the dance tunes with his band, Lionel and the Locomotives. Leonard wasn't much for dancing in the first place, so that led to standing around, which led to drinking and talking, both of which had given him far more trouble than they ever proved to be worth. Though he did not believe in sin per se, he was acquainted well enough with its wages. As for the music, if he *was* going to listen to somebody singing "I'm Movin' On," it would be Hank Snow and not Lionel Grooms—no offense.

"This is one-a-them box dinner social deals like they used to do," said Lionel. "Women's club at the Colona Grange is raisin' money. You can ride down with us, help unload, bid on some boxes. Don't need to win one, just drive up the price for somebody else. It'll be good."

Colona was a tiny farming settlement at the throat of the Uncompahgre River Valley. With two blocks facing open fields, the town wasn't even a wide spot in the highway and, anyway, the highway had gone elsewhere.

"Forget it. Ain't interested in no corn farmers' daughters," said Leonard.

"The truth is, the van broke down and we need your truck."

"In that case, I'll go, but I ain't dancin'."

"No shit."

Colona had built a schoolhouse in 1915, and more than fifty years later, it was still the town's most substantial structure. Its grand entrance foyer with the arching window spoke of a time when every community on the western slope—fueled by free land, railroad-driven speculation and mercantile optimism—believed it was destined to grow into a bountiful city. But the town discovered how reliant its farming economy had been on filling miners' bellies when the mining industry caved and a bankrupt Denver & Rio Grande lost interest in running trains to ship apples out of the mountains. After the school shut down, it was kept alive as a community center by the National Grange of the Order of Patrons of Husbandry, which had used it for meetings since day one.

The band was playing in the second-floor gymnasium, a low-ceilinged cracker box with basketball hoops nailed to the end walls and maple flooring that could still be seen through three different shades of varnish. At the end opposite the riser where the band was setting up, two older ladies unpacked decorated boxes from grocery bags and arranged them along the edge of a stage, where a hand-painted curtain advertised the two-digit phone numbers of long-gone businesses.

After lugging a boxy bass amplifier and a drum kit up the stairs, he elected to wander. An unlocked door opened to a former classroom, bright with afternoon sunshine streaming through tall windows. A half-circle of mismatched chairs faced a 48-star flag and the insignia of the Colona Helping Hand Club carved into a plank. Framed photos showed different clusters of women hanging on fence rails, sitting in a grandstand, having tea on the porch of a ranch house and, he noted, wearing uniform bloomers and clutching a basketball. A dusty, glass-front cabinet displayed an arrangement of purplish geodes, blunted arrowheads and an unidentifiable lump of ore; a train schedule with a railroad inspector's lantern; and fading ribbons from county fairs with the corresponding domestic arts entries. There was a fancy patchwork purse, ancient green preserves with the crisped label fallen off the jar and a disturbing quart of skinless canned tomatoes turned the pinkish grey of a medical specimen.

A box social seemed to fit right in.

The squawks and microphone foolishness from the band's sound check began to reverberate, attracting a few early arrivals up the stairs. The ladies in the gym were running through their checklist, too, comparing a lineup of boxes against the auctioneer's manifest, nodding to each other as they recollected paper snares they had once set.

"You can look, but you can't touch," warned one of the custodians.

Most offerings appeared fashioned from shoeboxes wrapped in Christmas paper slathered with ribbons or glued with magazine cuttings and construction paper hearts. Among the outliers, a box upholstered in gingham and lace, with a buttoned clasp holding fast the lid, another beaded like an Indian's moccasin. A third bid for attention with a box top field of fresh-cut asters and wild onions.

Then there was item number 17: three tubes (Quaker Oats containers?) painted red and bundled together with black sash cord. Pipe cleaner fuses rose from their tops, twisted together and, at the tip, threw off mock sparks made of gummed red and gold stars stuck to short snips of fishing leader. Leonard wondered which of these packages might be spoken for already, and which were private jokes or hopeful clues no stranger was supposed to fathom, and whether number 17 represented fire-crackers or dynamite.

Maybe he would try to bid on something.

To get people going, Lionel ran through bouncy numbers by Buck Owens, Frankie Yankovic and Elvis Presley, casting each one into the pool to get a read on his crowd. Merle Haggard's "The Bottle Let Me Down" drew the first women onto the floor for some line dancing, while the men kept to the wall holding Dixie Cups containing punch or catching spit. Leonard was with them and could feel feet tapping, from nerves and impatience as much as the beat. His Uncle Abner thought a radio was a waste of electricity, so Leonard didn't have much music to shape his ear. But Lionel's band was not bad. Even he could tell that.

Lionel switched from accordion to fiddle and started a patter that urged the dancers into squares. This sent some people heading for the folding chairs and others rushing onto the floor. He started them out with some easy calls. One square of older folks was pretty smooth. Another eight made up of high school kids knew the cues, but they seemed more interested in goofing around. After calling a few more tunes, Lionel changed gears again. He dug into an up-tempo "The Last Thing on My Mind" that had the crowd clapping in time as the fiddle screed through a run of the chorus and then skated above the harmonies in a second and third round. Barely pausing, he signaled the keyboard player, who banged out the introduction to "Good Golly, Miss Molly," and the floor filled suddenly as if a call had gone for volunteers to stomp out burning embers that imperiled the town.

Confident the band had the pulse now—it was rockabilly beats they wanted—Lionel plowed straight into "Whole

Lotta Shakin' Goin' On." He talked up the auction through the instrumental break, and then, when he got back into the chorus, he leapt off the stage and led the delirious dancers to the other end of the gym singing along to "shake, baby, shake!"

No, not too bad. Leonard straightened up from his slouch against the wall and yanked his belt square. He ambled in the slipstream of the dancers like he had nothing better to do, but he felt his chest ticking with anticipation.

An elderly fellow with eyebrows like albino caterpillars stumbled slightly as he climbed onstage. He laughed at himself and did a little juke step to the apron. One of the box dinner ladies followed him up, and the second helper handed her the first item, a blue-paper-covered box stuck with fold-cut snow-flakes.

"Are we ready, boys?" He took a sheet of paper from a vest pocket and waggled those eyebrows. The woman on stage held the snowflake box aloft.

The old man wasn't a regular auctioneer, but he kept up a rhythmic barker's chatter that wove a new story with each sale—exaggerating the attributes and mysteries of a box and questioning the capacities of various men in the audience for romance, risk-taking, eating or stinginess. He knew a lot of the people in the room, and it was clear by the way he presented a box or called out a certain bidder by name that he was sprinkling hints designed to guide the bidding as well as entertain the crowd. Leonard had assumed only young single women were in the game, but the third box went to a grandfather type who headed up to claim his prize with granny on his arm. Not all the couples kept their signals straight. One homemaker set off laughter as she swatted her cheapskate husband because her beaded box went to the wrong man. A few bidders appeared to be in it for sport, playing chicken with the more determined ones and veering away when the prices approached twenty dollars—a handsome sum considering tickets to the bean feed later in the evening were only two bucks. With so many cross-currents in the room, Leonard pushed his hands deep into his pockets and thought he would leave them there, though he kept a particular eye open for anyone hovering around number 17.

Although number 16 had just been claimed, Leonard's pulse jumped when the barker announced, "And now, gentlemen, it's s-s-s-s-seventeen!" and his assistant lifted up the firecracker box and made the sparks dance. Leonard drew a hunter's deep, calming breath and blew it out slow. *Let's just see.*

The auctioneer detonated a back-of-the throat sound and yelped, "This one looks like a blast. Whatta we got—a Fourth-a-July picnic lunch? The Fourth is over, so who'll gimme two, gimme two dolla?"

"Two!"

Leonard looked around too late to match the voice to the bid.

"I got two, who'll go four?"

Four came quickly from a square-shouldered man along the wall. Four was still cheap.

"We're doublin' here, so I want eight. Do I hear eight?"

A pause, then a higher pitched voice came in, a boy, slight and long faced, with straight black hair coming down too far from his hat. Not a hippie, but not your average country kid, either. The emcee looked him over, brows down a notch. "You're sure about that? Okay, I got eight now, do I hear ten?"

Ten came quickly from the man who'd just bid four. He smoothed the hair on top of his head, away from the knife-straight part two inches above his ear.

Leonard looked over at the boy. Would he keep going or not?

"All right gentlemen, you can see this here is an unusual entry, with, it looks like, three separate compartments. And that could mean... Well, it could mean anything. Hot dogs, kraut and buns... Drumsticks, mashed potatoes and gunpowder milk biscuits... Three cans a Coors... What do you say to twelve?"

"Twelve," said the boy.

"Now, if it's got the Coors, I'm gonna have to check some ID, Elliott."

The boy blushed as a voice shouted, "Them Ferrins don't drink!" Someone behind Leonard muttered, "You can say that again."

"Thirteen," said the plastered-hair man, without being asked.

Only a dollar more. Was he getting ready to drop? Along with everyone else, Leonard looked to the boy.

"Fifteen!" shouted the kid.

"Okay, fellas, if you don't need me up here, just keep goin' and let me know when I should come collect the money. I have fifteen."

The other bidder looked left and right, then held up a bill.

"Twen-ty dollars," he said.

"I have twenty dollars. Equals the top so far today. Who'll take us over the top? Can I have twenty-one?"

Elliott looked beaten down. Twenty dollars was a good ten hours' pay for the kid.

"Twenty-one? Twenty-one? Let's get out those wallet stretchers, boys. Twenty-one? All right, twenty going once..."

The man looked too triumphant, the boy too downcast. This was not for fun.

"Twenty twice…"

"Twenty-one!" said Leonard.

Heads snapped around, and it was Leonard's turn to blush.

"We had somebody layin' in the weeds!" cried the emcee. "Well, all's fair in love and war."

"What'd you say?" demanded the other bidder.

The emcee came back, "About the weeds or about love?"

"All's *fair in* love and war?"

A conversation was going on between the two that Leonard didn't understand.

"I still have twenty-one. Twenty-one one time… Twenty-one twice… Twenty-one sold to the fella in the weeds over there."

And just like that, he had his dinner. He looked toward the boy. Maybe if Elliott still wanted to go the fifteen, Leonard thought, they could work out something—and then he remembered there was a woman involved.

"Will Inetta Ferrin come up here and meet the lucky winner? And now we're off to number eighteen."

Leonard snaked through the curious crowd toward the stage. People stepped aside without looking up, and then heads turned to follow him. To his right, he saw Elliott coming forward, too. Something was not quite right. Inetta Ferrin had the same slim build, same black hair, a wide mouth set in an angular face squared off with a strong jaw. It was disconcerting to see Elliott's features on a woman. She looked at Leonard with amusement, stuck out her hand, and said, "Inetta Ferrin. You must be real hungry."

"Not sure what I am, but I liked your box."

"It took you a while to say so, whoever you are."

"Sorry. Leonard Self. Seemed like you had enough fans biddin' already."

"Elliott's my little brother. He was going to save me."

"Save you from what?"

She sighed. "It's a long story."

"Well, good. I was wonderin' what I was goin' to talk to you about."

He unpacked the dynamite sticks one at a time: three ears of roasted corn standing on end in the first one, interspersed with three dill pickle spears. Second stick: three buns and three kielbasas, each wrapped in waxed paper. Third stick: container of baked beans stacked on a container of sauerkraut stacked on a divided container of chopped onions, catsup and mustard. All fit snug.

"Expectin' company?" he asked.

"I never met a man who was satisfied with one of anything," Inetta said. "Don't tell me you're it."

He inspected the sausages inside the buns. "They look raw."

"Given my luck, I figured it was fifty-fifty a man'd even notice. You passed the first test."

He imagined she might be kidding. "Thought the idea was to impress."

She laughed. "By the time a woman's twenty-four in this town, if she could impress a man, she'd've already done it. The best I can do now is blow up the past."

"What about that long-story bidder I beat out?"

"Hank Albery. Let's just say even raw pork's too good for him. You may've noticed he dropped when he figured out he was bidding *for* me instead of *against* Elliott."

He didn't notice, but he nodded and said, "Got a propane torch in my truck. We could do them sausages—assumin' I qualify for the cooked."

"You pass the second test—be prepared for anything."

"There a third test?"

"Well, you didn't ask me how long they've been out of the refrigerator, so I guess you trust me."

"Guess I must."

"Then don't worry, Elliott's working the grill. We'll get your sausages cooked right. And your sweet corn warmed up, too."

He didn't want to start thinking dirty about Inetta Ferrin, but by the time he'd loaded the drums and amplifiers for the night, she had him about as hungry as he could remember.

Leonard was in no rush with Inetta. Not that she was pushing. She had her job in Montrose, surrounded with choices and carried along by town life. She wrote him, but he wasn't that much of a writer, so he drove the eighty-odd miles to see her when he had the gas money. He wasn't ready to call it a courtship, which seemed to require putting out the good dishes and buffing everything to a shine, including himself. In his case, a woman would get a better idea of a life together from meeting Abner, opening their cupboards and touring the trash pit, but Leonard had no idea how to nudge things forward in that more natural direction. He had so little experience with women, and what there was—from when his natural instinct had been to catch whatever was thrown at him—had not been good: some summer-job dude-ranch tack-room grab-ass, made more urgent by the smell of saddle leather and his dead certainty that fraternizing with the guests would get him fired. Mistaken nights spent buying rail drinks for women with sad eyes and party faces. That man was not really him, even then, so he felt no obligation to fill in that part of his history, but the tale of how he came to be could not be deferred forever. Inetta would ask about his parents. She'd wonder how a grown man came to stay on with his bachelor uncle. And if she was serious, she'd surely want to track his bloodlines back to whatever old countries were responsible for putting the Self family in Colorado.

How could he tell her of the hard black seed his father put in him? Of burying it so deep and keeping it dry and away from the light so maybe it would turn to stone instead of sprouting. And how, when the darkening visited him, as he saw it do sometimes with Abner, he learned to work his chores, hold his chin to his chest, hood his eyes, and move one foot after the other, one heavy second at a time, until the cloud passed. He couldn't spread the unexplainable thin enough for a cracker of conversation.

Even at this awkward pace, he thought maybe he was getting ahead of himself. He and Abner had worked out a way of living together—the ranch was in Abner's name, including the stake left by Leonard's folks—and there were two habitable structures on the place, but it was a delicate situation that a woman coming in couldn't help but want to change, and Abner had made it clear that if he'd wanted a woman around, he would have married one himself.

Scales

One winter day Abner didn't come back in from checking on a calf, and Leonard found him ice cold, looking like he'd expired trying to make a snow angel face-down. Only after Abner's passing did the plain arithmetic of the Reverse Dollar Ranch fully assert itself. The place made work for two backs and four hands, but not enough income to support an owner and pay a wage. He should have figured this out on his own, since he was the underpaid hand, but the family aspect of the arrangement blurred the economics of it. So he did as Abner had once done, kept his gate open and took in strays— a neighbor boy tossed out of his house, a son brought by some relative hoping hard work and a change of scene would straighten him out. When Leonard came to this place, Abner had made clear his staying was going to be a working deal, not charity or even plain kindness, which made it the deepest kindness of all, and now he would not change those terms for others. The efforts of random teenagers proved a poor substitute for his own, however, once Leonard stepped into Abner's shoes, so when Vaughn Hobart came knocking, Leonard was willing to have him back, even though it was clear enough why Vaughn was out of a job and looking for a bed.

Vaughn had been the last of the boys Abner took in, and

he and Leonard had bunked together in the homestead cabin, which made him not quite a relation, but close enough. Back then he had not distinguished himself in the industry department. Leonard had learned from branding with him in those days, you didn't want Vaughn around a hot dehorning iron or handling snips or even holding a leg. Picking the nuts out of the dirt and saving them for the skillet was about his speed. Just make sure you washed them again after he said he did. The years since had broadened him but not sharpened him much. Vaughn had drifted through a number of trades, lasting long enough to pick up an array of half-assed skills that could get a job done if you didn't care what it looked like or how long it lasted. More important for a drinking man, he also picked up the shop talk which, sprinkled into a stream of friendly b.s., could be enough to land him his next passing employment.

Leonard wasn't about to mistake the flush in Vaughn's face for the fruits of honest labor. Through the winter, Leonard had been feeding cattle on his own. It was tedious, stop-and-start work for one man to load the hay, drive the Ford out to the cows and spread a square, pull forward and drop another. He liked being out in the crisp cold, and inefficiencies were part of the deal on a small ranch, so you might as well enjoy the time. A little help would be nice, was all.

He told Vaughn how many bales to load onto the truck, which was still parked next to the rick after yesterday's feeding. When he came back, Vaughn was sitting on a bale and the bed wasn't full. Instead of standing in the truck and sliding the eighty-pound bales from the stack into the back, it looked like he pulled each one down to the ground, then hoisted it back into the bed.

"Figured you'd remember how to buck hay," Leonard said. Or at least pick the easy way to do it.

"It ain't that. It's my wind. Got a allergy or somethin'," Vaughn huffed. "And this elbow ain't been right since I busted it in three places."

Leonard wondered if he meant three bone breaks or three different bars. Once the load was arranged, it seemed a good idea to recap a few points while Vaughn caught his breath.

"Some of the cows'll be down around the crick, but they'll come up when they see the truck, so we'll drive over where that grass stubble over there's pokin' through—less chance of gettin' stuck. Just creep along in four-low. We kick off a bale every so many. Cut the twine and drop the flakes out as we go—you'll see how it spreads out. I like a nice line of hay, not all jumpy and clumpy. While we're at it today, we'll count 'em. Okay?"

"Okay," Vaughn said, clapping his hands together. "Let's get after it."

"Got a knife on you?"

"Nope."

Leonard didn't want to hand over his Case knife to Vaughn. Abner's old utility knife was in a kitchen drawer and he went in to fetch it. When he got back, Vaughn was behind the wheel of the idling Ford.

"Ready?" he said through the window. "Where's my knife?"

"Uhn-uh," said Leonard, holding the knife beyond Vaughn's reach and thumbing him into the truck bed. *Jesus.*

He coaxed the truck over the frozen ground where it still bore ruts from the wet fall and followed the line he'd scribed in his mind, calling to Vaughn to start dropping the flakes and monitoring him in the mirror as he went. Vaughn seemed to have the hang of it, and when they'd left eight bales, he had Vaughn hold up and waved him into the cab while they drove to the other side of the ranch where another bunch of cows huddled.

"How many did you get?"

"How many what?" Vaughn asked.

"We was countin' cows."

"I figured you was countin'."

"When I say *we*, that means you, too. I had thirty-nine. Let's see if we can come up with the same number next time."

They rode across the snowy pasture with only the thrum of the diesel passing between them. As the truck rocked along in the February sun, windshield cracks flashed like lightning. Approaching the herd, he stopped the truck, and Vaughn got out without being told. All the hay from the day before was gone, so he had Vaughn drop the rest. When they finished, Vaughn got in, folded his arms and said, "Twenty-three."

"Don't take it personal."

"We used to be more like friends," Vaughn said.

"Still are, but work comes first."

"Well, that's one way of lookin' at it," Vaughn said.

After they reached the house, Leonard looked in the bed and turned to Vaughn. "Where's the strings?"

"I cut 'em like you said."

"Didn't you hang onto 'em? I don't like the cows eatin' twine."

"All right, but if you don't like somethin' you might try sayin' so in advance."

Vaughn had a point. Saying so was not one of Leonard's strengths, but directing every move of a half-assed hand was not one of his preferred activities, either. He was used to Inetta, who seemed to enjoy dragging words from him and kept going until she had pulled his point out by the roots.

Just yesterday, Inetta had finished a drugstore Green River, except for the cherry, which reposed in the ice at the bottom of her glass. "Do you believe in fate?" she asked.

He did not sense fate was going to be the topic for long, so he answered with care. "Things happen for a reason."

"They do, but I'm not talking about how rocks roll downhill or yellow and red make orange. I mean how things that shouldn't happen *happen*," she speared the cherry with her straw, "and then seem as right as gravity."

"Even if you can't see it, there's still a reason," he said.

"There is," she said, "and I'd think you'd want to know it. You seem like that kind."

That kind of what, he wondered. "Sometimes it pays to know. Sometimes it don't."

"What do you mean?"

He thought of the rendering truck that had just visited a neighbor. "A man's cows was droppin' dead outa the blue. Turns out a hot wire'd fell in their stock tank. Good thing to know before he dipped to check the water."

Inetta frowned and studied the impaled cherry. "Okay, but not everything's a straight-out problem to be solved," she said. "What about the real mysteries of life—like why are we here? Does that need explaining in your book or not?"

Her book, he knew, was the Bible, and her church was some kind of holy-roller outfit. He meant to keep his distance from that subject, forever, if possible. "What I think don't need explainin' is one of them things I don't need to explain," he said, hoping that would get him off the hook.

"Amen," she said. "Most men can't wait to explain everything, or at least act like they know it all. But you—" she waggled the straw under his nose and he could smell the sweetness there, "are you going to do something about this, or am I going to have to bask in the mystery of your thoughts forever?"

"About what?" he said. Did she want him to eat it? Maybe this wasn't going to be the God talk after all.

She plunged the straw back into her glass so it rattled the ice, then snatched up a coin from the counter. "Got change for a nickel?"

He knew he didn't, but he dug in both pockets anyway to keep his hands from shaking. Finally, he had to show her what he'd dredged up: thirty-seven cents.

"Never mind," she said, picking through his offering and leaving her nickel in his palm. "Two pennies'll do." She took his hand, led him to the front of the store and stopped before a yellow enameled machine with a mirror on the front. *Your Weight and Fortune One Cent. No Springs.* She stepped on the brass platform and began to twist a knurled knob that advanced questions under a thick glass window. "Look," she read. "*What is my main talent? Am I to have money? Shall I go into politics?* It isn't so bad to ask questions." She looked at him over her shoulder. "Why are you so scared of me?"

"Ain't scared of you."

"Good! Then don't act like it." She turned the knob a few more times. "Here we go: *Where will I be married?*" She handed a penny back to him. "Let's see."

Inetta was on the scale. It was her question, but if he dropped the coin did that mean he was in on it? He thought he knew the answer. The door concealing the fortune drew aside with a clunk.

"*In Utah!*" she cried. "That's only twenty-five miles from here."

"A lot farther if you want to find a town," he said.

"Aren't you romantic!" She gave the knob another rotation and stepped off the scale. "Your turn."

He mounted the platform carefully and peered at the question: "*When will I be married?*" Inetta's hand was still firmly in control of the selection knob.

"Ready?" she trilled. This time she inserted the penny herself. "What's it say?"

"*Sooner than you think*," Leonard croaked, and Inetta began a laugh it seemed would never stop.

As time went on, it became clear Vaughn was accomplished in the varied arts of looking busy and staying out of the way—holding the ladder, banging on stuck threads, looking for tools he hadn't put away, taking a break, eyeballing and giving an opinion and, best of all, offering help once none was required. He treated keeping you company while you worked like it was his contribution, and when he couldn't avoid the heavy lifting, he wiped off sweat like it was worth time-and-a-half. Not much help and proud of it, that was Vaughn Hobart.

"It ain't workin' out, Vaughn." Leonard tried to make it sound general, like he was intending not to keep an extra hand anymore, but truth was, Vaughn wore on him. He wasn't a bad man, he just took up mental space where Leonard didn't have much to spare—worrying, planning, thinking about what needed doing. On his own, he could just get it done. The arrangement with Vaughn taxed him in a way he didn't care to explain.

"Sorry to hear that. It was workin' for me. Clean air, decent company, good food." Leonard noticed he forgot to mention honest work. "But if it ain't, it ain't. Maybe just a couple more weeks? I could part out some of them cars out back for you."

"The parts're right where I want 'em for now. What happens in two weeks?"

"Then…" Vaughn yawned and stretched. "Then maybe I'll be ready for one day at a time."

"They already got a place for that up here, and this ain't it." Some osteopath from town had brought trailers up to Glade

Park and established a treatment facility based on the theory that a drunk getting fresh air in the middle of nowhere might become interested in reform out of pure boredom.

"I know, but I don't wanna live in a trailer with of buncha chronics. I'm tryin' to set my goals a bit higher."

Goals. Leonard didn't want to hear about it, especially from Vaughn. If you did your best and persevered, good things might happen, but goals were better left to kids playing games, where the baskets were nailed down and the posts were buried. In real life, things moved on you. People turned. Time ran out. Goals just pointed you toward disappointment, but who was he to tell Vaughn that?

"Two weeks then, and see what you can do about holdin' up your end here."

"I owe you," Vaughn said. He stood wavering and red-eyed for so long, Leonard sniffed for that fermented alcohol breath. Vaughn came away clean, so maybe he meant it.

Leonard was fixing breakfast when he heard the horn and the ripping of tires sliding over the gravel and then the thump that usually signified someone might be taking home fresh venison. He listened for the rumble and crunch of a vehicle pulling away and when he didn't hear it, he set aside the eggs and stepped out the back door facing the road. He didn't see anything from there, but the road dipped where the creek and the deer cut through. He went back in and got the keys to the truck in case the driver was gone and the deer was out there dying in the brush.

When he reached the road, he recognized Stony Jackson's truck and saw Stony crouched in the grass along the shoulder. Stony lived on the far south end of Glade Park and parked his grader north so it was closer to the roads he maintained under contract. Stony waved him over and called, "You don't got a phone, do you." A declaration. Just about everyone on Glade Park knew who had a phone and who didn't. "Oh, well. I think he's okay. I just clipped him when he jumped out to wave me down. How the hell did he get way over here?"

Stony was referring to the rehab camp a few miles away. Leonard had a feeling he wouldn't be seeing one of those drunks—and the motionless body in the grass confirmed it. "Can you move?" Leonard asked.

"I can move, goddammit, it just hurts like hell," said Vaughn.

"Well then don't move," Leonard said. "What hurts?"

"My back feels twisted."

"Wiggle your fingers. Move your feet—I can see your jaw's still workin'," Leonard said. Vaughn complied, grimacing for effect, he suspected. By the time an ambulance got there they could already be at St. Mary's. To Stony, he said, "Got an army cot back at the house. We could strap him down and take him in."

"You know him?" Stony asked.

"Unfortunately."

"I winged him, I guess I should take him," said Stony.

"Don't want to get in an argument, but he wouldn't be here if I'd booted him out last week," said Leonard. "I'll haul his ass in."

Vaughn said, "Do I get a say in this?"

"No!" said Stony and Leonard in stereo.

"What the hell were you doin' Vaughn? It's the first time you got up this early since you been here."

Vaughn squinched up his face before he answered. "I thought I could flag me a ride to town and get back in time to help you some. What can I say? I love the juice."

From the barn, Leonard retrieved the army cot, which he left dotted with spider egg sacs, and a two-by-twelve they worked under Vaughn and used as a backboard to lift him onto the musty canvas. Leonard slipped a wool cap on his head, wrapped him in a blanket, roped him to the flattened cot and slid it into the bed of the truck.

"Is he gonna roll around back there?" Stony said. "We might want to pack him in with somethin'."

"I'll drive easy," said Leonard. "You just go ahead and yell, Vaughn, if you start to move outa the grooves. In fact, why don't you make a siren sound for me on the way. Then I'll know you're not in shock."

"That ain't funny—it hurts!" Vaughn cried.

"You wanna stay up here and wait for an ambulance?"

"No, let's go." Vaughn said. "Just get me there in one piece."

"You got it, then?" Stony was eager to move on but he wanted confirmation.

"If he dies on us, I'll be sure to let you know," Leonard said. "Otherwise…" He shook his head and threw up his hands in a gesture that released them both from responsibility for the ongoing adventures of Vaughn Hobart.

As Leonard headed into the sharp curves down Monument Road, he checked over his shoulder through the cab window. He couldn't see Vaughn's head, just his body from the belly down, his hands at his sides. He tapped the horn a couple times and shouted back, "You okay?" Vaughn's left hand waggled what was either a wave or a *so-so*.

Yeah, so-so was about it for him, too. Leonard imagined from Inetta's side of things his caution was starting to look like perversity, but in fact, when he was around her he got stuck somewhere between dumbfounded and petrified. He didn't know how to act except to crack jokes and keep his hands to himself. A woman had only been around in Leonard's life until he was twelve. Who'd he ever had to show him what he was supposed to do with someone like Inetta? For sure not his father, who had lumbered in drunken, snow-blind circles, strewing family the way a hypothermic man discards his clothes. His Uncle Abner had embraced deprivation as a way of life; it made random calamities seem less of an inconvenience and misery just a turn of the dial up from everyday suffering. However that philosophy worked for Abner, it was not a hit with the ladies. Leonard's menfolk had a piss-poor record all around, and Vaughn was of no use on the subject of women, either, except as one more example of what not to be.

Leonard had found other ways to cook in his own stew. He had a piece of land, but the beef business knocked him sideways and upside down every couple years. His house had never had a woman inside—and looked like it. Without much reason to change clothes on a given day, he wore his pants until they were practically waterproof. Vehicles at the ranch that didn't run outnumbered the ones that did. Why shouldn't Vaughn think he'd fit right in? Maybe that's why Leonard was dragging it out with Inetta. He was afraid what she'd think if she could see all of him, and he didn't know how he was going to change just by trying harder. He didn't have a goddamn goal beyond getting through tomorrow, and for all he knew, tomorrow Vaughn would be out of the hospital, and Leonard was going to have to decide whether he could convalesce at the ranch or had finally run out of chances. Either way, friend or employee, if Vaughn was the best he could do, it didn't reflect too well on his prospects with Inetta.

He found the emergency room and left Vaughn while he

located some people to bring him in. They came hustling out and arranged a gurney while Leonard dropped the tailgate.

"What happened here?" asked a nurse as she applied a blood pressure cuff.

Vaughn's eyes were closed, but he still had color and he was breathing all right. "Bumped into a truck," Vaughn said.

"Hitchin' a ride to town," Leonard said. "Most people know to stick out their thumb. He had to go jump out and wave it down."

Vaughn opened his eyes and rolled them to where he could spot Leonard without moving his head. "I thought it might be my only chance," he said.

The hospital had a pay phone. Leonard called directory assistance for the number at the dry cleaner where Inetta did alterations. The way his heart was pounding, it felt like an emergency, so he tried to make it sound like one in case she wasn't supposed to take personal calls at work. As he waited for her to come on the line, he wondered why what scared him worst seemed to be what he wanted most.

"What is it?" Inetta said. "Is everything okay?" He remembered the time he'd called after he found Abner. Drove down to the store and phoned her even before he notified the sheriff.

"Was wonderin' if you were free for a movie."

"In general, or did you have a day in mind?"

He did, though he had no idea what movies were playing right now. "Tomorrow," he gulped. "Night."

"Okay," she said. "Saturday night, say six thirty. Is that all you wanted?"

"Pretty much." He couldn't tell if she was relieved, irritated or just in a hurry to get back to work.

"Can't wait," she said.

Or maybe amused.

A Man Called Horse was sort of a love story once it got past the bloody parts. It was the best he could find on Saturday, and it was at the Star-Lite drive-in, which was cheaper than the movie house and had more privacy for what he had in mind. Richard Harris played an English aristocrat who was captured by the Sioux, and eventually he became their leader after he learned to respect their culture. From what Leonard knew, the captive part was common in the old days and some of the ceremonies were supposed to be authentic, with them talking the Indian language and all, but once he stepped back and thought about it, the story still seemed preposterous.

Inetta was squeezed close to him on the bench seat of the pickup, and he kept his arm across the back until a part with nothing but Sioux Indian for the dialogue looked like it would drag on for a while. He twisted down the knob on the metal speaker hooked into his window and took her chin in his hand and turned her face away from the screen toward him. The drums rattled hollow and metallic from the surround of other car windows, and the native chant rose from the distance to an even more nasal register. He'd parked in the back, partly because the Ford was jacked up tall for clearance, but mostly for this. She knew what was coming, and she looked so willingly into his eyes he knew it wouldn't matter one bit he didn't have a ring.

"You 'spose they let Gentiles marry in Utah?" he said. He had hoped he could ask without asking, and she would let him joke his way through this.

"Gentiles, maybe, but what about a Christian with a heathen?"

Inetta smiled when she said it, but of course she would want to get married in her own church. The whole thing with the penny scale was just a flirtation. "Either way, I am kinda outside the fold on this thing," he said. "I'm not real big on religion, but if it's a church weddin' you want..."

She stopped him with a finger to his lips. "What do *you* want?"

Thinking about it was bound to tangle him up, so he said the first thing in his mind: "You."

"Good answer," she said. She brought her face to his and kissed him, and unlike any of the cautious front-door pecking that had gone before, this one made him feel like his chest had just been unbuttoned, and if she'd asked him to come to Jesus in that moment, he might have done it. Instead she said, "If I've got this straight, you just asked me to marry you. If not, you better say so right now."

He should have rehearsed a speech, but it was too late. Up on the movie screen, Richard Harris, dangling from the two hooks piercing his chest, turned slowly in a mystical light. Leonard took a deep breath. "I did, and I hope you'll have me. Can't make any great claims for myself beyond I promise not to ever be any worse than the man you see right now. Life'll be different—for both of us—and you gotta know I work on things at my own speed. Church, well, I got a pretty fair idea of my shortcomings already and don't need any weekly reminders. If Jesus comes into it down the road, he does, but if me bein' a heathen's a deal breaker... Well, I wouldn't count on me bein' anything else."

"Everyone comes up short some ways," Inetta said. "All I'm counting on is your good heart." She turned toward the screen, but he could tell she was searching for something beyond it. As the images shifted, colored lights flickered and jumped in unison across random surfaces of the parked cars. Leonard waited for her to come back with whatever it was she went after. When she finally did, he saw the remains of tears on her cheek. When did that happen?

"Is there anything else you want to know about me?" she asked.

He was only beginning to learn about the depths beneath a woman's questions, but he had experienced enough mishaps around the ranch to know the dangers of assuming too much. "Plenty, but I wouldn't know what to do with it yet."

"Well, I don't want to surprise you later."

"You kiddin'? Surprise got me here in the first place."

Inetta moved in close again and wrapped herself around his stiff right arm, which had been locked to the top of the steering wheel since the conversation turned to Jesus.

"You're pretty smooth with the answers tonight," she said and then turned serious again. "I believe when the Bible says there are better days to come, and the way to heaven is not to live rigid or in fear of damnation. It's to surrender that part of yourself you don't want to give up. That's what love is, and whether it comes from God or somebody else, you'll know it. I'll never push my faith on you, but it'll always be there, and I'll pray for you to accept it someday. All I ask is for you to let me be who I am, as I will let you be. It was a heathen I fell in love with, and so it'll be a heathen I marry."

Leonard was beginning to understand better when kisses were called for, so it was a while before he got around to his question. "What'll your church have to say about me?"

"My pastor's going to want to instruct us. About the obligations of marriage. Of faithfulness. About living in Christ."

"I'm all for faithfulness," he said.

"We'll work it out," she said. "When I come to live with you, I'll have to find a new church in Glade Park anyway."

It struck him she had never seen the ranch. "We don't

have churches. Glade Park ain't a town, it's more of a place where people just live—like a big island away from regular civilization. We don't have much but a little store."

"I heard it's beautiful. Come here." She slid her fingers up the back of his head and found the hard little bumps under his scalp. "What's this?"

"Got it when I was a kid, runnin' across the road to Abner's." It wasn't a lie. Let her think it was gravel for now.

She pressed. "Does this hurt?"

"Nope." That was almost the truth, too.

The cars began starting and turning on their lights, washing out the credits on the screen. Leonard waited for the exit to clear.

"That penny scale. You already checked it out before I got there."

Inetta nodded and tried to hold back a smile.

"And the way it works, them fortunes come up the same every time, don't they?"

"They do," she said. "You're supposed to ask a different question the next time."

"Seems like everybody's fate turns out the same, then."

"Only if you want to believe a machine," she said.

Inetta must have told someone about his proposal at the Star-Lite, because when they came out for the first dance at the wedding reception—it was supposed to be *Unchained Melody*—Lionel's band started out with tom-tom music and Lionel singing this fake Indian *hoh-na-tonka-hey-ey* kind of stuff. Later, Lionel said Elliott put him up to it, and Leonard had to admit, it was a pretty good joke, just for the two of them.

Misdirected

He CANNOT BEAR TO DRIVE straight into the setting sun, hemmed in by the thickening creep of mall-drawn drivers hunched sideways into their cell phones, so he turns north on 26 Road toward the Book Cliffs. He does not have a particular route in mind and doesn't need one to keep working his way south and west. The section roads follow the public land survey's range and township lines that rule the valley, running in a mile-square checkerboard of letters and numbers, subdivided into halves and quarters as required. The quadrants break down where they encounter the river and squeeze up against the Monument, and the grid logic barely survives the climb to Glade Park. Though the roads by the ranch are still named by survey points, they appear only where needed and wander where they can, before petering out entirely.

I Road takes him past alfalfa fields already baled a week ahead of Glade Park's hay, ghost farm buildings, clusters of ranchettes and the occasional hacienda surrounded by steel equine fencing that costs twenty dollars a foot. Where the road dips, a man totters behind a line of cattle and uses his red wool cap to whap the flanks of the last cow slow to follow through the gate. He waves to Leonard, and then mounts the cap back on his head. His asparagus-colored ranch house is for sale, its roof dating stages of neglect in a money-green-to-carbon-black patchwork of shingles. In the distance, someone drives framing nails by hand—*tunk-Tunk-TUnk-TUNk-TUNK!* The steel sings a rising tone as it's buried deeper with each hammer strike. Leonard wonders if the carpenter, working against the dying light, wishes he had a nail gun to bang them home the way they do it now, each note the same as the other.

He comes to an intersection where a plump foil balloon lolls from a stake, its helium gone inert. An attached sign says *Miracle Class of '07* with an arrow underneath. Leonard recognizes it as a common family name in the valley, not a commentary on the graduate whose party is surely over by now. He considers following the sign (he has to turn south sometime), but a car is approaching from the other direction. An arm reaches from the driver's window and waves urgently. He slows and can hear music turned down as the car glides up to his side.

"Sir, do you know where we can find Loma?" a young woman inquires. There are three more like her in the car, issuing a spoor of cigarettes, mingled perfumes and, he can see from his perch, the slop from plastic cups.

"You want to go west." He points the way he's headed.

"I told youuu!" wails a voice from the back seat.

The driver shrugs her bare shoulders, waggling the arms of a silver cross suspended between her breasts. "We're meeting some people at Country Jam."

Leonard focuses on the roof of the car. "Then your easiest way back is down to the freeway." He indicates the direction of the Miracle arrow.

"Nu-uh. They're checking cars when they come off the exit. That's why we're sneaking in the back way." She puts up a shushing finger to her lips.

"Yer choice." Not his problem. Nothing is anymore.

"*Mis*-ter!" One of the women jumps out from the other side and wobbles in exaggerated tiny steps around the car to block his way. She clings to her cup with one hand and thrusts up the other like a traffic cop. "Help us out. We're not from around here." She's wearing cut-off jeans and cowboy boots with a black halter top that has *WANTED* stenciled across the front. She approaches with her hand out toward the truck as if it were a dog she wants to befriend and slides her palm along the hood as she edges toward his door. When she reaches the window, she deposits her cup on the hood and declares, "We're totally lost!"

"No we're not," chimes the driver. "We're just a little misdirected."

"Whatever," says the woman at his window, concentrating to articulate every syllable. "We're *not sneaking* in. We got tickets. Are you headed there? You can be our guide—the faithful scout leading us on the secret passage to Country Jam." She grips his side mirror, and Leonard is afraid she's preparing to swing herself onto his running board. "Pleeese?" she slurs.

The voice from the back seat calls out, "If you do, Candace'll show you her tits!"

Candace whips around and slaps the car door. "Shut up!"

Her release of the mirror allows Leonard to crank the wheel toward the ditch and pull away. The plastic cup spills on the windshield and falls to the road, bouncing with a hollow sound. He hears Candace howl, "Real nice, Grandpa!" and when he checks the mirror, she is still standing in the road with her hands on her hips.

By the time they get turned around he should be out of reach, but just in case, he takes the next road south toward the Monument.

The Doing

Living with Inetta introduced Leonard to new mysteries, such as why it was necessary to drive a hundred miles to stand around holding Hawaiian Punch and Spanish peanuts while listening to apple farmers he'd never met talk about cross-pollination.

"It's what you do in a family," she said, "even if you don't care for it."

He didn't. But Elliott had graduated from high school, and that meant Leonard's second-ever trip to the Ferrin orchards for a dose of Inetta's parents and their neighbors. He didn't understand how people as bright as Elliott and Inetta could've come out of a dark-curtained house that felt like a waiting room for the Second Coming. He was glad to see the reception held outside in the fresh air and sorry for Elliott that the guests were mostly adults from the family church.

Leonard found Elliott scraping off red icing from a piece of graduation cake decorated in the colors of the Montrose Indians. "Congratulations," Leonard said. "What's next—you gonna work for your dad?"

"I'm not sure," said Elliott. He had seemed happy when he walked off the stage with his diploma, but glumness had settled over him now. "Things aren't too good out there."

"There's the Army. The war's about over."

"Maybe. I was thinking more like California." Elliott shook the frosting off his plastic fork into a garbage can. When he turned, Leonard noticed a trace of color under one eye. Purple edging to yellow, a fading shiner.

"What'd you walk into?"

"A fight. It was stupid."

"Fightin' usually is over somethin' stupid."

"Or *with* somebody stupid," Elliott said. "No big deal."

"Main thing is to let bygones be bygones."

Elliott took a bite of cake and made a face. "Still too sweet," he said. He looked around to see if the cake baker was watching and dropped the paper plate into the can. "Thanks for coming."

"Elliott didn't seem too overjoyed to be done with school," Leonard said on the slow drive home up Monument Road.

"Oh, he's happy," Inetta said. "He can't wait to leave."

"He told me maybe California."

She said, "He would die down there at home. He'd dry up or blow up, I don't know which. In California, he'd have a chance."

"Chance at what? He didn't say much about his plans."

"It's going to be hard. For a long time, Dad thought he'd take over the orchard."

"Doesn't sound like it now," he said.

"No, he probably never was going to do that, but it took a while for everyone to figure it out."

He wondered what a long, slow estrangement felt like, whether it could be worse than a sudden end to things, what drove a young man to leave land that had been in his family for generations. He waited for her to say more, and when she didn't, he said, "Elliott's sharp. He'll do all right."

She said, "I'd like him to stay with us for a while, before he leaves for good. Sort of a transition."

"The ranch ain't much closer to California."

"No—but it's closer to what he needs right now. He wants to get away from home, and he hasn't thought it through. I don't want to see him head off in his present state of mind."

"Did you see he'd been in a fight?"

"He's been in a lot of fights," she said quietly. "And he always will. He's going to play too large for a small town."

When Inetta wanted him to know something, she told him plain, and when she thought something was none of his business, she didn't say anything. She put this one somewhere in the middle, which meant she wanted him to figure it out on his own.

"You used to *live* in here—and you made kids *stay* in this place? Where did you bury their bodies?"

Leonard was showing Elliott the old cabin where he'd be staying for the summer. Despite Inetta's suggestion, he hadn't done much with it since Vaughn moved out. This was a ranch, not a hotel.

"It's gross! I can't believe my sister would make me live in a root cellar." Elliott was pushing it. The root cellar had caved in years ago.

"You done?"

"Okay, it's perfect—really. I was thinking about finding a room in a penal colony when I got to California anyway."

Leonard stepped out of the doorway and turned back to the house. "If I'd known we had a baby on the way, I'da painted the walls blue and put in a crib."

Elliott followed him, waving his hands. "Ah, I guess my

sense of humor's too warped. It'll be fine. Just don't be surprised if I fix the place up a little. I mean, seriously! I feel like Abe Lincoln."

Later, he told Inetta, "That brother a yours, he had me goin' out there. He was runnin' around, *ooo-ooo, spiders*! Next time you tell me to *think* about somethin' I'll know it means *do it*."

"He always makes me laugh," she said.

"S'pose you'll miss him."

"I will," she said, "but I'll still have a man to make me laugh."

Inetta settled in only to read or work a quilt, and even then she tasted pages and flickered over stitches with the energy of a hummingbird. Around him, she wore a mindful quiet that she left behind when she went out, like a housedress hung on a peg. When she returned from her trips to town, the world gusted in with her—from church, from the truck radio, from book club or the library, from people on the street, from the newspaper she bought. He would not say Inetta ever bubbled over, but she fizzed at the brim, especially after her classes at the quilt store.

Early on he made some journeys with her, some of it a new husband feeling his way, most, thinking it was a more judicious use of fuel to combine their errands. While she attended class, he could pick a load from the feed and seed, stop by Western Implement for necessities, prowl Surplus City's surprises and absorb a long coffee at the Mesa Drug soda fountain. From there his mission dwindled to time killing, and when he found himself picking through a pawnshop jumble of rusty tools, still waiting for the class to break up, he figured saving gas was costing him one way or another.

To his eye, Inetta's craft seemed advanced already, her sewing too meticulous to require a teacher's correction. She rarely made another version of the class project, and if her quilting improved after the Saturday instruction, the change was too subtle for him to detect.

"I don't go there to copy somebody," she told him. "Class is mostly a way to find something in myself I didn't know was there. Learning doesn't fill me up so much as opens me up. Shakes me loose and throws me off my habits—might even rearrange me. It's like if you only rode Brandy and not Geronimo or Elvis. Once in a while I want to get on a horse that scares me sideways."

He considered offering to give her a ride himself but let the joke go. Whenever he voiced a stupid thing that popped into his head, she took it as commentary, as if he had been working on it for a month. She informed him man jokes were poison darts tipped with the jester's own hurt. He didn't think so, but there it was in a book she left out for him with his truck keys marking the page. The woman's way was more indirect—a hint here, a nudge there, a question that appeared offhand but somehow nailed his shoes to the floor and sewed his tongue to the roof of his mouth. Inetta often laid things right under his nose. Like the barn cat that dropped mice in their bed, she wasn't necessarily trying to feed him, only expressing her nature. What he did with the information was up to him, and sometimes it took a while. When she told him on that first night she was a Christian, for example, he assumed it was her way of saying he better not try anything. Eventually, he understood she meant that her faith was essential to her and he better know it, the way he needed to know what time his train left the station.

Elliott had not grown up around cattle, so when they went out for the first time, Leonard put him on his best cow horse. Smitty could do a lot of the work on his own. "We're just gonna look over the calves on the range today. If we gotta cut pairs, I'll tell you what to do."

"Cut pears, what pears?"

"Cow and calf gotta stay together. If we need to bring one in to treat for somethin', the other comes, too."

"Oh, *pairs*," Elliott said.

"What did you think I said?"

"Never mind. You already think I'm a flake."

"You'll fit right in in California."

"Have you ever been there?"

"Farthest I been is Utah." The only other state he'd seen, in fact.

"You like being here, then," Elliott said. "I mean, around the people."

"The people." He didn't think much about that one way or the other. "They're fine. You take the ones you like and ignore the ones you don't."

"But it's harder in a small place to find someone you really like."

Leonard didn't have a good answer for that and he wasn't about to get into girlfriend talk with Inetta's little brother. "If you think you want to go to California, now's the time. You don't wanna get stuck where you ain't happy."

"I've been saving money, but it's hard."

"Got a skill?"

"I know orchards. A little car mechanics."

"You know someone out there?" Leonard asked.

"Not really."

"Big step, then."

"Yeah, one giant leap for Elliott Ferrin."

They came to a gate into the rangeland. Without being told, Elliott jumped down, opened it and closed it behind them.

"You must've never felt stuck when you were young," Elliott said.

"Hell, I'm only thirty-eight."

"I meant my age, like you didn't have any choice in life."

Leonard thought of Inetta standing on the weight and fate machine. "Not stuck, exactly, just a ways too far down a certain road. My uncle took me in and he raised cattle a little. It wasn't somethin' I chose. When he died, I just picked up the slack. I prefer the horse side of it."

Elliott said, "I can see why. The riding. The relationship. You don't send horses off to the slaughter."

"Cows're meant to be food. Horses, too, some places. It don't bother me, but yeah, the relationship."

"So why would you keep the cows and not raise horses? It's not like you're getting rich."

"Rich ain't the point."

"I know that. You were the one just saying you were on the wrong road. Isn't it easier to turn around than to keep on where you don't belong?"

None of the other boys he'd had help out at the ranch had talked to him this familiar way. Elliott was a relation, but they hardly knew each other. He scanned the brush for a change of subject.

"Look at that calf over there. I don't like the looks of that belly. Let's see if we can get it to mother up."

"How do we find its mother?"

"They usually find each other," Leonard said. "We just wanna provide some encouragement."

Trees are mostly wind and sign language, animals survive by staying still and mountains cause the weather by awaiting it. He had always kept his shades drawn, his talk necessary, his actions to the problem at hand, leaving it to others to fill in the silences, worry the what-ifs and tease out additional meanings. If his actions were straightforward and his word was good, that should take care of most of life right there. He was of the mind that talk got people into hot water more often than out of it, while Inetta believed humans would be better off if they communicated more like they prayed. She read him a magazine article about how elephants could convey their movements to each other over long distances, warn of trouble and signal their readiness to mate. That's what prayer can do, too, she said, if people just knew how to pay attention. He didn't know about elephants or prayer or how unspoken things were transmitted but something in what she said must be true. Otherwise, how could he know what love felt like?

From early on, they were different but well matched—salt and pepper, knife and fork. Churchgoing was where they were set on opposite sides of the plate. He suspected Inetta still prayed for his conversion, but she kept her silence on the subject and never pressed him to do more than what he chose. For his part, he would bow his head for grace and keep his opinions to himself. When Inetta found her new church in town, Word of Faith Assembly of God, she asked him if he wanted to come along.

"Just to see where I go," she said. "There's music, fellowship. Nobody's going to bite you."

"It ain't only the church," he said. "I'm no kind of joiner. I'd go once for you, but I ain't givin' myself over. It's wrong to keep showin' up if my heart ain't in it."

"I'm not out to make you miserable," she said. "Or to have

you make yourself miserable just for me. Let me know if you ever change your mind."

He didn't and that was that.

Their labors naturally divided—not as man and woman, but as farm-raised and ranch-raised. Or as he said, she grew up with Haralson apples and cherry pies while his were horse apples and cow pies. They wheeled about the ranch and across the valley, square dance partners obeying silent calls before returning home. Outdoors, Inetta worked like any hand. Inside, she made supper appear and dishes disappear. Corners became dustless. Bedding was aired, shirts folded, eggs sorted, letters answered, bills paid, tomatoes canned, books balanced. He noticed the transformations but knew only vaguely how the tricks were performed.

She did not change the house, except with small touches, like curtains for the windows and open pantry shelves, a lawyer's bookcase with up-and-over glass doors, rag rugs and coffee mugs she bought at the artist co-op. When he questioned replacing his perfectly good rubber soap caddy with a breakable clay dish, she answered, "Beauty's meant to be used, not just gawked at."

He could be a gawker, he had to admit. When he first visited Artists Point with her, he looked and then set the view aside, as if he'd just examined a picture postcard. Inetta approached the prospect new each time, remarking how the light repainted the scene as the sun crawled over the landscape. He half supposed the name drew her. Under its signpost she could fill her sketchbook and commune with the beauty without quite presuming to declare herself an artist. He understood some line separated picture-taking from art-making but not why she hesitated there. She could make sense of the big view—the red cliff canyons and monoliths, the moody ever-green mesa, the dry, elephantine Book Cliffs and the flat river bottom with the city sprouting out of it—but his eye found no place to rest. He didn't care to face eternity every time he turned around and his work made him focus closer to hand: on the keeper in the auction ring, the rattlesnake in the rocks, the leg-breaking badger hole, the slot canyon ready to boil in a rain storm. Between her dramatic vistas and his foreground of small particulars, the desert's middle expanse dissolved into a blur of browns and greys. Such a divided landscape almost demanded an extreme perspective—God's or the sparrow's.

Elliott turned out to be a good hand who more than earned his keep around the ranch. He had Inetta's ability to focus and restless energy that outlasted normal chores, so Leonard put him to work on one of the Pontiacs in back of the barn and let him strip parts from other cars.

"Hope you can get 'er runnin' before you leave," Leonard said. "I wanna surprise Inetta, so if she asks, let's just say this's a car you're workin' on for practice."

Elliott knew his way around an engine, which was eighty percent of the car's trouble, and Leonard rarely had to weigh in with advice. If the ranch stockpile didn't have what was needed, they prowled the salvage yards in town. The boy worked late, kept his cabin clean and never dragged the next day. He seemed lonely but never spoke of his parents or talked about missing friends back home. All his talk was of California and then, once he narrowed his target, of getting to San Francisco.

"He won't make a good hippie," Leonard joked to Inetta. "He works too hard."

"He's going to be fine," she said. "He just needs to get his bearings before he lands in a whole new world."

Inetta was right about summer at the ranch being enough of a transition for Elliott. One morning he brought the Pontiac keys to Leonard and said, "Your car's running now and my duffel's packed. I'm really ready to go. Can you get help for the fall?"

"We'll manage," Leonard said. "You got bus fare?"

"I do."

"Good, 'cause you'll need somethin' to cover your gas," he said, handing the keys back to Elliott.

Elliott took in a deep breath and puffed it out before he replied. "I thought you said you wanted to surprise Inetta with the car."

"Didn't say she'd be the only one surprised."

Alone again, they found a life, slow but sure, and the places he thought he had known forever opened up some more for him. The house, the pastures, the trails into the backcountry, even the settler cabin heavy with thwarted hopes. They sold off the cattle, bought a stallion for the brood mares and declared themselves in the horse business. It did not work out as clean as that, of course. Sometimes you have to charge money to discover how little the rest of the world values the things you hold most dear. So after the foaling season, Inetta handled more of the ranch chores and he'd find work in town—jobs that never stayed filled because they were low paid and started at daylight six days a week. Jobs where he never saw a boss all day. Jobs where he knew more than the one giving the orders. Jobs where they kept him waiting and then called him up and said never mind. Jobs where he had to know somebody. Jobs where nobody wanted to know his name. Jobs where they paid in cash. Jobs where they didn't pay in full. There were times when the work dried up, even for the ranchwise man looking for a few extra hours, and then Leonard and Inetta turned to barter, making do and doing without. After the work around the place was done—well, it was not ever done, but brought to completion, exhausted for the day—they leaned into each other without ever once thinking about it until they gradually became one, the way an old barn acquires sheds and coops and cribs. Their original lines were still distinguishable but they would never return to a freestanding state.

Now and then Inetta sold a consignment at the quilt shop, which, though it hardly compensated her, pleased her greatly. One evening, she beamed as if she had sold her entire stock. She drew from her fabric bag a bulky bundle wrapped in kraft paper, and placed it before him on the table. She slit the taped closure with a coffee spoon and reverently lifted the wrapping. "Will you look at that?"

He did—and saw a worn wool blanket. The predominant red had held up, but it was difficult to tell whether the stripe running around the border had always been gray, faded from black, or was once white and begrimed beyond reclamation. As she unfolded the thing, it got no better. The edges looked mouse-chewed and one corner was rounded and charred. At least it didn't smell worse than any other camp blanket.

"I got a commission," she said.

He thought he knew what a commission was, but wondered if a special meaning applied in this case.

"Someone brought it into the store looking for a quilter who could do something with it."

"Besides lettin' the dog sleep on it?"

"It's precious to them," she said. "It's wool. Just 'cause it's gone ratty doesn't mean it has to be the end."

That was true enough. He held onto things that weren't

quite done with because he never knew what might come in handy down the road. His repairs and solutions might be ingenious but the problems were usually straightforward. He knew what the outcome was supposed to be, and he either got it or he didn't and he tried something else. But this art business was a different deal. Taking a rag from a sentimental lady—it had to be, what man would ever think of such a thing?—and turning it into some unspecified treasure, well, that was the kind of job that could make tears run down your leg before it was over.

He knew he shouldn't say it. "How much?"

"Oh, don't spoil it. The money's not the point."

"What is, then?"

"Somebody has faith I can do it."

Inetta looked about as happy as he had ever seen her and he decided to remember the moment. It would help him keep his mouth shut if this went to hell.

"What about hearts?" he said as he toed open the door, bringing in the cold with his arms full of kindling.

Inetta had just flicked another domino of butter into a bowl of tamped-down potatoes. She sloshed in the milk, then mashed and whisked some more. "Hearts? What *about* hearts?"

"They're red. Like the blanket." He was trying.

Inetta looked at him. "Hon, hearts are pretty…obvious."

"Well, quilts're obvious, ain't they?"

She laughed. "Some. Most. But come to a quilt show with me sometime. You might be surprised."

"Wouldn't be surprised to find I'm the only man at a quilt show."

The potatoes were about the right consistency, judging by how they flew when she shook the whisk at him.

When he rose the next morning to poke the wood stove and put the heat on under the percolator, he found Inetta's sketchbook face down on the kitchen table. She had worked late on something, he knew, but they always put away their work, tired or not, finished or not. The place was too small to let things pile up. That she had left it out meant she wanted him to see it without having to submit it for his opinion. She knew he harbored sentiments deeper than his wisecracks, but they took all his concentration to surface. He had to grope after them like a drunk picking up change from a sticky bar top.

Looking at her papers terrified him. In the world of horses and machines, he easily connected what he saw with what it might mean. Hers was a world of yawning gaps and invisible connections. To him, anyway.

He turned the book over.

Even in outline, he recognized the plump bodies and rufous topknots of the Gambel's Quail, whose coveys scoot through the brush, intent on the ground like nuns late for evening prayers. Here, pairs faced each other, drooping comma forelocks almost touching. On other pages, he saw how Inetta examined different views—full-breasted; in cameos; framed in blocks; heads, beaks and crests abstracted into geometric shapes. Another study layered them, as if each bird were a feather. Without the red applied, it took a moment to register the form she was working out.

Hearts.

He turned back to earlier pages, lifting each sheet as if the sound might wake her. He recognized the pinnacles and sandstone sweeps of Monument Canyon. A page of geometry and another of jagged and crazy shapes. Throughout, Xs were slashed across sketches and some were abandoned half-finished. Inetta's restless mind was evident even in the rejections. There was no fine-tuning of a drawing, no erasure. Going forward again toward the last page, he could see her tracks wandering, scrambling over blind hills, before she gained her sense of direction and the images grew confident and strong.

Someone had faith in her, she said, but what did that mean? His business required trust, but trust was still based on reality. People proved honest or they cheated. They followed through or they dropped the ball. They delivered or made excuses. But faith concerned the unseen, the unsaid and the undelivered. The faith of millions had never brought God down out of the clouds, so how did the faith of one woman move Inetta?

They were back-to-back in the stable, currying a pair of bays he was getting ready for sale. Curry to dandy to brush, front to back, top to bottom—mirroring each other's motions already felt like a conversation, and so he dove in further.

"Y'know, I always do this before I deliver a horse, even when it's already been sold. You could say it's part of sayin' goodbye to the horse or it makes a customer want to buy from us again, but I don't think about it that way. Ain't that smart. Just like doin' it, and it works out to be right for everybody. The knowin', the doin' and the rhythm of it are the same single thing. Couldn't separate it all now if I had to. I can feel it right now with you, and the new owner's gonna feel it, too. Guess what I'm sayin' is, maybe there's somethin' like this in cuttin' apart an old blanket."

Inetta didn't say anything for a while. Then: "The cow. She has to be milked twice a day. Her milk goes in the pail and then I have to decide what to do with it. And then there are the chickens, and my job is to keep them healthy and fed, keep the coyotes and bobcats and skunks away, collect the eggs, rake out the manure, compost it. I may cook the eggs, sell them or give them away. I decide when we eat an old hen and how to cook it, just like I can decide whether we should sell the cow and buy our milk.

"It may seem I'm in charge of the chickens and that cow. But even with the power of life and death, I submit to those creatures. My submission is the same every day, no matter what, and it has nothing to do with me or the tiny little choices I make. I'm hardly separate from them. My responsibility commands me to serve them—even though I hold dominion over them. I wonder if that's how God sees us.

"And then there's my husband." Inetta put a hand on his hand, as if to reassure him she was not talking about him, but about all husbands and all wives for all time.

"A woman is supposed to honor and obey and submit to him, too. No matter how men and women try to slice and butter it to their own taste, that's how it's always been. That's how it seems to work. I'm blessed to have you as my husband, Len. I thank God for sending you to find me."

She took up the dandy brush and began stroking out the bits stirred up by the curry.

"I don't mind all this routine, Len. This is my life, my place in the world since I was a little girl, and I'm at peace with it. But then along comes this blanket, and there's no plan, no commandment, no boss, and nothing in its broken-down nature that dictates what I must do next. This woman, Terri Barclay, has just put it in my hands and I don't exactly know why. Whatever happens is all up to me."

"But ain't it always been up to you when you make a quilt?" he asked.

"I guess. But there's also the pattern books, the other

quilts in the shop, the classes, the pictures stored in my head. Things you don't even think about that tell you a quilt is a rectangle or a square and it's made up of blocks and you do this and you don't do that.

"Maybe everything that comes along is like you and that blanket, blessed surprises, and I just haven't seen it up till now. Maybe that cow's been waiting all this time for me to come up with a new way to empty her milk bag. Maybe all the times I thought it was the devil trying to get me to sin, it was really the Lord saying, *Inetta, maybe you should try this out for once.* But I honestly believe that would wear me down in a hurry, figuring out what was what every day. Going around in a white heat of creation all the time. Even God had to rest from it. Even He just lets the world run. It would be foolish for me to think I could do better. That I could go out on my own and make something that had never been made before. But once... just this once... I don't know, this is what I'm feeling. This is why that raggy old blanket has got me up at night."

Artifacts

BETWEEN THE BOOK CLIFFS AND THE RIVER is country he recognizes but doesn't quite know. As he drives his zig-zag course, Leonard remembers names on mail boxes, places he bought or delivered horses. Though the houses and outbuildings and corrals aren't much different from his, the open range is farther off and more of the land is in crops. These parts seem well settled into the grid, the alfalfa waiting for the sewer district to expand and plant a fresh cul-de-sackery named for tropical paradises and developers' daughters.

Ahead, a stretch of open field bangs up against a sheep fence that hems a tangle of push mowers, bicycle frames, rolls of barbed wire and miscellaneous appliances half parted-out, spilling their guts into the dirt. A pale yellow trailer slouches off its blocks against a flaking plywood vestibule. Behind it, pink beards of insulation sprout through another trailer's missing panels. An International pickup slumps on ruined tires. Its bed is a patchwork of past paint jobs, and the cab, partially buffed down to the bare steel, has acquired a brown patina that, in this climate, may take another decade to qualify as rust. Other vehicles in advanced states of decomposition point at a mysterious arrangement of obsolete farm implements. It's hard to imagine anyone voluntarily crossing the sagging wire fence line, but just in case, an eight-foot sign painted on a clipboard-brown sheet of Masonite guards the gate. With an out-of-place precision, the text is executed in white block letters, except for the NOs, rendered in a pomegranate red. He stops to take it all in:

NO TRESPASSING NO HUNTING NO SOLICITORS
NO BOY SCOUTS NO MORMONS OR JEH WITNESS
NO LONG-LOST RELATIVES NO DO-GOODERS
NO LOST DOG SEARCHERS NO LAND AGENTS
NO BILL COLLECTORS (OR TAX) NO TOURISTS
NO CAMERAS, ILLITERATES OR OTHER EXCUSE
IF YOU THINK THIS DOESN'T MEAN YOU
THEN IT MEANS YOU DELIVERIES ONLY
                              – C EDWARDS

Leonard doesn't know the owner, but he knows the impulse, and if he'd thought of it last year, he might've put up such a sign himself. As it happened, the traffic through his gate dwindled soon enough without one. It was June when Inetta died, a dry month when the weather was too moderate to prop up uncomfortable conversations. While she was alive, Inetta's prayer circle came in ones or twos, sprinkling prayers and wringing out handkerchiefs. They rejoiced and gave God credit for any lull or stutter in her disease's advance, and when death finished its dirty work, they took that as a triumph, too. With Inetta in her Glory and the Lord's greatness, mercy and everlasting love confirmed once again, their ministry was done. Apparently, the prospect of saving Leonard was too remote to keep up their interest.

By August, only Winnie Bonniver still called on him. Most of Inetta's friends, he was sure, reached the end of the brief mourning period with relief. Winnie seemed to take it as an opportunity to interest him in jigsaw puzzles. One afternoon she brought along a three-hundred-forty-piece "Millpond" puzzle in a can, spread the pieces on the coffee table and left a corner started for him. Next time by, she did not seem at all put out that he had not touched it. She spent several hours snacking on the pound cake she brought him while picking over pieces until she'd almost finished it.

He'd have to say he couldn't place Winnie when she was around during Inetta's last days. Winnie had a full square face, a thin lip line without a trace of red and a sort of workhorse disposition that tended to blend into the crowd. She tried to prime his memory one time with *I used to be a Lingenfelter* and when that didn't help his recall, she took it cheerfully, as if being overlooked were a sign of familiarity.

He thought Inetta was the only woman on earth who could endure his quiet cussedness, and so he relied on it too long to deter Winnie's continued visits. Instead of giving up, she traded the finished "Millpond" for a six-hundred-piece "Hoover Dam" and then showed up to check its progress, which proceeded only when she was on the job site. When she brought out a thousand-piece "Cupid's Kiss," he began to fear something else was going on, but he didn't know how to cut it off without hurting her feelings, so he moved the coffee table out to the barn and left the puzzle box on her porch the next time he was in town.

Winnie's efforts to move him to something new helped Leonard realize he had no expectations left, led him to see the year ahead as a continued unwinding, at the end of which dangled his promise to Inetta. There was no precise moment his plan began to form. It started shapeless and quietly wrapped itself around him, until the notion of the end felt like a comfort, and the walk to Artists Point seemed a fitting declaration that he was done.

Winnie had told him removing Inetta's clothes would be the hardest thing, and she offered to come in and take them away while he was out. But clothing in their house carried no sentiment as far as he was concerned. Her dresses did not come in Christmas packages, and she kept each article for its plain function until it wore down to rags or was pieced out to quilts. Despite Winnie's warning, he thought he could face the finality of an empty closet, so he put his head down and worked quickly one afternoon, scooping up shoeboxes, stripping shelves and dumping entire drawers into plastic trash bags. While this decisive work felt cleansing, the sight of the lumpish black bags slumbering on the floor spooked him, and he decided he should take them to town right away. With half the dresser already emptied, he could do without it, and he moved his pants, socks and underwear into peach boxes. He loaded up the coffee-puzzle table, too. It wasn't quite a full truckload, so he packed away more household goods—how many plates and cups did one man need?—then he covered the bed with a tarp and drove to the Goodwill.

He returned to the house and saw more things of use but no longer of value to him: pots and pans; books and the bookcase; two stuffed chairs where the kitchen chairs would now do; a floor lamp; the end table where the telephone sat; the telephone. He marked them all for future shipments. Then there were possessions worth something: the horse trailers; a couple saddles worth five hundred apiece to the right buyer; the tractor; the welder; Inetta's sewing console. He could sell these off to make a few pride payments against her bills. An auction would have been the easy way to go, but he couldn't bear his neighbors poking around and asking what he was up to, so he found a consignment house to take things off his hands and keep his name out of it. He sold off his remaining stock gradually to keep word from getting around that he was selling out, but the prices didn't stop some buyers from whispering that Leonard Self was losing his grip.

As the personal items disappeared, salvage came to the fore. All his life, he could no more discard pulled nails than watch a child drown, and the right scrap in his board pile could save a trip to the lumberyard. He kept the blue Oldsmobile with the broken axle and rusted-out body as a repository for any General Motors kin that someday might come coughing in search of an organ donation. The old icebox would have made a dandy smoker if he'd found the right piece of channel steel to hold the burner. Miscellaneous bits, buckles and cinch rings still waited to be mated with new leather. That odd length of rope could be spliced and inner tubes beyond patching still had useable rubber. He never knew what might come up, but like a man with money in the bank—maybe like C. Edwards—he had always felt ready for it. And then, over the last months, he wondered if anyone would even haul away his orphaned scrap for free.

Except for this purging, he cleaved to familiar chores, letting routine shuffle him past disquiet and dread, much as it had always done, and as there became less to do around the place, he started walking to fill the void. He never used to walk when he could ride, but now he followed the creek until it hit the fence and then he circled the fence line back to the house— mornings clockwise and evenings, counter-clock. With each day's circuit, he brought some random useless article and dropped it along his path—a church key, a carburetor float, a broken pocket watch, a faucet seat grinder, a suspender clip, a mechanical pencil with a rotary dialer on the end, a rotted rubber sink stopper and chain, a potato masher, a handful of used horseshoe nails. He imagined his junk rediscovered someday, its importance elevated by the mysterious pattern of distribution and the passage of enough time to scrub the names from the land.

Out of all the artifacts only two snuck up on him. A stout nickel Ingersoll alarm clock sat on Inetta's side of the bed. She'd always been the one to keep it going and afterwards it seemed beside any point of maintaining. His trouble was sleeping, not waking, and now he had fewer reasons to arise on time. Before he put it in the donation box, he wound it to make sure it still worked. The clock came alive in his hands and dragged him back to the nights when it stepped through the hours like a man with a bad leg hauling himself up the stairs— the tic stronger than the toc—*TIC-toc, TIC-toc. HEAVE-rest, HEAVE-rest.* He would try to tune it out the way he did the irregular electric train treadle of Inetta's sewing machine, but time never stops climbing the stairs and so he sometimes went out of range to find sleep in a chair, never considering that Inetta was left alone with the sound. And in the day, it must have measured her visitors' silences and concentrated everyone's thoughts upon the time of leaving. He tried to recall when he last heard the clock but could not fix the day Inetta gave up winding it.

And the other, a spiral-top Gregg steno pad containing nothing but hen scratches. He'd found the tablet in the last few days, saved like an ancient rune awaiting translation. When he flipped back the cover, he could hear again the rap of a card deck against the kitchen table, the castanet whir as the halves riffled back into each other, and the tick and slither of cards cast across the blue oilcloth into each other's hands. He and Inetta had often played gin rummy on winter nights. They had kept score with hatch marks in ranks of five so they didn't have to add up numbers, and though they recorded all the points, the columns were never totaled and the game never ended. They just picked up the tally where they'd left it, letting the marks flow from one night into the next, page after page, as the notebook changed hands and pencils blunted and sharpened again.

Inetta's scorekeeping came in crisp down strokes as regular as pickets, while Leonard's lines rose and fell, leaned or curled at the ends like bending grass. Looking down the columns—Inetta's to the right of the rule, Leonard's to the left—he remembered how the gap would spread apart and close again, as if they were caught shuffling up parallel aisles toward a common exit. Any evidence of those spikes and squalls and troughs and twists of daily play was now gone. The tracks through the tablet attested only to time and attention paid and how well matched they had turned out to be.

The cards would go fast at the Salvation Army, but who would want a notepad with only a few pages left? He flipped back to the last month, where he had begun to pull away, his column nearly full. Inetta's ended on the first line—ten wavy hatch marks tethered by their crossbars and the last two teetering into infinity.

Leonard lingers a while longer outside the tangled yard of Mr. C. Edwards. Impossible to tell if his jumble is a happy treasure trove or an insurmountable burden. Maybe one naturally becomes the other when a man lives too long.

Screening

LEONARD PUSHED BACK FROM THE SUPPER TABLE, a move that normally coincided with Inetta jumping up to clear the dishes. Instead, she remained seated, her hands in her lap, and for a time she stared at a whorl of Swiss chard left on her plate. He scooted forward again, studying her face for a sign of what was to come. During the day, they talked mostly in passing, across distances, hands busy, backs turned, gazes focused on something else that needed attention. Important words were left for the table. She brought up a bundle of envelopes and sat for a while longer, holding it with both hands. They didn't pick up the mail every day, and most times, she got it and presented him what he needed to see, which was little. Even the credit card companies didn't bother with Leonard Self.

"I guess I'm going to tell you," she said finally, taking off a rubber band and fanning the envelopes like she was getting ready for a card trick.

He waited. Wherever it was headed, this was not a good beginning.

"I was hoping to hold off." She spread the envelopes face up. He tried to decipher the sideways names. "But everybody says no."

"Everybody?" Leonard said dumbly.

"The clinic, the doctors, the Medicare, the Medicaid."

The only doctor he really knew was a veterinarian. Inetta wouldn't reach Medicare age for more than a year. He had applied for Medicare grudgingly and never used it except for that checkup where the doctor told him his enlarged prostate wasn't going to kill him unless he got in a wreck racing for the bathroom. And Medicaid. Wasn't that welfare?

"I got cancer, hon. Pancreatic. It's not good."

Cancer. They stayed work-fit, ate with balance and restraint, didn't smoke or drink. The strongest medicine around was for the horses; all they had in the house was aspirin and Absorbine Jr. He could see no outward signs of illness. Her mood was good. She didn't seem any slower at her work. She'd always been thin, so not much for cancer to carve away. Had her color changed? Maybe a little. He finally exhaled the breath he sucked in when he first heard the word. The chair clattered to the floor behind him, and he pivoted around the table to enfold her. He bent over her from behind and started to wrap his arms across her chest, and then he hesitated in case she was tender—*Where's her pancreas?* But then he recovered and warmed her neck with his breath and hoped the stillness he felt was her calm and not surrender.

"I should've told you but I was thinking it was mine to deal with. I just had a backache and I'd shake it off. Then I felt it in my chest and then in my belly. I wasn't even sure it was the same thing, but the hurt got worse and I saw the doctor. Then one thing leads to the next, one test to another, a doctor to a referral and then a bunch of things come in a hurry. Somewhere in there, I let my silence drift into secrecy, until the secrets became too large to tell. And then it turns out to be a big deal, and I don't want to spring it on you out of nowhere. I thought it might get better after the treatment and then, well, why upset you at all?"

"Me upset ain't as bad as you carryin' around a cancer."

"But what would you have done, Len? Even the doctors can't do much. Why make you worry about what can't be helped? What would you have done?"

"Comforted you."

She dropped her head a little. "Well, yes. Sometimes it seems Jesus has his hands full. I didn't mean to lie."

"You didn't lie. You just kept it to yourself too long."

Well, she'd told him now—that was the main thing—and he had to catch up. He slipped one hand under her knees and threaded the other arm around her back. He made as if to raise her out of the chair and she said, "Hold on, old man. One invalid in the family's enough."

She stood, reached around his neck and took a little hop into his arms, light as a bride. Too light. He toed open the cracked front door, elbowed off the outside lights, butted the screen and carried her out into the night where the heavens had spilled their star sugar across an indigo tablecloth.

Inetta pulled back from the sky to tell him, "I picked a bad one."

"How long's it been?"

"Months. Long enough to figure out I don't have emphysema, gas or gall bladder. Long enough to hear the difference in the doctor's voices."

He couldn't bring himself to ask the other how-long question, so he held her in the cool night until his arms were numb.

"We're being screened," said Inetta. On the top of the statements, bills and official letters she showed him a pamphlet: *Colorado Indigent Care Program.*

"Not for welfare," Leonard said. They were not *indigent*. They were not a *case*.

"Don't get all in an uproar. They're trying to help us. It's just how they do it when you don't have insurance. They want you to put it on a credit card or show you can pay or show you can't. If you can't, well, you do this form…"

"We'll pay."

As he said it, he knew what it meant. Not the exact dollars and cents of it, but the simple choice: the ranch for Inetta. The life they had here for another, smaller life somewhere else. Selling off only part of the ranch wasn't viable, not now. Any smart buyer would want the good pasture, the creek frontage and water rights, and there was already plenty of land out there for even the dumb buyers to choose from. Something was happening just below the bustle of the oil and gas development—unfinished buildings, lots with new curbs overgrown with tumbleweeds, for sale signs that never went down. He didn't count on someone else to pull out his bacon. Not insurance, not the government, not even his neighbors. He'd known that all his life. All you had was yourself—and, if you were lucky, one other. But they still had a chance. Surgery, radiation, chemo, whatever the doctors knew how to do against the thing. He wasn't going to let his wife be consumed—not without a damn fight.

"It's not going to be a fight," she said gently, as if he were the patient. "It'll be more of a walking to God."

Schism

Leonard considered Inetta the most tolerant person he knew. Her parents had not been, and they had driven away Elliott and Inetta by treating any spark in them as willfulness and every bit of difference as a sin. The Bible was supposed to be their guide, but Leonard saw how easily they made it conform to their own judgments and fears. Their version of the Word was so thick with reproach that its message of love and redemption seemed merely a salve applied to well-deserved wounds. Inetta's tolerance he judged by her acceptance of him, of course, and by the fact that she never spoke ill of her parents or anyone else. So, whenever the smallest reproaches came from Inetta's lips, they sounded scathing to him.

"You should have come with me—Easter of all times—to see it yourself," she said, describing Word of Faith's elaborate pageant that Leonard annually declined to attend because, he said, he already knew how it came out. "Nothing like this ever happened with Pastor Evans."

Maybe the new pastor just needed to make his own mark. That was the kind of thing Inetta would usually say, and since she didn't, he kept the thought to himself.

"You know when Jesus is on the cross with the thieves, and the Romans come to make sure they're dead?"

Leonard nodded. The story had stuck with him, even if the point behind it hadn't.

"This tall-skinny boy playing a soldier, he takes his spear and... you know what the scriptures say?"

"Maybe if I hear it."

Inetta said, "*But one of the soldiers with a spear pierced his side, and forthwith came there out blood and water.* Well, when the boy put up his spear, bloody water gushed out from Jesus!"

"Just like in the Bible," he said, as if he might appreciate that the scene was true to the account. In fact, he was thinking of ways he could have rigged the illusion. "Stickin' spears in people makes a better story. They must've put it in the book for some reason."

"To show Jesus really perished—but here the gore was unnecessary," she said. "We're celebrating the Resurrection, not Halloween. Ever since Pastor Zeb took over, things've been more show-businessy, more about money."

"Church always seemed about money to me."

"I'm not talking about the offerings," she said. "It's his emphasis on having money as a sign of God's love and approval I find distasteful. Jesus didn't die so we could get rich, and I don't go to church to see Calvary treated like it was some cowboy movie."

"Well, maybe this Pastor Zeb ain't right for you."

Inetta gave him a look that meant she didn't need to hear more on his side of it. "It wasn't just the blood, hon. And it's not just Zeb's preaching. It's the people he's starting to attract. You should have seen that boy who put in the spear. He was all solemn, but he acted proud—like he was the star of the show."

Expectation

CHOIR WAS SO WEIRD, Helen Vavoris thought. It was the only place in school you could find boys and girls who normally wouldn't be caught dead together doing stuff that was totally embarrassing if you thought about it too much. Druggies, brainiacs, prom queens and sluts, jocks, wall flowers, rich kids and poor spending forty minutes a day in eight-part harmony. Madonna and the Eurythmics were pushing Donna Summer and the Bee Gees off the radio. Prince and this new band called Nirvana were blasting new sounds and attitudes into rock music. And Helen was probably going to spend December in a nightgown and cap singing "It's Beginning to Look a Lot Like Christmas" everywhere she went. That was the trouble if you loved to sing in high school. They put you in a robe, just like you were in church. If you were good enough for Swing Choir, you got to perform for Kiwanis and the old ladies of Eastern Star, supposedly as representatives of Today's Youth, acting like kids who hardly existed in 1989 except when they visit their grandmothers. Helen could hardly wait to be on her own in life so she could stop acting fake just to make other people happy. At least by Christmas, the ordeal would be over. Poor Joe Samson, on the other hand, had to spend the entire summer crooning "Lida Rose" in a bow tie and straw boater with Neulan Kornhauer.

Joe and Neulan had been cast together as school board members for the Junction High production of *The Music Man*. Singing cornpone barbershop quartet songs in a musical production on stage was one thing, but then Mr. Genolia, the choir director, sent them out in the community on what he liked to call *gigs*. Crooning to Eastern Star ladies for free on a Tuesday night was not a *gig*.

Joe Samson was cute and popular enough to be kind of stuck-up. Besides his sweet voice, he was co-editor of the school paper and cross-country co-captain. It wasn't football, but smart guys with curly brown hair and blue eyes didn't have to be quarterbacks to be dreamy, Helen thought. Neulan, though, oh my God. He acted as if the summer circuit of retirement homes and Elks Clubs were Showtime. He didn't sing the leads, but his voice rumbled beneath the quartet in a register so deep and powerful that, like a great river, it demanded you trace it to its source. As far as real life was concerned, though, Neulan was the wrong Righteous Brother, Mr. Bassman at the punk party. He practically violated the school's dress code by going too far out in the uncool direction; with his waxy butch cut, heavy-framed glasses and unvarying black and white dress, Neulan could have stood with the soldiers in the photo of Helen's dad from the Korean War. Okay, Neulan was sort of smart—but in a model-airplane, ham-radio kind of way that *might* appeal to a girl who wasn't allowed to date or watch cable. You had to give Neulan credit. It took strength to be that peculiar. High school was cruel enough, even for those who weren't members of Bean Pole Baritones for Christ.

Neulan's mom didn't give him much choice, pumping him so full of Jesus like that. The lady was notorious. She let him be in *The Music Man* because it was wholesome, but she forbade trying out for other plays. Supposedly, she wrote a note to get

Neulan excused from gym class for life and when that didn't work, she told the teacher he wasn't allowed to wear shorts! No wonder he was so excited about being in a dumb church production of *The Ten Commandments*.

"Pastor Zeb really liked my audition," she heard Neulan telling Joe. (Neulan obviously thought singing barbershop made them friends.) "Mo-ses. Mo-ses," he intoned, then switched voices: *I am here, Lord.* "Put off thy shoes from off thy feet, for the place thou stand-est is ho-ly ground."

"That's great, man, really, really biblical," Joe said.

"He asked me to play the Voice of God."

"Is God a good part?" Joe asked, not so innocently.

"It's okay, but I said, Charlton Heston did God and Moses both."

Neulan's thundering laugh told Helen that Pastor Zeb must have bent to God's will.

Once a month the Film Society showed classic films in a college lecture hall with a raked floor and hard oak chairs with straight backs and desk arms for note taking. Helen thought Room 102, with its pull-down screen and scratchy sound system, was perfect for the semi-rebellious act of watching old movies. Going to the dollar double features was like skipping high school and going straight to adulthood, which, the more time she spent at Grand Junction High, became her goal.

When she arrived in her sophomore year, it seemed like everyone had already decided Helen was a coming attraction they didn't need to preview. *I had your sister Margaret*, a teacher would say, which meant, anything less than National Honor Society will be a severe disappointment to us all. "I'm not Margaret!" she wanted to shriek. "She studies. She's serious. She writes poetry? Fine, but I'll have poems written *about* me. If you can't tell the difference, too bad! Someday, you'll all figure out what you're missing."

Margaret was still okay to have as a sister. She had painted the night's combo of *Joan of Arc* and *The Blue Angel* in a vaguely redemptive light so their parents would allow Helen to go along with her on a school night. In Margaret's version, the Joan story reinforced the lesson that headstrong girls get burned, and *The Blue Angel* sounded like a harmless musical featuring nuns and Air Force stunt pilots.

Most of the audience was college students, with a few people from town. There was Mr. Philipp, her English teacher, accompanied by the formidable Miss Wright, the Speech teacher. No rumor material there, though. In hallway whispers, Mr. Philipp was linked with Mr. Genolia. The fact they'd never been seen together outside school practically proved they collaborated on more than directing the musicals.

Margaret said Ingrid Bergman was already thirty-three and a big star when she made *Joan of Arc*, and the director was famous for *Gone with the Wind* and *The Wizard of Oz*. "He died right after the movie came out," Margaret whispered as the film began. "Either Ingrid Bergman broke his heart or the movie did."

The film offered support for both theories. Bergman looked stunning in her silver armor during the opening credits before reappearing as the Middle Ages' most unlikely farm girl—the camera caressed her peach complexion stretched over impeccable cheekbones, luminous hazel eyes, impossibly full lips. And then, after her visions, Joan sits at her uncle's house, about to leave on her quest to save France. To disguise her for the journey to meet the Dauphin, her country braid is shorn to a Prince Valiant bob. As her uncle enters, Joan stands and the sheet around her shoulders falls away to reveal her grey doublet and tights.

"Why, you... you make a handsome lad!" stammers the uncle.

From somewhere in the hall came a student's cry: "Why, you... you... jeez, you're stacked!"

The room rocked. The breasts unnoticeable beneath Bergman's prim peasant layers had been thrust onward and upward, so any British soldier would seek to waylay this French "lad." Helen hated the mocking reduction of the heroine to her boobs, but the scene deserved it, and from then on she couldn't help but view Bergman's every gesture as fake—a famous actress who'd already been screwing her previous director, playing this beatific teenager. By the time of the big battle scene, when a wounded Joan pulled an arrow from her shoulder, Helen felt nothing at all.

In contrast to the spectacle of the first film, action in *The Blue Angel* crept past shadowy, foreboding images. Clucking chickens and honking geese for sale in a street marketplace. A dead pet bird tossed into a boiler. A student erasing a blackboard. Each time, the smart aleck in the audience called out "Ooo, foreshadowing!" until someone told him to shut up. Helen had never seen a foreign-language film before, and at first she felt disoriented by having to read the subtitles while gathering nuances from the actors' expressions and the German inflections. But the lingering pace, spare dialogue and broad acting soon allowed her to slip into the tale of the pompous professor overwhelmed by sexual attraction, his mouth puckered like the knotted end of a balloon as the cabaret performer Lola Lola hauled him down to utter humiliation.

On the drive home, Helen vented to Margaret. "Joan seemed so limp—even when she was supposed to be afraid or defiant. All the men were so bloodless, too. The churchmen standing around waiting to make their speeches. I don't get it.

Her lawyer, or whatever he was, and that monk. They hardly did anything to save her. Did the church make all the good people into zombies?"

Margaret was studying to be an English professor and she liked to practice on Helen. "Only that jailer-rapist showed any desire for Joan as flesh and blood. The rest were titillated by the possibility she could increase their power. But she also threatened them. A *girl* with a vision—that made her more dangerous than Lola Lola."

Helen responded quickly. "But not more interesting. Lola seemed real even when she was obviously acting. Like when she practically tapped the professor on the back with her spotlight and he turns around and sees her for the first time. She's like, *Yoo-hoo, forget finding those schoolboys. What you're looking for is over here.*"

Margaret nodded. "Do you think she really wanted the professor?"

"He sure thought so, but I bet she did it every night, making fun of someone who'd fall for her act. A fancy professor was probably a nice change from the drunken sailors."

Helen wanted to see below the surface of things the way Margaret did, but she'd always been too impatient to study as hard as her sister. She thought if she simply opened herself up to the world, the world should reveal itself to her, like the eggs the magician produced from the professor's nose at his wedding with Lola Lola.

Margaret said, "I wanted to like Joan more—the woman leading the army and not the cabaret singer showing men her panties. But you're right. Lola seemed more real and alive than God's girl."

"Lola Lola!" Helen cried. "Joan needed more Lola Lola."

They drove home laughing, chanting *Lola-Lola, Lola-Lola, Lola-Lola!*

As Margaret parked under the carport, Helen thought of the disgraced Professor Rath, reduced to playing a mournful clown with the cabaret, returning to be humiliated in his hometown. "Both those movies made me sad," Helen said.

"Because it was saint or temptress, God or panties," Margaret said. "What a choice they gave us. At least Rath went for it. A fall from grace is always more interesting than ascending into heaven. Joan fell for God and he used her. Then he dumped her and she just took it, right to the end. *Then* she got sainthood? Big deal."

Margaret turned in the seat and put her hand on Helen's knee. "It's funny to think of Lola Lola making those Inquisitors crow, but they would've burned her, too. Remember that, Hel. Don't take any crap and don't wait around to get saved. It's your choice, and you might as well be dangerous."

Three days later Mr. Philipp posted the audition announcement for the all-school play: *Joan of Lorraine*, by Maxwell Anderson. Alongside the notice, he'd tacked a tattered cover from *Newsweek* magazine showing an armored Ingrid Bergman from when she starred in the original. "Queen of the Broadway Season," it said. Helen wondered what Mr. Philipp thought of Bergman's performance in the film, if he adored women from the other side of the aisle or if he was more the Professor Rath type.

The Queen. That's why Bergman's Joan had been so unmoving! Joan of Arc was a peasant, not prom royalty. It was the 1400s. She probably wore the same dress all the time. Her whole family lived in the barn with the animals and had to pee in the fields. But she was still a teenager. She wouldn't just kneel there all glisteny-eyed if St. Michael the Archangel showed up out of nowhere. All the girls Helen knew would totally freak. *You want me to dress up like a boy and sneak behind enemy lines and sleep in tents with a bunch of farmers and have people shoot at me with crossbows?* That would be an exciting request all by itself, and with God saying he'd picked her, Helen imagined she'd shudder and whip around like a downed electrical wire. It would be religious passion, of course, but still. Put her in Joan's tunic, and she'd find a way to make the boys in the audience crow like the professor did.

First she had to win the part. It was true that Bette Campion looked more like Ingrid Bergman, and if Mr. Philipp had the Queen in mind, then Helen might as well forget it. But Bette Campion would never crop off her hair to play Joan. Bette had never suffered that much in her life.

Helen found the pages from *Joan of Lorraine* that Mr. Philipp distributed for the audition very disappointing. Unlike the movie, more than half the play wasn't about Joan of Arc at all, but about the rehearsals of a play about her. The actress who plays Joan doesn't like the way the director tells her to act the part, because she thinks Joan shouldn't compromise her ideals or something. Since that was how Helen felt, too, that part of the play should have been interesting. Instead, the big moral dilemma was sort of boring. Mr. Philipp said the author himself cut out all the play-within-a-play stuff for the film. Good move, as far as she was concerned. But Maxwell Anderson couldn't cut Ingrid Bergman, and so Helen knew exactly what was going to happen in tryouts. In high school, kids didn't act—they imitated what they saw in the movies or on TV, so they'd all show up pretending to be Ingrid Bergman. And people were so brainwashed, they'd go, wow, that's really a good Joan of Arc! Then it would come down to looks, and of course Bette Campion looked more like Ingrid Bergman than anyone. The whole thing was sickening.

If she was going to win the part, Helen had to forget everything she'd ever seen in the movie and everything she'd learned so far about acting, which was mostly about being fake. Besides imitating other people, you put on lots of makeup and unusual clothes to disguise yourself and pretend-listened to other people—because in a play you knew what they were going to say and because all you really cared about was what you were going to say next. In fact, you knew everything that was going to happen until the curtain fell and you were just trying to look good and get more applause than anyone else at the end. Kind of like high school.

Mr. Philipp made his honors class read this Russian director-actor guy named Stanislavski, and if you were in a play, he made sure everyone knew *there are no small parts, only small actors*, like that quote was supposed to make you feel better about being stuck with a crappy role. Some of the Stanislavski Helen read was too detailed and old-fashioned, and he wrote about plays she'd never heard of, but Stanislavski said some good stuff, too—like about finding a true way of walking, which was about how actors walked, but also about truth and locating hidden parts of yourself. She had even copied out one quote and taped it above her dresser:

> Bring yourself to the part of taking hold of a role, as if it were your own life. Speak for your character in your own person. When you sense this real kinship to your part, your newly created being will become soul of your soul, flesh of your flesh.

Helen used to think of acting as the opposite of real life, but Stanislavski persuaded her that an actor's job was learning to see, hear and love life and to carry it over into her art. Great actors were in a search for truth, and truth was, the French weren't just following some bimbo in shining armor to the Homecoming bonfire—it was war, and lots of them would die. In real life, Joan charged into battle, she stood up to the bishop, and she climbed right onto that pile of kindling. Who really wants to die for their beliefs, even if they believe they're right? How could Joan face burning alive without fear, unless… *Unless she was already burning inside!*

So far in Helen's life, passion seemed about wanting things, not giving herself up to something else. She had to learn what religious passion felt like. She'd never come close to a mystical experience before and didn't know how to go about finding one. She couldn't exactly invite the Holy Ghost to her house. According to Stanislavski, observation was the best way to start, but she had to find someone to observe—and fast. This was the best part for a girl she'd ever see in high school, and she had to go for it. Next year, the best she could do might be putting white shoe polish in her hair to play Elwood P. Dowd's sister.

Her parents were lax (or was it lapsed?) Methodists, Margaret thought she was a Transcendentalist, and Helen wasn't really anything. There were two Catholic churches in town, which was still a long way from fifteenth-century France, but that was about as close as she was going to get in Grand Junction. St. Bernard's was downtown in an old brick church—old for a town that was barely a hundred—and the priest there ran a soup kitchen for the poor. That was where the Mexicans went, too. Assumption had a modern-looking building that reminded her of the part of the Holiday Inn with the indoor pool. A peasant girl would for sure pick St. Bernard's.

Helen positioned herself in the balcony, where she could spot any impending signs of spiritual transport. Father Vincent's vestments were in the same ball park as what the inquisitors wore in the movie, but the entire Mass was in non-mystical English, and instead of the chants she'd hoped for, the music was Olivia-Newton-John-sounding folk performed by an overweight woman whose dress came down to her ankles, backed by a guitarist with a monk haircut who strummed every song with the same heavy stroke. The girls her age in the congregation were those pale, dark-haired ones that didn't know how to dress, who showed up in high school out of nowhere because they'd been in parochial school through junior high. Father Vincent did some mumbo jumbo with his back to the congregation, and then he talked to them about Nicaragua for so long she thought she was in Social Studies class.

When it came time for Communion, she stepped out in the aisle to let others pass to the altar. Methodists had Communion, too, but Catholics had started the franchise, so she expected a bit more ritual and old-fashioned fervor. No dice. It was like they were waiting in line at McDonald's; returning, they looked like kids trying not to get caught chewing gum in class. Just when she thought she'd never discover anything approaching Stanislavski's *real kinship*, Father Vincent called for the Kiss of Peace. She'd moved over when the communicants returned and was now trapped in the middle of the row. A grey old man with wiry hair escaping from every opening in his shirt turned his watery eyes toward her. The granny on her left was already engaged with someone. Leaping from the balcony was not an option. Helen raised her eyes heavenward for deliverance as the man clasped her hand in both of his and asked her, warmly, where she went to school.

After the big letdown from the Catholics, Helen didn't want to waste another Sunday on her search for religious ecstasy, so where to turn? The mainline Protestant churches seemed like different flavors of Methodist—vanilla with sprinkles, strawberry sauce or chocolate syrup. Of the million other fringy sects in the valley—Nazarenes, Brethren, Adventists, Witnesses, Mennonites, Christian Scientists, Foursquare— how could she possibly pick one? Mormons? They seemed the exact opposite of passionate, even with the polygamy stuff. There might be some Jews in town, though she'd never met one, and they were probably going to be too cerebral anyway. Quakers? Greek Orthodox? Unity? All in the phone book; all wrong for different reasons. The Indians had a vision quest, but that seemed like too much physical fitness mixed with starvation. From her vague grasp of Buddhism gained by watching *Kung Fu* reruns on TV, she decided Zen enlightenment would take way too long and, besides, Buddhists seemed even less interested than the Catholics in anything to do with enlightening girls.

Although she was a classmate, Vonda Rae Fitch might as well have gone to Central as far as Helen was concerned. Since Vonda Rae took the easy classes and worked after school, she and Helen only crossed paths in gym class, and even there they were in different worlds. Tallish and boyish, Vonda Rae threw a softball so hard it stung when you caught it, so Helen did her best to play on the other team. Helen's friends regarded laps around the track as an opportunity to stroll and socialize, while Vonda Rae loped circles around them. Her bobbed hair allowed her to blow out of the locker room without even using a dryer.

On Monday, the gym teacher handed out lacrosse sticks

and placed the class in two lines to flip balls back and forth, under the theory this would inspire girls to join the lacrosse club. Everyone expected Vonda Rae to wing it, so no one was too crazy about pairing up with her. Instead, she surprised Helen by offering soft lobs that Helen sometimes caught but was unable to reciprocate. Watching the girl stride after her wildest tosses, Helen had a small epiphany: if she were casting the soldier Joan purely on looks, Vonda Rae would win the role on the spot. And even better, she went to Neulan's holy-roller church!

"Vonda Rae…" Vonda Rae's eyes narrowed slightly. Helen had never spoken to her before. "I'm wondering… have you ever… like, heard strange voices speaking to you… just you?"

"What do you mean *strange*?"

"I don't know—because it's in a language I don't understand?"

Vonda Rae snatched up a low toss and sent it back. "Yeah, so? There's lots of languages I don't understand."

"It's not just the words, it's like where they're coming from… *heavenly* voices?" Helen should've worked this out first. Lying didn't seem like a good start for her research into religious ecstasy, but maybe she could make up for it later.

Vonda Rae looked wary, but interested. "How do you know they're heavenly? You're not making fun of me, are you?"

"No-no-no. I'm trying to figure out if God's trying to reach me."

"He's trying to reach everybody," Vonda Rae said. "How do the voices make you feel?"

"Scared, I guess. Mostly good."

"Yes. Well, they should—*if* they're from God."

"Who else would it be?"

The teacher blew her whistle. They were supposed to run a lap around the field before heading in. Vonda Rae started jogging backwards so she could hold Helen's eyes, then raised the lacrosse stick above her head and said, "So… if you really want to know… Word of Faith Assembly of God. Wednesday night. Seven o'clock."

Wednesday at Word of Faith was youth group, which was called Jesus Trek, but all the kids called it Trek for short. Helen supposed it came from the march up Calvary, but Trek made it sound slightly more cool and ambiguous—an adventure hike or a space exploration kind of thing. All she knew about the Assembly of God was the grownups who ran the church didn't want little kids to believe in Santa Claus or drink pop, the older kids were not supposed to date, and at services they played music you could almost dance to except they weren't allowed to dance—at least before marriage.

Word of Faith was built after the bigger churches started imitating shopping malls instead of cathedrals. Trek met in the Fellowship Hall instead of the basement like at the Methodist church. Still, it had the same lunchroom-and-linoleum feel covered with a hint of bleach.

As soon as she walked in, the youth pastor wanted to make eye contact. Helen knew about practicing in front of a mirror, and she believed he had spent major time perfecting his Staredown of Bliss. It said: *I am so happy with my life you can't make me blink, not even if you stare me in the eye for a million years.* He said, "Welcome. I'm Pastor Ryan. Everybody just calls me Ryan, hold the Pastor, heh-heh-heh."

Helen definitely wasn't going to do either one, and she looked around to see if anyone else seemed alarmed by Pastor Ryan. In one corner, boys were shoving each other and swaying as they talked, as if dodging ping-pong balls rapid-fired at their heads. They had a coltish cockiness that came from catching footballs and pinning opponents, but she knew from having classes with some of them that they'd soon fall into a new hierarchy of selling cars, fixing them or stealing them. Then there was Neulan Kornhauer. Definitely in the category of boys she did not want to lock eyes with outside school—the boys who think they're in your league if you're nice to them, which also means they think *you* are in *their* league. It felt even worse being around him in church, where she couldn't be a bitch.

Despite being in choir together, Neulan had never paid any attention to her before, yet he immediately swooped down as if she'd come to Trek especially to see him. He didn't actually say anything. He just hovered over her like he was about to offer her a spoonful of baby pudding. Kind of icky. Vonda Rae was more like, *hi, okay, you came*—almost shy, as if she hadn't been the one who invited Helen in the first place.

Pastor Ryan said, "Let us pray," and the random little groups quietly morphed into one circle. Neulan reached for her near hand, and a girl came up on the other side and took the other. His hand was surprisingly soft and his touch light. Everything else about him seemed so sharp-edgy—all ribs and elbows and knees and the tips of his bony shoulders that made two little tent poles in his shirt—it just seemed like his fingers should be that way, too. If she didn't know she was holding hands with Neulan Kornhauer, it wouldn't feel all that bad, and that realization made it even creepier.

Pastor Ryan's prayer unfolded like every prayer Helen had ever heard, starting with *Dear Lord*, like he was typing a letter when most of the time a prayer's more of a phone call that should start out *Hello, God*. Next came a bunch of flattery and stuff God already knows, and then thanks for the obvious, life, et cetera, et cetera. Then finally, he kind of nudged forward why he was really calling—not that he wanted to *ask* for anything special because man is so unworthy and God's real busy and what we really care about is Him, but just in case it's not too much trouble… And after some more super-backpedaling humility he said *in Jesus's name*, and everybody knew to say, *Amen*.

She moved her lips, but no sound escaped.

The group started to reshape itself again and move to a new circle of folding chairs. If the present configuration held, she risked being stuck with Neulan all night, so she darted for the opening between Pastor Ryan and Vonda Rae. Too late, she realized she had put herself at the top of the circle, where all eyes were on Pastor Ryan, who said, "Let's all take a moment to share something we're grateful for."

She was immediately grateful that Pastor Ryan looked to his right instead of his left.

This was obviously not the first night for the gratefulness question. The answers percolating around the circle seemed selected from a familiar master list: my parents, the beautiful day, a new dress, a postponed exam. God also confirmed his awesomeness by paying close attention to Janine Reed's cold and inspiring Todd Loman to set a personal pushup record. Instead of showing his boundless love by simply sending down a cure for cancer or making everybody smart in math, God sent personal reassurance by helping kids find their glasses or making sure their team won the football game. But if he let the team lose, that was showing love, too, the way parents keep their kids from eating too much candy.

Helen was only half listening to the litany of thanks until Neulan expressed gratitude for *seeing things in a new light*. She hoped she was not one of the illuminated things, and it dawned on her that she was not truly grateful for anything. She could get away with repeating one of the other responses but didn't want them to get the idea she fit in with their crowd. That would be the worst—word getting around school that Helen Vavoris had *joined* the Jesus freaks.

The moment passed to Vonda Rae, leaving Helen only one tick away. Vonda Rae hunched forward into a tuck and hugged her knees, peering across Helen toward Pastor Ryan with her head cocked like boys did in the middle of a cannonball to see if anyone was watching.

"So... I'm grateful because Helen came here tonight. She told me about some experiences she was having, and I thought at first she might just be teasing me, but I said she should come to Trek, and here she is, so... And also I'm grateful because this reminds me I shouldn't judge people who act different..."

Vonda Rae's shoulders fell and her eyes shifted downward—so different from the lithe Amazon of the playing fields. As she unfolded from her anxious crouch, she exhaled a final "So..." that handed the thread over to Helen, who took it with a tight smile, thinking: *YOU were judging ME?* It seemed like a good time to channel some of Joan's humility.

"Why am I grateful?" Helen raised her hands, a pianist poised over the keys. Then she cocked her head and asked, "What am I grateful for?" as if it had just occurred to her to rephrase the question so she could move it into a better light. Everyone knew she was stalling. Some of the faces were encouraging and expectant. Others clearly wanted to cry, *Come on, you had the most time of anyone!*

"You can pass, if you want," said Pastor Ryan.

"No, no... It's just... I'm not saying it's the voice of *God* I'm hearing, but..." But let them think that. She closed her eyes and bowed her head, listening for any murmurs from the circle.

Pastor Ryan tumbled right in. "And why wouldn't you?" he asked in an almost giddy tone. "He speaks to us."

"Out loud?"

"Heh-heh-heh." Pastor Ryan blinked. The circle rippled with perplexity. Some girls, eyes bugging, covered their mouths. Only Neulan Kornhauer looked at her directly, one eyebrow cocked, the opposite corner of his mouth drawn inscrutably. He might be doubting her. He might be curious. Oh, God. He might be *interested*.

"What do you mean, *out loud*?" Pastor Ryan asked.

Since she was making it up, Helen decided to go all out. "So you can *hear* hear it, not just in your mind... Like it was on headphones. I was hoping you guys had some experience with this."

"What does the voice say to you?" Pastor Ryan, half grilling, half ecstatic. He really wanted to know.

"It's hard to explain. It's not English."

"Is it like baby talk?" Janine Reed asked. She was intense, spooky pale and half-emaciated. In the old days, never would have made it out of Salem alive.

"Kind of," Helen guessed. Did these people speak in tongues? Excellent!

"It's more like music, I bet," said Neulan. "Like listening to a beautiful song on the radio, before you've learned the words. After, you can't get rid of the tune."

"Praise the Lord!" cried Pastor Ryan.

Okay, fine. So the Trekkers didn't burst into tongues at every meeting. But God, why weren't Charismatics more charismatic? Helen couldn't wait for the tongues of fire to descend on Pastor Ryan. It was time to check out Pastor Zeb himself.

The service at Word of Faith trickled to a start about ten after ten Sunday morning. People wandered about greeting each other and a mild man in a cardigan who clearly wasn't Pastor Zebulon Miller made some announcements while a quartet played dentist office music in the background. Neulan and three others eventually came forward from the choir, which hadn't sung a note, and a man in the front row of the congregation stood up and joined them. He moved to a microphone stand and slowly withdrew the mic from its mount as if he were lifting a long-stemmed rose from its vase. He opened his free hand in a sweeping signal to the keyboard player who ran a glissando down the scale to land on a chord that left Helen expecting another one. The man—who else could it be but Pastor Zeb?—stood poised with his head cocked, and smiled slightly, as if the decaying notes whispered him their secret.

"This is a song I wrote," he said, "called, 'He Won't Mind.'"

A wind-chimey tinkle led into a new progression of open-ended chords, and Pastor Zeb began to sing. Not just sing—*perform* like he was on a stage! Helen had never thought about religious music as being music you interpreted and sold to an audience. Her Methodist choir's main job was keeping the rest of the congregation in the right key. The hymns they sang sounded as if they'd been written for sewing machines by men in powdered wigs. This ensemble sounded like Air Supply, with the pop-song choruses repeating and building. Worshippers swayed and lifted their palms as if they were checking for rain or waved overhead the way people do when they're trying to attract the attention of someone who's beyond shouting distance.

Pastor Zeb called his wife Cindy onstage. Her helmet of blonde hair could withstand whatever whirlwind the Last Days might throw her way. Definitely a part Bette Campion could play. Cindy told how their old washing machine had quit and a repairman had pronounced it dead. There was no money in the budget for a new one, she said, and the dirty clothes from their large family—Praise the Lord!—had begun to pile up.

"It's getting bad," Pastor Zeb said. "Cindy has to wash my socks by hand."

Cindy, as the script must have called for, waved away an imaginary odor. The congregation obliged with a laugh. Nothing like a good old stink joke for utter hilarity in church. Pastor Zeb gave Cindy a little squeeze that dismissed her from the skit, and he straightened from a hapless husband into a commanding head of the household. "So what's to be done?" he asked. "What *is*... to be *done*?"

He looked out to the congregation with a *w-e-l-l?* sort of expression. They knew he was all ready to go with his words of scripture, so they waited for the answer. Helen knew what her family would do. Old machines gave up the ghost and life went on. You read *Consumer Reports*. You bought on credit or saved your money for a replacement. But Pastor Zeb was treating the dead washing machine like it posed an immense test of faith.

"What do most people—even many Christians—do in a situation like this?" Pastor Zeb spread his arms and looked heavenward. "They get mad and they cry, *why me? Why me, Lord?* Then, they calm down. They get a little perspective. Maybe they're even a little bit ashamed, because they know the Lord occasionally tosses tribulations toward believers. So they accept it as a test of faith. But then what happens?"

He waited again, but it was a dramatic pause, not an invitation to answer. "They flunk the test. They *flunk* the *test!*"

He strode to the other end of the stage so he could lean into a different part of the congregation. "And you say, 'Come on, Pastor Zeb. *They prayed!* What's wrong with that? They didn't expect God to deliver a new washing machine.' And you say, 'They were willing to go out and earn the money. They just hoped and prayed a solution would be found.' And you would be right, that is exactly what many people would do. They would hope their prayers would be answered."

A weary look crossed his face and he stepped over to the lectern and snatched up a Bible. "But that is not the response of someone truly living in the Word, is it? What does the Bible teach us?"

The Bible was just a prop. Without looking, he said, "Paul in Romans 15:4 tells us 'that we, through the endurance and comfort of the scriptures, might have *expectation*,' and Romans 15:13 goes on to call God 'the God of *expectation*.' It says, 'May the God of *expectation* fill you with all joy and peace in believing, so that you may *abound* in *expectation*.'

"The scripture tells us there is joy and peace in believing. We can *abound* in *expectation!* Some translations do say 'hope,' but hoping is different from expecting, isn't it?"

Yes, I am hoping you will wrap this up soon, but I expect to be disappointed.

"*Hoping* is: maybe it will, maybe it won't. It's all about a wish or desire of yours that remains unfilled. But when you *believe*, you *expect* things to come to pass. When you *believe*, you await that which you *know* shall be fulfilled. There is no maybe. No uncertainty. Because *you have God's word* on it!" He drummed out four slaps on the Bible in time with the words, and cradled the book in his hands for a moment. He was radiant now, as if he had shaken off years of worry.

"When you were a child, do you remember your father going off to work in the morning? You didn't just hope he would come home at the end of the day, did you? You *expected* him. You *knew* he would be back, and you *carried* that knowledge throughout the day. And as the time approached, as your mother started preparing dinner or you heard a car coming down the street, you would get all excited because you were brimming with *ex-pec-tation*."

Pastor Zeb watched the imaginary street for the imaginary father. His head was bobbing and the tips of his fingers were waggling. "Your faith in your father made it possible for you to live in a childlike state of pleasure and joy!"

He ran in a toddler-like shamble toward the imaginary father in the imaginary doorway and stopped there, with his back to the worship hall.

When he turned, he was an adult again.

"But we are not children. We have put away childish things, haven't we? And we know not all families are happy and not all daddies come home at night. And we know God is not the Maytag Repairman. So what then is the basis of our expectation? God tells us in Luke 6:38, 'Give, and it shall be given unto you; good measure, pressed down, and shaken together, and running over, shall men give into your bosom.' Did you get that? This verse calls for rejoicing, for emotion, for *jump*-ing-*up*-and-*down*!"

Pastor Zeb channeled the little child again, grinning and staggering around the stage. People began to hoot and clap and shout *Amen!*

"Amen!" said Pastor Zeb. "A-*men*."

If this was how Vonda Rae's church was going to be, forget it. Helen didn't come to come to Jesus, and she didn't want to hear boring home life turned into Bible lessons. She wasn't going to drive to the God store like she was sure it was going to be open, even though the lights were off and no one was answering the phone, because God would have told her if it was closed. She didn't want a new washing machine. She wanted to forget about the laundry, forget what other people thought, even forget how to speak her own language.

"Helen! Are you coming tonight?"

Oh, God. Neulan, shut up. After being so into her at Trek, he'd been ignoring her at school, for which she was thankful. Neulan was strange but he was still a boy, and he was acting the way boys did who made out with you at a party and then the next day wouldn't even look at you.

"Haven't decided."

"Do."

Had he gone out of his way to intercept her? Now he had so obviously fallen into step with her, chopping that long stride of his. They both walked to school. She from the south, he from the east. She was far enough away to ride the bus, but somehow that was even worse than walking.

Then a thought. It wasn't evil. It was just a question. "Do you ever speak in tongues?"

Neulan stopped, but didn't act surprised. "Me? No. *Tongues are for a sign, not to them that believe, but to them that believe not*—1 Corinthians 14:22." He looked pleased with himself.

"Come on, you're making that up."

"No, I'm not. I've been studying."

"Studying what?

"The Word. About voices. You said last week you were hearing voices."

"I didn't say anything about speaking in tongues, so why were you studying that?" She thought she had him there.

"Because you sounded confused about what was being said to you. God doesn't speak to people so they can't understand. If that was God you heard, it would be clear, not a puzzlement."

A puzzlement!

Neulan went on. "The Apostles spoke in tongues so unbelievers from other places could understand the Word. *Tongues are a sign for them that believe not*—and you are an unbeliever, aren't you? So if you truly heard a prophet speaking in tongues, you would understand him, too. It wouldn't sound like *Ah hama hr-r-reeshma cala bah xhota dohbalala to ma sha-lah.*"

"You said you didn't speak in tongues."

"I don't. It's not biblical to talk babble. And it's not biblical to hear babble and believe it's the Word of God. So if you heard something that sounded like HebrewLatinGreekApache, then it was the devil or..." Neulan left it there.

"You don't believe me about the voices?" she said.

"I believe you are seeking something. I don't believe you've found it."

They stood at the light waiting to cross North Avenue. She focused on the walk sign, unsure what to say. Neulan lived on this side of the avenue, but he seemed to be planning to cross with her.

"Your question is really not about hearing voices or speaking in tongues," he said. "The right question should be: what is it like to be visited by the Holy Spirit?"

The light changed, and he continued with her. "Of course, if you had been, you would already know the answer."

Who is this guy?

"Okay, so what's it like?" she asked.

Neulan looked down at her. She hoped she looked sincere.

"Have you ever changed the oil in your car?"

"Oh, all the time."

"Well, you know when you're underneath breaking loose the drain plug?"

One minute he seems like he gets it, and then...

"And then the oil starts coming, and you do the last couple turns by hand so the plug doesn't drop in the drain pan? And then the warm oil starts oozing over your fingers? That's kind of what it feels like—like your whole body, starting with the top of your head, is suddenly being covered in warm oil."

"And what does it feel like inside? What do you do?"

"You feel like laughing," he said.

"Laughing? What's funny?"

"It's not like laughing at a joke. It's like you're overjoyed and you can't contain yourself."

Neulan was smiling, light-footed. Radiant, if that was possible.

"Do you jump around or anything?"

He laughed in that big, resonant voice. "I have some cousins in Missouri who do that. Southern Baptists. But no," he said.

"So you just laugh…"

"I *feel* like laughing. Sometimes I do, and sometimes I don't. Sometimes I sing. Sometimes I just sit there rejoicing in the Spirit."

It sounded like what being stoned was supposed to be, but she decided not to say it. "Does it happen a lot?"

"You wouldn't want it to happen a lot," Neulan said. "People who speak in tongues must believe that's how they're supposed to receive the Spirit because they see it in church or their minister talks about it. Maybe they want a sign that they're anointed like the Apostles, so they seek after it. I'm not saying it's wrong, not if it's a genuine response to the Holy Spirit. They're just like you, chasing after something they think they're supposed to have."

He was getting way too personal. "So it's like laughing," she said.

"Laughter's the real tongues—the universal language. Everybody speaks it. Everybody understands it."

If Neulan was right, she could imagine it now—maybe even feel the breeze. Jesus or the Holy Spirit or even St. Michael in the play would grab you and tickle you until you couldn't stand it anymore. Once he had you, it was like you didn't dare try to get away because you knew Jesus would come after you and he could find you no matter what and he wouldn't stop tickling you so you would throw up your hands and grab for things you couldn't reach and you'd struggle to get away but you couldn't and you weren't sure you should because Jesus loved you so very, very much. It wasn't his fault that his love made you ecstatic and scared the shit out of you at the same time. Your heart would be bursting and you'd be gasping for air, you'd be laughing so hard. And when you were through, when he finally let you up, even breathing regular would feel like the most amazing thing in the world and it would change you forever.

Something like that.

Of course, it wouldn't really be Jesus doing it. It would be you, doing it to yourself, because you had this huge longing in you. The world was so immense and heartbreaking if you couldn't fill more of it. You had to forget how tiny you were and just go for the whole thing. But if you truly got sucked into this parallel Jesus universe and forgot about everything except pleasing God, you'd just be lost in a different way. You had to have a real purpose in life—outside of God, outside yourself— like Joan, like saving France.

Didn't you? Didn't you have to look into your own soul first, before God got hold of you?

"Have you ever read Stanislavski?" she asked.

"Who?"

"Never mind."

Helen was at her front door, and she couldn't believe she had just let Neulan Kornhauer walk her home from school.

Helen was excited all over again about playing Joan, about bringing this new information from Neulan to her part. Mr. Philipp was going to be amazed when she came out of nowhere and showed him this girl who threw off sparks, who jumped out of her skin, who rejoiced in the spirit, who heard St. Michael and the other saints and was overcome with divine laughter. That was how she'd finish it, too—with the lines near the end where the inquisitors threaten her with the fire, when Joan says:

> Every man gives his life for what he believes. Every woman gives her life for what she believes. Sometimes people believe in little or nothing. Nevertheless, they give up their lives to that little or nothing. One life is all we have, and we live it as we believe in living it, and then it's gone. But to surrender what you are, and live without belief, that's more terrible than dying—more terrible than dying young.

Then she would laugh the laughter of Joan's *certainty*. She was sure Bette Campion wouldn't be laughing.

Pastor Ryan was so glad to see her, Helen wondered if he was working on commission. He tested Neulan's theory that laughter is a natural language. His laugh came in these delayed *heh-heh-hehs*, like his Laser Eyes of Happiness were drawing so much juice that the laugh signal was getting interrupted on the way to his brain.

Instead of the "why am I grateful" round robin, this time

Pastor Ryan wanted the group to react to Pastor Zeb's washing machine dilemma. He recounted the tale of the broken washer and even repeated the joke about the smelly socks. Helen could tell the biggest suck-ups by who laughed again at the dumb joke like it was the first time they heard it. Not Neulan.

"What do you think?" Pastor Ryan folded his arms and leaned back in the chair. "What would you do if you were in the pastor's shoes? Anyone."

Helen couldn't help herself.

"I would do exactly what he's doing."

"Good. And what's Pastor Zeb doing?"

"Telling everyone in church he believes God will give him a new washer. If he gets one, it will prove God cares about believers, so of course they'll buy him one!"

Pastor Ryan's Adam's apple dropped, his eyebrows popped up, and his Laser Eyes stopped lasering. "Heh-heh-heh. Praise the Lord!"

Yes, it was like he was wired all wrong.

"Pastor Zeb instructed us that we must demonstrate our expectation of *salvation*. The washing machine was a met-a-phor." As Pastor Ryan emphasized the word, Neulan left the circle and went over to a short stack of two-by-four lumber piled against a wall. He moved the boards to the middle of the room and aligned them across the floor.

Pastor Ryan found a passage in his Bible: "In Hebrews 10:23, Paul says: *Let us hold fast the confession of our expectation without wavering; (for he is faithful that promised)*. He's telling us the Lord is *trustworthy*. But it's easy to waver, isn't it? The world is always giving us excuses to doubt or get distracted by circumstances or go back to our old ways. In fact, it's pretty darn convenient to *expect* without getting off our lazy behinds!"

Pastor Ryan made a show of looking around the entire

circle, but he made sure his gaze landed on Helen at the end. He went to one end of the boards and said, "I'd like a volunteer over here to walk all fifty feet of this line."

Todd Loman jumped right up and sauntered over.

"Okay, Todd," said Pastor Ryan. "I'm looking for you to get to the other end without wavering or falling off."

Todd stepped onto the board and crouched a little, holding out his arms like a surfer before he moved briskly across the full distance, hopped off and took a bow.

"Piece of cake!" said Pastor Ryan. "Piece of cake. I bet any of us could do that. Now, let me tell you a story from back in 1859. There was a French acrobat by the name of Charles Blondin who wanted to cross the gorge below Niagara Falls on a tightrope. Like Todd, he was a show off."

He waited for the titters. "It was a spot about a quarter-mile wide and one hundred sixty feet above the water. No one had attempted this before and lots of people called him a lunatic. The top surface of his rope was about two inches wide."

Neulan turned all the boards on edge.

"So imagine. Imagine this line extends twenty times farther. It sags and sways in the wind. There's nothing to grab onto or catch you until you hit the ice-cold river more than twelve stories below. Anyone want to try now?"

Todd Loman bounded back and mounted the first board. He moved cautiously, but the boards twisted underfoot and he fell off. After repeated tries, he never made it beyond half way.

"Well, Charles Blondin made it, but that wasn't enough. He went across again, blindfolded. Then he did it wrapped in a sack. Each time bigger and bigger crowds appeared. They wanted to see his next trick, and they wanted to be there in case he fell. One time he pushed a wheelbarrow across the gorge. When he got to the other side, he asked the crowd, *Do you think I can make it back?* Everyone said yes! *Even if I do it with a person riding in the wheelbarrow?* They said yes again. *Shall I try it now?* Everybody said yes!"

Pastor Ryan, as Charles Blondin, looked over the circle and said, "All right, who's my volunteer?"

Neulan pretended to be someone in the Niagara Falls crowd. He looked up in the air and tapped his fingers on his chin in an exaggerated fashion.

Pastor Ryan pointed to him. "You, sir! Do you believe I can do it? I need a passenger."

Neulan struck a self-important pose and said, "Oh, I believe you can, but I was just about to leave for an appointment."

"How about you, sir. Will you come with me?"

Neulan became another spectator. "I would, but my family depends on me, and I dare not put their well-being at risk."

"And you?"

Neulan said, "I'm petrified of heights. My trembling would put your life in danger."

Turning back toward the circle, Pastor Ryan was clearly pleased with his corny playlet. "It's easy to waver when you're tested. It's easy to profess faith, but *belief* is getting *in* the wheelbarrow! They *flunked* the *test!*" Just like Pastor Zeb, Pastor Ryan thumped his Bible to emphasize the words. "And how about you? Everyone said they believed, but no one was prepared to get in. Belief is not words or feelings. It's *action*. It's living in *ex-pec-tation* of your belief!"

Helen felt embarrassed for Neulan during these theatrics, but he didn't seem to mind. He stood with his palms out, eyes closed and face upraised. She looked to Vonda Rae, who had tears running down her cheeks. Other girls sobbed quietly, like they'd just gotten a breakup note. The boys sat rocking themselves as if listening to God on the radio.

Vonda Rae held her hand aloft. Eventually, it dawned on Pastor Ryan she was not worshipping, but had a question. "What about Charles?" she asked.

"Who? What do you mean?" Pastor Ryan said.

"Charles Blondin, who walked the tightrope. What happened to him?"

Good question, Vonda Rae. Did he keep doing ever-more risky stunts until he broke his neck? Did he chicken out one day? Maybe he died of old age, surrounded by his fans. That's what should've happened. He was the original brave one in the story, the one who risked everything.

"After Niagara Falls? I don't know. The story was a parable about trusting Jesus."

"I know *that*," said Vonda Rae. "But was he saved?"

"I don't know," said Pastor Ryan.

"You can't ever know!" Helen blurted.

"Heh, heh, heh," said Pastor Ryan. "Heh, heh, heh."

Original

HELEN PEDALED UP A LONG, GRASSY HILL on her dad's old three-speed. Each time she pulled the little trigger on the shifter, another gear materialized and she climbed faster. As she breached the top, suddenly she flew free of the bike with her arms and legs trailing her curled body, as if she'd been blown away from the center of an explosion. The reverse dream physics that hurtled her upward now slowed her descent and she landed gently on her side in soft grass that swaddled her in a snug embrace. A sensation of being paralyzed woke her and still she couldn't move. Something was pinning her covers.

"Margaret?"

A shape on the bed did not budge but the voice was Margaret's. "Where the hell have you been going at night?" she hissed.

"None of your business."

"I knew it! You're doing something stupid."

"Get off my bed!" *How could she scream in a whisper?* Helen tried to throw an elbow, but was hemmed in up to her shoulders.

"Look," Margaret said. "I don't care what it is—or who it is. I'm not going to tell. Just don't... be... stupid. Do you know what I'm talking about?"

"You're the one who doesn't know what you're talking about."

"Then tell me."

"You'll laugh," Helen said.

"I won't. But so what if I do? I don't want to go around worrying about you."

Helen thought: *Margaret's worrying about me?* But she said, "You're not mother."

"Well mother's going to notice you sneaking around, too."

"I'm not sneaking."

"True. Sneaking would require subtlety."

What did Margaret want from her? She usually didn't care what Helen did. She probably was maneuvering to get Helen grounded so she could use the car on Wednesdays, too. Well, screw her. There was no way their parents would ground her for going to a church youth group, even with the Assembly of Godders.

"I'm going to church," Helen said.

The pressure on the blanket released. Helen sat up and tried to make out her sister's face.

"Oh, Hel," Margaret sighed. The old nickname used to torment Helen when she was little. But now it sounded tender. "That's even worse than a bad boyfriend."

"I started out doing it for the play," Helen said, "because I really wanted the part. But the part isn't what I thought. Now I think it's the real Joan I care about. She got to become a saint, but I don't think she ever got to be herself."

Margaret said, "She stood up for what she believed."

"I don't know. I mean, she was thirteen when God or whatever voice first came to help her *govern herself.* That's what she thought was happening when they made her change and dress like a boy and play a soldier. And then she became a heretic and martyr. Then history made her an icon, and the movie made her gorgeous. It's not like she couldn't be any of those things, but was any of that what she really chose? Why didn't she just laugh in God's face and say, hey, I'm underage?"

Margaret put her arms around Helen. "They had to grow up sooner in those days," she said.

Helen laid her head on her sister's shoulder. "Having God's babies isn't growing up—it's giving up."

The whoosh-clang of locker doors. Three octaves of voices trilling and booming across the scale. Levi's seams whistling. Books slapping terrazzo. The white noise of shuffling feet.

"Where were you last night?" Vonda Rae said, a little too urgently.

Suddenly everybody cares about where I am. "I didn't have a hat," Helen said. She'd bailed on Hat Night at Jesus Trek.

"Oh, that didn't matter. We missed you."

Somehow I doubt that.

"Okay. Look, I'm supposed to tell you. We don't have Trek next Wednesday. We're busy getting ready for the Faith Jamboree." Vonda Rae took a deep breath, as if the preparations were already exhausting her. "Then," counting the Wednesdays on her fingers, "it's the middle of Jamboree—no Trek again. So plan on coming the Saturday or Sunday of Jamboree."

"Oh, Vonda Rae, I don't think…"

Vonda Rae would not be shaken. "I know it's Homecoming weekend, and I know it's not easy coming to God when you're so smart. You think you need proof for everything. Well, come to this, and you'll see." She pushed a piece of paper into Helen's hand and wrapped her fingers around it.

"Promise me? Please? I'll sign you up." Vonda Rae hugged her for a second, then bounced away. Seen in the chaos of the hallway, it could have been the random collision of two people headed in opposite directions.

The canary-colored flier featured Independence Monument and the photo of a long-faced, balding man with side wings of unclipped hair. At first glance it appeared the special guest speaker was a Golden Retriever.

Special Faith Jamboree Speaker
"Rocks, Fossils and the Biblical Record"
October 20-21, 1989

Dr. Woodman Nasby, author of *Genesis, the Flood, and the Young Earth: A Biblical Interpretation of the Geological Record*, will give an illustrated lecture on the topic at Word of Faith Church at 7 p.m., Saturday the 20th. Sunday the 21st he will lead a bus tour of the Colorado National Monument leaving from the church at noon following the 10 a.m. service. Luncheon provided.

Secular science claims the dramatic landscape of the Monument was caused by uplift and erosion over millions of years. Come witness with Dr. Nasby as he explains how key geological formations and the fossil record in the Grand Valley confirm the Lord's handiwork. Learn how all of this beauty we enjoy is consistent with God's plan and creation as revealed in His Word.

Dr. Nasby is a professor of Flood Studies and chair of the Biblical Science Department at College of the Redeemer in Ft. Smith, Arkansas. He is also author of *The First Manager: How Noah Saved Civilization.*

What a perfect way to spend a Sunday. A ride up the Monument with a bus full of Trekkers who were convinced the earth was six thousand years old, with Vonda Rae and Neulan both mooning over her. No matter. After the audition, they'd be history. She'd have new places to go and bigger things to do by the time the Word of Faith bus rolled backward through the Old Testament.

Down by the roller dam a keg flowed and sparks ricocheted against a black October sky while the Fine Young Cannibals sang *She drives meh crazy—hoo-hoo.* Since it was still cross-country season, Joe Samson shouldn't have been there, and that went for all the partiers around the fire—a few dozen kids working hard at being nonconformist but too good to be hood. Colorado had raised the age for beer consumption to twenty-one the year before, disappointing the seniors who'd entered high school looking forward to being legal at eighteen. This would be his only woodsy of the fall, he told himself, one symbolic act of solidarity with his fellow outlaws before dedicating himself to serious partying in the spring.

Helen Vavoris orbited the bonfire holding the arms of her sweater overhead, trailing it like a drogue chute as she swooped and dipped, twisted and yipped. Her ululation as she darted in and out of the flame-wobbled shadows made Joe think of a movie Indian, but her movements weren't tribal. She danced by herself and, if she was drunk as she looked, she was going to need a ride home. She looked good, but a lot of girls appealed to him that night and it wasn't just the beer. He was in the phase of life when most experiences and thoughts seemed exceptional simply because he had them.

Joe wasn't the only one following her. Some girls rolled their eyes; others squinted with lemony expressions. The boys standing with them pretended to scan the entire scene so Helen's act didn't appear to be of special interest.

She could be worth a shot.

Finally, she paused, heaving, away from the heat. She picked up a cup set on a fallen cottonwood, drank deeply and sat down to watch the river.

Now.

"With those moves, you should try out for Swing Choir," he said. "I know you sing."

"Oh, the great Joe Samson remembers me! Maybe I would, if you guys weren't always doing my parents' music."

Feeling his advantage shifting, he decided to change the subject. "What are you drinking?"

"The world."

"Funny." Palmed joints were being passed along the dark edge of the fire circle. Maybe her ecstasy wasn't from the Coors. "Are you sharing?" he said.

She gave her head a slow shake that Joe could read two ways—*no*, or, *you're an idiot.*

"Why don't you like me?" he asked.

"Who says I don't?"

"Your body language. Your language-language."

"So you know how to read girls the first time you talk to them?"

"Sometimes, but you're different."

"Original," she said. "It's not the same thing."

She locked onto his eyes for a moment before spreading her arms and pin-wheeling away. A spray from the cup spattered his face. Water.

Definitely worth another try.

Joe waited by his car, watching the kids filter up from the river. Orange coals from their moving cigarettes wavered like fireflies under the cottonwoods. Couples emerged from the trail plastered together. Darting packs of boys shadowed tight bands of girls. No sign of Helen. Sure, he'd noticed her in school but the girl he glimpsed tonight crackled with an invisible charge that had raised the hair on his arms. He wasn't drunk. Maybe a little. He steadied his thoughts against the beer buzz that gave him the courage to wait by the roadside, hoping for another chance.

"Miss me?" The voice from behind startled him.

He turned. "How did you get here?"

"I flew," Helen said.

"If your wings're tired, I could give you a ride home."

"I've got till one," she said.

Helen's idea to drive up Monument Road and count the stars had sounded like an invitation to something more but still kept the tone light and goofy in case someone changed their mind—as Joe was doing now, arms locked and clinging with both fists to a pipe barrier while Helen poised atop it, teetering on her belly above Cold Shivers Point.

"Do heights bother you?" she asked.

"I just suffer from an over-active imagination."

"Me, too, except I don't suffer. Think I can balance?" She arched her back like a trapeze artist and released her grip on the rail, toes pointed, arms spread to the sky.

Joe thought he was going to vomit. "Whoa-ho," was all that came out.

Helen slid back to the ground. "Have you ever been over here?"

She led him away from the protected overlook to show

him the buff sandstone smooth as a blackboard that formed the top of the cliff. They strolled past the moonlit names, initials, dates and hometowns carved by tourists, lovers, sailors on leave, angry teens and happy families. The newer marks defiled older ones that had attained the weathered dignity of gravestone inscriptions. He heard his mother's voice: *Fools' names and fools' faces always appear in public places.* But time had already softened the fools' work. Today's vandalism, he thought, tomorrow's petroglyphs.

"What do you think the story is here?" she said. She rubbed her toe over a Jana + Harlan enclosed in a heart, with the date, Nov. 17, 1974. Underneath, a series of updates: '75-'76-'77. "I'm suspicious of people who make a big show of being love birds."

"Maybe they broke up after high school," he said. "Or maybe they graduated and moved on."

"Or maybe they got busted for defacing the park. I mean, how many Jana + Harlans can there be?"

"Or maybe their parents opposed their love, and they decided to jump and be united forever."

She said, "I think we would've heard about that one."

"Yeah, you're right," he said. "It's more the kind of thing forlorn Indian maidens are supposed to do."

She laughed like she was supposed to.

"Want to do it?" she said.

"Do what?"

"The Point."

The official Cold Shivers Point was a toadstool the size of a card table, reached by a clamber across a forty-foot arm of sandstone that narrowed to a finger. Anywhere else, it would be a stroll along a sidewalk, but here the gutter was a three-hundred-foot drop.

"No thanks."

Helen shrugged. She skipped over the rock to the cliff edge and probed the line where sandstone became air. She mimicked a diver trying to generate some spring from the board. "Greg Louganis," she said.

"Greg Louganis hit his head."

"And then he won the gold," she said. She continued along the canyon lip to where the tombstone surface roughened and formed potholes. She trotted casually, a walked batter on her way to first. "What about here?"

She chose an irregular fin of rock and plopped down on it, dangling her legs into space. Water had eroded a crack between her perch and the main wall, and Joe could see straight through the gap to the canyon floor. She looked an invitation over her shoulder, but he maintained his distance, pretending to study the black and orange epaulettes of lichen at his feet. She turned back to the canyon and leaned forward into the abyss. He fixed on the curve of her back. His mouth began to water. A breeze blew from behind him toward the canyon. How much more than the wind would it take to send her over? A flushed bird. A sudden sound. He tried to imagine what he'd tell her parents. A hand at her back and she'd be gone forever. He tried to deepen his breaths before he made himself puke.

Helen rose easily and came over to the juniper where he stood. She took his hand. "Too much to drink?"

"What is it with you?" he said.

"It feels amazing!"

"To you, maybe. Don't you consider what could happen?"

"You don't have to consider," she said. "Death's right there in front of you and it still can't touch you. You feel your heart going in your body and you know you're alive, and whatever happens, it's up to you."

"But what if…"

"Everything's what if, every single moment. You usually don't get to see it so clearly," she said. "The cliff's real, but the fear is all in your head."

She turned him back toward the car and stopped at a segment of rock, shaped roughly like a grand piano with the lid sharpened to a point. Its tip angled out into the canyon, while the keyboard was anchored to the cliff.

"What about this one? See?" she said, bounding across where the leap was not so fearsome. She landed on the corner and executed a hopscotch turn as if she'd just reached the 9 and 10 and was heading back to 1. With oblivion behind her, she stretched out her hand and purred, "Are you coming?"

Crazy. The distance was short, but the landing mattered and her presence halved the landing zone. How could she trust he wouldn't miscalculate? His momentum could send them both over the edge. Flight signals hammered every synapse; his pores gasped to be in a different skin; panic leached from his palms. It wasn't worth it. She wasn't.

When she saw he wouldn't cross, she knelt and pretended to pray, then sprawled on her back with her hands behind her head like a sunbather on the petrified sand. She rolled over on one elbow and pretended to feed herself grapes. After each move, she looked back to Joe with a playful smile.

"Okay," she said, standing up and extending her arms. "Now you'll have to catch me!" She closed her eyes, turned three times and jumped.

Finally

"AND FINALLY," said Mr. Philipp, glancing at the cast list before turning it over and lowering his arm slowly as if his fingers pressed to earth a paper that might otherwise rise to the heavens, "we have the role of Mary Grey."

Bette Campion inclined her head as if in suspense, but a calm expectancy remained in her eyes. What could be more certain than choosing the prettiest, most popular girl in school to play the principled actress who wouldn't compromise her interpretation of Joan of Arc?

A *travesty*, that's what it would be, Helen thought. *I worked for this.* And she was perfect for the role, not in the Bette Campion way, but in the real Joan of Arc way. Did Miss Perfect do research? Did she want it so bad she prayed for it? Okay, Helen didn't pray, either. Her *PleaseGodPleaseGodPleaseGodPlease* was more like an incantation. But she *was* Joan, and anyone who couldn't see that was too stupid to be in theater, too stupid to teach high school and too stupid to live.

"Helen, would you please meet me in the classroom in a few minutes?"

A tight circle had pressed around Bette, offering congratulations. Other students were gathering books and making quiet exits. Mr. Philipp was handing around mimeographed copies of the cast and crew list with the rehearsal schedule. She could leave now and never come back, say she'd never heard him or forgot or went to the room but he wasn't there and she couldn't stay. She didn't want to talk to anyone now—she wanted to scream. She wanted to send Bette Campion's perfect nose and plump lips and ice-blue eyes back through the openings in her skull, until her smug face was nothing but worms of red pulp. She wanted to cry.

At the injustice.

Still, she found herself sitting at a front row desk, listening as the classroom clock ticked off the seconds, something she never noticed when the room was occupied. She wondered if Mr. Philipp could hear his pathetic life leaking away as he waited at his desk for his class of the stupidest sophomores who thought he was a faggot and who only studied the clock. All he had going for him was directing these boring plays that people only came to because their kids were in them. The same thing over and over, year after year—telling kids where to stand while they overacted, just so he could pretend he was doing something artistic.

She was glad she didn't get Joan, because now she wouldn't have to take part in such mediocrity. There was just no point in trying to do something better and deeper, because nobody around here could tell the difference.

Mr. Philipp came into the room and perched on the corner of his desk. "That was quite an interesting audition you gave last week."

"Not interesting enough, *obviously*." She did not look at him. She did not want to look at him unless her gaze could burn holes through that stupid "creative" Hawaiian shirt he changed into for rehearsals.

"You clearly put a lot of thought and a lot of work into your interpretation. I give you credit for originality, but it was also eccentric, indulgent and wrong for this play."

Wrong for your stupid version of the play, you mean. Your boring, safe interpretation that only needed Bette Campion to make her eyes go all sparkly.

"The important scenes are not about teen ecstasy. They're about a mature actress who has to overcome her own doubts about the character, who disagrees with her director and has taken a stand against compromising her interpretation. I hope some of this sounds familiar…"

Helen shrank from his smile. What next, a consoling hand on her shoulder?

"You'll have another year. Bette won't, and she's been very dedicated to the Drama Club. That's not the reason I gave her the part, of course, but…" He held out a blue-covered copy of the script. "I'd like you to be my assistant director and understudy the lead. The chances you'll ever perform it are small, but you'd attend all the rehearsals, work up your lines and observe how everything develops. I could've cast you just to put you on stage, but I hope you'll get more out of this—learning what works as a whole and what doesn't. Then in the spring, you can audition for *You're a Good Man, Charlie Brown*. You do have talent, Helen, I can see it, and who knows where that might take you. What do you say?"

Watching Bette Campion over and over? Impossible. Charlie Brown? Sickening. Screw you, Philipp, and fuck your pitiful consolation prizes!

"Hel—what's going on? What's wrong?"

"Nothing," Helen said. How did Margaret know to come in? Helen had broken her mirror hours ago and there was no possible sound coming from her room now, not with her head buried under the pillows.

"Oh God, the mirror. It's the play. You didn't get the part…"

"Mmmmmh. I don't want it!"

"You worked so hard. Oh, baby, I'm so sorry."

She was glad about smashing the mirror. It was bad enough seeing her pitiful self reflected in Margaret's eyes.

"I heard," was all Neulan said when he caught Helen after class and ushered her down the hall.

"Mr. Philipp basically said it wasn't my turn."

Neulan scoffed. "Taking turns is for the water fountain. What about merit?"

"Exactly. Otherwise, why pour your soul into something? Well, too bad, I'm not going to act like a martyr over it."

"That's funny!" he said.

"What is?"

"That you're not going to act like a martyr because you didn't get to play the martyr part."

She laughed. Sometimes she thought it was too bad a guy so clever had to be so geeky.

"I've been working on a little production where I might need some acting help," he said. "Would you be interested?"

Wary now. "In what?"

"Revenge." Neulan said it lightly, with that smirk of his.

"Against…" The one-minute bell rang.

Neulan took her hand and traced letters in her palm. It was amazing how clearly her skin could read:

E-V-E-R-Y-B-O-D-Y.

Neulan hung across the street from school near the mortuary grounds. Helen stayed on the school side and headed toward Safeway. She wanted to hear his plan, but not badly enough to start gossip about Neulan and her. He met up with her at Seventh Street and they continued east until they reached Lincoln Park.

"What's the worst thing that could happen to this stupid high school right now?" he asked, sweeping his long arm to take in the town's complex of football field, ballpark and the old pavilion called the Barn.

"We're ruling out a nuclear bomb?" she said.

Neulan's movements quickened. He didn't really want her to guess. "The Homecoming game has to be postponed at the last minute!" The Tigers were a football power with a good chance to win state. The jocks would be in no mood to dance with the game still to be played. The beauty queens would freak.

Neulan pointed to the field. "Eight stanchions, eight lights apiece, sixty-four bulbs to loosen. No one will figure it out—at least not in time. They'll think it's a power problem, a switch, a systemic failure, because sixty-four light bulbs don't all burn out at once. And even if they catch on, the only way to get the lights back on is to screw them all tight again. By then it'll be too late!"

"It's brilliant," she said.

"And you-know-who'll be waiting in her tiara to be introduced with her Homecoming royalty. No lights sparkling off those rhinestones. No bouquet from the captain." Neulan gave a dismissive wave. "Buh-bye, Bette."

"Buh-bye," laughed Helen.

"So Thursday night, we meet here, after the bars close and North Avenue quiets down. Can you get out at three a.m.?"

Why not? She had to see what else this strange boy was capable of doing.

He said, "I'll meet you over there under the home stands. You can be my lookout. Wear black, but don't dress up like a cat burglar. Bring your Bible. Then, if anyone sees you out, you can be like, *I fell asleep at a friend's doing Bible study*."

It should have been funny hearing Neulan's deep voice trying to imitate an innocent Bible study girl, but it wasn't. Helen envisioned herself in her role on the ground while Neulan scaled the towers. Offered the understudy once again. "If this is supposed to be my revenge," she said fiercely, "I get to help unscrew the lights. We'd be done twice as fast."

Neulan didn't respond at first. Looking up at the towers, he seemed to be pondering. "You can't be afraid of heights," he said.

"Don't worry, I'm not."

Neulan stared back at her, his gaze steady. "Okay," he said, extending his hand. "But just us. Don't tell anyone."

Helen thought she felt a tremor as he withdrew his hand from hers. "You didn't think of this for me, did you?" she said.

Neulan's smirk returned. "I want this town to wonder forever—to realize whoever did it was smarter than everybody."

"What good is that, if no one knows it was you?"

"*I'll* know," he said.

"I'll know, too."

"Yeah," said Neulan. "Just us. That'll make everything so much sweeter."

No one actually came home for Homecoming, so playing the game a day late didn't matter that much, except to the visiting team, which got an extra sixteen hours to contemplate being crushed by the Tigers. Meanwhile, since rescheduling football teams proved easier than rebooking the band, the Homecoming dance went on as scheduled, creating plenty of opportunity for speculation about who was responsible for the lighting prank that forced the game to Saturday. Top suspects: the cross-country team. They hated the football team, mainly because the football team disdained the runners, who they thought were too unathletic to play football. Other fingers pointed to the tennis team. They hated football players even more for calling them fags. On similar grounds, the Drama Club had the most reason to resent the jocks, plus, they had the most experience hanging lights.

Joe Samson didn't believe anyone on his cross-country team had done it, though he wished they'd thought of it. This was going to be a great story for the school paper, and when he arrived Monday he had already compiled a list of interview assignments and outlined a *Rashomon*-style narrative that would work whether or not the culprits could be identified. Walking into first-period choir, he found girls clumped together and openly crying. Mr. Genolia stood in the corner with his hands on Mr. Philipp's shoulders. Neither of them looked very good. Steve Lovering hunched over the piano pounding out the intro to "96 Tears," which didn't sound nearly as cool as it did on the Vox organ.

"What's going on?" Joe asked.

Steve kept bumping between the G and the C7 chords. "It's too crazy... I can't believe it... Helen Vavoris..." Joe slammed the keyboard cover to make him stop. "What the fuck!" Steve rubbed his fingers.

"What happened?" Joe demanded.

Steve lifted the cover again but didn't touch the keys. "She was off with the Assembly of Godders. They were up at Cold Shivers. She fell or something."

Joe grabbed his shirt and twisted it hard. "Fell—like off?"

"Of course off. Geez, don't be pissed at me she's dead."

Fell, it turned out, was the least vicious version of the

story. Other theories were circulating; the most popular—that she'd committed suicide because of Mr. Philipp's casting decision. Another rumored pregnancy. She was crazy, according to some who'd seen her wild and solitary dancing along the river a few weeks before. The most farfetched claim was that she'd experienced some sort of religious ecstasy and thought she was leaping right into the arms of her Savior. Then there were whispers about Neulan Kornhauer, the only one who'd actually witnessed what happened on the cliff. Traumatized. Yeah, right. He must've dared her to do something stupid. Or he was trying to put the make on her and she was trying to get away. Or he pushed her. Whatever. *She never should've been with that weirdo.*

Joe went to Helen's memorial service at Cold Shivers. He held to the fringes and watched Bette Campion lead the sniffles. She told about competing for the lead in the play, and how she would've gladly relinquished the role if only she'd known how much it meant to Helen. No one bought it. Vonda Rae Fitch released a clutch of helium balloons at cliff side, and for a second it looked like she was going to jump herself. Someone found Helen's name scratched in the rock. Speculation said it was Neulan, while others insisted he would've used some kind of power tool and done a better job of it.

After everyone left, Joe made himself peer over the drop-off. Visible in the daylight, the canyon was less frightening to him than the dark void he'd experienced with Helen, and somehow seeing particulars of the terrain below made her flight more abstract and difficult to imagine. She didn't belong down there among the rocks. She didn't deserve to be the object of rumor. And attention-seeker or not, she certainly was too nuanced to be a supporting player in the self-dramatizations he'd just witnessed. Original, she'd called herself. Now no one was going to find out if it was anything more than an aspiration.

Neulan hadn't attended the service. Joe thought of him standing here as he once did, how Neulan's panic must have also surged if Helen had tried the same blind, spinning leap. Did he draw back? Did Helen miscalculate? Or did she improvise some other craziness? Neulan didn't deserve to be blamed for Helen's experiments with recklessness, but high school was a petri dish for cruelty. Police had checked inside his locker, the gossip ran, where they found handcuffs, straight razors, satanic robes and pictures of dead babies. Poor Neulan. He probably looked shifty when he was interviewed because his lazy eye didn't let him make full eye contact, but he was just an awkward outcast who wanted to share in the fun. His idea of troublemaking was wearing Bermudas under his choir robe or lip-synching to Steve Lovering's falsetto.

Joe couldn't reverse the social tide, but if Neulan was in real jeopardy with the law, speaking up was the right thing to do. Joe thought he had enough exposure to both Helen and Neulan to be credible without being mistaken for a friend. He'd simply tell the police his story, describe Helen's wild behavior on the canyon rim, and before, at the woodsy. She wasn't suicidal and Neulan wasn't a bad guy. They were just kids who wanted to be somebody else and they tried harder than most to be someone special. Kids were allowed to learn from their mistakes, but what could Helen have possibly gotten out of her terrible final seconds? Editorializing about her death couldn't make a bit of difference for her now, but telling the simple truth might still rescue Neulan from torment.

The investigation declared Helen's death accidental. Perhaps Joe's account made a difference or maybe the police weren't that serious about Neulan after all. At her final performance in *Joan of Lorraine*, Bette Campion received a bouquet and raised it to a heavenly spotlight. The principal suppressed Joe's investigation of the Homecoming prank, to discourage similar stunts. Mr. Philipp resigned at the end of the year to sell insurance for Allstate. Joe composed his college admission essay about youthful mistakes, forgiveness and finality and got accepted to Missouri. He laid Helen's memory to rest and forgot about Neulan. And except for an occasional pounce of dread when he stood on a high place, there they stayed.

Margaret Vavoris had never been very respectful of Helen's room, but this time when she opened the door and crept in, she felt she was about to despoil a sacred grotto—one that already looked looted thanks to Helen's casual jumble. Her parents had left the space untouched out of fatigue and reluctance, and Margaret hoped they would never muster the detachment to tame it into a guest room or a home office. Margaret knew the apparent chaos was ordered in layers by time and in deposits scattered according to Helen's enthusiasms. She had no difficulty locating *An Actor Prepares*, the book she needed to return to her college library. It rested on the far side of Helen's bed, alongside Mircea Eliade's *Shamanism*, a cassette of Cat Stevens's *Catch Bull at Four* and a plastic holy water bottle from the Mother Cabrini Shrine. Inside the Stanislavski, a slip of notebook paper with a verse written in Helen's hand.

The breeze at dawn has secrets to tell you.
Don't go back to sleep.
You must ask for what you really want.

Don't go back to sleep.
People are going back and forth across the doorsill
where the two worlds touch.
The door is round and open.
Don't go back to sleep.

Asking

LEONARD DOESN'T BELIEVE IN GOD, at least the one that exists independently of people's minds, but it's impossible to live here without thinking about the possibility. Even if, like C. Edwards, he banned the visits of Mormon missionaries and Jehovah's Witnesses, it would barely dent the valley-wide bucket of church signs, bathtub virgins, dream catchers, radio sermons, bumper stickers, cardboard panhandler blessings, roadside *descansos* and cleavage crosses. But sweep all these manmade reminders aside, and there was still no escaping questions about creation. Here wasn't like the city, where civilization's handiwork could block the horizon and fill the sky. No picture could fill this frame.

Just past the crumbling crossroads of Appleton, though, Word of Faith Church tries its mightiest. Depending on the angle of approach and time of day, the complex might be a college campus, the fairgrounds or a military base. Right now, all Leonard sees is a dust devil escorting a yellow soft-drink cup across the empty mall-sized parking lot.

Inetta left Word of Faith after the girl's accident on Cold Shivers Point, but her discontent had been festering ever since Pastor Zeb took over. The first change she'd noticed was how the praise music sounded more like what she heard coming out of radios or in the grocery store, and the singers started dressing differently—no longer like the worshippers in the pews, but in outfits meant to be looked at. The altar, she realized, was becoming a stage. The seasonal pageants took on a more theatrical tone as well with more spectacle than word of God, and that boy she'd never cared for seemed to be everywhere, ravenous for attention. Pastor Zeb appeared more interested in attracting new worshippers than ministering to the ones he had, and there was too much talk about money. Churches always had to ask for support, so that wasn't it. Instead of presented as a caution, wealth had become a subject of study and glorification, a sign of godly approval.

"God doesn't want his people to be poor," Pastor Zeb had preached on Inetta's last day in the flock. "In my Father's house there are many *mansions*, Jesus said. He didn't say pup tents. He didn't say trailers. You think when you get to heaven you'll be asking, hey, Lord, where's the trailer park?"

Once Inetta found a new church that suited her, Shower of Blessings Holiness Temple, she relayed to Leonard bulletins about people they knew. "The Halbergs brought the cutest little girl to church," she said.

He continued studying the circular for Cattlemen's Days. He thought he recognized where this was going. "That ditch rider was up here. Guess whose gate was stuck open?"

Inetta gave him a one-eyed frown. "Guess who's changing the subject. She's a foster child, the sweetest thing."

"I'm sure. I'm thinkin' to skip the horse show this year, just go for the rodeo." They had long put to bed the subject of children, he thought. Early on in their marriage, Inetta assigned his quiet avoidance the meaning closest to her own desire, that he wanted children. That was not quite the way he saw it—*wanted* was too strong a word. He took what came—the good with appreciation and the bad with acceptance—and he turned away from desire, because that road led to disappointment and regret. She wanted a child, well okay, and once it was clear they couldn't conceive, that was okay, too.

"You took in some young people before Elliott."

"That was different. They weren't foster—they just found me. I didn't go lookin' for 'em." And no one was looking over his shoulder, either. No one was giving him rules to follow or paperwork to complete. If a boy paid attention to his way of doing things, it worked out for them both. If not, so be it. He had no intention to reform anyone or foster anything.

"You helped a few boys straighten out."

Inetta put a more positive light on the facts than he thought warranted, but that was how she looked at everything. The idea they might salvage some kid—she could have a different word in mind—made him uneasy.

"A few stayed bent, too," he said.

"It could be a blessing," she said.

And it could be asking for trouble for all concerned.

The traffic he'd meant to avoid begins to thicken and nudge around him, like cattle nosing to the hay feeder. Slow. He's borne past a billboard announcing a department store that's decided not to come to town after all. Someday the forsaken parcel will bring a payday, but not for the last old boy who tried to kick up a living from the dirt. The boxy buildings plunked down across the roadway barely register, indistinguishable bunkers with a mysterious power to draw a crowd even on a weekday and hoover local dollars to faraway places. Stop. As he waits, traffic lights and turn signals and digital signboards descend with an alien urgency. Artists Point seems unreachable as a memory.

Good Dogs

Junior Crimmins was alone in the duplex with Brutus and Daisy, his father's pit bulls. He sat on the bare floor with his back against a moldering green couch, its cushions too broken down and sticky with spills for comfort. Brutus dozed against one leg and Daisy the other. Junior stroked their short, smooth coats and felt the warm skin glide back and forth over taut muscle. He felt Brutus tense, then Daisy. They rose together and trotted to the door.

The knock and the word came together. "Police."

The dogs squirmed, but stayed quiet. They were trained not to bark in their master's presence without the signal.

"What do you want?" Junior said through the door. "No one's here. Just me."

"Open the door."

"Okay." Junior knew the value of superficial cooperation.

The drooping front stoop was too small to hold both officers. One, a woman, stood off to the side behind the open screen door. The man was no taller than she was. His dad could take them both.

"Can we come in?"

"All right."

They stepped in and quickly assessed the room. The woman

looked toward the kitchen; the man fastened on the dogs.

"Lay down," Junior said, and they both dropped to floor.

"Good dogs," said the man, taking a hand off his pepper spray.

"Anyone else home?" asked the woman.

"I said. Just me."

"And what's your name?"

"Hardy Crimmins, Junior."

The officers gave each other a look.

"How old are you, Hardy?

"I go by Junior. I'm eight."

The woman said, "We're going to take a look around, okay, Junior? Just in case you forgot someone else was home."

"I told you, but go ahead."

"Your dogs won't mind, will they?" said the man.

Junior snapped his fingers and Brutus jumped to his side. "You can pet him."

"That's okay."

Their look around was quick and efficient. The bedroom. The closet. The bathroom. No basement, no attic access. Not much to see. The woman opened the refrigerator.

"What's this?"

"Lard."

"You've just got lard in the fridge?"

"Mom keeps it there 'cause the dogs'll lick it."

"Do you have anything to eat in the house?"

"Scooters."

"Scooters?"

"You know, Honey Nut Scooters."

"Oh, yeah, them. We'd like to talk to your dad. Do you know where he is?"

"Not really."

"How about your mom? Where's your mom?"

"Out."

"Did she say where she was going?"

"To work."

"Where does she work?"

"Different places."

"When's she coming back?"

"Not sure."

"When did she go out?"

"Wednesday, I think."

The cops looked at each other again.

"You have a sister, right? What's her name?"

"Shannon."

"Where's Shannon?"

"With a friend."

"Does Shannon live here?"

"Not anymore. She doesn't like sleeping on the couch. Me, neither."

The male cop made a blowing sound from the corner of his mouth only he wasn't smoking a cigarette.

"Junior," said the woman cop, "we're going to call some people who are going to help you. Do you have anything you could pack some clothes in? Your pajamas... a toothbrush?"

"We're out of garbage bags."

"I was thinking more like a backpack."

Junior shrugged. "Where are we going?"

"A place where people help kids."

"Do you have a pillowcase? You could put some things in a pillowcase," said the man.

"Sure... Maybe we do... What about Daisy and Brutus?"

"Oh, don't worry about them," said the man. "Someone'll take care of the dogs."

Nadine Grenier did her best to help Junior after Officers Hostetter and Jensen brought him in. For a social worker, help first meant getting him into a stable situation. With a boy left alone in a house with no food, it was easy to do something that made a difference right away. The challenge would be setting his life on a track better than where it was heading, keeping the connections that would support him and determining which might have to be severed. From the changing addresses in the public records, it was clear Junior had spent his childhood in cheap apartments, decaying motels, off-the-grid trailers and run-down rental houses, almost all of them monitored by local police departments. Sometimes the moves were due to evictions and other times to avoid prosecution.

She learned what she could from Junior and his sister, but she also had to sort through caseworker files, school transcripts, court records and even news stories to piece together a picture of the Crimmins family. Junior's mother, Vickie, rode out of Walden, Colorado, on the back of Hardy Crimmins' motorcycle, and whatever the two of them did before or since had created such a wall of ill will that Nadine couldn't get Vickie's parents to admit their daughter existed. Relatives on the Crimmins side were also out of the question for placing Junior. About the only roots the Crimmins family put down were attached to marijuana plants.

Hardy Senior's main talent appeared to be intimidation. His skills were always in demand for second- and third-tier jobs doing security, collections and witness tampering. The mother cycled between fighting with school officials to get Junior special help and abandoning the kids for days at a time. The daughter was a pistol. Shannon seemed far older than thirteen, perhaps thanks to her experiences dodging the attentions of her father's co-conspirators. She had moved in with a friend and was doing all right in school.

It was unclear how she had maintained her self-possession amid such a stream of unreliables with the extent of parental guidance being, according to Shannon, *get knocked up before you're eighteen and I'll effing kill you.*

The first foster couple Nadine found for him was kind, but they approached parenting with an intensity that frightened Junior. They saw raising other people's children as their calling from God. While they surely did not wish to smother him, that was how it felt after eight years of neglect. Junior ran away three times after awakening in a panic, feeling the combined weight of their love and God's pressing on his chest. Nadine asked him some questions and removed him from the house. The next place felt more normal to Junior. Dinner came straight from cans and the couple sometimes fought.

One of the records in Junior's file contained a special needs label intended to protect him, but it also meant he was routinely shelved as past his expiration date. His needs were not always apparent, and in a new school they could escape a teacher for a time unless Vickie Crimmins was in one of her coherent phases. Each school change had run him through a new steeplechase of appointments, assessments and searches for parental paperwork, and by the time he'd been classified, each fresh set of classmates had already identified him as an alien. They'd seen enough of such kids already to know not to invest any energy toward them. They'd disappear soon enough.

On Junior's second-grade classroom wall—he was already a year back—Nadine picked out his grey shoe-box-shaped drawing amid the paper subdivision of hand-holding families living in white houses with peaked roofs, their chimneys puffing cheery smoke clouds toward sunny blue skies. He was not the only child in class who had lived in a trailer, but the others had already learned how to produce the picture the teacher expected. For Junior, the trailer was the happiest place he could remember.

He received classroom questions with crimson dread and cupped his hand to hide the lack of stars atop his graded papers. Summoned to the board, he accepted the chalk with the anticipation of a prisoner receiving his final cigarette. Why did his new teacher expect him to recite multiplication tables he had never seen before? By what hidden signs were the other kids able to chip apart words into things called syllables? How could they lay down a ruler with only twelve numbers on it and know that a line was seven and three-quarters? He was afraid to ask.

So much information seemed just beyond his reach, like cookies placed on an upper shelf or a marble left in another pair of pants. He attempted once to convey this to his teacher—*I know it... in the book*—but that answer didn't count.

When he could, Junior removed himself from the yellow problems chalked on the cloudy green slate. He imagined the background flutter of papers, whispers and skritching pencils into a stand of cottonwoods. Between his legs, he milked a pilfered bottle of mucilage to release its comforting aroma of decay. Thus calmed in his alternate world, he appeared to be listening, and his over-matched teachers might believe they had trickled in some knowledge that would follow him home, like a piped-in tune overheard at the mall.

Junior never caused trouble. Trouble followed him though, and he was jostled in hallways, punched on buses, humiliated in lavatories, excluded from all the reindeer games. *HardyFarty FartyHardy Farty Crimmins.* His dad had heard that too, he'd told Junior, and look at what a man he'd become. People call you names, you laugh in their face. You kick their ass. It's good for a boy to learn to defend himself. To learn early how bad the world can suck. He tried to forget the words and move out of range of the sticks and stones, but how can hunted creatures erase their own scent? The teasing pushed him farther out to the fringe of the herd, beyond the intermittent protection of his mother, playground monitors and teachers at the front of the room.

Going by Junior was preferable to HardyFarty but it didn't help his prospects in Grand Junction. Locals had been reading about Hardy Crimmins for years—the last time because his partial remains had been discovered in the desert, just weeks after Junior was taken from the duplex. The investigators favored the theory that the missing body parts had been delivered to a party not inclined to report receiving them.

Junior's mom got him back for a while. Her new boyfriend kept on Junior, trying to make a man of him, forcing him to do pushups and drop quarters on his bed to show he'd made it right. He'd assign Junior a chore and make it impossible to do. Junior was supposed to take out the kitchen garbage every day and bring back the wastebasket so it was pristine inside. The old plastic had little brown cracks he could never get clean. He'd scrub with a toothbrush and try to bleach them out with cleanser, but the inside was never pure white, and the boyfriend would scream at Junior like he was in the Marines. His mom started drinking again and that meant she'd start the drugs again and Junior knew what was coming next. So when the boyfriend called him a limp dick, Junior popped him one, and the boyfriend beat him up.

So much for the family reunion. Nadine found an older

couple on a small ranch that could take him. She thought it might be a good change.

"You lived on a ranch once before, didn't you?" Nadine noted.

"I guess."

"The ranch or farm in Crawford. Did you like being around animals?"

"We didn't have any animals. Just corn. A big cornfield where my dad wouldn't let us play. He had to guard it."

"He guarded corn?"

"He said his job was to keep people out of the cornfield."

Hunt Club

VAUGHN HOBART HAD THIS WAY of showing up at the ranch that was neither predictable nor surprising. He regarded the Reverse Dollar as a former home and Leonard as something approaching a relation, a feeling that hadn't been dampened by his collision years ago with Stony Jackson and his ride to town in Leonard's pickup. The accident and an impatient convalescence had set Vaughn's torso cockeyed from his pelvis, so he appeared to be heading three-quarters on and one-quarter off to the left, holding his arms out in parentheses like a man about to pounce on a chicken. As he approached the house this late fall evening, a plastic jug of milk dangled from one hand.

Vaughn's progress with alcohol proceeded as crookedly as the rest of him, veering among the stages of quitting booze, thinking about quitting, pretending to quit, drinking only for social or medicinal reasons and falling hard off the wagon. Under his latest regimen, he had stowed bottles of Old Crow with friends and sworn to limit his drinking to their supply, eliminating the chance to pick up yet another open container violation, and reducing somewhat his exposure to DUI charges. While he could count on finding his whisky at these scattered bottle clubs, they didn't always stock his favorite mix.

Bourbon and milk sounds worse than it is. The milk mellows the edge of the whisky and disguises the color. Vaughn believed it cut the smell of alcohol and prevented ulcers, to boot. Leonard simply accepted that this drink-as-you-go program might turn out better than the others, which hadn't seemed to work at all.

Inetta didn't approve of this arrangement, so Leonard met him in the yard with a coffee cup and the bottle. The compromise had the added advantage of keeping winter visits to a minimum. This stay might be short, too, since Vaughn had left two people waiting in his current ride, a copper-colored Mercury Marquis. Like each of Vaughn's cars, this one had the look of having been transferred from owner to owner with mounting degrees of relief. The hulk slouched over sprung shocks on the driver side, and silver duct tape had been applied to keep the peeling fore-edge of the cream vinyl roof from flapping.

Vaughn stirred his drink with his forefinger, took a sip and declared, "Mother's milk."

Leonard nodded toward the two figures in the car. "Who's that?"

"Bryce Deaver and Pinky Allred. I need you to help me talk some sense to them boys."

Bryce and Pinky were distant cousins whose Jack Mormon forebears had left Utah and the Latter-day Saints for territory more forgiving of foul language, strong beverages and petty crime. Last Leonard knew, they summered together in a trailer on Piñon Mesa that made up for its lack of plumbing with a lack of rent. Now into their thirties, they'd avoided long-term gainful employment by taking whatever opportunities came down the road and dodged jail by working out of sight of witnesses. Bryce, riding shotgun, was trim and semi-handsome in that bland Mormon way that kept people thinking a little inbreeding wasn't all that bad. He tempered the impression some with a snaky way of squinting you knew was only going to get worse when your back was turned. Pinky was bigger and softer. Orange-brown skeins of whiskers hadn't quite formed the quorum for a beard and a calf's kick to the face had left him looking a bit like an orangutan, though if you said frog, nobody would argue.

"Ain't gonna be much help with them two," Leonard said.

"You don't need to wrassle 'em. Just set a example."

"A example."

"They don't think too much about other people, and they won't listen to me on it. It's only a matter a time before all hell comes down on their stupid-ass hunt club."

"Hunt club?"

"They're supposed to be the caretakers on that actor's ranch—what's his face, Devin Magruder. As you know I been workin' on certain prospects in that field myself." Vaughn had talked for months about the easy money to be made watching properties for absentee owners, but Leonard hadn't seen any actual activity in that direction. "On the side, they been sellin' so-called memberships to friends at two hundred a pop to poach when he ain't around."

"So if you're not in on it, what do you care?"

"They keep fartin' around where I'm at, somebody's gonna think I'm the stinker," Vaughn said. "Money talks to money. I don't want no suspicion cast over the local help by them two. But they think they're so smart. They ain't gonna take no lecture from me."

"You think they'll take one from me?" Leonard said.

"I was hopin' you could be more subtle."

Pinky leaned over the front seat to give a few whaps to the horn.

"They wanna show you the setup."

Leonard said, "Last thing I want to do is go traipse around another man's private property with those two. If we have to sort this out, let's talk it through right here."

The window switch didn't work, so Bryce opened the door and stuck his hand through without getting out of the car. "Bryce Deaver," he said. "You knew my dad."

"I did," said Leonard. "He could quit an outfit better'n anybody I ever seen."

"He had his standards. Didn't take any shit."

"No, he definitely believed it was better to give than to receive."

Bryce snickered. "Vaughn says you like to hunt."

"Well, Vaughn ain't wrong but he's a little out of date. My huntin' days're about wound down."

"We got a place you should see. Maybe he mentioned it."

"He did."

Bryce stepped out of the car and leaned against the rear door. Pinky took the signal and came out the other side. "This is Pinky Allred. You probably know his folks, too."

"And his grandfolks," Leonard said. "Marlon drilled my last well years ago. I think that was you with him."

Pinky, pleased, hunched forward, then back. "Yep, it was."

The four men stood with their arms wrapped across their chests waiting for someone to get back on the subject. Their vaporized breaths rose and disappeared in the cool dry air. Inetta's dog, Stitches, came around for some attention. Leonard thought he could smell burning juniper drifting over from the Fokken place, some of the sweetest smoke there is.

Bryce snuck a glance at Vaughn and turned to Leonard, "Look, we heard you might be interested. If you aren't, I won't say a word more."

"Well, I'm interested in not seeing you boys end up in jail."

This time, Bryce glared at Vaughn and shook out a cigarette. "Here's the way we look at it. One, we got permission to be on the property. Two, we don't let just anybody come up there. And three, nobody's doing anything they wouldn't do somewhere else. We just provide what you might call… a more welcoming environment."

Pinky chimed in. "He's got maybe two hunnerd elk pass through there."

"Or more," said Bryce.

"Or more," Pinky agreed. "They could stay there all huntin' season if the snow doesn't drive 'em down. That's not right."

Bryce said, "The man who owns all those acres doesn't own the elk. He didn't raise 'em. It's the principle. Magruder brings in his California friends, and they can't hunt for shit. We make sure they know the difference between shooting a movie gun and live rounds, what's a clear shot, what isn't. We might try to drive something their way, then we have to track their misses."

Pinky stirred at this. "I'd like to track his missus. Hwhoooo! You should see Magruder's wife."

"She looks hot," said Bryce, "but she thinks her shit don't stink."

Pinky whistled. "Hell, she's got people who take a shit *for* 'er!" They slapped hands. "He's no better'n us. He puts his pants on one leg at a time."

Bryce was on a roll, too. "But if I had a shot at that, I'd be taking off both legs at once—so fast my cheeks'd be clapping!"

Pinky made a move to pretend-hump Bryce. They giggled and wrestled for a bit. Leonard looked at Bryce's boots, cheap black Dingos cinched tight with a concho strap. No cowboy in high rut was stopping to get his pants all the way over those.

"So, anyway, okay." Pinky rolled his eyes up as if examining the underside of his skull. "Some of his friends tip pretty generous. But it ain't like they *belong* here. We always hunted up on Piñon Mesa, my dad, my granddad. Me and Bryce. It's traditional. Now these new owners come in and they push us out like we're fuckin' Indians. We don't bother *them*, why do they have to fuck with *us*? It's still a free country, right?"

"It is still a free country if you got big money," Leonard said, "and big money wants big places to go. Pretty soon even the edges of big places start lookin' good, and that's when we find out how much freedom we really got. People with money don't just want the land, they naturally want to control things, and they usually get their way. You and me're free to do what we want off to the side"—he looked at Bryce—"but anywhere they got their eye, we don't get to decide who gets pushed around and who don't."

Pinky shoved his hands deep in pockets that almost reached his knees. "But they ain't *connected*. You know what I mean."

Leonard did know. He didn't need Pinky Allred telling him.

"They don't *rely* on bein' here," Pinky whined. "You don't think that makes a differ'nce? My granddad was huntin' to feed his family. He said if it came down to takin' government game or government welfare, no way the Allreds were gonna take the welfare."

Leonard knew those stories, but he also knew the feel of it. The cold of it. The root cellar and government cheese of it. The rags for underpants of it. The don't-ask-me-again of it. He said, more gently than he felt, "You and your hunt club boys ain't huntin' for food now, are you? You want entertainment, go to the movies. You want to hunt, wait for the season like honest

143

people do. You owe the man a day's work for a day's pay, not sneaking around behind his back."

"But he doesn't own us—or the elk."

"No, he don't. But if you don't manage yourselves better, somebody'll own your ass, and you won't like it."

"Fuck that shit," said Pinky.

Vaughn looked at Leonard as if to say, *see what I mean?*

"Almost sounds like you're on their side, Mr. Stableman." Bryce perched like a crane and ground out the coal of his smoke on his boot heel. He pinned the butt under the nail of his index finger as if he were about to flip it away, then winked at Leonard and tucked it in his shirt pocket. "All we're sayin' is, money doesn't mean the same to them. My old man always told me, don't ever buy a horse unless you need one to make a living. Shit, Magruder pays to keep 'em around just so his ranch looks pretty. He paid a frickin' wildlife biologist to walk around for the whole damn summer, when he could've just asked me and Pinky things. He rebuilt those ranch buildings twice over, almost. He's got a good hundred grand worth of cars, snowmobiles and four wheelers that mostly just sit around."

Pinky didn't want to let it go, either. "He's a fuckin' *actor*. What kinda work is that? Sit in a fuckin' trailer and some girl puts makeup on you and hands you cold drinks and you go out to play pretend until it's time for your blow job. And you know what's really fucked up? Devin Magruder played a fuckin' cowboy! Got millions for pretendin' the same shit you or me does every fuckin' day!"

Not every day, Leonard thought. Not you two.

"Then he turns around and buys the land right out from under our ass! It's a fuckin' insult and a injustice, too." Pinky looked around triumphantly, case closed.

Leonard said, "It grinds my guts, too, when people waltz

in here like they know more about this country than I do. But it's hard for me to judge another man's heart—what he appreciates and what he don't. What he deserves and what he don't. Devin Magruder must do his job good enough. He liked Piñon Mesa good enough to buy there. From rich or poor, it's wrong to take somethin' when it ain't been offered. You think he won't catch on, that this won't bite you. It will. That's my whole speech on it."

Vaughn stepped in. "I told these boys I thought you were interested. I can see you don't think it's a good idea. My mistake. We should get goin'."

"No problem," said Bryce. "It's always nice to hear advice from the elders."

Pinky said, "How about some of that Old White Crow before we go?"

Leonard picked up the bottle. Vaughn tipped the cup toward Leonard as if he was requesting a final shot but the look in his eye said they were finished for the day.

"You give them keys to Bryce," Leonard said. When Vaughn trailed him back to the stoop, he said, "That subtle enough for you?"

"It'll have to do." Vaughn said. "I don't think it's badness got 'em this way so much as doin' for yourselfness. Once that branch's on the campfire, you can't stick it back on the tree."

Vaughn clapped Leonard's shoulder, handed over his cup and rocked his way back to the Mercury. Pinky was still carrying on about injustice, while Bryce squatted over Inetta's dog, working its ears and squinting toward the house.

Chores

THE DAY WAS HOT, nearing a hundred, and Nadine knew her car would be a furnace. She parked facing east so the sun didn't heat up the door handle so badly, but the first minute would be hell until she could get rolling with all the windows down. She waddled to the parking lot and sighed as she pushed some case files across the seat. The exhalation came from the effort of moving her bulk in the heat but also from the weight of Junior and the other kids passing through her cubicle. She always had to watch herself. You didn't ever sigh in front of a child.

Junior rode with Nadine to his new foster home, far from town. Up the road to the Monument, winding and scary, then up some more above the red and sand-colored rock. He had never been so far in that direction and it seemed several times the road would hit the sky but it kept climbing. From the car, he could see very little but twisted juniper with sage scrambled at its feet and unpaved tracks that led to houses tucked out of sight behind signs that said Private Road. The road crested and dropped away again to reveal a broad open land rimmed by hills topped with pale pinkish sandstone that reminded him of Brutus and Daisy lying on the couch. At the farthest edges, blue-grey mountains jagged into a bright blue sky. He sucked in his breath, not like he did when Nadine swept around the turns on Monument Road, but like the one Christmas he opened a wrapping and found exactly what he'd wanted.

The car wiggled west toward a red-roofed log house. One side looked like an old fort with a tower on the corner, but with a silver observatory on top. On the back, an antique-pink iron bridge span poked upward onto the roof of a garage with an orange rail car parked beside it.

"What's that?" Junior said.

He didn't understand Nadine's answer. "It's so people don't think they're in Kansas."

Across the road, a sign said "Glade Park Store." It had a gas pump out front, but it didn't look anything like a Loco Mart. More like an old red barn with some buildings behind it, a phone booth and a faded, bug-eyed fire truck sitting under a shed roof.

Some cows grazed along the road but there weren't many houses to be seen, not even in the distance. The flat, open country he saw from above started to roll and pinch between the bluffs, and they went miles without meeting another car.

"Do they have any other kids?" he asked.

Nadine kept her eyes on the road. "You're it, but they have horses, chickens. There'll be plenty for you to do."

She slowed the car and turned through a green steel gate that had been propped open. The dirt road led to a V-shaped cluster of cottonwoods, and set deep in the notch of trees, a small house the color of brown sugar sent up white puffs of smoke from a metal stovepipe. The steep tin roof flattened out over the front door, the corners held up with rough posts that showed where the branches had been trimmed. It covered an open stoop with two turquoise metal porch chairs that had backs shaped like the Shell Oil sign. Two small windows were divided into fours and he could see the square pattern repeated in the curtains behind the glass.

He got out of the car and stretched; the air was cooler than in the valley. A stream flowed away from him beyond the trees, dividing the land between green pasture and bare dirt where corrals and ranch buildings scattered. The man and his wife came out of the house together. They both wore jeans, boots and flannel shirts. The man looked old, like he imagined his grandfather might be. The woman was younger but still a lot older than his mom. She wasn't as pretty, either, but something about her face made Junior want to keep looking at her.

They invited Nadine and him inside the house through what he thought was the front door but it went straight into the kitchen—actually into a main room that had everything in one, with the kitchen table closer to the door than the sitting area. It was neat but not fancy. A floor lamp with a plain shade stood between two stuffed chairs, and where he thought the couch should be was a cabinet that had a table on top and a straight-backed chair. He wondered where he would sit when all three of them were in the room, and then, where he would sleep. Something else was odd but it took him a couple turns of the room to pick it up. There was no television.

Another door went out the back, and when they took him through that way, he could see that maybe the front of the house pointed away from the road instead of the direction you'd expect. It faced a one-room log cabin, set back a ways under the trees. The doorway leaned a bit, but the door had been shaved so it fit snugly without sticking. "I'd give you your own key, but it don't have a lock," said the old man, who told Junior to call him Len.

A bunkhouse entirely to himself! Grey linoleum and an oval rag rug covered the floor, which sloped a little in the same direction as the door. The windows were small and square, with hemmed flour-sack curtains slipped over a rod that would let in a soft, white, morning light. The walls were covered with a fiberboard that Len had painted white, but he said Junior could have any color he wanted if he cared to paint it himself.

The iron twin bed creaked when he climbed on, but the mattress was new, and the quilt was a fine blue-and-white one handmade by the woman, who asked to be called Inetta. She pointed out the paperback dictionary and soft-cover Bible sitting between a pair of horseshoe bookends on a small pine table. Its soft surface showed traces left by children who must have pressed too hard into their schoolwork. Besides the ladder-back chair for sitting at the table, his room had a solid mahogany armchair stained dark brown with a thick seat cushion that might have been covered in leather, but the smell had gone out of it, so Junior couldn't be sure. Its high back and wide, flat arms made him think of a throne, and he thought he would prefer looking at it to sitting on it.

A single light fixture hung from the center of the room, and if he came in after dark, Junior would have to wave his arms until he found the pull chain. He was welcome to use the bathroom in the house any time, and Len showed him the one-holer behind the bunkhouse, just in case nature called deep into the night. Junior thought he might use the outhouse all the time. Having the place off by itself made him feel like he was a hired hand, living on his own and working for room and board.

Len and Inetta said they would give him regular work to do, and they sounded like real jobs instead of those made-up chores that people pushed on foster kids to teach you some sort of lesson, as if you'd had things too easy in life and needed to fold laundry or scrub toilets so you'd grow up right. But before he started work, Junior had to get used to being around horses.

The horses intimidated him at first, and it did not help when Len cautioned him: "A horse has got blind spots, like people. Only with horses, you know where the blind spots are—front and back. Most times, when you get kicked, it's your fault. The horse ain't tryin' to hurt you. It's tryin' to stay alive."

Every time Junior turned around, it seemed a horse was about to crush him, out of startle, meanness or animal indifference. He grew up with pit bulls and had no fear of their blunt carnivore nature, but horses were alien and unpredictable. Most dogs wanted to please more than anything, and he could read their displays. He wasn't so sure about horses. It seemed they could run over him without knowing it, like semi-trucks turning a tight corner, and this was more worrisome to Junior than the thought an animal might come after him on purpose.

The boarded horses concerned him the most because Junior encountered them in the close quarters of the stable that stood off from the storage barn. One or another always seemed ready to rub him into a wall or corner him so it could plant a hoof in his chest. They belonged to people who didn't have somewhere to keep them. Sometimes men came by, but mostly it was women who showed up to exercise the horses and ride on weekends. Len and Inetta took care of feeding the animals and turning them out during the day when the owners didn't come by.

The ranch had breeding mares with one stallion that Len told Junior to steer clear of and some other horses kept half-wild in pasture for rodeo stock. Sometimes as part of a trade he'd take in rejects—lame, half-starved, listless, skittish or crazed horses he thought he might reclaim, but he didn't keep them for too long or at too much expense. God and man supplied the horse business an endless stream of malformations and mistakes, he explained, and not all of it was worth fixing.

"You gotta love horses in general, but don't get too attached in specific," he said. "Otherwise, you'll end up keepin' the ones you can sell and feelin' sorry for the ones you should send to the cannery."

Len showed him the big book where he kept track of what he knew about each horse, its condition, vaccinations and costs, its brands, arrival and departure. Most of it was in a kind of shorthand code, he said, because if he didn't lay out his losses plain, it kept him from worrying as much.

After a week of tromping around without Junior getting kicked, Len took him to the stable for his first lesson.

The horses needed their stalls kept clean, Len explained, so they could stay healthy and their hooves wouldn't go bad. "You wouldn't think God would invent an animal that could kill itself so many different ways," he said. "Colic. Thrush. Laminitis. The feet's the worst. In the wild, they're okay, but when they're stabled up, they don't have a choice about what they eat or where they stand. And sometimes when they do, they don't make the best choices.

"So," he said, tapping an index finger in the middle of Junior's forehead, "we got to look out for 'em. A horse can't think of but one thing at a time. So you, Junior, you gotta plan ahead, and look past the oat bag."

Len showed Junior how to move the horse into the tie stall before mucking its own stall down to the rubber mat. He demonstrated forking out the manure and raking the wet straw, telling Junior not to load the wheelbarrow too heavily, and how to lift with his legs instead of his back. To reinforce the lesson, Len let him push the wheelbarrow back to the manure pile. Junior staggered a little across the uneven ground, trying to build up a speed that would help him dump the load. He heaved the handles abruptly when the front wheel hit the edge of the pile, and the wheelbarrow twisted in his hands.

As Junior rubbed his wrist, Len smiled and said, "It ain't a race. Just go steady."

Next, Len showed him how to distribute the clean straw across the floor.

"The straw's yellow, in them bales over there. Put the right stuff down. The green's hay for eatin'. Feel of it." He pulled a bale of hay off the stack and let it drop on end, to show Junior how it bounced, then had him squeeze a handful to feel its give. "Smell that? It's cut while it's still growin', so it keeps some moisture. Good hay smells sweet. So does good manure. When things stink bad, there's usually a good reason for it."

Len filled the water, led the horse back into the stall, removed the halter and closed the half door. "Your turn," he said, handing Junior the pitchfork. Then he walked back to the house.

Junior did not share Len's opinion about the smell of manure.

In the next stall was a short, cherry-brown gelding named Brisket. He snuffled and shifted when Junior entered the stall, but let himself be led out. Junior tried to imitate the way Len had run the fork across the floor, but his stroke was not so smooth, and he was not sure what he was supposed to let through the tines and what he was supposed to lift. In places, soggy hay and manure stuck to the floor and if he shoved too hard through it the fork skidded into the good straw. The mat was set over crushed gravel and wasn't perfectly even, which left damp pockets he had to come back for. He remembered scrubbing out the plastic wastebasket and wondered what he was missing that would get him yelled at. By the time he had Brisket back in his stall with clean bedding, almost an hour had passed.

There were three stalls to go, and with no sign of Len, he assumed they were his to do. He would have to work faster if he didn't want to be here all night. Junior was well into the second stall when he heard Len and Inetta come in behind him.

"Thought we'd see if you were interested in dinner," Inetta said.

Junior didn't know them well enough yet to tell if their look meant they were amused.

"I'm not done yet," he said.

"No, not quite," said Len, looking into the stall Junior had already finished.

"It's hard work."

"Yep."

"You should have a Bobcat. You could drive it right in here and dump everything in the bucket."

"And cows should poop ice cream," said Len. "But that ain't the way it works."

Len and Inetta exchanged a glance, then left him alone again.

Junior ached by the time he got to the third stall. He wasn't used to physical labor, and his hands felt like they might blister. Did they expect him to do this every day? It didn't seem fair. Mucking stalls wasn't like doing house chores. The ranch was getting paid for this. He was just a kid.

Inetta came through the stable door. She brought in a red Coca-Cola serving tray with a glass of milk, a coffee mug with a spoon in it and a roll on a napkin. She set it beside her on a straw bale.

"Soup," she said. "Why don't you finish up that one and take a break?"

He was hungry, he realized, and maybe he hurried too much with Inetta watching him work. When he shut the horse back into the stall, she stood there next to him. She put her hand on his shoulder and led him back to the first stall that Len had cleaned.

"Take a look," she said. She steered him past the second stall. Junior peered over the half door. It looked clean to him. He'd spent almost an hour on it. Then the third and the fourth. He waited for her to tell him what a good job he'd done.

"Have a seat," she said.

He noticed her jeans were tucked into the same kind of rubber boots Len had told him to put on over his tennis shoes. Inetta stepped to the fifth stall and led out the dappled mare named Daphne, guiding her, it seemed, with no more than a hand placed on the horse's cheek.

Inetta turned to Junior. "Eat. And watch."

With her wrinkled face and grey-streaked hair, Inetta seemed much too old to be doing this work, and she was small—small as Junior. She raised forkfuls from the floor without the grunts that accompanied Junior's lifts and deposited the sticky mixture in the wheelbarrow with a quick stab. She took two half loads out to the manure pile instead of one big one, but otherwise, she moved through the stable just like Len. Smooth, economical, never straining. She had Daphne back in the stall by the time Junior finished his soup.

"Ten minutes, more or less," she said, checking her watch. "In the morning, I can get all these done in an hour. You're learning, so it takes longer, but you'll get it down."

"Len said it wasn't a race."

"It isn't. But if you want any time for yourself, you'll have to figure out how to get it done. Without"—she threw back her head toward the third stall—"leaving stuff in the corners."

Junior was tired or he wouldn't have said it. "We do it again the next day, so I'll clean it then. What's the difference?"

She didn't answer in a mean way, like she wanted him to feel bad. But her eyes flashed so he knew it was serious.

"The difference," she said, "is that every day is a new day the Lord has made. He doesn't just hand life over to you in one big piece to make a mess of it however you see fit. He gives you this day, and then another, and then another. Same with these horses. Same with the world. One day at a time.

"Doing it right is a way of giving thanks for the day you're given. Leaving a mess behind is a way of saying today didn't matter. *I can always do it tomorrow.* And then that pushes into the next day and the next, and then no day is special and there's no hour when your labor is done. You can never truly enjoy the rest God intended."

She dropped the tools into the wheelbarrow and pushed it into a corner, then sat down next to Junior and pulled off her boots and clapped them together.

"You'll be fine. Just listen to Len and follow his lead. We don't talk alike, but what he says, I would say. And what I say, goes for him."

Inetta picked up the tray with one hand and ruffled his head with the other. "Come on in," she said. "There's more of this soup and then there's pie."

"Hay for the horses. Manure for the soil. Fertile ground for the alfalfa. That's about what the world comes down to if you don't make it too complicated," Len was saying. The old man picked up a carrot from his plate, rubbed his thumb over its fine, unpeeled orange ridges and snapped it in half with a sharp cracking sound.

"Smell that. You ever taste a fresh carrot? Prob'ly not. Now they scrub off the soil, trim away the greens, peel it down, run it through a tumbler full of chemical water, poke the nubs in a plastic bag and drive it across the country." He took a bite. "They do that with everything now, so nobody knows the difference."

The food *was* different on the ranch. Junior had eaten well enough in other foster homes, but here there were no ready bags of chips and cookies, no frozen vegetables, nothing cooked in a microwave. The bread didn't come full of air in a plastic bag. Inetta made dense, crusty loaves from scratch, and Junior began to see bread as a food with taste and texture instead of a slab for serving peanut butter and marshmallow crème. He learned to eat chard and other greens Inetta didn't name, braised with onion, garlic and bacon grease. Even the sweets were different—jams made from prickly pears and chokecherries preserved in stubby Mason jars. He noticed that despite Len's esteem for manure, Inetta still washed the eggs before cracking them over the skillet.

The old man was particular about how things were done, but most of it wasn't difficult if you paid attention. Len wasn't like other grownups who told Junior what to do and then pestered him about whether he had done it. As in the stable, he showed Junior what was required, left him alone to try it and then offered correction. Len expected mistakes and slow going at first and didn't treat them as failure.

"Never ask a horse to do somethin' it ain't ready for. It won't go from scared to not scared or can't to can in one step. Give it the time it needs, build little by little. Don't punish it. A horse don't like pain any more than you and me. It can get used to it, but you don't want a horse that gets used to pain. It'll give up on you."

Junior got the feeling when Len talked about horses, he was talking about him, too. He was always trying to get Junior to notice some little thing.

"See them ears pinned back? Shows she's mad. You don't want to tussle with a angry horse. Some horses know that, and they try to fake you out."

"How do you tell whether they're faking?" Junior asked.

"You got to know the horse. Or else you can get bit a few times."

Sometimes Junior wanted to write things down so he could remember what Len told him, but the ranch wasn't a paper and pencil kind of place. He tried to recall the way the rancher said things, too. Junior felt stupid when he talked, so he tried to use as few words as possible. He liked how Len could make a few words sound smart.

Junior was worried about a wiry pinto gelding that had kicked at him once or twice and almost caught him.

"That horse is a little pig-eyed, so he sees worse than most. Some think pig-eyed horses is mean, and I guess so, if they been picked on 'cause they can't see good. You gotta talk to him. Let him know somethin' good is comin'."

Len would say something that sounded like the truth, and then he'd wink like it was a joke he expected Junior to get. "A horse ain't that smart, but it's got a real good memory and it can learn. Trouble is, you train it wrong and it won't straighten itself out. Not like people do."

That was Len. He'd come straight at you with something, and then he'd park it sideways at the last minute so you could see it better.

Oil Change

RANCH DOGS GET ENOUGH PROVOCATIONS to entertain them all day. Leonard expected them to exercise better judgment after dark: announce trespassers in the yard, but not howl at every coyote that crossed within a half mile. Inetta had trained Stitches from a pup to act more like a housedog, and she was well-behaved enough to sleep inside. Stitches knew what brought her praise or banishment, so the wet nudging Leonard felt meant the sounds coming from the yard must've fallen somewhere in the middle.

He sat up to listen. Not that he could hear anything; his tinnitus was worse at night, or else he noticed it more when vision didn't distract him. Nothing. He got up and looked out back through the bedroom window. As it should be. Horses tranquil in the pasture. Barn door closed. Stitches kept circling, making *mmm-mmm* sounds and shoving her nose against his hand. Maybe a skunk invading the hen house.

Might as well look before the commotion woke Inetta. He took down her .410, chambered a round of birdshot in case he needed to make some noise and told the dog to stay. Something kept him from flicking on the pole light over the barnyard. He pulled on his pants and stepped barefoot to the front door, meaning to feel his way around the crunch of pea gravel surrounding the house.

He waited on the stoop, surveying the yard and letting his eyes adjust to the night. No stirring from the chicken coop. Underneath his truck, a glint caught his eye. A flash of something, illuminated by the half moon. It flickered, moved a few inches then winked out.

A cat out for a midnight hunt? Hell.

He scanned the perimeter one more time before heading back in. Then he saw the shape on the road, just beyond the drive. A car. He looked back toward his truck, trying to sort out the shadows, then began a quiet advance.

A pair of black boots with silver concho straps stuck toes-up from behind the front tire. He checked the safety, eased the shotgun barrel between the legs and pushed until the muzzle made soft contact. A satisfying dull thud came from the darkness as a head banged the undercarriage.

"Hello, Bryce," he said quietly. "Where's Pinky?"

"H-h-hold on."

"I will, as long as you tighten whatever it was you was loosenin'. Then come on out."

"Uh, Pinky's up on the road."

"Well, then for your nuts' sake you better hope he don't surprise me."

Bryce Deaver slid from under the truck, a socket wrench and channel locks in his hands, and a dark smudge on his forehead. He started to his feet, but Leonard gave the shotgun a little thrust that Bryce correctly read to mean he should stay on the ground.

"You givin' midnight oil changes?"

"No." Bryce didn't make eye contact. He was focused on the .410 pointed at his crotch. "I guess I screwed up," Bryce said softly.

"Guess you did. My brake lines okay? Fuel tank clean?

Don't bother bullshittin' me. I'll check."

Bryce nodded. "I just started to break out the plug. Nothing leaked."

"Bryce, what the hell?"

"They fired our ass. As if you didn't know."

"I don't," Leonard said. "But I warned you. Be glad if fired is all that happens."

"Somebody squealed on us."

"And you thought it was me? I don't concern myself with the daily activities of lowlifes. You got what was comin' and your plan was what—loosen my damn drain plug so it'd shake out down the road? Bleed my brakes? What'd you think'd happen if I was headed down Monument Road when my truck give out?"

Bryce tried to look defiant and contrite at the same time. "What're you gonna do?"

"Ought to shoot your ass and bury it in the manure pile."

"Pinky knows I'm here."

"Fine, but he won't know to look where you're gonna be."

"Come on, Leonard..."

"You tell me which'd leave the world better off—Bryce Deaver stealin' off people for the next forty years or Bryce Deaver fertilizer?"

He lifted the shotgun and signaled Bryce to stand. Bryce stayed on the ground and glared back. "Shoot me here if you're gonna."

"You're a cocky sonofabitch, but you don't know a thing about people, do you? I don't care a damn what happens to you, but that's a long way from shootin' your shifty ass." He lowered the barrel and looked toward the car. "Pinky really up there?"

"No."

"You get to tell him what he missed, then. Take off your boots."

"What?"

"Take 'em off or you'll be dealin' with the sheriff."

Bryce pulled at a boot and wiggled it off. He set it on the ground and worked the other one loose.

"Now the pants."

"Come on!"

"Your choice. Drive home in the breeze—or trespass and vandalism."

Bryce stood. "Can I keep my wallet?"

"Sure. Wouldn't want you drivin' without a license. Keep your undies and your shirt, too. You want the rest back, they'll be at the store in a bag with your name on 'em."

Bryce stripped to his briefs. "You didn't tell Magruder?"

"Don't matter who did, Bryce, get it through your skull. You should be out lookin' for a job, not for somebody to blame for the mess you created. And next time you got a problem with *the elders*, I suggest you raise it in the daylight. We old folks don't see too good in the dark and might mistake you for a skunk." Leonard motioned up the drive with the gun barrel and Bryce took the suggestion.

Leonard watched until the white of Bryce's skivvies disappeared. If the truck checked out in the morning, he'd let the matter drop. Mad as he was, he shouldn't have pointed the gun at Bryce, even with the safety on, and he knew he'd work the damn thing over a dozen ways before he got back to sleep.

Smokes

JUNIOR LIKED BEING AT THE RANCH. The clear air and the clean smells—Len was right about the manure—and the land with no other person in sight made him feel like he was part of forever. He felt more grown up there than he had in town, more like if something happened, it was because of him. But living on a ranch for the summer didn't make him a ranch kid. The real ranch kids at his new school would sniff him out in an instant. He was still a foster kid to the social worker, still a Crimmins to the teacher, still a HardyFarty to the bullies, and beneath the notice of the Redlands kids from the nice houses. He wasn't a band kid or a sports kid or a smart kid, either. He admired the skaters with their attitude how clothes didn't matter, but he was awkward, and even if he had a board, the ranch had no pavement for practicing, and he knew Len and Inetta would not understand.

In those first weeks back at school, he could see his classmates declaring themselves. The secret codebooks were being handed out, the styles established, the clusters forming and the doors already closing. He wanted so much to pick a side—even if it was just for this school, this town, this year. Who else could an outsider join but the other outsiders—the hoods and the heavy-eye-shadow girls who acted hard in front of everyone.

Junior thought he could act hard. They acted bored. He could act bored. They walked like they knew how to drive and just didn't have the money for gas. He'd already driven Len's tractor. They cupped cigarettes stolen from parents or bought by big brothers. He would have to learn to smoke, just like his dad did.

Maybe being named Crimmins wouldn't be so bad behind the school.

Junior told someone on the bus he had been kicked out of his mom's house for fighting with her boyfriend. It wasn't quite a lie, and when the boy looked interested, Junior let the story stretch into him beating up the boyfriend. The new account got around. Though he lacked his father's disposition and stature, Junior realized he could grow into Hardy Senior's reputation.

It didn't take long for a boy to pick a fight to test the new kid.

"I heard you're supposed to be bad."

"Not really."

The boy crowded him and kids started to gather, watching. "You look like a pussy to me."

"I'm not."

"Then what's that smell? Did you just shit your pants, or do you always smell farty?"

Had the other boy not been so sure of himself, he might have noticed the steel thermos bottle Inetta had packed with Junior's lunch. Once Junior swung from his hips, it was too late for both of them. The tough guy dropped, and Junior earned a suspension, after some debate over whether a 24-oz. Aladdin wide mouth violated the school weapons policy.

When he returned, Junior discovered the air around him contained a new charge. Before, he felt blocked by a force field of contempt. But now it seemed he was the one who controlled the space. His stare, written across a version of his father's face, was now read as the cold gaze of a gangster, and the foot-bouncing that relieved his anxiety suggested a simmering ferocity. Instead of being shoved aside, he seemed to have set himself apart. He started telling people to call him Hardy and they did.

He watched the real toughs more closely for clues about what else he should be doing. They mocked sports and learning. They wore the same uniform—baggy pants and dark T-shirts that skirted school policy against slogans. They joked a lot in class and seemed to be having fun hanging out after school, too. They threatened loudly but didn't seem to actually fight much. And smoking, of course. They stood together one foot off school grounds, shaking out cigarettes to greet each other, passing them to the girls who hung around them. When they said goodbye, they flicked their butts sparking into the street or ground them into the dirt, as if putting bugs out of their misery. Throwing up a smokescreen would be one more sign you didn't mess with Hardy Crimmins, Jr.

First, he needed to practice.

Filching smokes would've been easy when he lived with his mom, but the Selfs didn't smoke or drink. He knew kids hung out by the air hose on the side of the Loco Mart and gave money to older guys to buy them smokes, but he was too shy to ask a stranger, and he rarely had the cash anyway. Picking up butts off the ground was too gross. He remembered an older boy in his last foster home who bragged about smoking grapevine. In the fall, the vines could be broken off in segments, stripped of the leaves and dried. The ones that were hollow worked best, he said. If the tubes had filled in, they'd be too hard to suck on. Junior had never seen any grapes on Glade Park, but the school bus went past a winery on Broadway. There was a bus stop nearby, where one kid got off, and he wondered if he could jump off there and sneak back to the vineyard. Broadway was the main drag and eventually it would take him to Monument Road, where he could hitch a ride with someone heading home to Glade Park.

He was afraid of getting caught at school with a knife in his backpack, so he brought along a pair of wire cutters from Len's toolbox. He got off the bus like he was going home with Michael Friedman and then backtracked to where the dormant vines snaked along trellises, waiting for winter pruning. The vineyard was next to a fake chateau a hundred yards away. He had no cover, from the road or the winery, so he planned to snip off the first dry-looking vines he found, stuff them in his backpack and run for it.

He wasn't sure how to pick out the best part of the vine for smoking. The ends seemed too thin and they got tough where they tied to the wires. He chose some lengths about as thick as his little finger because they were close to cigarette size. The wire cutters weren't ideal for pruning and he had to work the blades around the vine to cut through. He kept an uneasy eye across the open field. Surely any minute someone in the chateau would see him and come charging after him. He coiled a length of vine and crammed it into his pack. One more and he was done. The vines pushed back, like the hands of someone buried alive trying to escape a tomb. He forced them down so he could zip the top of his pack closed, and their fingers sprang against his back as he ran.

The cars sped by him as he stood on Broadway with his thumb out. Maybe they didn't want to look like perverts picking up a lone boy. He began to wonder how he'd ever get back to the ranch. There was no way he'd be back in time to clean the stalls. Finally, a red convertible pulled off Broadway onto the crossroad. It seemed too cool to have the top down, but the driver was happy and red-faced with a knit cap on his head.

"Where you headed?" he asked.

"Glade Park."

"Can't help you there. I'm going to Redlands Mesa."

"Where's that?"

"The new golf course." The man pointed east.

Junior's hopes of getting to the ranch were fading. "How far's that from Monument Road?"

"A mile or so. If I take you up to the clubhouse, there should be someone coming off the course who can drop you there."

Junior got in and placed his backpack between his feet. The windshield cut the chill and Junior felt the car's heater blowing warmth from under the dash. The man seemed happy in his own world. They turned at a big stone sign where a side road flared on the right and climbed a wooded hill with a stream trickling beside it. Some apartments appeared, shoved together like in the city, then the road forked at a pond and climbed in both directions. The man took the right turn toward the open land. It felt to Junior like they were going out of his way, and for the first time, he wondered if the man had told him the truth.

Near the top, giant houses sprouted from bare ground. Roofs covered in red clay tiles jutted above walls of stacked stones. One house had a circle drive that went under a canopy and the one next door had two-story windows beside a front door that looked like a pulled-up drawbridge. He could see a tangle of elk antlers with lights on them suspended over the entry. It seemed the houses wanted to look very old and brand new at the same time. The road curled around to a tiered parking lot and the clubhouse, which was also new. The man drove right to the top, stopped and jumped out.

"I got a tee time," he said. "You can wait out front."

Junior could only stutter a thanks before the man got on a cart with another golfer and disappeared down a hill. He wasn't certain he was allowed inside, so he stood by a wall and waited. Junior saw the Monument to the south, but he had no idea how to get there. There wasn't a road in that direction—just expanses of bright green grass running between dry, rocky ridges. A woman carrying a huge purse came out the main door and walked to her car, her hoop earrings bouncing. Two men who smelled like cigar smoke strode through the side door past Junior, snatched golf bags off a rack and clattered off. He didn't know how to hitch a ride from a place like this.

The sun dipped behind the Monument and he felt the temperature start to slide. A young man from inside the club-house opened the door and stuck out his head. "Can I help you with something?" he said, making it sound like *maybe you should leave now.*

"Can I use your phone?"

It was dark when Len's pickup pulled into the parking lot. Junior darted out of the shelter of the building's overhang and stepped onto the running board before the truck had even stopped. Len looked across the seat at him, but did not speak. Junior flushed and avoided his gaze.

Len circled through the lot, still strewn with the cars of people inside the bar. He proceeded slowly down the hill, look-ing sidelong at the houses. "Didn't even know this was here," Len said. "Think Vaughn used to trap bobcats up this way. "Huhn," he added after a silence, as if closing a door behind him.

Junior had told Len he'd missed the bus and hoped that

would do for an explanation. It seemed to, until they hit the tunnel part way up the Monument.

"We can't be missin' the bus."

"Sorry."

"You got schoolwork?"

"No," he lied.

"Good, because the stable's waitin'."

"I figured."

Another silence from Len. Then, "Anything else you want to tell me?"

Junior thought for a moment. "Thank you for picking me up."

"That ain't what I meant."

Junior knew what he meant, but he didn't know what to say.

"Me'n Inetta want to see you on the right path, but you got to pick it for yourself. Sometimes you can get off actin' stupid, but don't stay stupid."

"I wasn't doing anything."

"All right."

They rode in silence to the crest above Glade Park. From on high, Junior could see scattered pole lights and the softer glow from distant house windows, winking like stars dying on the ground.

"You have troubles, Junior, you have to tell us. You want help, you have to ask us. Can't put it more simple than that."

Inetta hadn't waited dinner for him, but she had saved some fried chicken and mashed potatoes. At least they had a microwave to warm it up. Microwave but no TV, how did that make sense? After he finished with the stables, they sat down with him at the table, so he was sure he was in more trouble than Len let on.

Inetta started in. "I suppose it's not so interesting up here compared to town."

"It's all right." What did she mean? Were they thinking of getting rid of him?

"It's different is all," she continued. "We have different things going on, jobs that need doing. They're not just ways to make money or kill time."

"I'm sorry. I just got on the wrong bus."

"That ain't what she means," Len jumped in. "You got a chance up here most boys don't get."

Besides shoveling horse manure was his first thought, but he said something truer. "I like it here, but I'm not going to be a cowboy when I grow up."

"Who is anymore?" Len looked over at Inetta and she smiled like he was saying this to her.

"What *are* you going to be?" she asked.

"Haven't decided."

"What do you like to do?"

"What's that got to do with work?" he said.

"Well, it's a place to start," she replied.

"Did you like horses when you were a kid?" Junior asked Len.

"Yep, but I guess I didn't have much choice. It was that or cows."

"Cows seem dumb. And chickens, too."

"It helps to think so when you're gonna eat 'em, but yeah, they are."

He'd watched Inetta chop a chicken's head off. Even dumb, it didn't want to die, but the smart got to eat the dumb. Junior saw that clear.

Inetta steered things back to the topic.

"There's different ways to go about it," she said. "Some people search for their heart's desire. They know what they want and they keep after it. Others, maybe like us, find something that doesn't feel like work and it turns out someone else thinks it is and will pay you for it. That's pretty good, too."

"That sounds like my dad," Junior said. Len and Inetta looked at each other funny.

"Could be," said Inetta. "What I meant was, there's different ways to find what you were meant to do. You find it or it finds you. That's why you want to try new things."

He was twelve. Junior understood well enough about wanting to try new things. "But what if nothing ever fits you? Do you just join the army?"

"That's one way," Len said, "cause they'll for sure make you try things you thought you never would."

"Were you in the army?"

"Nope. Missed out because of the ranch. But here's what you'll learn—from there or anyplace you pay attention. No matter what the job is, somebody likes doin' it. If you think you're stuck in the wrong job, you got two choices. You can quit or you can find the guy who's crazy about that kind of work and try to see what he sees. Look for the good, not for the bad. I guarantee you'll learn somethin' that'll make the job easier."

Junior thought he saw it. "You mean like how you like manure so much."

Len frowned like he didn't get what Junior was talking about, but Inetta laughed and laughed, so Junior figured he was on the right track.

The grapevines were a failure. The segments Junior broke off were too dense to draw and keep lit, and when they did burn, it was with a hot, harsh smoke that burned his lungs and made his head spin. He needed real cigarettes.

The bus driver smoked, and for a few days Junior rode in front, hoping he might get a chance to lift a pack from the jacket draped on the back of the driver's seat. When that plan failed, he worked up the nerve to approach Rocky Weiss after school. He had a quarter in his hand in case Rocky wouldn't let him bum a smoke, but Rocky just gave a nod and passed one over without looking at him, like they were in a prison movie. Once he got started, Junior found others who would share their cigarettes or sell him onesies. He still didn't smoke in front of anyone. Before he did it at school, he wanted to have everything down right and be able to inhale and blow the smoke back through his nose.

The bunkhouse was too confined and he didn't want Inetta to smell smoke when she came in to change his sheets, so after dinner he went for walks along the creek, where he could experiment in solitude. The creek carried enough water to have a name—Swift Creek—but like most things, it had been christened in a moment of optimism. It was swift after the winter snowpack melted, and when Junior first came to the ranch the stream trilled over the rocks, but it slowed in the summer, with barely enough water to keep the creek bottom green.

Junior learned to take in shallow puffs spaced well apart. Most of his rehearsal time was spent handling the cigarette until it began to feel natural in his fingers. It never felt right to have the smoke in his body. He had a rock where he liked to recline afterwards, clear his head and let his heartbeat slow as the sky turned from the daytime's enameled blue bowl into a deep black broth filled with fairy dust. He knew about the constellations but he preferred the swirl and mystery to locking the stars in place with names. If he held still, he thought he could feel the temperature fall one degree at a time as the heat left his rock. He listened to coyotes calling across the mesa and yipping in celebration when dinner arrived at the den. He saw them often in the evening, cutting through the ranch as if they owned it. They must have known they were safer here than up the road where Kurt Fokken liked to string their tails along his fence. The Fokkens had a boy who rode the bus, too, but Skye Fokken had purplish smears under his eyes, wore camo pants and shot a crossbow at anything that moved, so Junior kept his distance.

One November night, when an icy spit was in the air, Junior headed back for the shelter of the stable. He knew it was off-limits to smoke there and told himself to be careful. Daphne's owners had taken her out for an event and her stall was open. He pulled a straw bale inside and sat with his back to the wall. It was warm and fragrant and dark without the stars, and the quiet nickering of the horses soothed his nerves about the next day when he would join the others who hung out by the Safeway on their lunch hour. He'd stand on one foot, with the other against the wall. He'd pass a quarter and palm a smoke, then wait a while, squinting down the row. He might ask for a light from another's cigarette or snap one of Inetta's kitchen matches against his jeans. He had that move down pretty good. He'd take in the smoke and then let it out like something he'd wanted to say for a long time.

Volunteers

SOMETHING WOKE HIM EVERY NIGHT and Leonard tunneled up from sleep, met the inner hiss-whistle that canceled every silence and surfaced to feel the finger of his prostate gauging the fullness of his bladder. Tonight, the squawking of a pump handle, the distant booms of coupling boxcars, ditch water tumbling down a flume. Were these from dreams? None of these sources came within earshot. Lightning flickered behind the eyelid of the bedroom pull shade. The tick and snap and rolling thunder he heard did not quite square with an approaching storm.

He stepped to the window and peeled back one edge of the shade. The tin-coated roof of the stable glowed hotplate red along its seams and dragon fire snorted from the peak ends. He ran for the phone, jamming his sockless feet into boots as he called, sorry to be rousting the volunteers from their beds. Whatever was left inside was already lost but the fire's spread had to be contained.

Inetta was right behind him for the dash into the yard. They raced toward the orange glow between the open double doors but the heat blasted a warning and he felt his lashes crinkle. They danced forward and back against the sear, trying different angles as if a secret passage could be found between the flames, while the whickers and chuffs of the stall-bound horses pealed from inside. Inetta hammered a pane of ice around the hose to the stock tank and he yanked the rope to start the pump. The engine coughed and caught. Inetta fixed a nozzle to step up the pressure but the feeble stream thrown through the stable window was like pissing into a forge. They heard screaming and booming hoof strikes against the boards. Then nothing but the whooming of the stable's hellish breath, choked with smoldering straw and roasted animal fat mixed with a branding iron stink. White smoke wept from the wrinkled ribs and over the rim joists like steam lifting a kettle lid. Tamped down by the metal roof, the flames seemed lazy, preferring to lick each other instead of bursting through to the sky.

They turned their energies toward the barn—Inetta sloshing down the near wall and Leonard bucking away lean-tos of flammables. The stable roof began to buckle and twist as the rafters collapsed and the fire assumed a new register, a low chuckling that rose to a molten gargle with a crackling top note.

Lights twitched up the road and they readied themselves to surrender to the fire crew. Only then did they think about the boy. Inetta ran to the bunkhouse and he shouted Junior's name into the smoke. The truck rumbled down the drive and yellow-cloaked neighbors spilled into the yard. Leonard was half glad to be done with the lost cause. He stumbled out of the way, still calling the dark for Junior. The crisp air slapped him awake to the unburnt world beyond the barn. He ducked under the electrified wire to where horses circled the pasture or nosed into the loafing sheds according to their tempers. He moved among them counting head, farther and farther away from the glow.

Inetta found him sitting there, back against a shed, elbows on knees, sighting toward the flickering light.

"He got out Brisket," she said. "He won't come up. He's scared."

"He got a reason to be?"

"Who wouldn't?"

The yellow slickers moved so slowly. The truck lights flashed white haloes across their backs.

"I'll go down then."

He gathered himself and walked stiff-legged through the hoof-pocked grass. He saw Junior, shivering and blowing on his hands beyond the bunkhouse, the gelding tethered and skittish, vapors rising from the both of them. The boy collapsed a little when he spied Leonard coming and reached for Brisket's flank, as if steadying the horse would steady him.

"You okay?"

Junior nodded, black circles under his eyes. Shook his head.

Leonard turned toward the blaze.

"Just the one?"

"I..." Nothing else came out.

Inetta made it a circle. "Tell him," she said.

"They wouldn't come," said Junior. "I unlatched the stalls but they wouldn't. It was too smoky."

"That's their safe place," Leonard said. "What about the fire?"

Junior dropped to his knees, planted his palms in the frozen dirt and lowered his head. The smoke ushered upward the ghosts of three horses. A radio blatted a faraway voice, flat and official. Men shuffled after sparks as the kiln of the stable settled into itself.

"So," Leonard said finally and stomped toward the ruin.

Mike Gundy squinted at Leonard through his visor, then tipped it up. "Not much we could do."

"No," Leonard said, "not much. The barn's good. The house."

"The house, that's the main thing," said Gundy. "We'll be here a while yet."

The water away from the stable was starting to freeze. Leonard finally felt the chill through his scorched and blackened long johns. Inetta, in a flannel shirt tossed over her housecoat, was still talking to the boy. He sensed the crunching step of fire fighters behind him and turned into Bryce Deaver and Pinky Allred.

"Comin' back from town, we seen the glow and busted on over here," said Pinky. "Almost beat the fire truck."

"Helluva thing," said Bryce. "Sorry it was too late."

"Yeah, well," Leonard said. "Good to see you volunteerin' now."

Bryce chunked a shovel against the hard ground. "Seemed time we should pay back some of what we owe, is all."

Some things look better in the morning. This didn't. The stable had collapsed into a pile of blackened, twisted tin and charcoal hunks that were still smoking in places. The corral opened like a U with two charred ends where the fence once terminated at the stable wall. He walked around the ruin and thought this must be what it smells like when hell freezes over.

Two of the owners had already been to the ranch. Brisket's owner, Lori Freeman, was alerted by someone on the fire department phone tree, and the Tollinses had showed up, too. He'd sold them their Appaloosa, a mare named Tucker. They were in shock when they left, and he wasn't sure his promise to replace the horse had gotten through. The others, the Hoekstras and the Nagels, had him worried. Faith Hoekstra was a lawyer with a tough reputation, and the Nagels were always on him about seeing the receipts for every little expense. His insurance agent said he'd have an adjuster up as soon as possible. If the insurance didn't cover this, Leonard could be in deep shit with both of them. In fact, he was in deep shit anyway. People didn't pay good money to have their horses barbequed. They'd all talk about it, far and wide.

Karen Nagel was due to come out to the ranch, and he wanted to head her off. When she didn't answer a phone call, he decided to go out to the house, one of the newer places southeast of No Thoroughfare Canyon. Her horse, Arkady, a fine registered Morgan, was the most valuable of the horses killed. Arkady, plus Tucker and Spinner, the Hoekstra horse, amounted to maybe fifteen grand, not counting their destroyed tack and the mental anguish he expected to find when he met up with Karen Nagel.

The entrance to the Nagel place featured an iron arch with a fancy *N* and matched Kokopelli figures blowing flutes from the halves of the ornamental gate. The red dirt drive climbed the hill to a big log house with a walkout overlooking a meadow. They had room to keep a horse on their acres, but as Karen explained, her husband had a complicated travel schedule and she liked to go along whenever he went somewhere interesting. He knocked on the frosted glass door and watched her ghostly shape move through the high-vaulted room on the other side. When she opened it, he already had his hat in hand but he declined her invitation to come in from the cold. He wanted to keep the conversation short and his escape route direct.

"We had a fire at the ranch late last night. The stable went up quick and we lost Arkady. I come out to tell you how sorry I am and that I'll make it right. He was a good horse."

He stood there, waiting for the curse, the cry, the blow, while she faced him, the moment stretching, her eyes frisking him, her knuckles white on the door lever.

"Lost..." she said. "You mean dead."

"Yes, ma'am."

She turned half away, then back toward him, looking through tiny cups of tears. "And how do you possibly make that right." She stated it as a fact, not a question, and the door in his face was its punctuation. It was true. He couldn't change what happened. Emotional restitution was beyond his means. This woman's horse could not be easily replaced, and the man who lost it might not be the right one to try.

He still had not heard Junior's account, only Inetta's version of it. The boy told her he'd been smoking in the stable and woke up to the blaze. Leonard had not laid down many rules, preferring to let the logic of chores lead Junior to the right side of behavior, but safety lessons were better not learned the hard way. No fire, no matches in the stable—that was clear as anything could be.

"You have to talk to him," Inetta said. "This is eating him up."

"What'm I gonna say?"

"He knows what he did wrong," Inetta said. "He doesn't know it's not the end of the world."

"It ain't, huh? There's a better day comin' sounds more like your department."

"He needs to hear it from you."

When Junior was taken from his mother and brought to the ranch, he acted like it didn't matter, and when Leonard came into his room, that was the blank face he wore. Sitting on the edge of his bed, Junior was hunched for whatever was about to land on him. Leonard took the big chair and leaned forward with his hands clasped between his knees. They each examined familiar parts of the room, letting silence pack the small space full.

"There was a boy once," he finally began, "about your age, livin' across the road from here."

Junior looked up from the rug to Leonard's hands.

"Back then, finishin' eighth grade was the big deal, like high school today. The school up here only went to sixth, so he had to go into town. Had to get himself down to where the bus would pick up, and he rode there, even in winter, and left his horse at a friend's place durin' the day. No stayin' at school or foolin' around—just straight home to do chores. Like you.

"Well, one time the horse got loose somehow and he couldn't find her. Kept lookin' until comin' home late got scarier than comin' home without the horse. See, the dad had his problems and one of 'em was the drink and another his mother called *the darkening*—sadness, temper, what all. This boy could see it comin' from way far off."

"Like when the rain comes in," Junior said. This was familiar territory. "Like you see the clouds all black, and sometimes the storm gets to you and sometimes it doesn't." He looked at Leonard directly. "Go ahead," he said. "I think I know who the boy is."

Leonard had not rehearsed this, and now he wished he'd worked out how to say it. Hitchhiking home. Trotting down the road to the house. Maybe this was the wrong thing for Junior to hear. Maybe there was a better way to tell the boy about mistakes and regrets and how they don't have to determine your whole life.

"Seen my mother kneelin' in the yard and my sister, Emma. They're both sobbin'. My old man there with a shotgun. First, I thought some varmint had got into the chickens, and then I seen our dog on the ground. The old man was on the warpath. He says to me, *get your ass over here!* and my mother screams *run!*"

Then the blast, his mother knocked back, her shins still flat in the dust. He didn't need to tell that. "So I ran. Took off for my Uncle Abner's—over here."

A second round racked and fired. Zig-zagging off the road, staggering over the uneven pasture ground. A third.

"Seems like I remember the buckshot zip across my jacket, sting my scalp and then sizzle past my ears, but the pellets had to've hit all at once."

"Your dad *shot* you?" Junior's eyes were big, intent on him.

"At me."

"Why?"

"I don't know."

"But you got away."

"Sorta," Leonard said. "Got just enough time from him shootin' my mother and sister. Now, what if my mother meant run *here* when he was yellin' at me to get over? Would he've shot me first or could I've done somethin'? What if I'd tied up my horse better and been home on time? Don't know any of that. Wasn't even in my head at the time. Just did what I thought my mother said and ran away."

He rose from the chair and sat on the bed next to Junior. The springs gave that porch-swing violin squawk he remembered from when this was his room. "You do a little thing wrong and a big thing happens. You save one horse but three die and you feel terrible to blame. Well, I felt the same only worse. I was just a kid then, like you."

Leonard didn't know how to describe to this boy the cure for blame. He didn't know how to talk about finding the one who loved you because he'd so stumbled onto it himself. And so he stumbled forward. "It don't matter anymore what you did and didn't—it's too late. Now, it's what you do with the rest of your life. Life is long and then it starts to shorten up all of a sudden. You're headin' into the long part, Junior. It's the part where you can still decide how the rest is gonna be. You're a good boy who made a bad mistake. We all wish it hadn't happened, but now it's up to you whether this makes you weak or strong."

He had to stop before he started to preach. The only words he had left were the platitudes that had never helped him. By now Leonard either was or he wasn't the man the boy would decide to become.

"Can I still stay here?" Junior asked.

"Don't know," Leonard said. He could promise to forgive, but his forgiveness would be tried. He could not quite see into the hard days ahead when the customers were gone and he struggled to rebuild and found no one who would take a chance on the place that burned up the horses, while the boy who did could do nothing but remind him. With his story, he'd meant to help Junior look ahead the way Inetta did with him. But the truth was, Leonard's past was still in him, like the pellets under his skin that never worked their way out.

"We'll just have to see."

Across the Road

He showed Inetta where they were after the insurance claim fell through and the letters from the lawyers arrived. Not good. Even without replacing the stable, anything they could try was just moving the leak to a different pocket. He knew it was a stretch, but he took his numbers to the bank, and the man behind the desk was only trying to be straight when he said, "We aren't just looking for borrowers with equity in their property. We loan money to people who can pay us back."

Leonard stood up. "Fair enough. I don't wanna borrow and you don't wanna lend."

The banker had grown up a farm kid. He knew about a few other things besides making money. He said, "You're already trying to pay those people back. No sense paying me interest, too. Can you spare selling off some acres?"

Leonard wasn't about to get tangled with some real estate agent in town who'd just poke a sign in the dirt, run an ad in the Sunday paper and expect his six percent. The best thing all around would be selling to another rancher, and on his end of Glade Park, that meant one man. Donnie Barclay.

"Where were you thinking?" Inetta asked.

"Across the road. It touches Donnie's land on the back."

"It wouldn't hurt to be rid of that—to let all of it go."

"Still be there to look at. Sellin' ain't the same as lettin' go," he said.

"What your father had in him isn't in you." She knew more than he did what he was saying sometimes. For all he knew the darkening waited in his brain ready to flower in years to come. "You're half your mother. More than half."

That was Inetta, always looking on the bright side. It was hard for him to think on his mother anymore, to get past her last word and his last image of her. He had to hold her in the abstract, in metaphor, not even mother, but water: soothing, life giving, beautiful, and most important of all, she could quench the fire. For a time.

The great part of being rich, in Donnie Barclay's humble opinion, was that it let him do what he wanted without thinking about money. He wasn't interested in the peace of mind bullshit the TV ads talked about—he enjoyed a little turmoil—and he didn't care that much about toys, though he had a lot of them. He could decide whether he liked a pair of boots or a new pickup without looking at the price tag. He could fuck off for the afternoon, buy drinks for the room or send his ranch foreman's kid to college because he felt like it. And even better, he could afford to say no. Forget freedom of speech and religion and all that other shit. He had the best kind of freedom on earth. As his father Buck Barclay would say, *know when you got 'er dicked.* Donnie pretty much did. He learned early on he did not enjoy sweating details in the middle of the night, so he found people he could rely upon. He still watched over his enterprises, but never obsessed over the day-to-day numbers. That was a good way to miss the thing that would *really* fuck him.

The Barclay family had prospered in western Colorado since the 1880s. Even before the Indian land on Glade Park opened to homesteading, Donnie's great grandfather Lincoln Barclay had staked some out with Winchesters. His grandfather Emerson held sway over the nearby rangelands by occasionally directing other rancher's sheep over cliffs before federal grazing permits formalized the Crown B's control. The larger opportunities represented by government propping up the beef market were not lost on Buck Barclay. While his cattle found all kinds of ways to kill themselves and lose him money, the government offered as many ways to make some. Buck rounded up farmers and ranchers to persuade the county that paving rural roads was going to help agriculture, and then he branched out into serving what the people wanted. By the time Donnie was old enough to work on a chip spreader, Barclay Paving and Excavation held road contracts in three counties. The father concentrated on the bidding, backslapping and political donations, as the son learned the business from the dirt on up. As the center of commerce began to shift from the tree-lined Main Street toward the prairie dog flats west of town, Barclay Paving moved with it, skinning off the brush and applying a poultice of parking lots. Somewhere in there, Donnie Barclay learned to delegate, climbed off the paver and never got back on.

Leonard had hoped to run into Donnie somewhere. Bringing up his land in casual meeting would make it seem less like begging. But the weeks dragged on.

"Just call him," Inetta said. "It's not like you don't know him."

Leonard had helped out at the Crown B on occasion as an extra hand who could cut pairs and vaccinate calves. Some years he'd also drawn a summer paycheck from Barclay Paving driving a dump truck. He remembered it as slow, backward and repetitious, the way a lot of work was, just more out in the open. Inetta didn't understand that having a man like Donnie in the neighborhood didn't make him your neighbor. Working for the man who owned the truck you drove wasn't the same as knowing him. But Leonard finally did call him, and Donnie made it easy.

"This is a good day to come on over," Donnie said. "I've got a horse I've been thinking about for the grandkids. You can give it a look and tell me what you think."

It turned out Donnie already owned the horse. "They could ride it anyway," Donnie admitted, "but owning something makes the whole thing different. Kids need something they can grow up with, instead of toss away after a few months. Not one of those damn Nintendo things. I'm gonna spoil my grandkids, but I'll be goddamned if I'll ruin 'em."

Leonard didn't know what a Nintendo thing was. And come to think of it, he didn't know why he was on his way over to the Crown B to look at a horse when he'd called Donnie about selling part of the Reverse Dollar.

Donnie didn't seem interested in looking over the property. "I know where it is," he said. "Let's us go for a ride. You can take Ninny, see what you think. The kids'll get to rename her, of course. She was supposed to be a cow horse, but let's just say she's not."

The Crown B sprawled across the west end of Glade Park all the way into Utah. Leonard had ridden through parts of the ranch, but there was more he'd never seen. Maybe Donnie wanted to show Leonard that he didn't need to buy any more land. Maybe he just wanted an opinion about a horse. With Donnie, it wasn't easy to tell.

They picked their way north, following a trail toward the ridge that roughly marked the border of the ranch. Above, he knew, was a high plateau where Donnie held the grazing lease. It was reachable on horseback, but the only access road from the ranch looped through Utah and around. They hadn't brought extra water, so he figured Donnie had something less adventurous in mind, an excuse to get out without any work waiting on the other end, and as they threaded through the sagebrush, it struck Leonard how long it had been since he did the same. Ninny seemed gentle enough for kids. He didn't sense anything troublesome in her temperament and suspected Donnie already knew that.

"Tell me what's got you wanting to sell now. That fire took a big nip out of things, I imagine," Donnie said. "You planning to rebuild?"

"Nope. Don't think I have much future takin' care of other people's horses now. This's just to settle up."

"I heard the kid staying with you started it."

"He went in there for a smoke. Thought he was bein' careful."

"Every man who ever shot himself in the foot thought he was being careful," Donnie said. "City kids, goddamn it, that's where it's all going."

"He admitted it, at least," said Leonard. "What's done's done."

They rode for a while, following a deep wash with a soft sandy bottom, listening to the song of a meadowlark scramble over the creak of saddle leather. "The original Utah Jazz," said Donnie. "Songbirds, saddles and horse farts." They pointed their mounts up an incline and followed a bench running along a buff sandstone cliff that shaded to red closer to the ground. Great arcs of stone had weathered or fallen away, leaving shaded coves forty feet high. Between the arches, the flat walls were streaked with desert varnish that, depending on the light, ran from maroon to purple to blood black. Ahead, a narrow keyhole in the cliff pinched between two towering formations. "You been back in here?"

"Heard of it," Leonard said when he realized where Donnie was taking him—a petroglyph site reachable only though the Crown B. They tied the horses to a greasewood and slipped through the slot to where the canyon widened again to reveal a billboard-sized catalog of human and animal figures etched in the varnish.

"See the sharp-shouldered spaceman guy with the horns?" said Donnie. "That's Fremont culture. Probably a shaman, a thousand years old. Same with those spirals, snakes and the squared-off deer. Then came the Utes. I think the bear claws, the mounted hunters and the rounder of the bighorn sheep are theirs. Those damn bullet holes are the white man. Happened when I was a kid, never found out who."

Three circles of rock were shot away from a two-foot-high striped figure with a triangular torso—face, heart and crotch. Someone proud of his marksmanship, no doubt.

"What the hell's going to happen to this place after we're gone, Len? My son and daughter're good people, but they're not much interested in the ranch. It's not the life they want. Wrong kind of responsibility. This was already a beautiful place, but funny how some dead Indians' pictures make it priceless. It's too remote for me to protect and too close to civilization to hide for much longer. You can't stick up a sign telling people to leave it alone—that'll bring the idiots with pocket knives and plastic bottles that much faster.

"That kid who burned your stable—bet he wasn't even trying to be bad—he just couldn't give a flying crap. That's where it's all headed after they put us under. From *Don't Tread on Me* to *Who Gives a Shit.*"

The afternoon sun illuminated a fringe of green growing along the upper rim. The meadowlark was back and a grasshopper buzzed around a clump of needlegrass.

Leonard said, "Got to sell the acres across from me. It's goin' to someone. I wanted to give you the first shot."

"I appreciate it," Donnie said, but he was still on his former topic. "Just a hundred and fifty years ago this was somebody else's home. My family didn't straight-up steal it, but we didn't pay for it, either. All we had to do was *improve* it, right?

"We think this is God's Country, but I'll tell you right now, there's beauty all over this earth. Places to take your breath away where you'd expect it to be a shithole. North Dakota. Puerto Rico. Vietnam. And places that truly are shitholes as far as I'm concerned—there's always somebody who'll want to put a bullet in you if you insult their holy site. Why is that? It's not just the scenery. Not just religion. It's home, Len. If it wasn't, the Israelis could give the Palestinians Nevada and call it square."

Donnie made a move back to the horses. "Your old man's place. Nothing wrong with it, but to me it's just more grazing land. I can spend my entire week listening to people who have *opportunities* for me, which really means they want me to buy their shit or invest in even worse shit. They think when you have money, you don't have standards, but that's when standards are even more important, because you have so many damn opportunities in your life. I'm not saying that's you; it's just reality. I'm sorry about your situation. I won't presume. Twenty-four thousand. You can take it or not, but thank you for offering me first refusal."

They mounted up. Leonard looked at Donnie sitting so

easily in the saddle. He thought of his family's fallen-down house across the road, his burned stable and the settler's cabin where Junior was packing up his clothes right then. Donnie was right. Those were all installments of a long decline, but it was one Donnie Barclay would never suffer. Twenty-four thousand would clear all he owed, and Leonard could walk away instead of run. He could hold his head up and never be sure if Donnie Barclay had meant to walk over him or do him a great kindness.

HALF TUNNEL

Newsblind

B<small>EFORE</small> <small>TURNING</small> <small>SOUTH</small> <small>ACROSS</small> <small>THE</small> <small>BRIDGE</small> to the
Redlands, the parkway snakes between the river and a waste-
land of rubble bill-boarded with promises of professional
spa installation, exceptional dental care and relief from DUI
charges. Leonard sees a ladder-racked pickup coming up on
his right, racing to pass before the road narrows to two lanes.
The truck bed is overloaded with yard waste, paint buckets
and miscellaneous unbagged trash that flits in the slipstream
coming off the back. Leonard's in no hurry, but the reckless
move irritates him and he holds his place against being over-
taken. The driver takes some shoulder before squeezing in at
the curve, spinning a salvo of gravel across Leonard's grille.
Through their back window he can see two yahoos bobbing
their heads toward each other in celebration of the maneuver.
Let it go, he tells himself, just as the driver swerves again only
to jolt over an unseen obstacle, sending up a shower of debris.
Leonard feels the thump, too, just as flapping newspapers burst
in a flock from the truck bed, twist and plaster themselves
across his windshield.

He ducks down to an opening where he can see to cross
the bridge and pull safely aside. By the time he steps out to a
clear view of the road, the offenders have disappeared over the

rise. He strips off the newspaper and mashes it into a ball. How long has it been since he even glanced at the news? Another habit that slid away with Inetta. Behind him, on the bridge, a stray tire bedevils the traffic. He considers walking back to clear it, but the spot is blind and there's no pedestrian walk on that side of the bridge. Let someone with a cell phone call it in. He's spent a year shrinking his attention down to a pinhole, and with it, his sense of obligation to clean up after the careless.

Time was, he took on such chores without thinking, hauling strangers out of ditches, offering gas to stranded tourists, snugging up a neighbor's sagging fence. That was how it was out here. You made your contribution to mutual survival—no recognition or recompense expected. Cowboy karma, he'd heard somebody call it. Inetta might call it grace. But for all that, what did such steadfastness do for his mother and his sister kneeling in the yard. Abner, alone and facedown in his field. Vaughn bent sideways for good. Junior banished. Inetta herself, slow walking away from him. No matter what Leonard Self decides about his importance in the universe, if he turns his back on this, the tire will still be off the bridge tomorrow and no one will even remember it was there. He wishes he could talk it out with Inetta, hear again why it matters not to let things slide. He used to step up without thinking on it because simple goodness needed a place to lodge, entrusted closer to the real world than with an all-loving and do-nothing God.

He thinks of his own father, for the first time in a long while without feeling a strangle in his throat. Had Leonard's sense of rightness only been the offspring of his father's crime, or had he inherited good examples, erased from memory by the final, bloody picture of the man? Leonard had always supposed in his father an anger that became a poison and the poison caused pain and its steady drip called for an end. But how big must a pain be to also consume a wife and a daughter and a son? His old man was a young man then, half Leonard's age. He should've remembered how things change, how the cold lifts and the desert greens and the hummingbirds come back. Leonard still couldn't see all the why of his father but he recognized a partial answer in himself. The darkening was not pain but bone-deep numbness. Not nightmares but short dreamless sleep and long wakefulness. Not chaos but an empty, unbudging sameness that Inetta had been able to wave away whenever it gathered, but left alone with it now, he was ready to roll to a stop.

He climbs back in the truck and sees Inetta's urn tipped on its side, the cork plug fortunately still in place. He molds the newspaper into a nest that he places on the floor and swaddles Inetta in the obituaries. As he pulls into traffic, it occurs to him his name is about to appear on one of those pages for the first time, for the sole achievement of ceasing to be.

Ice Walk

IT WAS POSSIBLE TO FLOAT UNEVENTFULLY above the treeless crags and half-greened slopes that marked the last few hundred miles of his flight from St. Louis to Grand Junction, but to Joe Samson, the purple majesty of the Rockies was best enjoyed from the fruited plain. Once he changed planes in Denver, he tried to shed memories of return trips from college in a bucking and plunging puddle jumper that vibrated like a giant sheet-metal alarm clock. In preparation for his demise, he inventoried the cabin and imagined which of his fellow passengers he would cleave to in the final moments. As the plane rose over the Front Range, he played alphabet games in his head. Either that or watch for a rivet to pop from the shuddering wings.

Apple, Bean, Corn, Date, Eggplant, Farina, Grape... Aspen, Beech, Cedar, Dogwood, Ewe, Fir, Ginko... Alejandro, Bastien, Carlos, Diego, Esteban, Francisco, Guillermo...

The flight finally descended over Bunkwater Ridge, and he relaxed a little seeing the spiderwork of gas field roads showing pure white against the snowy scratchboard of brushland. Then the little propjet crested the Book Cliffs, and the Grand Valley burst forth below, as if winter's curtain had been pulled aside on a window overlooking Egypt. Globe willows had begun to leaf into green puffballs and farm fields lay in pregnant patches that seemed too perfect to be made of lowly dirt. A yellow ATV bounced away from a cluster of vehicles parked in the desert north of the irrigation canal, and Joe felt a sudden urge to be down there, too, without an engine between his legs, biking hard over trails and the checkerboard of section roads that had none of the traffic he had to navigate back in Missouri.

Safely in the terminal, he cut through the circling greeters and travelers, their eyes searching for what they could no longer gather into an embrace. Behind a sagging brocade rope, a dusty brown bear and a snarling mountain lion faced off over a plaster of Paris dinosaur track. A child oscillated on a coin-operated rocket ride, while a woman hovered nearby clenching her unlit post-flight cigarette. He wondered whether the town had more than one cab by now. His mother wasn't supposed to drive, and his younger brother, if he was still in town, had never owned a car or even had a license. If he and Shelly were to move back here, by default Joe would become—in his mother's stroke-addled phrase—*the house of the headhold.* For now, he just wanted to know if it would be possible to live here again. Taking his chances on the cab, he planted himself at the curb and for the next half-hour watched the sun walk west along the maroon uplift of the Monument.

Joe quick-stepped down the driveway, his bare soles licking gingerly over the cold the way a cook's finger tests for heat. Winter here was always warmer than it looked, yet no matter how he tried to adjust his expectations, it was never as warm as he wanted. *The Clarion* lay just off the drive in an orange plastic bag scuffed by the toss from the deliverer's car. He turned to see the black apostrophes his feet had made in the near-invisible rime.

With its circle drive, featureless brick front and non-functional pillars, the house his parents built after he left home resembled a poorly situated Ramada Inn. Behind it was the pole barn his father had filled with all means of motorized escape—all sold off now, including the Winnebago that, as far as he knew, had rarely made it out of the shed. He tried to imagine his father on vacation. Carl didn't actually need to visit paradise. He just wanted it to be within bitching range.

His mother seemed to do well after Carl died, until the day they found her unconscious in the parking lot at work. As Marian put it, she forgot to faint sitting down, but doctors called it a stroke, and so began a process laden with hopes and lurches and setbacks that Joe slowly accepted would not end with a full recovery. The kids were young, and they'd adapt to a new place. Shelly could find a job with the school district. His career was the sticking point. He'd be leaving a great job with a St. Louis PR firm; they'd already informed him he couldn't serve his clients from Colorado.

He separated the slick Sunday inserts from the thinner front news section, which featured stories about the Lion's Club parade and a vehicular mishap above the announcement of Enron's bankruptcy. Despite its nickname, "The Carrion," *The Clarion* wasn't terrible. It was local, and like everywhere, people complained as if the news were the newspaper's fault. The crime sprees carried out by interchangeable sets of violent stepbrothers and their feral girlfriends weren't so much sensationalism as a sign of a deteriorating quality of life since meth came to the valley. In contrast, *The Clarion's* business coverage was unfailingly positive. Even oil spills and food poisonings in Chinese restaurants were treated as the bearable price of retaining jobs in a global economy. *The Clarion* had recently lost a sharp young reporter to the *Houston Chronicle*, and the opening should have been good news. But Joe was sitting at his mother's kitchen table in a town he thought he'd outgrown, preparing to interview for a job like the one he'd had a decade ago. It felt like a giant step backward toward the person he wasn't anymore.

But maybe it would be a process.

Clarion managing editor Ed Whiteside met Joe in the lobby and walked him back to a room on the other side of a vending area that contained a modest-sized conference table. Whiteside indicated a seat for Joe and remained standing with his palms planted on the table, leaning forward as if about to devour whatever had been brought to him.

"I've seen your clips from the business daily," he said. "Agri-business, real estate and development. Not bad, but that was a while ago. Your PR writing… we don't see too many agency people who are trying to make it back into journalism."

Joe wondered if the interview was going to be a short one. "I'm back here for family reasons, not a career change, but the agencies in town don't have a place for someone with my experience."

Whiteside tapped a file folder on the table. "I saw you grew up here. You graduated in the same class as Neulan Kornhauer. Have you been following the story?"

Neulan? It was not good to be surprised in an interview, but Joe had no idea what Whiteside was talking about. He tried to finesse it. "I've been back and forth from Missouri. I may have missed some developments."

"Yeah, I suppose you don't see the *Herald Times* back east." Whiteside opened the folder and handed over a tear sheet.

Rio Blanco Sheriff says Meeker, Gunnison deaths may be linked

MEEKER – Authorities are revisiting their investigation into the death of a Meeker woman, citing similarities with the fatal plunge of a Grand Junction woman last year.

Rio Blanco County Sheriff Fred Jeep said Wednesday his department has been in contact with Montrose County investigators into the death of Caroline Kornhauer, who perished from a fall into Black Canyon near Gunnison last October.

Christi Queen was 21 when she disappeared in July 1994. Hunters discovered her remains in a rugged area east of Meeker that November. A coroner's report ruled the cause of death suspicious. Blunt force injuries were consistent with a fall, Jeep said, but investigators found no explanation for the woman's presence in the remote location.

Caroline Kornhauer's death remains under investigation, according to Montrose County Attorney Jeff Carstens. Jeep said his department may renew its investigation after reviewing information from the Kornhauer case.

Asked about a potential linkage between the deaths, Caroline's husband Neulan Kornhauer said, "Like the Queen family, we have experienced a terrible tragedy that left unanswered questions. I hope and pray any investigation helps us both find peace of mind."

Neulan's wife off a cliff! Unbelievable. The story made no reference to Helen Vavoris, and the Meeker paper was unlikely to connect its story to the even older accident. But surely if Joe saw the pattern… *Neulan. Of course.*

"Kornhauer's playing up the good Christian husband act," said Whiteside with a grimace. "He invited us to cover his wife's funeral, where he got up and sang, but we can never pin him down for an interview. Somebody here remembered he was a witness to a girl falling at the Monument—back in your time, right? So were you buddies with Kornhauer? Was he a ladies' man back then?"

Joe had to laugh, despite his discomfort.

"I thought so," Whiteside said. "Look, I've lost my guy who reported on the Kornhauer story, and we need to pick it up again."

"Are you offering me a job?" Joe asked.

Whiteside pushed the file folder across the table. "For now, it's a freelance assignment. I see you can write. Now show me you can still report."

Risky

Joe didn't start his test with much besides tenuous ties to Neulan and his public relations-encrusted reporting skills. The background file would help get him up to speed, and his memory of what happened at Cold Shivers Point might draw out Neulan, but he reminded himself he only needed to write a good story, not solve the mystery.

Caroline Kornhauer had an appointment in Montrose to show her wedding portfolio and planned to scout locations in the Black Canyon while she was in the area. On her way, she dropped Neulan and his gear at the Bridgeport trailhead to Dominguez Canyon where he would camp for the weekend. When she drove away early that Friday morning, it was the last time he saw his wife.

Two days later, when Caroline didn't arrive to pick up Neulan, he caught a ride back to Grand Junction with a day hiker. When she hadn't returned late Sunday night, he called the police. The next day, the Kornhauer Cherokee was found parked at the Black Canyon's South Chasm View, a sheer, nearly two-thousand-foot drop to the Gunnison River. Neulan was logged in at the Dominguez Canyon trailhead and witnesses reported seeing him over the weekend. The man who gave him a ride to town was located and corroborated his story.

There were at least forty miles of rugged country between the Black Canyon and where Neulan camped. None of the material, including a copy of a police report, suggested Neulan was under suspicion, although in Joe's limited experience with crime reporting, police guarded their files, and he wondered why investigators had shared this report.

Whiteside had included clips on Christi Queen, too. The local paper found nothing remarkable to report about the young, church-going dental hygienist who'd disappeared from her parents' home, except for her father's grief. In a forlorn photo he knelt alone on the rocks where her discovered bones had washed out of a canyon. Without this context, the file's final, mundane item might have escaped Joe's attention: the notice for Christi Queen's memorial service.

"Yes, of course, I remember Christi," said the Reverend Gordon Dash of The Grace Assembly Church. "A nice girl, very devout. That was very hard on the family."

"What about Neulan Kornhauer?" Joe prompted. "If he was visiting in your area back then, he might have stopped in for services."

"No. That's a name I'd remember, I'm sure."

"You'd probably recall him if you ever heard him sing."

Reverend Dash was silent for a moment. "Tall fellow?"

"Yes."

"That could be James King."

"Someone who attended your church?"

"A traveling man. As I understand, he worked for Halliburton, and when he was in town, he came to Sunday worship, sometimes Wednesday night Bible study. Such a glorious singer. He had a voice that could part the Red Sea."

When Neulan answered, Joe sang four ascending notes: "How can there be…" After a brief pause on the other end, six responding notes rose from an octave lower: "An-y sin in sin-cere?" Then half the old quartet joined in harmony: "Where is the good in good-bye-eye, in good-bye-eye?"

Neulan's booming voice laughed, and said, "Who is this?"

"Don't you recognize one of your fellow school board members from River City?"

"Samson?"

Joe sang: "Your apprehensions confuse me, dear…"

"That isn't funny. Is it you?"

Joe picked up on the last notes of another of the quartet's numbers—"It's you-ou, yes… it's… you-u-u"—and admitted, "Yeah, it's me. I'm back in town."

"And you decided out of the blue to call me," Neulan said.

"I'm a writer now. I have a freelance assignment to write about your wife's case."

"Her *case*. If you want to talk about her case, call the police."

"Okay," Joe said. "I'd like to talk about her and what's happened to your life since she died. Can I come over?"

No answer. Joe heard a scuffling sound, then Neulan came back on the line.

"When?"

"Now?"

"Who's it for? The story."

"*The Clarion*."

Another pause.

"If you've got my number, you must have my address."

Neulan lived on Roan Avenue, an old street lined on its west end with workingman's cottages barely thirty by thirty feet square. The houses flared larger in the middle blocks, with articulated rooflines, porches and facades from the twenties and thirties. Farther east, the street grid shifted, the boulevards and sidewalks disappeared, and the houses shrank and grew plain. Neulan lived near where Roan expired in a dreary wedge between downtown and the industrial hypotenuse of the freeway business loop. Joe checked the street number on a drab white shoebox with a low, cement-colored roof. What did he expect? Appearances had always worked against Neulan, so naturally he would disdain them.

Neulan was less pale than Joe remembered, more filled out. He still wore heavy-framed glasses, but at least these looked like he'd selected them himself, and he projected the same half-twinkle, half-flat gaze, as if one eye were following you with interest and the other remained fixed on something inside Neulan. His hair had lengthened, or perhaps, freed from the wax, had simply relaxed.

"You're looking good, man," Joe said.

Neulan swept his arm toward a fat brown couch that looked as if it had been upholstered with a waffle iron. His silent gesture suggested they dispense with the charade of being interested in each other's lives. Above the couch, Jesus stood in a lithographed blue monotone of clouds, his arms spread before a dove descending in a burst of celestial luminosity. Calvary's three crosses, still occupied, hovered on another cloud at the light's edge. A dark-stained coffee table displayed two lemonade glasses, a pitcher and a family Bible, thick as a school lunchbox. At the narrow end of the room atop a laminated bookcase, a sleek Bang & Olufsen stereo system seemed to have landed from another planet.

Joe set a cassette machine on the table next to the Bible and poised his fingers over the buttons. "Okay to record?"

"Let's go," said Neulan.

Neulan recounted his two-plus days far back in Dominguez Canyon's roadless areas. Every detail he shared about the campsite and trails he could have noted on earlier trips. He made a point of telling Joe his company pickup remained at the house over the weekend and offered the names of people he'd tracked down from the trail registry who'd seen him at the canyon. He anguished that while he slept under the stars, Caroline lay dead on a granite shelf in Black Canyon. Neulan set forth each answer in the manner of a waiter presenting patrons dessert-tray choices for the twentieth time—neutral, ingratiating and bored all at once.

Joe asked about their marriage. Neulan loved his wife. They shared two children and their faith. They had their conflicts—what couple didn't?—but he was proud of Caroline's new career and tried to adjust his work travel and his own passions to accommodate her wedding photography. He showed Joe the calendar where they'd kept their schedules, the fateful weekend circled. They were saving for a new house, Neulan said, but tithing to the church came first. He watched for Joe to make a note and seemed disappointed the tithing comment didn't rate.

Joe was unhappy with all Neulan's answers, surely honed from previous telling. He leaned over and shut off the machine. "Has anyone asked you about Helen Vavoris?" he said. "I've always wondered what happened there."

Neulan straightened. "Helen has nothing to do with anything."

"Isn't it odd that your wife died the same way Helen did? I mean, people do fall off cliffs, but lightning doesn't strike twice so close to the same person."

"Are you calling me the person... or the lightning?" Neulan's face expressed amusement, but his eyes didn't. "I'm disappointed. A professional writer using a cliché—and a myth, on top of it. Lightning strikes where the conditions are right."

"All right. Where were you when it happened?"

"When what happened?"

"I'm talking about Helen now."

"Nearby," Neulan said.

"Nearby…"

"I didn't bring a tape measure. I was maybe five feet away."

"And what was going on when she… fell?"

"She was riding in God's wheelbarrow."

"What does that mean?"

Neulan closed his eyes for a moment. "I don't feel like explaining it right now. It's a metaphor for risking to believe. Helen wanted to become a pure spirit. She was testing herself."

How would Neulan know that? "Is that what she told you?"

"You and I may care what happened to Helen," Neulan continued, "but no one else does anymore—except to make it look like I did something to Caroline. That's sick. Keep Helen out of this."

But Helen was right in the middle of this for Joe. Helen and the weight of his own complicity. He could only feel innocent if Neulan was.

"I've sworn on the Bible," Neulan said. "I've volunteered for lie detectors. I have witnesses and an alibi, and some people still won't believe me."

"Why do you think that is?"

Neulan paused, pinched his nose. "Everything was so easy for you."

"Maybe your story sounds too perfect," Joe said.

"When people expect you to lie, even the truth sounds false."

Joe tried a new tack. "Caroline's camera was never found."

Neulan looked disgusted. "Is that a question? Have you seen where she fell?"

"Those pro camera bodies are pretty tough. You'd think something would turn up. A strap, a lens cap."

"Maybe she dropped it on the rim and it was kept by whoever found it."

"Any photos from before she died might be important evidence."

"I have no idea about that. Here's the only picture I care about." Neulan stood up and lifted the Bible from the coffee table. From its pages, he withdrew a photo of Caroline. She was contemplatively posed, looking upward toward light filtering through a blossoming orchard. Short, dark hair framed her strong cheekbones and full eyebrows lifted toward heaven. If Neulan's devoted pose in front the cloud-Jesus poster was supposed to convey something truthful, it was failing.

Neulan said, "I don't expect you to make me look goody-goody, because I'm a sinner. Let's have the truth. There were times I was selfish in my marriage. But please don't think you can trip me up or get me to admit something I didn't do." Neulan reached over and restarted the tape recorder. "Let's have this on tape. I know you want a good story. *I* want a good story. It's not that complicated. The woman I loved died while I was off enjoying myself in the wilderness. As her husband, I'd sworn to protect her, and I failed miserably. My kids will grow up without their mother, and because of that, for the rest of my life I will feel like s-h-i-t." Neulan actually spelled it out.

Kids. Joe saw no sign of kids.

"If you want to write about how I'm guilty of something, write that! But approach it with some empathy and originality, not like those other hacks at the paper who just want a murder story."

"And do you feel guilty about Christi Queen?"

Neulan's fingers began to curl, then he relaxed and laughed. "That's a good one! That sheriff is like you, wondering if lightning can strike three times. He has nothing, and he still mentions Caroline's death in the paper like it's connected to his case. That's evil, Joe. These people are after me. They think they see some pattern." Neulan thrust a forefinger in front of his face and said, "*If* I was going to kill my wife… if I *were*…" He checked to see if Joe noted his switch to the subjunctive. "One, I would not be so stupid as to push her off a cliff. Not after I was practically accused of doing that to Helen. No way. Two, husbands are always suspects. Twenty-six percent of murdered women are killed by husbands or boyfriends, and those are just the ones who get caught. So, knowing I'd be a suspect no matter what, I would have made sure I had a better alibi that didn't rely on being seen by random hikers."

"Like what?"

"I don't know. I don't need to come up with an alibi. I'm just saying if. Three, murders of spouses are either surreptitious and arm's length—slow poisoning… accidental overdose… hired killer…" Neulan paused to see if Joe was following his argument. He placed Caroline's picture atop the Bible. "Or, they're crimes of passion and the violence is over the top. And then the killer, horrified by what he's done, feels compelled to dispose of the body. Do your research. These are signs of the murderer's emotional involvement with the victim. So if you're going to kill your wife, make it quick and clean and leave the body where it lies."

Wasn't a two-thousand-foot fall quick, clean and disposed of? And for that matter, arm's length?

Neulan was pacing now. "Four…"

Jesus, how many points had he figured out?

"There's a caveat to my previous one. Without a body, there's no murder, so a killer *might* think the Black Canyon gorge is a good place to dispose of the victim. In that case, I would have moved the car, maybe abandoned it in Montrose. Leaving the Jeep parked at the overlook was like a flashing neon arrow… Look here… Look here… But I wouldn't've picked the Black Canyon at all. It's a national park with one way in and one way out through an entrance gate. You need a pass or have to buy a ticket. Very risky if you don't want to be placed at the scene."

Yes, thought Joe. *Very* risky. But the entrance wasn't staffed early in the morning, and if you rode in with the victim…

"However, even with all that," Neulan said, hovering over him, "I would never kill anyone—because murderers burn in hell."

Joe tried one more time. "Did Helen say anything?"

Neulan looked perturbed. He glanced at the tape recorder. "Is this stuff about her for the story or for you?"

Joe hesitated. "For me. Off the record, if you want."

"I don't care. We talked, yes, but that's not what I remember."

"What do you remember?"

"The kiss."

Joe absorbed this. "She kissed you?"

Neulan stared through him. "Yeah, I know—hot girl kisses geek—that's too hard for you to believe. So you see what I mean."

Once again Joe saw Helen slouched on the canyon rim, her legs dangling into space, the thin question mark of her spine leaning away from him in casual reproach. He recalled his trembling, from both dread and desire. Is that what Neulan felt up there? The difference was, Neulan didn't shrink. He went right to the brink with her. Kissed her. If that really happened, how would Neulan find a kiss like that ever again?

"You travel for your job, right—weeks on location?"

"You know I do."

"Who's James King?"

Neulan exhaled. Even his sighs seemed like notes from a great organ.

Joe said, "You don't know him? I talked to some people…"

Neulan leaned into him. "If you're going to play prosecutor, we're done! I only let you come here… and interview me… because I owe you."

"What do you owe me?"

"You know what I'm talking about."

Joe did, but he didn't want to think about what he'd done for Neulan. In fact, at the moment, he wished he could undo every bit of it.

"I just did what I thought was right." Joe closed his notebook, capped his pen and shut off the tape. "I just said what I believed was the truth."

"Then do it again," Neulan said. "Just write the truth." He stepped to his front door and held it open.

The Plan

THE LORD WAS ALWAYS TESTING NEULAN KORNHAUER, but He was also bestowing signs and other forms of divine help such as sending Joe Samson—long ago, to absolve Neulan of suspicion and, this time, to warn him of approaching danger. So funny how Joe, who believed he was God's gift to women, had almost flinched when Neulan came up with Helen's kiss. Joe, who always thought he was so superior and smart, trying to corner him with a question about James King!

Neulan watched Joe get in his car and drive away. *Go listen to your tape and mope about Helen Vavoris. Go to hell.* He cleared the lemonade, spilled the remaining ice into the sink and watched the cubes disappear in the soapy hot water as he washed the glasses. By itself, his connection to Christi Queen was innocent. Unlike other men who went to bars and casinos, he attended church when he was out of town. She happened to go to that church. The fact he'd used a different name up in Meeker proved nothing. King and Queen was a coincidence or maybe it was how God brought them together. He knew better than to act according to a pattern. Things happened. Things happened. He was not a killer. Things happened.

Now it was time. He had to move quickly. The investigators, slow and plodding so far, had been suspicious of his alibi yet unable to place him at the scene of Caroline's fall. They'd sifted through other possibilities, looking for evidence in an ever-widening circle while he continued to be the grieving widower, the hardworking father, the faithful choir director, the fierce campaigner for safety signs and railings in national parks. Once they discovered James King, they'd start coming at him from two directions, perhaps three, if they decided to dig up Helen's death all over again. How unfair! Helen started this. She introduced him to temptation. If anything, she had harmed him by showing him where to stand so he could feel its pull and still resist it. She had lured him and awakened his desires, but he remained blameless, on the righteous side of the line.

Any pattern Joe imagined he saw was not of Neulan's making; God was the great patternmaker. Neulan had only surrendered to God's plan. Temptations, even if visited upon him by Satan, were all part of the larger plan that reflected God's will. He had not sought out these women; they were presented to him. He had not compelled them to do anything; they had their own ideas, desires and volitions. He had not made them go to those places; he'd simply been present, as the Lord knew he would be. Other women he knew had made other choices and returned to their beds and continued on with their lives. But now, with police and reporters coming around and stirring up suspicions, he supposed some of those women would come forward to speak against him—instead of being grateful to God for showing them a safer path.

Neulan called his parents and arranged for the boys, who went there after school, to spend the night. Since Caroline died, this had become routine when a sudden work trip came up. He packed a suitcase of everyday clothes, his hardhat, work boots, coveralls and running shoes. His Bible. From a panel under the carpet in the closet, he extracted the plastic tub containing his emergency cash, methodically skimmed from ATM withdrawals so nothing would seem amiss. Before he loaded the Cherokee, which he kept outfitted with his camping gear and roadside emergency kit, he drove to the Loco Mart and filled the tank and a jerry can. Upon his return, he made himself a sandwich, hardboiled all the eggs left in the refrigerator and placed them in a cold sack with some apples, raisins and salami. Just like packing the boys' school lunches, he thought. He went out back and filled his water cooler from the hose. Scarcely more than an hour after Joe's departure, Neulan was ready to disappear.

He thought briefly about leaving a note behind, something about secretly harboring a fatal disease that was driving him into the wilderness to make a final peace with his Savior, but with no medical records to back up the story, it would probably be discounted. No, it was better to evaporate. He walked through the house one more time. Whoever came here next would not consider it abandoned, just a little threadbare with its sun-bleached couch and Jesus print, unoccupied like a counselor's waiting room at the end of the day. They could pull it apart for all he cared. They'd find nothing. No residue from those relationships. No messages or photographs, no diaries or books with inscriptions, no hair samples or cigarette butts with lipstick, no missing earrings or incriminating articles of clothing. None of those clichéd shrines that turned up in the movies with candles and news clippings taped to the wall. You could not be guilty of knowing what someone wanted. You could not be guilty of leading someone to think they had found it.

If he had one regret, it was leaving the stereo behind.

Neulan sat in the Cherokee for a full three minutes without turning the key. The minutes were not critical. It would take some time for Joe Samson to decide what he really had, since Neulan had given him nothing. The newspaper would be cautious. As far as the town was concerned, Neulan was still a decent Christian man who had lost his wife, and no publisher was going to offend the religious community by getting ahead of the police investigation. If Joe knew about James King, though, it was possible the police did, too, and that's what concerned him. As much as he wanted to stay and defy them, he could also prove his superiority by disappearing from under their noses. But disappearance would look like flight, and flight would look like an admission of guilt, leaving his story to be embellished and blown into a sensational horror story. Without defenders, he'd forever become the town monster. The wife murderer. The serial killer.

People had to understand he wasn't like that.

Who would be his character witnesses? His parents? Neulan was not certain he'd ever heard his father speak a complete sentence in public. Mother, on the other hand, would be too fierce a defender, just like all the mothers whose drug dealers and child abductors were innocent angels. Long ago, her fervor had convinced neighborhood children the Kornhauer gingerbread house concealed a giant oven. His Pastor Zeb? It was his job to protect his flock and not to judge, but he would turn his back on anyone whose sins threatened his churchly kingdom's building fund. Though Neulan had never slighted his job, the cops would be digging into his travel reports, and his boss would turn on him for involving the company. Friends? Best to have a woman. They were the ones attracted to piety and music and challenging cases. He ran through the choir sections in his mind. Jane Heenan could be counted on to speak adoringly of his character, but her breathy, unconfident soprano barely made it past the front row. Too bad. With more time, he might have been able to do something with her.

Who else? Neulan went back in the house to find the church directory. Not helpful. The names were like the others in his head—he could already see them hedging their words, brushing his taint from the hem of their garments. Next to it on the shelf were Caroline's high school yearbooks. He'd given his to the police, with circles around the pictures of boys who might still harbor prurient interest in his wife. He paged quickly, hoping to find one forgotten classmate who would remember him fondly. So many girls… Imagining how they must have blossomed since, he wanted to linger. And then a familiar face stopped him cold: Margaret Vavoris, Senior Class Secretary. Caroline had been older than Neulan, and he'd never have thought of Margaret had he searched his own annuals. There was a reason why it happened. Everything happens for a reason.

"Could I speak to Margaret?"

"Who's calling, please?" The voice on the line stirred a memory and something more.

"This is Neulan Kornhauer. I…"

"I know who you are. How did you find me?"

"I thought the class secretary might be organizing a fifteenth reunion."

"You weren't in our class," she said.

"No. I fibbed to your father. I wasn't sure he'd give me your number." When she didn't respond, he added, "For a long time, I felt I should offer you some comfort."

"You're a little late now."

"Yes," he said, "I am. I'm ashamed it took my own loss to

see how painful mysterious circumstances can be. I could have offered you some closure if I'd only reached out before. I want to make amends for my silence."

"How thoughtful," she said. "Why don't you just write your memoir and leave me out of it?"

Neulan had been ready for some resistance but not hostility. After all, he'd been absolved in Helen's death. Unless he won her over, he now sensed, the family could be an epicenter of malice against him.

"I *loved* Helen," he said. "I lost my *friend*." He paused to test the effect. There was silence, but he knew how to do this, so he plunged on. "And now my wife, too. Reminders are everywhere. Caroline's death brings flashbacks to Helen and it just goes around and around. I need a new start. I should've called you sooner, but I've only now decided to tell you some things…"

He wrung off the last line as if he were choking. He needed the break to think. What could he use? Their walks, Stanislavski, sneaking out for the football prank? Should he try the brain tumor after all? He waited for some cue to come back over the line.

"Things?"

Neulan struck without knowing exactly where it would take him. "Secrets," he said, "I wasn't supposed to tell you."

Neulan carved the reverse *S* over the canal feeding the Redlands power station and continued slowly through the cottonwooded draw, a speed trap made more perilous at this hour by the possibility of deer bounding across Monument Road— and by his trembling hands on the steering wheel. It was impossible to read Margaret over the phone, and he needed time to sharpen his appeal, so he'd suggested getting together.

Margaret's response had dumbfounded him.

"Okay. How about Cold Shivers Point? Maybe we both should exorcise that spot forever."

His headlights picked up a fool's gold glitter of colored glass left against the wasted hills by generations of target practice, some of it his, some teaching his boys to shoot. He really was leaving all of himself behind. God had given him the warning and this chance with Margaret and then no matter what happened, he would keep going and everything after would be new. He thought of his life ahead. His voice would be his fugitive's identifying mark and he'd have to forgo singing. Perhaps he could still direct a choir.

Neulan tightened his grip against growing tremors of anticipation as the road twisted through the three-mile climb to Cold Shivers. The exposures and walls of rock brought back flashes of the Faith Jamboree bus laboring up the grade and the guest professor leading the tour trying to project his comments over the whine of the engine and the chatter of kids in the back. Helen, sullen, contemptuous. Why had she come if she didn't want to have fun? He recalled how she'd stood at the overlook while the professor droned on about dinosaurs and Genesis and she hissed *This is boring,* then slipped away from the group. She'd scuffed along the canyon rim, telling him how this would be their last adventure, how Jesus Trek had simply been research for the role she had failed to win, how she was tired of living in a place that only rewarded playing it safe, praising Jesus and being like everyone else. A warning had burned in his nostrils. At first he'd thought it was his fear she might slip, and then, plainer, that she had daringly placed herself at death's very edge, while he, the believer in eternal life, held back. Oh, God, how he'd quaked beholding his weakness—and felt the power he reserved over her in that instant.

Then the terrible ride back down. Silence except for the saurian wail of the brakes and the sobbing Trekkers, too shocked to pray. At home, he'd fought off drowsiness and chattering teeth to search his Bible for the meaning of what he'd encountered. Temptation, he'd thought, was supposed to be a proposition you could resist with the help of the Word, as when Jesus in the wilderness turned away the three temptations of the devil. But as he'd watched Helen scamper along the dividing line between rock and air, life and death, what had seized him was beyond words, and whatever force overwhelmed him came inexorably from within.

One winter night he had forgotten a gallon of apple cider left on the porch to chill. The next morning, relieved the jug hadn't frozen and burst, he went to bring it in. The instant he touched the glass, a cloud began to branch through the liquid in a stunning, slow-motion firework of ice. In seconds, the jug had shattered in his hand, leaving the neck ring dangling from his finger. That was Neulan, touched at Cold Shivers, observing the beautiful transformation in himself while anticipating the inevitable result. Helpless.

He parked the Jeep and walked the short trail to where he could see the pedestal of Cold Shivers Point. Margaret materialized beside him. How had he missed her approach? She was Helen and not Helen—taller, darker and sadder, but with the same smoldering intensity. He had not expected the effect.

"So you're Neulan, all grown up," she said.

He waited to answer until he was certain he would not stammer. "Please forgive me," he whispered.

"I thought you weren't guilty of anything," she said.

"I was under suspicion. The disbelief made me *feel* guilty, and that feeling made me afraid to speak. The forgiveness I seek is for my silence."

"About what?" she asked.

Good.

"There was once an acrobat, a kind of daredevil named Charles Blondin," he said. "He pushed a man in a wheelbarrow across a wire strung over Niagara Falls. It's a true story, but also a parable about the nature of belief."

Margaret pulled back her head as if she'd just walked into a bad smell. "I didn't come up here for a Bible lesson," she said. "What about Helen?"

"Helen was thinking about Blondin's story. She was searching for answers about limits of all kinds and Blondin was one of those fearless people. Most of us hang back. She didn't. She was the most alive person I've ever met—beautiful, passionate and pure in spirit. I've missed her every day since." He saw Margaret relax ever so slightly. "We walked away from the group. She wanted to go over this way."

Margaret glanced toward the dark line of piñons before walking with him, placing her feet carefully, keeping a comfortable distance from the edge. "You're leaving for good, then?" she said.

They were close to the spot. He felt unbalanced, pounding with adrenalin as the canyon sucked him sideways. One way or another, he'd only helped move things in the direction they were already headed. He was just a bystander. A witness of himself, as he was now.

He knelt on the flat rock. "Have you seen this?"

HELEN V
RIP 10-21-89

He reached for Margaret's hand to draw it to the inscription, but she shook him off.

"No matter how many times I retraced it, it could never be deep enough," he said, "because every sign of man ends up erased. I think Helen came here to test her faith against this immensity. She was measuring herself against Charles Blondin, against Joan of Arc. A high standard, maybe impossible. But she was happy to be skipping along these rocks. When she slipped, I promise you, she was full of joy. When she went over the edge she was ready for whatever God..."

Margaret stiffened. "That's it? That's all you had for me is some God bullshit? You didn't know my sister. She wasn't one of your Jesus Trekkies!"

How disappointing. Why did she have to talk to him this way? He had come here with good intentions. He wanted to offer her some peace and leave with her blessing. That was all—unless God decreed otherwise. He liked Margaret, but she was apparently just another person who underestimated him, who felt superior without knowing his good qualities. Helen knew he was smart and imaginative. He was the reason she kept coming to Jesus Trek. She'd snuck out of the house in the middle of the night and climbed lighting poles for him. With all the seats open, she'd sat with him on the tour bus.

But Margaret continued to blister him. "She told me all about your little adventures. She wanted to know what to do about your attentions. She came up here that day to let you down in a nice way—not to be nudged into the arms of your fucking Jesus!"

This was so unfair! His desire *had* filled the space between him and Helen, the vibration from his pounding heart set off waves the way a woofer on high volume made him feel sound in his chest. But he had only tried to kiss her. It wasn't a nudge or a push. Helen *wanted* to be on that edge and he didn't. Her falling wasn't what *he* wanted to happen. But she did fall. She did, and the look on her face as she broke in the air and those seconds of being alive they both knew were her last and how everything was sucked into that moment! God! How could you go on after that eating Cheerios and driving to work and talking about the Broncos?

"She was standing here," he said, moving closer to a wedge of rock projecting into the canyon. "She was daring me to jump across." When he turned back to see if Margaret appreciated the gap, he noticed the compact man in the shadows leaning on a metal baseball bat.

"No, I didn't trust you," she said and moved closer to the man, whose face was set and stare was cold. "And did you?"

"Did I what?" Neulan asked.

"Did you jump across? Did you trust in God to command his angels to lift you up in their hands so that you would not strike your foot against stone?"

"You *do* know the Bible."

"I studied literature. It's not the same thing."

And now she was using it to mock him, just like Helen. He had tried to tell Helen that belief in God's love and mercy was the most important thing. Helen laughed and said life was about belief in oneself—God had nothing to do with it. He thought she would understand love—God's love—but she laughed. He tried to kiss her but she laughed and laughed.

Neulan checked Margaret and the man in the shadows. He could get past them and make it to the car. His plan was still forming but he knew how to improvise. He'd find people who would offer him shelter, give him work, enfold him in their congregation. His ribs vibrated at the prospect of a new life and his breath quickened as he gathered himself to beat

Margaret and her stony bodyguard. A familiar sensation here where, brought to the edge of desire, he had discovered the breathless rim of heaven.

Gravity. Surrender. Angels. Flight. Which way?

He ran for it.

Being Positive

JUNIOR CRIMMINS INTERVIEWED at the call center company where they hired anyone: college students, retired old men, sad guys from halfway houses trying to act positive, mothers with kids in school, women sending money to their boyfriends in jail, chicanos with tattoos from their wrists to their cheekbones. They didn't care about his experience. They said don't worry, we'll train you. What we're looking for is a positive attitude. That didn't sound so hard, so he took the test, and they said, oh yeah and you have to be able to read from the script better than that. What about being positive, he wanted to know, and someone said, try McDonald's.

McDonald's was okay for a while. He worked mostly in the back setting up the cook line, but sometimes he came up front to fill the cones or the coffee cups or change out the fryers. The store was seven miles from his sister's and he had to bike or take the bus in his uniform, which didn't make him a retard, but when some kid called him one Junior couldn't do anything about it. He was representing McDonald's, sort of like representing your country when you were in the service, and he couldn't disgrace the uniform. So Junior had to take whatever some idiot said. Once he wasn't in school anymore, they didn't care if he was Hardy Crimmins. They weren't scared of him when they saw him in that shirt with his feet sore and his ears cramping from smiling wearing the visor. Most people acted nice, and many were too busy to even see him, but then one person who wanted to feel big could just step up and ruin his whole day.

Then Shannon said, what did he think about helping at her Wee Amigos Day Care? He could earn his room and board instead of paying her and Richard rent. Watching little kids didn't seem like a job for a man but no one would see him or be making fun of him for it. She told him it was to give him a better start in life, be a resumé-builder. No one would know that Shannon Diaz was his sister, so she could give him a good reference if he did a decent job and stuck with it long enough.

Your main thing will be no fights, no bites and no blood, she said. You'll read to them, help them wash hands, serve snacks, give hugs, wipe boogers, rub backs at nap time, keep track of turns, make sure nobody escapes, sing ABCs and Itsy-Bitsy Spider. Be peaceful, be happy—just be Junior.

That's all?

It's a lot—you'll see.

Do I have to do diapers?

You take care of the snot patrol, she said, and Luisa will handle the other end.

The kids liked repetition and so did he. The day had its shape and Shannon had her plan, with new activities and familiar songs and favorite books and places everything belonged. Junior's job as the aide was mostly to swim through the children, point them in the right direction and respond as they bumped up against the rules. He rolled on the floor with the toddlers, who bobbed around him like wide-eyed rubber dolls, lurching, colliding and falling all over him. He felt more like a coach or the gym teacher with the pre-schoolers. He could tell them what to do and sometimes they would listen, and sometimes they would tell him what they wanted to do and he would do it with them, eating pretend birthday cake or being a scary monster. They liked being chased and snatched up into the air where they flew and flipped and dove and spun around his shoulders. Then he would give them the power and they would be monsters or arrest him and put him in jail until they were ready to be chased again. It was a fun routine. They had a Playland at McDonald's but he couldn't make up anything there, especially around the customers.

Shannon showed him some things he was supposed to do—like the nose count each time they went out or came back in, wiping down the lunch table with bleach, and using certain Spanish words—but other things he already seemed to know. He could see how each child was different. He knew not to push too fast or too far past what a kid was ready to do. He started them with the familiar before moving into something new. He watched out for the ones that bit and the ones that kicked. All this made him think about the ranch.

Sometimes Junior got surprised. Little kids could go from acting like babies to sounding like geniuses. A sweet boy suddenly swore at him. A smart girl who called herself a princess came in one day and said, *I don't want to be me anymore.* A four-year-old told convincing lies. Some sat on the toilet without lowering the seat and Junior always had to be alert for what the children were flushing.

It was still better than mucking stalls.

He learned to anticipate tiny disasters. He rescued teetering sippy cups, plucked kids off high perches, extracted Legos from mouths and crayon stubs from nostrils, limited squirts from the soap dispenser, kept cupboards locked, sorted out spats, intercepted flying toys, dried tears.

Always, it seemed, drying tears.

Drop-off time presented the morning's first challenge. *Mommy will come back* didn't stop the tears and *It's going to be okay* only filled time until the crying stopped on its own. Some distractions worked one day and not the next. Mommy-want could bubble up at any time, for no apparent reason. Finally, Junior stopped trying to talk them out of it or hug them out of it. He understood. He still wanted his mommy, too. Some wants only mommy could fill.

He taught them the Robot Game his dad used to play with him. He'd press the buttons on the TV remote like it controlled the robot, and he'd say, Stop or Go or Fast or Slow. When he said Talk, the kid would have to say I-am-a-ro-bot-my-name-is-whatever he wanted his robot name to be.

A girl named Serenity wanted to be the robot, but it was Terence's turn so Junior wouldn't point the remote at her. *I hate you!* shouted Serenity.

You don't hate me, said Junior. You hate waiting your turn. We all have to take turns.

Serenity glared at him, but when it was her turn to be the robot, she took it. Junior pushed the Go button and told her because she was patient she would be the first one ever to get the Smile command from the Robot Controller.

The children were supposed to pick up some Spanish as part of the program. Junior had a little Speedy Gonzales Spanish and he knew words like *leche* and *queso*, *puta* and *cabrón*. At McDonald's, he sometimes understood what someone wanted when they asked in Spanish, but he couldn't answer back. His new job made him want to learn the language. When Shannon read stories in English, she translated some of the words into Spanish. They had to learn the class rules in both—gentle hands, *manos apacibles*; walking feet, *pies que caminan;* and his *favorito*, peaceful words, *palabras pacíficas*. Junior liked to urge them on, *lávese las manos!* That made hand washing sound fun, like a battle cry instead of some teacher bossing them around.

Shannon told him he was doing fine, and Junior believed her because the kids showed him he was fine, with their laughter, attention and trust. And he felt good. He would be tired at the end of the day, but the next morning he was ready to go again. Each day he saw some little thing that was better than the day before. A squirmer who sat still for a story. A boy who threw his blocks and then picked them up. A girl afraid to jump off the climber, finally believing Junior would catch her.

The kids never improved in a straight line. A good one could go bad for a day for no reason he could see. But when someone who was trouble had a good day, Junior was pretty sure he knew why. Those were his kids, the ones he watched closest of all.

The day Shannon asked him about Cody Markuson, she looked so serious, almost stern. Cody was a happy and rambunctious three-year-old who seemed older. He was always trying new things, throwing balls over the fence, urging Junior to chase him across the yard. Junior didn't expect it when Shannon said, *Cody told his mother you touched his peepee.*

One day Cody was peeing without holding his wiener and it was spraying around and hitting the wall. Junior just straightened him out. Touching another penis *was* kind of interesting—feeling the live, meaty weight of something so familiar, yet unconnected to his own body. The sensation only in his fingers, not down below. He knew this was supposed to gross him out, but it didn't. He wondered what that meant. He wondered why holding Cody's penis made him think about himself instead of Cody. He thought about it afterwards, more than once, but not in a real bad way. It didn't turn him on or anything. It was just information.

Did you?

Junior explained. He brought Cody in from playing outside because the boy had to go. Cody was toilet trained, but that meant he was off diapers and knew to tell someone so he didn't have an accident. Junior didn't realize Cody usually sat down to pee—that he hadn't yet worked out the standing up and aiming part.

So you held his penis?

More like grabbed it. Cody wasn't holding onto it and he was missing the pot—he was pissing all over the wall. It was just a reaction.

That's all?

I told him he had to hold onto it and point it into the bowl. I cleaned up the wall. I took Cody back outside. I didn't even yell at him.

You should have told me.

It didn't seem like that big of a deal.

Well, now it is.

The Markusons called the Fosters, the Debenhams and the Castros. The Castros talked to the Delgados. Everyone who had children at Wee Amigos started talking to everyone else, and by the time the sheriff and Child Services got into the act, they had four complaints to investigate. Three boys, one girl. A peepee, a pecker, a wiener and a bottom. All pointing at one Hardy Crimmins, Junior.

Turnaround

In his Seven years at *The Clarion* the child sex abuse cases were the worst kind of story Joe Samson had to cover. The staff voluntarily passed around the assignments, sparing each other from prolonged exposure to the putrid air that surrounded each sad episode. Child cruelty and deaths were no fun, either, but other tragedies at least carried the possibility of catharsis or redemption or healing of some kind. Even after justice was done, the sickness of child molestation continued to drag everyone down.

Joe had started out in journalism thinking he'd enlighten the public, and it wore on him to see his work received or rejected based on how well it reinforced reader prejudices. He didn't want to reproduce those miserable stories all over again, and after writing about the arrest of Hardy Crimmins, Jr., he decided to do more than simply deposit this latest molestation story at the curb. If Crimmins was guilty, he wanted him put away, of course, but he vowed to dig more deeply into why these cases happened. He knew abusers were often victims themselves, and he had an idea if he looked closely at the Crimmins family, he could find the wretched thread that connected Hardy Junior to a cycle of abuse. The boy had ended up in foster care for some reason. Hardy Senior, a big Elvis-gone-to-seed type with poor impulse control, was at the very least a lousy role model.

Junior himself came up clean in the files. His booking photo showed a long face that might have been assembled from a scrambled Identi-Kit. Hooded almond eyes over high Indian cheekbones split by a blunt nose. His jaw was delicate, his lips full, almost womanly. His skin marked by acne and possibly a shattered windshield had etched his forehead. His thick black brows were raised as if in surprise, but the eyes registered nothing. In close-up, such a face would warrant crossing the street, yet the man in the picture only weighed in at 135 pounds. Joe traced him through schools and jobs but he seemed to have stuck with only one person at McDonald's, and she couldn't be quoted: *I knew he was kind of a retard—I just didn't know he was a pervert.*

Shannon Crimmins Diaz ran Wee Amigos Day Care out of her house on West Orchard Mesa. A cheery sign in front proclaimed *Welcome/Bienvenido,* and Joe saw colorful play structures in a back yard covered with green artificial turf. Shannon's husband Richard worked for the city's public works department, and his handyman skills were apparent in the wooden fence and sturdy access ramp that led to the front door. Flower boxes and Tyrolean-style shutters tacked around the windows softened the telltale rectangularity of a manufactured home.

Shannon had ignored Joe's phone messages and did not look happy to see him. Planted in the doorway, her posture could not have been more ferocious if the toddler wedged on her hip had been a firearm. At moments like this, he didn't enjoy the work. He'd gotten soft as a corporate hack, always telling positive, supportive stories, and he'd never had to deal with people in pain.

Shannon narrowed the door opening, so he placed one foot over the threshold and put forward his questions, pushing and probing the way a wrestler tries to set up a takedown, feeling for an opposing movement he can turn in his favor. But his questions only exposed him to her unspeaking glare, and he felt himself in danger of losing his balance. He made a show of putting his pen in his pocket and closing his notebook. "Are you doing all right?" He hoped he looked sincere and that she understood the inflection aimed at her personal well-being. Her business was clearly not doing all right and might never again.

Shannon had grown up in a household where she learned bullshit as a second language. Her expression showed her opinion of Joe's question. She stared down at his foot, still thrust through the doorway. Her resistance had made him step forward, and now her resignation caused him to draw back.

"Have you ever made a mistake?" she asked him. "Do you know how to tell the difference between evil, a bad choice and an honest mistake?"

Joe didn't know if she was talking about herself or Junior. "If I have the facts…"

"Facts! No one in this town is going to care about the facts. They won't care I have my childcare certificate or that we've always passed all the county inspections. They won't care that these kids were learning and happy and safe. All that matters right now is that Junior is a Crimmins, and so am I. He's in jail and they want me there, too."

"Do you think that's all it is? Something must've happened here."

"I'll tell you what happened when you can answer my question."

"Okay. It's about intentions. Evil's intentional. A mistake is unintentional. A bad choice is somewhere in between. That's how I'd draw the lines."

"All right, now suppose you're Junior, and you make a mistake. Not even a bad choice. A mistake. How much room do you think there is between your lines? I'll tell you: there's no room. When you have nothing and you're nobody, there's no difference. You live just one mistake away from jail. And after you make it there once, even a half-mistake'll get you back."

Her lips were tight. She frowned back her tears. "Don't write about this. Please don't make me a complainer. That's just the way it is. This is what we get."

The moonfaced toddler on Shannon's hip maintained its claw grip on her blouse and stared dumbly at Joe.

"Get for what?" he asked.

"For thinking things could be different."

"I am going to write a story about this," he said. "I can't say I'm going to help your brother. But if you think there's something I should know, you should tell me."

Shannon pulled a step back into the house. Joe realized the child she held was the only one in the place.

"I can tell you what Junior's really like, and you could even write it," Shannon said, "but people will see what they want to see."

"Let me show you my map," Captain John McLearn said, pecking two-fingered on the keyboard behind his desk. McLearn looked like Claude Rains in *Casablanca*—the same pencil moustache and cheerful manner of a man who had more information than he let on. McLearn ran the police department's support services—all the administrivia no law enforcement officer wanted to do, like HR, professional standards, facilities, court services and records. The computer screen was not cooperating. Message boxes appeared, but no map. Tapping harder on the keys only summoned more of the alien syntax and sketchy graphics of government software.

"We're not quite ready to unveil this," said McLearn. "It's still in what they call *alpha*." He picked up the phone and punched a few numbers. "Is Sig around?" He mouthed *computer guy* to Joe as he listened for the answer. "He's not in yet?"

It was ten a.m.

McLearn shook his head, said "Never mind" into the phone, and to Joe: "It'll be something when we get it on the Internet." He went to a cabinet and withdrew a thick roll of paper, filed longwise in the drawer. As he returned to his desk, Joe wondered if McLearn longed for the moment he could stop sucking in his gut.

The captain unrolled his bundle, a county map covered with colored plastic tapes, the sort used to mark legal documents for signature. "Every one of these tabs represents a registered sex offender," he said. "About half of these are in Grand Junction, the rest in the county's jurisdiction. The vision is to be able to generate a map from the database and see all our sex offenders in one place." He paused. "So to speak."

The map covered McLearn's desk. In places, the tabs were stuck atop each other, as if a load of autumn leaves had been dumped on a neighborhood. Joe's eyes scanned immediately to the Redlands. No flags close to his house. He looked for the Crimmins-Diaz address. There was a scatter of red and yellow tabs on Orchard Mesa, but none very near Wee Amigos Day Care.

McLearn said, "County-wide, we're watching more than four hundred. The number'll just keep growing, because once these guys register, it's tough to get off the list. If they stay clean, they can petition for removal, but who wants to be the judge who decided a guy was not a threat—then he goes out and abducts a little girl?"

"So the numbers keep growing, the problem looks worse, the public cries out for more protection and the numbers grow some more." Joe meant to phrase it as a question.

"You could put it that way," said McLearn. "I didn't. There are definitely predators you want to supervise forever. But that's only about four of the four hundred guys we're tracking. The rest—especially your child molesters—their risk of re-offending is way lower than your average criminal."

"And why is that?" Joe asked. "Do the extra restraints work?"

McLearn shuffled through a drawer, then gave up looking. "A while back, there was a big hue and cry over child molesters living near schools and playgrounds. The state did a study before passing a new law restricting where they could live. It found their distance from schools and such didn't make any difference. You know what mattered most?"

"I'm guessing it wasn't some extra-special public humiliation," Joe said. McLearn gave him a sharp look. "I mean, it seems like a funny system, where a paroled drug dealer or murderer could move in next door and you wouldn't know it, but you get notified about a guy who got a sixteen-year-old pregnant. So what does matter most?"

"Support systems," said McLearn. "The guys are more likely to succeed if they have treatment, a job, friends and neighbors who support them. The trouble with shaming these guys—they're more likely to move away from their support network to get out of range of the pitchforks. We have people come here from out of state exactly for that reason. I don't want to say community notification's a joke, but most of the people we have here are unlikely to reoffend. For the most part, you're already going to know the person who molests your child, and it's someone you trust."

"Like in a day care?"

"Were you going to ask me if Hardy Crimmins is registered?" McLearn said.

Was McLearn leading him? Under the sex offender system, Junior could be one of those yellow flags indicating an offense as a minor. The names weren't listed publicly, but McLearn would have to disclose it if Joe inquired.

"Yes, is Junior registered?"

"No," McLearn said, rolling up the map.

"What about Hardy Senior? Was he?"

McLearn paused before answering. "For statutory. Sometimes those things happen. There's no indication Hardy Senior abused his kids. Neglect, sure. And some guys lose interest in supervising their kids when they have to do it via jailhouse correspondence."

After leaving McLearn's office, Joe stopped at the detention facility to see if Junior had accepted his visitor request. The clerk told him Junior had been released on bail. Joe called the home number for Richard Diaz and no answer. Though it seemed pointless, he tried the Wee Amigos number, too.

Shannon's cheerful recorded voice answered: *Thank you for calling Wee Amigos Preschool and Child Care! We're busy with the children right now, so please leave your name, number and a brief message, and we'll get back—*

He hung up. Chances were zero Shannon would get back to him as soon as she could.

Hello

"LOOK AT THIS, LEN." Inetta brought the newspaper back from the Glade Park store. She'd folded the front page so nothing showed but one story and a forlorn photograph. "Look at this," she said again.

The picture of the dazed young man did not register at first. It had been years ago. "Junior," he said. "Damn."

"He was helping at his sister's, it says."

"Helpin' what?"

"She did day care. In her house."

He remembered the sister. She seemed all right. Both the kids seemed all right given how they'd been raised. When Junior was living at the ranch, she'd been up once and told them she meant to take him when she was old enough for the county to approve her as his guardian. It sounded like the talk of a girl trying to rope in more than she really could, but maybe she did it, after all.

"He never did catch on quite," he said. "Me neither, I guess."

"You were patient... It breaks my heart."

"He just wasn't much cut out for the horse business. But messin' with kids? I don't know."

Inetta was hopeful. "Being in the paper doesn't mean he's guilty."

"No, it don't," he said. "But once he's newspaper guilty that's almost as bad."

Richard came like he had promised, even though Junior said he didn't care if he stayed in jail until the trial. Richard said it was fine for him to come home. There were no children at Wee Amigos right now. Maybe after things settled down. Junior's bail bond was already set up like a loan on the house, Richard explained. He and Shannon would only have to pay it off if Junior ran away, and he knew Junior wouldn't do that.

"You've got to just settle down," Richard said, "and get your mind clear."

But Junior's mind wasn't clear. It was all beaten down by the noise and crowded stupidity of the jail. It was jumpy with the blame and confusion of the past week. It was throbbing with fear that he had ruined it for Shannon. His mind swirled with the memories of all the times—all the times!—he'd fucked up, been rejected, forgot, didn't know, couldn't hack it. His mind was full and heavy and dead and empty all at once.

It was everything but clear.

Richard dropped him in front of the house. Welcome, said the sign. *Bienvenido.*

"Shannon's at the doctor," Richard said. "She'll be back soon."

"What's wrong?" Junior asked.

"She's breaking out all over. I don't know. Can't breathe. It's probably nerves—she'll be okay. You wait for her to get home. I have to get back to work."

Junior couldn't remember being in the house alone. He'd never been there when it was so quiet. There were always the kids, little Richard, the television, always Shannon. Now he'd made her sick on top of everything else.

He hadn't been able to eat or sleep when he was in detention and his head was spinning from the emptiness in the rest of his body. Even his arms felt hollow. Propelled by what he thought was hunger, he went into the kitchen. So tired. His feet could barely clear the cracks between the tiles. Thank God the refrigerator door swung open at his slight tug. The light inside illuminated a package of hot dogs, a covered bowl of Jello cubes quivering in four flavors, half a jar of pickled beets, a plastic tub of herring, a can of fake whipped cream. He tried to taste each thing in his brain, but nothing tempted him. It was all the same, sitting inert like an aspirin left to dissolve on the tongue.

The newspaper lay on the kitchen counter, the page folded in half and half again. The face hovering above the orange jump-suited shoulders didn't look like his face. It looked like a fucking criminal's, and the headline said he was a criminal, and the story said he was a criminal. And no one in the world could be blamed for thinking he was a criminal because he looked exactly like every other person in an orange jump suit whose picture had ever been in the paper. The face in the picture didn't feel like his. The name in print didn't look like his name the way he wrote it out. The words—he couldn't stop reading them as *child mole station*, like there was this cute little stuffed mole in an engineer's cap riding around and around the tracks on a toy train—the words didn't describe what he had done. None of it was right. None of it was real.

He walked out the back door and took a circuit around the green swing set and the bright red and blue climber that Richard built out of cargo netting and plastic culvert and the yellow sand box where there weren't any kids playing, and he came into the house again and shouted *I'm home!* like that would summon Shannon from the back rooms to answer him.

But all that greeted him was his picture looking like a criminal, so he went back outside and walked around the yard, and as he walked he felt like he might explode if he went anywhere else, like he had found the one path through a minefield, and any step to the left or right would be the end, so he walked around the play equipment again and again and again and again.

The route was safe, but everything around it pushed in, trying to take over the space he occupied, and everything inside him pushed out. Out through his head, his eyes, his ears, his mouth, his skin. He wasn't thinking his thoughts anymore. They were just shoving on their own to get away, flinging themselves into outer space where no one could hear them. Everything wanted to be out of him. Everything. Maybe that was it. If he kept moving, maybe his thoughts would trail off behind him. They would stay where they were. He had to keep moving. Forever. Around and around. In and out.

He dared himself to go back inside the house, not looking on the counter, just feeling the four walls around him. He tried to hear the voices of the kids, their morning song, the dance to calm them down and get them ready to learn, their mats stacked against the wall, and the books on the shelf and the toys in the box and the paints in the Tupperware and the empty cubbies where they used to keep their stuff to take home and show their moms.

If he kept moving, maybe it would be okay.

But there was his picture in the paper. And his sister at the doctor. And Richard with a bail bond on the house. And everything he ever did was just a fuck-up, just a burning stable, just his mom on drugs, just his dad's dogs…where did they go? And there was his picture in the paper staring at the girl at McDonald's who hated him, staring at the kids he bummed cigarettes from and didn't pay back, staring at his teachers, staring at Len and Inetta, and they were all saying *see?* His picture staring at the ceiling in Shannon's kitchen, staring at himself, staring at nothing.

He turned the newspaper over and there was Shannon's cell and by the phone was a card and on the card was the name of the newspaper and on the newspaper story was the name on the card, Joe Samson. The one who'd left messages for him at the jail. Joe Samson, who wrote that he molested kids and whatever. Someone Junior never met who made him look like a criminal in the newspaper.

Junior walked around the yard again, but it didn't help. Richard said to get his mind clear, but it wasn't clear. He came back into the house. He headed all the way back to his room. He stepped down the middle of the hall and felt the difference in the floor where the house had been joined together after the two halves had been hauled to the lot. One foot on each side of the division, one foot a fraction higher than the other, like he wore two shoes and only one sock. He knew the seam was there, even though the floor joists had been hung together and sheets of plywood nailed over it. He couldn't see it, but his entire skeleton could tell where it was because it put all his bones out of whack. He felt as if he were straddling a crack in the earth that was about to open. He didn't know which side was going to be swallowed up so he lurched forward, shifting his weight from one leg to the other until he reached his room.

His room was clean and neat and nothing of Junior was visible in it. It could have been a motel room or a hospital room waiting for the next occupant. It was his room because Shannon and Richard said so. They could have called it the spare bedroom, but they called it Junior's room. The Kleenex box on the dresser was Shannon's touch, and so was the night-light that pulsed an apple-cinnamon scent. He didn't know if this meant his sister thought he was a baby afraid of the dark or smelled bad or both. The only thing that made it his room were the clothes on the hangers and in the drawers, and some of those came from people who had given them up to Goodwill for adoption. In the top dresser drawer were the keys to the van that was practically Junior's. Richard's old work van that was ugly and beat up but ran. Junior was going to buy it once he had a job that paid cash.

He was never going to have a job that paid cash.

He was supposed to stay and wait for Shannon and clear his mind, but something was onto him, something was trying to crush him or smother him or suck everything out of him and if he stayed his body would be there on the floor when Shannon came home. He would scare little Richard and Shannon would scream and say *why did I ever let you in here!*

Maybe he would hear her and maybe he wouldn't.

Maybe one time Shannon thought she wanted to have him back, but she'd had four days to think about it while he was in jail, to look at the story in the paper, to have all the parents come and take home the kids' paintings and their extra clothes and ask for a refund for the rest of the month. When she saw her brother the criminal in her house once again, she might be disgusted. She would know for sure what a mistake it was to let him live with her. Junior didn't want his sister to have to throw him out of her house. He had to get out before she returned. Back in the kitchen, he cleared the counter—took the car keys, newspaper, cell phone, the business card—and stumbled out to where the van sat under the carport. The tires were low but not flat. The tank was short of empty. The battery was still alive. The van coughed and shook like an alkie hacking his lungs inside out, then idled back to a tremor.

Clear your mind, said Richard.

When you want to clear your head, Junior thought, you hit the road. You just get in the car and go.

Junior took their street to the frontage road and the frontage road to the highway and sat there at the stop sign staring straight ahead. Cars on his side of the road were still slowing after speeding across the desert and on the other side they were speeding up. He was not used to driving the van and it was hard to judge how to get across the four lanes. In the distance, he saw the fairgrounds, where boys in helmets rode bikes over the dirt BMX track. They circled the banked turns, popped up the jumps and went out of sight again like little flying fish.

Pointing the van in the direction he wanted it to go was something he never thought about, but now just turning the wheel seemed like the hardest thing he had ever tried to do. Pushing down on the gas pedal a quarter inch felt like too much to take on, like it would burn his last bit of energy and he would slump over in the seat and go to sleep and never wake up. He turned right because it was easiest. As long as he was headed that way, he thought about going to the newspaper office downtown, driving right up to the address on the card and plowing through the front door. He thought about going to Cody Markuson's house and asking Cody to show his mother what really happened. He thought about going to California. His cheekbones felt like grenades.

Clear your mind, Richard said.

The ranch, he thought. The van rolled on its own with nothing to stop it. It coasted down the hill and across the bridge and around the edge of downtown and into the left turn lane toward the Monument. Over the railroad tracks and the river again. Once he pointed the van onto Monument Road there'd be no more coasting, but also no choices to make and the van would follow the switchbacks up if he just kept his foot light on the gas. At the top, he could turn toward the ranch, where the creek would be flowing, the pastures greened up, and Inetta would be cooking something he could eat without feeling sick to his stomach. Scrambled eggs and thick bread toasted over a burner on a fork, with butter sinking into it like a late morning sleep. Len would be there to show him what was growing where the stable used to be, where the manure made the soil better and there were no hard feelings. And they would let him stay in his old place until he had to go to court or else he could sleep outside under the stars and not even bother them. He could live under an overhang of rock and no one would know he was up there. He could disappear for good in that country.

The metal box of the van baked in the sun and he was moving too slowly to create much breeze through the open window. The hairs inside his nostrils were curling up and ready to sizzle. Junipers clawed their way across the rock past the twisted dry stumps of their ancestors. Maybe time just hardened everything, alive or dead. Maybe the Selfs had forgotten all about him. Maybe Len would get his gun when he saw the strange van pulling through the gate and Inetta would call the cops.

A bus came toward him—one of those high buses with the silver sides and the seats that recline and the blue tinted glass. It took up the entire width of the other lane and it went slow so people could look out the window and see the sights. They were high enough to see the canyon, even though they were on the wrong side of the road. They were surely cool, and they didn't have to worry about going off the edge because they had a professional driver who did this all the time. The destination sign above the windshield said SPECIAL, and all the heads looking over the top of his van were white as cotton balls.

The turn. The bus had blocked the turn to Glade Park and Junior had gone right past. It didn't matter. He was letting the van take him now and maybe he would go all the way to the top of Black Ridge or back into Rattlesnake Canyon… Except Richard had trusted Junior not to run away. He should have stayed in jail where he had no choices to make. Jail was a terrible, boring, jittery place, but at least he knew where he was going when he was there.

Duh duh tuh-duh tuh-duh-dee—Tuh-duh.
The happy, tinkling sounds pulled him back into the van. It was the morning song the kids sang: *Hands say hello to your knees—Hello!*
Shannon's cell phone.
Hands say hello to your hips—Hello! Hands say hello to your nose—Hello! Hello, hello, hello.

He let the ringtone run out, but the song kept circling in his head: *La-la-la. Dee-dee-dee. Hands reach high, high as can be. La-la-la. Dee-dee-dee. Hands together, friends we can be.* It wasn't fair. He was their friend. He took care of them. He reached across the seat for the phone and punched up the missed call. It wasn't a number he recognized. Who else would be calling Shannon's number now, except someone to call her names? She was even more innocent. They had no idea. He hit Send to call back the number. He would tell them.
"Joe Samson."
"Who is this?"
"Joe Samson. Who were you trying to reach?"
Joe Samson. The guy who wrote the story was after Shannon, too. "This is Hardy Crimmins. You called my sister."
"I called you, too. Thanks for getting back to me."

"I'm not getting back to you. I want you to leave us alone."

"I'm sorry you feel that way. Your sister said I should talk to you, and I was hoping we could meet."

"You called me a child molester."

"I wrote a story that gave the reason you were arrested. If you want to give your side to it, I'd be very interested in talking to you. Where are you now?"

"In my van."

"And your van is where?"

"On the Monument. Would you please leave my sister alone? She didn't do anything wrong. And I didn't either."

"Then why do you think some parents are saying you did?"

"I don't know." Junior knew and he didn't know, but why would he tell such private things to the man who had already made him look like a criminal? How could Joe Samson put the kids back in Shannon's school and give him back his job? That's what Junior wanted.

"Are you driving right now?"

"No," Junior said. "The van is driving itself." It was almost true.

"If you're driving on the Monument, don't you think it would be a good idea to pull over while we talk?"

"I can drive fine."

"There's road noise. It's hard to hear you."

"Too bad."

"Hardy, is there someone who was at Wee Amigos, a parent, who I could talk to—someone who knows you? Maybe they…"

"I don't know the parents' names. I just know the kids. The kids would tell you."

"Can you give me some names of the kids? I'd need their last names, too."

Joe Samson didn't know anything about this! He had called Junior a child molester and he didn't even know the names of the kids. "I need you to write that my sister's school was a good place. Nothing bad happened there, I swear to God."

"It doesn't work that way. I need someone else to tell me. Do you know a person who would say that?"

Junior tried to think. He thought of the mothers and sometimes the dads who dropped off their children at the front door. In the mornings they seemed in a hurry and in the afternoons they usually looked tired until they saw their kids. He couldn't remember talking to any of them. He wondered if anyone even knew who he was.

"My sister is sick because of this."

"I'm sorry to hear that. This must be hard for her."

"So you can't do anything, then."

"Only if you answer my questions."

"Like what?"

"Have you ever known anyone who was abused—molested as a child?"

Why was he asking that? Who was he talking about now? He was just looking for a way to trick him. Fuck him. Junior ended the call. I should've told him to fuck himself, Junior thought. But then he imagined Joe Samson, not yet knowing the line was dead, trying to ask another question, hanging like a stupid, gasping fish. That was even better.

He was passing the high point where the road moved away from the canyon and was almost straight. He sped up, blowing his horn at some people taking pictures. They waved happily. Shannon was probably back from the doctor by now, looking for him, calling Richard—*didn't you pick him up?*—wondering what she did with her cell phone, noticing the paper was gone, noticing the missing van that had sat so long it seemed like part of the carport. Standing there in the empty house, the empty pre-school, her skin broken out. Ready to throw up all over again. Shannon who came for him, who protected him, who always did her best for everyone. Richard confused, pissed, worried, walking around at work hammering shit because he couldn't come home after taking off once already. Breaking things he'd have to fix tomorrow. Shannon checking his bedroom, wondering what to do. Little Richard bobbing around. Would he know something was wrong? What was wrong? Uncle Junior was out of jail, wasn't he?

He wasn't going to be found innocent. He could dress up in one of Richard's nice shirts and put on some fake glasses like the guys in jail said they were going to do to look respectable in court, but the parents had nicer clothes. And like on TV, the prosecutor would look all sad and say, *These children have been scarred for life. Why would they lie?* He would say to Junior, *Tell us about your family, Hardy Crimmins*, and then his public defender would jump up and object and the judge would say *Overruled!* The prosecutor would go all serious and ask him, *Do you think it's okay to touch someone's penis, Hardy Crimmins? Did your sister tell you it was okay to hold a little boy's penis? When you held their penises did you tell anyone, Hardy Crimmins?* He would say penises a thousand times and Hardy Crimmins a million times. The jury would look at the parents and think, *What if that happened to my kids?* And people would be watching Shannon, thinking how could she not have known what was going on in her own house? It almost didn't matter what happened to Junior now, whether he got off or not. Shannon would be the one hurt. She'd have to face all the people while he'd be in prison. She'd be dragged down to the bottom with him.

Duh duh tuh-duh tuh-duh-dee…

"Hello."

"Hardy? Joe Samson again… We got cut off."

"What if I told you the truth?"

"What's the truth?"

"That Shannon always checked on me, made sure the kids were all right and I was doing what I was supposed to. Ask anyone about her, how she is. Ask about Shannon. People will tell you. Ask about Richard. He's as good as a man can be. They took me in. They took me in and tried to help me. Maybe I screwed up, I don't know, but not my sister. You can check it out. Ask the neighbors. Shannon didn't do anything wrong."

Junior gulped for air.

"Hardy?"

"Little kids don't care. They don't even pay attention to that stuff. They poop and pee in front of each other all the time. That was my job, to help them. That's what I did. Cody was missing the pot, and I grabbed his pecker. That's it. That's all it was, and I cleaned it up and didn't even think to tell my sister."

"One kid, one time? What about the others?"

He wasn't going to listen. Junior tossed the cell phone on the dash. He could hear Joe Samson's voice coming out over the whine of the engine.

"Hello, Hardy?"

Little kids didn't care. That was why they were so great. They didn't care what your name was. They didn't know the difference between you and a real teacher. They didn't pay attention to whether you could sing good. They knew certain stuff was dirty, but they didn't know why. They could tell in a second if you loved them—and they loved you back. That was all finished for him now. Kids didn't know about things being finished. They'd scribble over what they'd just colored. They thought going to jail was like a time-out and being dead was like playing dead. When it was over, they got to come back. They got to decide when they weren't dead anymore.

"Hardy, are you there?"

It had been a while since he was up here. He'd forgotten this part of the road. Now he rode in the van as if he were back in the bus, in a comfortable seat, looking through the blue windows, listening to the man on the microphone at the front. You really could see a long way, much farther than when you looked up at the mountains from down below. You really did feel like the world could just keep going without you. You went around on the ground spilling, making dents in whatever you touched, but up here, you couldn't see the mess. The earth didn't even notice. It said, *Don't worry. There's nothing you can do to ruin things. So many people have fucked up before you, and look—the mountains are here, the sky is still blue, the sun rises and sets. Really, what have you done that can't be scribbled over? Don't look down—it'll only confuse you. Look at the sky. Get your mind clear. Reach high as can be...*

"Hello... Hello... Hello?"

The sign said Monument Road would be temporarily closed the next day between the Visitor Center and West Glade Park Road. Leonard asked the ranger at the gate about it, but there was a line of cars back and the ranger just said *removing that vehicle* before waving him through. He kept an eye out as he drove the crooked miles beyond the center. After all these years the road no longer made his palms sweat, but Half Tunnel, just ahead, came close. In the all-day shadow cast by the cliff, ice stayed on the road far into spring. The drop demanded attention, and the curb of low sandstone blocks dividing road from air concentrated the mind. Guardrails here were pointless. If terror won't keep a fool on this road, why should taxpayers waste the money?

The road's history carried its own chill. In 1933, as builders blasted a route across the cliff, the face hanging above the road sheared off. Suddenly, nine local men earning their first dollar for a day's work had to choose between leaping into the canyon or being crushed. Most of them came from Glade Park's Depression-flattened ranches. Some of the families were still his neighbors.

A car was pulled over on the shoulder before the passage squeezed along a ledge with cliff leaning above and falling below. Two young men on foot edged along the outside lane where scarcely a foot separated the pavement and the air.

Leonard slowed to a crawl to match the walkers. "What's up here?"

One of the men pointed. "You mean down. That dude's van that ran off the road yesterday."

"What dude?" Leonard asked.

"Higgins, or something, the one who was in jail for molesting those kids."

"Making his getaway," said the other.

The two paused and peered into the canyon, bending cautiously and bracing their hands on the low redstone slabs set to deflect a slow skid or a drifting wheel.

"This obviously didn't stop him," the first one laughed.

"Holy shit, how they gonna get that out of there?" his friend said.

"Crimmins…" Leonard said before sending up his window. Before he gave into the impulse to get out of the truck and take a shovel to their heads. "His name was Hardy Crimmins, Junior."

"Whatever."

Leonard drove until he found room to pull over. A cool spit of rain was blowing in from the north as he got out—the kind of mountain squall that would pass in a few minutes. The van was out of view from there, but he was looking beyond the crash site, further back in time. He'd always thought he could feel the CCC men's spirits wisping up from the Half Tunnel drop-off as he passed that stretch of road. Now he tried to sense if a new strand had joined them.

Junior was what, barely twenty? Why couldn't he see the years ahead of him left room for a comeback? So much time, not like where Leonard stood, looking back at ashes and smoke.

"Shouldn't've give up on you, boy," he said softly, and let the rain sting his face until he couldn't feel it anymore.

When Shannon Crimmins called, he was relieved it was not someone who'd require him to make an excuse for Inetta. They still hadn't told anyone. Inetta wanted to see her friends, but wasn't ready to bear the weight of being sick in their eyes. They had passed the time since her news got worse in even deeper isolation, except her disease also lived there now, uninvited company that at any time could come walking in from another room.

"I've been all month getting up the guts to call you," Shannon said, and he understood the black tang of the fire must cling to her thought of him, just as he felt the shame of not calling her after Junior died. "Would you mind if I came out to see you?"

"The road's pretty washboardy right now."

"You'd rather me not, then?"

He told himself he was protecting Inetta from company, but the truth was he was tired of tiptoe talk on delicate topics, and this had to be one, whatever Shannon had in mind. He heard her breath over the receiver. Or was it his? A decent, distancing answer did not come to him, so he said, "Come on out."

He met Shannon at the door so a knock wouldn't waken Inetta. She clutched a tote bag in front of her as if she'd been caught skinny-dipping and just snatched up her clothes. He stepped out the door and invited her to sit in one of the metal yard chairs. Some days they were too hot to use, but on this afternoon they radiated a pleasant warmth. She stowed the bag under her chair and turned sideways to talk to him.

"Junior was doing real good. The kids called him Mr. Teacher. He liked that a lot. He always talked about your ranch. He said it was the best place he'd ever lived until he moved in with me and Richard. I suppose it was hard for you to tell, though."

"It don't bother me when people don't talk," he replied. "You can usually tell what you need to know without a lot a jabber."

Shannon said, "He felt so bad about the fire. He wanted to pay you back, but of course he had no way." She touched her nose with a tissue and her eyes opened and closed like they were gulping the light. "I don't know what you did with him. He never put it in words to me, but I know he had a lot he meant to express. It just didn't work out." She reached into the tote bag and handed over a thin square wrapped in bright paper. "He made this in industrial arts way back then, but I guess he was too shy to give it to you. Then he moved to that group home and things sort of got away from him for a while. But he always saved it, so I'm sure he meant to get it to you someday."

She bit her lip before she said, "Open it later, if you don't mind. It's still hard."

"All right." Through the paper, he felt a slight ridge around three sides. A lacing, maybe.

"I mainly wanted to tell you about Junior so you wouldn't think bad of him at the end. He messed up sometimes, but I don't believe he did what they said." She rose from her seat and shifted her tote bag. "I also have a favor to ask, if you don't mind. Junior didn't have many happy places in his life, but he talked to me about a little creek? He thought it was special."

"He was right," he said. "Around here water makes any place special."

"I hope this doesn't sound too forward, Mr. Self. I brought along Junior's ashes."

He realized this was a request. "It's pretty much all dust around here already. Don't see how a little more could hurt."

Inetta's voice came through the screen. "Don't mind him. That's how my husband says we'd be honored."

The three of them walked the creek and Shannon picked a nice green spot near the far end of the pasture where the water had exposed some slick rock. Shannon told them the pasture reminded her of a field where she once watched Junior when he was little. She remembered a group of children careening after a ball, and a man with a whistle trying to turn their play into soccer. Junior never kicked the ball or even tried. He simply fluttered behind the pack, riding its contrail. Whenever the ball sliced in his direction, he'd leap out of its path and let the others overtake him. One breathless boy who'd been tracking the ball finally fell on it and the others collapsed with him in a delirious dog pile. Junior was laughing, too, the last to drop. He plopped on his seat and rolled onto his back, not quite touching the jumble. The man with the whistle urged the children to rise and reform, and when they did, Junior remained there, staring open-mouthed and happy at the brilliant blue sky.

Shannon trickled a first fistful of ashes over the water and said, "My family never did things the way regular people do."

Leonard tried his damnedest to find the right words for her then, but the best he could do was, "Amen."

DEVILS KITCHEN

West

ATOP THE RISE where the reckless pickup disappeared, a stoplight marks Leonard's next turning point—head left to the east entrance or drive west and climb the far end of Monument Road. Estimating the difference between the squirming alternative routes, he realizes his choice is not simply a matter of knowing the shortest distance. One direction will take him back the way he came down; the other will draw an uncompleted circle, bringing him to the rim of the great open bowl of Artists Point.

He turns west to follow the base of the Monument. He seldom has reason to travel this back stretch, and its long-past incarnation seems more familiar to him than the version that now stretches along the highway. Past the Loco Mart and the school, he remembers when the Redlands was covered with orchards that fed a baby food factory. Sometimes he would ride with his mother to pick over dented cans of industrial applesauce rejected during the war by the military inspectors and sold at a discount. Nothing wrong with baby food or rations but it seemed to him an apple deserved a better fate than applesauce. A chance to make a run for the teacher's desk instead of going straight to the grinder. Here and there he spies a few barren stragglers stranded like tumbleweeds against back fences. By the time the apple had reached this valley, he guesses, it had fallen about as far as it could from the Garden of Eden.

He passes churches and a shopping mall and little houses with their mailboxes set along the road and then the ground opens up a bit, with a winery and hobby ranchland and a big horse barn of the kind he never had even in his dreams—the kind one man built for his wife just because he could. This was Buffalo Run, named after the bison that used to graze the base of the Monument. They were transplanted here by a peculiar hermit who'd fought for decades to preserve what he called *the heart of the world*, sending countless letters to the editor and the governor and Congress and the president about God's creation, women's suffrage and the eight-hour work day. He wrote in red and blue pencil for emphasis and because ink bottles froze in the tent where he lived year-round. He hacked out the trail that became Monument Road and climbed sheer rock faces to drill holes and pound in pipes so more timid people could follow. Strung fence from juniper posts marked with tin cans and railed against the *sheep driveway* ranchers had cut to Glade Park. And the crazy sonofabitch won! There's a statue of John Otto in town that makes him look like Stonewall Jackson instead of a burro-riding crank. Now rangers guard the entrances and the old buffalo fence marks the line between parkland and the oversized houses crowded up against it to enjoy the view.

But John Otto mostly fought the Park Service and the local Chamber of Commerce. At least in those days, everyone knew who the robber barons were. Now there were so damn many moneymen. They could afford to build another house just to show people somewhere else in the world how smart they were. The way things were going, someday they might stampede right through their side of the buffalo fence and set up housekeeping in the park.

No point resenting the fortune of high-dealers breathing heavy and dreaming of numbers. Someday they'll all be down to the same six feet or scattered to the same winds. Back at the ranch were tax deal papers telling him all he needed to know about how men like that must occupy themselves, and he is grateful not to have been one. He feels unencumbered now and he can go easy, finish his slow disappearing act without leaving another mark or occasioning a regret. There're probably better words for what he's thinking but there's no Inetta to tell him what they are.

Shopping

To Leonard the craft gallery on Main Street was just one more sign of the times. Downtown he could buy a drink, ladies' fashions, antiques, a tattoo, a bicycle, healing crystals, records and incense, a plan to manage his investments, or a sandwich that had one piece of Italian ham sliced thin as a playing card. Nothing against people who wanted gelato and a three-dollar cup of coffee, but he was out of luck if he wanted a haircut, nails, ammunition, a work shirt, an aspirin, a pencil or a coffee cup that got refilled until you were good and done. The boots and saddlery shop was hanging in there, but these days it was getting by on steel-toes for the oil patch.

Inetta saw it differently. The winding street was lined with sculptures and trees and places to sit outside for lunch with your dog. Except for the banks, the businesses were nothing you could find at the mall. The gallery offered her a chance to chat with the artists who ran it as a cooperative and to praise the work she admired—mostly ceramics, which she occasionally purchased, and jewelry, which she did not. Once, she might have imagined working there.

She brought him along with her to shop for an urn. He figured he was along for moral support, but he couldn't be sure because Inetta had a way of turning expeditions into something for his betterment.

"If I'm going to hang around the house for a year, I want to be in something nice," she told him. "I don't want you keeping my ashes in some old Folgers can."

"I was thinkin' your flour canister."

He was joking back, but her notion was not so far off. He had held things together all his life by making do with what he had and he might not have thought this far ahead without her prompting. What kind of husband planned where to store his wife's ashes when she was still breathing? He groped for the right pace and tone with her, tried not to look ahead, even as his life slid headlong into the unspeakable.

The woman at the shop asked if she could help them find anything special. He tried to be protective, saying they were just looking, but Inetta came right out with it. "We're looking for some stoneware to put my ashes in."

"We don't have anything here in quite that size with a lid," she said. "Have you checked the antique shops? Sometimes they have those vintage flour crocks and sugar canisters."

He wondered if the woman had simply misheard or if she had handled this kind of request before.

Inetta smiled at him. "We thought of that but I'm looking for something more… handmade."

The woman brightened. "Then you ought to see Beryl Moore, Beryl and Martin. I'm sure they'd have what you're looking for in their studio. They make these wonderful storage pots and bread bins." She showed them some of the Moore's mugs, which to his eye were eccentric and oversized, but Inetta saw something she liked, and the woman scribbled an address for her.

They left the co-op and passed one of the antique stores.

He paused before the window. "Sure you don't want to go in and look at the cookie jars?" She threw an elbow to his ribs, and at that moment it was impossible to accept she was dying.

The Moore's studio was toward Palisade in an area that had been orchards before it turned over to housing development sometime in the 1960s. They'd preserved a couple acres on a corner that still had a few fruit trees, with a guesthouse and two-story pottery shed behind the residence. All the clapboard buildings were painted barn red. Next to the shed was an arched yellow brick kiln tall enough to walk into. Two iron rails ran between the shed and the kiln. The four structures defined a shaded flagstone courtyard.

Martin Moore looked like an artist—at least, an artist in his seventies. He was thin and slightly stooped, with a goat beard and the pale blue eyes of a malamute. He absently combed his fingers through his hair so it poked up in little grey artichoke spikes. Beryl could have been Mrs. Claus—a round, beaming woman with half glasses perched over rosy cheeks. As soon as Leonard and Inetta walked through the studio door, Beryl offered them tea.

The sunlit front of the studio featured an assortment of elegant pottery displayed on shelves, tables and windowsills. Through a doorway he could see an old potter's kick-wheel and a motorized one, a long worktable and racks of white, unglazed pieces ranging from simple tableware to elaborately impractical objects—dragons, goats and rocket ships melting into pitchers, teapots and flower vases. Something that might have been a man-eating saxophone, finished in fiery colors, stood up on hind legs next to a watercooler.

The couple quickly sized them up. Martin invited

Leonard for a tour of the back while Beryl took Inetta around the showroom. Seeing Leonard's eye drift to the kiln, Martin showed him how an L-shaped brick-lined cart rode on the rails, carrying pots from the shed into the kiln for firing. The bed of the cart fit precisely, becoming the floor, and the wall at the back of the cart sealed the kiln after it was rolled in place. The bricks in the sides were dry-stacked three courses wide, interlocking without mortar.

"I built it myself almost thirty years ago, before I knew totally what I was doing," Martin said. "After a few tweaks, it works beautifully, but you couldn't do this today. There's asbestos in the roof and uranium tailings under the footings. Probably nothing about it is to code. Whoever buys this place may have to knock it down and haul it to the landfill."

"You been makin' pots that long?"

"Longer. And teaching. You don't do this to make a living. You do it to make enough money so you can keep doing it."

"Like ranchin' these days."

He saw in the kiln's design and the shed's rough carpentry a kind of artistry he understood. What had to fit, fit right. What needed to work, worked. Tools were where they were supposed to be. Take away the pots and there were no flourishes in the plain grounds—just color, proportion, order and the quiet side-by-sideness of the Moores as they moved around their establishment. It was so familiar it made him ache deep in his bones.

He went back into the shop and found Inetta cradling a squat ceramic container. A red streak chased by corn tortilla speckles shot through a midnight blue glaze. Rough-bark cork stoppered the wide opening. Inetta said, "Beryl calls this style Heavenly Caprock. They brought the cork back from Portugal themselves. It's perfect."

He reached for his wallet. "How much?"

"Already taken care of," said Beryl. "You sure you don't want it wrapped?"

"I'll carry it home just like this," Inetta said.

When they got to the truck, he said, "I know it comes out the same, but I was goin' to buy that for you. How much was it?"

"She was going to give it to me. I shouldn't've told her what it was for, but I'm trying to get myself used to the idea by saying it. I'm trading her for it."

He pulled out of the drive and waited until Moore's property was out of sight. "You liked that place, didn't you?"

"I did."

"Portugal! We never got as far as Mexico." He drove for a while. "I'm sorry if I held you back."

"Len, that's not the way I see it." It was her turn to be silent.

He kept his eyes on the road.

"You liked it there, too," she said.

"I did."

"Maybe I liked it because of the art. Maybe you liked it for the bricks or the shed, I don't know. But we both liked it because they were right together. Well, that's what you gave me, mister. If it was a choice between you and a little studio somewhere, there'd be no question."

They were headed down North Avenue, a busy commercial four-lane that sprouted when drive-in cruising and strip malls were king, now given over to converted motels, Walmart, taco joints and discount furniture. It didn't seem the right place for this conversation.

He spoke anyway. "Haven't figured out yet how to do this."

"Yeah," she said. "Tell me about it."

They drove the length of the avenue and turned south for Monument Road.

Inetta unbuckled her seat belt and slid next to him.

"I'm trying to be brave, hon. I don't want to leave you. It's been good. But… it's not going to get better than right now."

He pointed across the river. He knew she didn't expect an answer. It was enough to be heading home with her head against his shoulder and her arms wrapped around the urn they came for. But it nagged him that he didn't have the words, didn't have the ease of a Martin Moore to turn his insides into something people could see and appreciate. The man's pitchers were ridiculous if you thought about them pouring ice water, but they opened a window that forced you to question this one little thing. He remembered Inetta's cow that might want to be milked a different way. He wondered what-all open windows he had walked right past.

They began the climb up Monument Road and he thought if he didn't say the right thing now, he might never get the chance. His heart heaved up and his throat felt stiff as conduit. He said, "I wish I could ride with you right up to the gate."

And she whispered, "Oh, you'll be there with me, all right. Then I'll go in and you'll keep on going."

"Where?"

"You'll figure it out, hon. But for now, let's take our time. Jesus can wait a little bit."

The Big Empty

THE REVEREND QUENTIN PEASELY, Inetta's pastor from Shower of Blessings Holiness Temple, was the first visitor she was willing to receive. Peasely seemed much too overjoyed to see people who were not glad to see him, and his conversation came wrapped like steaks passed over a butcher counter, but Leonard gave him some credit because Inetta did. She said Men of God had an obligation not to appear troubled.

Inetta had a difficult Saturday and missed Sunday services, unsure she could bear the hard sit in church, so Peasely came to see her. Leonard left them alone to pray and whatever else goes on when a minister corners you in your own house. As he was leaving, Peasely located him in the barn and fixed a grip on his shoulder. "Inetta tells me she's spoken about seeing you in heaven."

"She has."

"I know it's hard to accept right now, but God has a plan for you both, Leonard, and He's reaching out to you through your love for her."

He thought of God filling his wife with loving tumors and didn't respond. The Reverend smiled and tightened his grip. "She also tells me you're a tough nut to crack."

"God's had plenty of opportunities to throw me a thunderbolt."

"Not all thunderbolts look like thunderbolts," said the reverend.

"That ain't in the Bible."

"Not in so many words," Peasely said, relaxing his hand. "Inetta knows where she's going, and she's not afraid, but she has her worries about you. She prays you'll accept Jesus someday, of course—she's also concerned whether you'll be all right in the meantime. You need to talk to her. This is not the time for either of you to hold back."

The reverend had something else he wanted to say. "She's hurting. A lot."

"She has her pills. She ain't said nothin'..." As soon as Leonard said it, he knew. He wouldn't have said anything, either.

Peasely reached inside a pocket at the back of his zippered Bible. He gave Leonard a card. It said Hospice & Palliative Care. "Call them. Call them today."

"We ain't going to town."

"You don't have to. They'll come up here."

"We don't have no insurance."

"I know. They'll help you anyway. Just ask for what you need."

Charity, then. Inetta had already laid out all their affairs at the hospital and they sent the paperwork to the state. Like they were paupers. Like they couldn't take care of themselves. He couldn't head off that humiliation but he didn't plan to go through with any more of it. Now she was hurting too deep and there was nothing else he could do for her except the things he'd never wanted to do.

"I know she's dying," he said, finally.

"She is," said the reverend.

"But we don't give up easy."

"Call them," said Peasley, and this time his touch felt almost a comfort.

A man from the hospice showed up in a van about nine in the morning. Inetta was still sleeping. He introduced himself, took a quick look in the house and directed a rearrangement of the front room. "Is there something we can move out?" the hospice man asked.

Not much to choose from. He indicated Inetta's sewing machine cabinet—a marvel of drop leafs, extensions, rolling storage drawers and an airlift that brought the machine out of hiding. "It'll be a bear," Leonard said, and he began to unpack the drawers, detach the sewing machine from its mount and remove the top. Maybe he should have asked Inetta, but sleep was so precious for her. Meanwhile, the man brought in the components of a hospital bed, which he unloaded quickly, and they used the dolly for moving the cabinet out to the barn.

"When's the nurse comin'?" Leonard asked.

"I *am* the nurse," he said. "Bed hauler, bagel slicer and bottle washer, too. You can ask me for just about anything." The man was short and beefy with hair cropped so close it was hard to judge the color. He wore khakis and a loose blue shirt with the tail out.

"What did you say your name was, again?"

"Ted. I think we woke your wife. Shall we show her what all the banging was about?"

Inetta shuffled in, her left arm bent and stiff, hand in a fist. Her right hand clutched the waistband of unstrung sweat pants too exhausted to stay up on their own. She scooted onto the edge of the bed, and Ted demonstrated the controls and showed how to use the sheet underneath as a sling to heft her into a comfortable position. Sitting up in the bed, she seemed lighter and heavier at once, anxious and at peace, her very essence trapped in unfamiliar flesh.

From a canvas bag, Ted produced an electronic device and began to attach tubes and wires to it. "This pump will help keep you more comfortable," he said to Inetta. "You can control your own pain relief with this button. You're probably used to dosing horses, right? Well, this is a lot easier."

Ted managed to be efficient, attentive and cheerful all at once as he reviewed medications, set up a schedule for when he'd check in and gave them papers to sign. When Ted finished, Leonard followed him out to the van. He intended to ask a question he couldn't quite shape about how Ted's good and kind spirit bore up against death's constant thrum. Leonard knew the signs of the end approaching from his lifetime on the ranch, and he'd witnessed death and its aftermath in many forms, but he'd never had to cradle it and so never had to master this slow letting go, watching another person empty of everything while he drowned in it.

"We can't have visitors just show up if I'm out here in bed," Inetta said. "Get me the phone."

"Who do you want me call?" he asked.

She stared at him, with surprise or confusion, it was getting harder to tell. "Lula," she said. Lula Tibbets lost her husband Alf a year ago. "She'll understand, and she'll know who I want and who I don't." The things he didn't know. "And Elliott. I want to talk to Elliott."

"I think you better call Elliott," he said. He didn't want his next words with Elliott to be on a phone call.

Elliott had done well after he left for California. He was a hard worker raised by fruit growers, and he quickly found work in a Sonoma Valley vineyard. The winery exposed him to people who appreciated that he carried an unaccountable judgment for things—what some people called taste. When a wealthy man from Washington state bought the vineyard, he acquired Elliott, too. Before long, he was working in Raimon Winterzee's other enterprises. His duties kept changing based on whatever Big Rai thought needed straightening. Elliott was circumspect about the details and claimed his job was boring unless you were in business. Big companies were full of people too scared to try anything, he said, and the people who weren't scared were usually just out for themselves. According to Elliott, if you were fearless and selfless, you could just about write your own job description—whatever that meant.

Inetta and her brother remained close, but Elliott rarely made it back to Colorado. A call from her would bring Elliott back for sure. Leonard would be glad to see him, too, glad for the lift Elliott always brought her and glad for a chance to deliver the kind of apology that had to be done in person.

Elliott had offered to fly them both out to California for his wedding, and Leonard had declined. "You tell him I wish 'em well, but somebody's got to tend the ranch," Leonard told Inetta, and when she insisted, he added, "It ain't 'cause he's queer."

She made a sour face. "They go by gay these days."

"Same deal, though."

"Pretty much."

"And they're gettin' married nowadays," he said.

"Pretty much."

"Ain't nothin' against Elliott. You just tell him I can't have him payin' my way."

"I think you better tell him," she said. It was as close to fighting as they ever got, and he let it drop. He was never much for travel—or for explaining himself, either.

Inetta once sat with Lula Tibbets the way Lula was sitting with her. Inetta had visited Joyce Barnstable in the hospital, taken food to the Clintons and the Rickerts and who knows who else, and sent Leonard out to mow for Tom Flannery, though he was about to do it anyway. She had joined prayer circles and vigils, attended wakes, visitations and church services, even a Catholic Mass for the Dead, and driven to gravesides with or without him. The deaths were coming closer and faster and their friends were falling right around them, as if a sniper had finally found the range. Now it was her turn. Soon. The medical people had told them as much—but never straight on or flat out. First in their expressions, in numbers about outcomes, then in pulling back from treatments, and finally in their silence once they turned Inetta over to him with instructions written on a discharge form. They had been given all the information but none of the plain truth. He thought he understood how the death conversation never happened with all the people hovering around. It was possible to think someone else would handle it, but there was no death specialist to step forward. Instead of the medical people, it was Reverend Peasely who let him know he had to be the one, because he was the one she wanted. But how could Leonard talk to her about the end, without sounding like he had given up and drawn the shade? He'd never been any good with words or with God, either.

The drugs that quieted her pain also muffled her spark and her eyes more often went to places he couldn't see. He picked up her chores as she let them go or, where they were out of her sight, he at least let her think they were being done. She leaned into him more and he assumed what she relinquished. Holding the glass of fresh water as she drank through a straw. Applying balm to her chapped lips. Helping her turn over. Rinsing her with warm cloths and with cool ones. Wiping crusts from the corners of her eyes. Changing her sheets and, eventually, changing her diaper. Even with all the washing, he could not stop the smell of death. It came from her breath, from her pores, from the solutions meant to cleanse the uncleanseable. He wondered if she could smell it, too. But he also began to see why Inetta had visited the sick. Tending to another's needs like this was neither servitude nor drudgery and not so different from caring for his animals, who expressed appreciation through their trust and submission. He found new depths to his patience. Even away from her bedside, he felt himself living outside of time.

He sat on the edge of the bed and held her hand and tried to come up with a way to take hold of the big empty and each night it got away from him until Inetta said, "Crank me down a bit." He found the switch and lowered her head and when she pointed, he took out some of the bend under her knees.

"C'mere," she said. She rolled a bit to the side and swept a hand alongside herself. He climbed next to her and sensed the slight warmth in the sheet where she had been. "Just stretch out here next to me," she said. "I want to feel your whole self, full-length."

They lay spooned like that for a time, exchanging only the heat from their bodies. He tried to send her something more, imagined molecules of love passing through their skins back and forth. He tried to press down the memories that came at him so he could simply be where he was, holding onto the woman who was about to sink into memory for good.

"Remember Elliott's wedding?" she asked.

"I do."

"When I went and you stayed?"

"I ain't proud of it."

"Doesn't matter now. You weren't ready at the time. Now, I'm going and you… you're not quite ready to make this trip, either."

"You came back from California," he said.

She became silent and he hoped he hadn't ruined it.

"Some ways we were so different," she said, "and some people wondered how I could love a man who never accepted Jesus, but I never had to push God's love on you, did I? You never were that far away from it."

He said, "You got me close enough."

"That was the miracle, how it worked out," she said. "And now we're almost done. I am, anyway."

He didn't have anything he could say.

"You gave me plenty in this life, Len. I don't need anything more, except one. Take me up to Artists Point. Hang onto my ashes for a year so I'm good and dry. Me and Jesus'll be watching and I want to float for a while."

A year. He couldn't even see past tomorrow.

"One year to the day I pass. We got a date?"

When he said yes, it felt to him like the whole world had come loose underfoot and he had nothing left but sand to grab. When he said yes, he closed his eyes and knew the darkening would attend the approaching year of days. When he said yes, he tried to locate Inetta's warmth again but could only feel it passing from her body into his and he had to rise before he took it all.

Nurse Ted came with donuts or chocolate truffles, fresh IV bags and an exercise ball and shooed Leonard out of the house. *Take a walk* he'd say and, when he learned better, he'd say *go saddle up.* Leonard never learned exactly what Ted did while he was gone, but Inetta always seemed a little better when he returned. Elliott arrived and spent a week, sleeping in Junior's old bed in the bunkhouse—surely the roughest accommodation he had suffered since leaving Colorado. He helped with the horses and brought Inetta picture books of painters, and the only time in the whole ordeal Leonard saw his wife cry was when Elliott left. By some signal, women from Shower of Blessings began to materialize at nightfall, the way a clutch of does appears at the edge of a break. They sat poised for hours to clear a glass or tuck the edge of a blanket but mostly to fill the room so there was life to spare. If they prayed, he did not hear it. No one asked what to do and nothing was requested, but sideboards were swept clean of dishes and laundry disappeared and returned. Stalls were cleaned, oats mixed, buckets filled and hay distributed. Casseroles and meat loaf, succotash and pickled beets, bundt cakes and raspberry preserves stacked up in the kitchen and were quietly consumed, mostly by the visitors. He found this revolving presence comforting, though not so much he was able to say it to anyone's face. Still, this was not the way he had foreseen their lives disentwining—Inetta in bed with her finger on the infusion pump and him left standing, lost amid the activity. Inetta was the one who had lived the selfless life. He was the one who deserved to go.

Talk of place-taking for the dying always sounded false to him, nothing but a cry for attention from the living. But he would have willingly gone first if such a bargain could have saved her. He imagined himself an untethered caddis fly, racing ahead of the hatch to alight first on the water. A death trout boils up through the pool's surface to take him. Inetta and the rest scatter at the warning splash, saved, then the slow backwater swallows the ripple. Instead, he can only watch his wife become less herself each day and hold his breath as she swims toward the deepest of all places.

The Visitations

PEOPLE WHO HAD BEEN FOCUSED on comforting Inetta passed in a line and made swipes at comforting him, but he wasn't ready for it and they weren't prepared either. *Inetta has passed on. She's in a better place. Wrapped in her Savior's arms. She's with the angels. She'll be in our hearts forever. She'll be missed. We'll all be reunited. She's returned home.* Like Inetta was a book that had just gone back to the library.

Elliott, in the receiving line beside him, was still trying to catch up to her death, though somehow he had managed to arrange the details of her funeral on his way to Colorado, leaving behind an unresolved crisis involving Mrs. Winterzee the Third. An overnight package bearing urgent papers concerning complications in the empire followed him up to the ranch. The delivery truck driver knocked on the door before the first condolence card arrived. Leonard didn't see how Elliott could stand it.

Elliott was poised on the balls of his feet, burning with the intensity of a man whose mind is accustomed to being four places at once. Even in his impeccable black suit, he carried some of the boy who'd pitched in all his wages to defend his sister from a man she despised. He enveloped each person in a practiced radiance, as if they had come to be comforted by him, then passed each hand to Leonard, ensuring the efficient flow of the line. Leonard wondered if this was the last time they would be together. When Elliott left, he would take the only earthly version of Inetta's face with him.

A taxi brought Elliott all the way up to the ranch. The driver waited to take him back to the airport, which was less than a mile from the hotel he'd just left. Across the road, Donnie Barclay's man was baling the first cut of summer hay, until this cursed June, the finest smell on earth.

"Didn't have to come say good-bye again," Leonard said.

"I wanted to talk money while I was still here," Elliott said, "and yesterday wasn't the day. Can I ask you about where her bills stand?"

"Plan to take care of 'em."

"I'm sure you do. I don't know what her care cost, but I can guess, and I do have a pretty good idea how this place cash-flows. I also know your feelings about accepting the tiniest help from me."

This was his chance to say it. "That wasn't personal—it was just...it was the money I couldn't accept. Shoulda said why better. And I was embarrassed. That gay stuff was new to me then. I grew up in the goddamn boonies."

"So did I," Elliott said gently. "So did I. Okay—if you won't take my financial help, maybe you'll take my advice. You two poured yourself into this ranch and your frugality held it together long past what most people could've done. I can't begin to know the memories it has. But this place is going to change for you without Inetta. Maybe not right away, but it will, and I can't say it will be for the better."

Elliott spread his arms toward the pasture. "You have an asset that's worth something here. You shouldn't think of selling out as some kind of moral failure. It's a piece of land, and when you're gone, someone else is going to come along and put their house on it and pay taxes and bury their dogs over there and think that makes it theirs forever, too."

"That how they think in California?" Leonard said. "You been a lot more places than me and maybe you're smarter than me, so tell me what I do after I settle up. Do I get a room in town and eat outa the freezer at the Loco Mart? Maybe for foldin' money I could mow some lawns at them big houses out in the desert."

"Sorry," Elliott said. "I spoke too soon."

"I'll manage."

"I know you will." Elliott's words betrayed no skepticism, but there was a hint of a sigh. "You're still my family, mine and Larry's both, and we'll help however we can. Just ask."

"Thanks. I'll let you know."

"Do."

Elliott stood close, searching Leonard's face. Leonard watched the taxi driver flip the pages of a newspaper back and forth. The cab idled, telling them it was time. Finally, Elliott said, "You know how much she loved you, Len. Take that with you from here on out."

"Ha-yep" was all he could say. He pressed his hands to the taxi door, surprised by the first warmth he'd felt in a month. Its thump was the last sound that passed between them.

Leonard followed them deliberately up the drive. The inattentive cabbie had left the gate open when he drove in and was likely to do the same on his way back to town. Elliott knew better, but Leonard wanted him to remain sealed in the cab now that he was headed away for good. Leonard needed to be the one to swing his gate against the rest of world. He turned back toward the empty house, expecting some relief at being done with all the hovering and creeping past his feelings. Truth was, he couldn't feel and wasn't sure he wanted to start again.

The sun had lowered to a squint above the bluffs and the shadows had begun their work, dampening the color, swallowing the details and reducing the landscape to voids and prominences. For months, he'd pulled a great shade against the painful brightness only to hide evening's stealthy approach. Now he felt rooted—no, mucked up to his knees and about to topple. He peered down the path by which he had come. The house seemed unaccountably dark. Surprised to be surprised, he knew what was coming next. A tunnel blurred at the edges. Air thickened with things forgotten and left undone. *Okay then.* He willed himself to move and could not. Something bumped against him from behind, soft and heavy like a rubber raft half-filled with water. *A year more standing in the current.* What a relief to stop resisting, to let the darkening sweep him under this time. To accept inertness the way the cottonwoods gave in to the drought. Upright and leafless, holding up long bones against the sky for the occasional hawk, then over.

He had been too young to observe in his father's rages anything but the sour-apple breath, the brow lowering into a curse, the eyes that saw right through Leonard. The boy never imagined his father's drunken thrashing was meant to throw off this smothering blanket of numbness. Once it visited, though, Leonard recognized the enemy and met it with sidelong resistance. Sometimes it was enough to swing his legs off the bed or brush his teeth or fire up the coffee. Chores and more chores, one at a time. But the darkening could fight guerilla-style, too, and it waited him out. Though his feet felt too heavy to lift, the weight he bore was in his head. He told himself if he made it to the stoop, he could wallow as long as he wanted, through the next 358 days if need be. But still the hundred-yard walk back stretched to furlongs. He imagined Donnie Barclay coming by and finding him stock-still in the yard, unable to lift so much as a finger in greeting. Not enough shame in it to get him moving. He thought of Inetta waiting for him, even if only in the metaphorical, in her blue ceramic jar, but for once he was beyond her reach.

He heaved himself against the darkening and managed only to sway.

A stirring next to the house. Stitches had hoisted her flanks from the shadows, stretched and was shaking herself nose to tail. Inetta had fed her as long as she could and Leonard had not yet worked the dog's dinner into the shambles of his new days. Stitches stood expectantly, woofed a reminder. Seeing no response, she woofed again and reared a few inches off her front feet, an arthritic effort at enticement.

The dog. The horses. Would they be the ones he took down with him?

"Gir-r-l," he managed, low and quiet. Stitches pricked her ears and cocked her head. She knew where the food was and it was not in his direction.

"Come." Not a command. A request.

He saw the dog check the hands limp at his sides. She was not prone to performing old tricks for nothing. He turned his wrist, cupped his fingers. Closed. Open.

"Come on, girl."

The dog waited. She'd heard no raised notes in his call and she knew Leonard had to come to the house. And so they stood apart, needing each other, until Stitches sniffed the air suddenly and looked around the yard in a single arc before centering back on him. Maybe she sensed something. Maybe it was just an act before giving in. She came slowly, half-submissive and off-kilter, as if her back and front were barely acquainted. A snuffle and a brief look confirmed the empty hand and she bumped her head under it and sat still with her shoulder pressed tight against his leg. He thumbed the ridgeline of bone that joined her skull beneath the bristled fur. She pushed up against his touch. A good girl, still able to do what a dog does best.

He looked down the tunnel shaped out of fear and time and obligation and God and all the things that had nothing to do with the angle of the sun. He measured the coming days in weight and time and distance against the strength of his word. His love. A dog's bowl needed filling. Ashes waiting on a shelf. The hospice bed still unfolded in the front room. He could tumble there once he got rolling and then see what the morning brought. *Food?* he said. Stitches hopped and pawed his leg and circled behind him, pointing the way. They started together, old man and old dog, and with each step the tunnel compressed a little until there was nothing to pass through but one last hoop of the doorframe, where he gathered himself and reached in first for the light.

Morning. The question: which one? A prickle of whiskers argued some days out. He lay twisted in Inetta's sheet, feeling bludgeoned but alive. Stitches regarded him with a mixture of hopefulness and reproach. The front door was open. Had he left it? Then he heard the voice.

"I brought some donuts," said Nurse Ted. "Thought you might be done with the bed."

Abandoned

LEONARD'S BONES FELT HER LOSS in the winter nights under the blankets and in the early mornings refilling the wood stove to drive the hard chill out of the house. Swinging his feet to the cold floor each day, he appreciated one more thing a younger wife had done for an older man.

He still had the habit of answering the telephone with the expectation the call was for Inetta. It almost always had been. Even the collection calls started out asking for her.

"Len, Donnie Barclay." Donnie's voice was flat. "You missing any horses?"

"They were all here yesterday," Leonard said. *Missing* wasn't the right word for what had been happening to his herd. He wondered if Donnie had noticed how it had dwindled.

"Yesterday I came across a black and white overo paint with your brand, a mare maybe ten years old. She's belly deep in a snowdrift up on Piñon Mesa. I thought I'd call you first. You know whose it might be?"

Leonard thought of the paints that had gone through his hands and who had bought them. He hadn't seen the Haxbys since selling them Maggie Mae for their daughter to ride five years ago. "Bald face? I've got an idea."

Donnie said, "I was thinking of making a run up there

with the county rescue team, but the next goddamn thing you know, they do a press release and there's a goddamn TV helicopter flying over. I don't want to embarrass anybody if their horse ran off. If you know the owner, we could all get up there with the snowcat and maybe walk her out... I could use a good horseman along, too, if you're up for it."

"Let me make a call."

The number he had for Rex Haxby rang into forever. The family lived in the Hatcher Creek Ranch subdivision where residents bought thirty-five-acre ranchettes with the prospect of an easy commute to town. A Homeowners Association was set up so members with horses had access to the former Hatcher ranch buildings and corrals. It was possible the horse could've gotten out and wandered up on Piñon Mesa, but a better chance Maggie Mae was not lost at all. All over Colorado, financially stressed owners were walking away from animals that cost a few thousand a year just to feed. At least Maggie Mae wasn't like some, left near a freeway interchange or tied up somewhere she could hurt herself.

Leonard heard Donnie's flatbed honking at him from the road, and he pulled out with his single-horse trailer and a load of blankets, halters and ropes. Donnie had brought a five-seat snowcat on the flatbed along with a couple of his men from the Crown B. At the store crossroads, they met Randy Springsteel, who worked in one of Donnie's construction companies. The plan was to dig the mare out of the drift and break trail for her with the cat. If she was too weak to make it out on her own, they had a heavy-duty rescue mat to drag her back to the road. Randy rode with Leonard, and they followed the road to the top of the mesa. The snow was churned up on the curves and the side roads were drifted over except for the occasional snowmobile track. It had been plowed once since the heaviest snow, but only up to the reservoir. Above there, the road was left to high suspensions, four-wheel-drive and the hubris of the men who owned the trucks.

Randy Springsteel also served with Donnie on the search and rescue team. The county didn't have a budget for rescuing animals, finding careless hikers or retrieving bodies from remote areas, so much of the work was done by volunteers. Donnie was a bit old for the physical part, but he had time and vehicles to spare, including a jet boat and the snowcat. Going along with his boss on side expeditions like this had to be part of Randy's job. He treated it as a perk rather than an imposition. Randy sat coiled in the seat like a bronc rider waiting for the gate to fly open.

"Donnie says this used to be your horse."

"Sounds like it."

"Has your brand, anyway—the Reverse Dollar?"

"My granddad wanted something to play off the S in Self. His idea of a joke, I guess. Not so funny anymore."

"What do these people think—they're going to turn loose their kid's pet and it'll just go on the mesa and turn into a mustang?" Randy was incensed.

"Hard to say. They turn loose their kids." So Leonard had heard, anyway. "You like workin' for Donnie?" he asked.

Randy stretched. His arms filled the cab and tattoos crept from his coat sleeves. "He's a good boss, if you know what you're doing."

"And you do?"

"Yeah, usually, but I've learned a lot from him. I worked for Samson Sanitation, and when he bought it, I was afraid he might bring in his own people and I'd be out of a job. He told me, nobody wants to jump into the shit-pumping business, they only fall into it. And he said, my worst fuck-ups have been putting the wrong people in the job, so since you're already here, let's see if you fuck it up before I take my turn."

"That sounds like Donnie," Leonard said. "He gets to the heart of things. Where'd he find the snowcat?"

Randy's laugh sounded affectionate. "Donnie says his wife won't let him go to auctions by himself anymore."

Leonard hadn't been around people much in the past few months and now he remembered why. He couldn't guard against a casual conversation bringing up words out of nowhere that knocked him breathless. *Wife* and *auctions* kicked him in the chest and *by himself* put him in a funk that lasted the rest of the way up.

The juniper-sage steppe graduated to scrub oak as it climbed the mesa. Near a campground, a lone towering spruce stood as a reminder of the sawmills that operated here a century ago. Farther up, there would be aspens. Leonard rarely got over to this side. Someone told him once Glade Park was about the size of Oahu. Oahu didn't mean anything to him except that his mountain island didn't show up on the map of the world.

When they reached the tracks left the day before by Donnie's sled, they unloaded the snowcat from the flatbed and transferred some gear from the horse trailer. Donnie's crew had brought safety helmets, four-by-four timbers, the rescue mat and rigging. The cat had a winch, which they hoped not to use because manpower was safer for the horse. First, they'd try to shovel her out and hope she wasn't too frantic to ride out on the rescue mat or too weak to get into the trailer on her own.

They bumped along for a mile or so through a tangle of scrub oak that still fluttered with crisp brown leaves. The snow depth didn't seem too bad until they reached a ridgeline.

Donnie slowed the cat and pointed below to where the snow built up when the wind released its load as it hit the ridge. The drifts appeared as a gentle incline, concealing the sharp drop. The mare must've headed down the mesa in the moderate snow cover, plunged over the hidden edge into the drift and gotten pinned up to her shoulder.

It was a beautiful spot, even under a winter blanket. Snow showed white through the brown snarl of scrub oak, thicker juniper greened the slope and, lowest down, Glade Park stretched flat as a runway. On the western border, loaves of sandstone, the river breaks and finally, forty miles away, the white-capped blue of the La Sal mountain range.

Closer in, an irregular black spot stood out in the white expanse. It was the mare's back, head and, as they drew closer, the discolored snow left where she voided herself. A blown-over rumple in the snow showed where she headed toward the ridge. Perhaps she was working her way back home before getting mired in the drift. It looked like Maggie Mae. White mane and tail and irregular patches of white along her side. He expected the mare to look back when she heard the roar of the cat, but she kept her gaze fixed on the valley. Perhaps she'd slipped into survival mode and was conserving every last bit of energy.

The cat made a wide swing so as not to panic the horse. As they neared, four curses released from the cab in the same instant. The mare was frozen in place, her lip drawn back, her unseeing eyes ice blue.

Donnie halted the cat. "Sonofabitch! I thought she was in better shape than that."

"Prob'ly was," said Leonard. Her left rear flank had been torn away.

"Goddamn it! I shoulda tried to dig her out when I found her."

Randy leaned between the front seats. "Too dangerous by yourself. You got us here as soon as you could."

Donnie was not ready to be reassured. "She was in here so tight, looks like she couldn't even fight."

Leonard surveyed the bloody snow scuffed over the wound. "Mountain lion. Tried to bury her."

Donnie said, "She used to be your horse, Len. What do you want to do, leave her?"

Leonard looked across at the sawtooths of the La Sals, beyond the mare's range of vision even when she was alive. At best, a dimming white line under the sky.

"Whose land we on?"

"Mine," Donnie said. "Or close enough."

"It's a nice spot to leave her bones," Leonard said. "But it's your livestock up here next summer. You want to feed a predator, it's your call."

Donnie stepped out of the cab. He wore Sorels and he sunk below their tops as he staggered over to the mare. He pushed against Maggie Mae's body. "Goddamn it. She's in here real solid. We'd have to saw her apart damn near. Sorry, girl," he said, running his hands down her neck. "Sorry."

Donnie slammed himself back into the seat and rammed the cat's levers forward. "Well, boys," he said, "thank you for joining me in this exercise in fucking futility."

Leonard was mindful of the trailer drifting as he took the snowy curves back down to the store. The empty metal cavity boomed over hidden frozen humps. The return took less time than he expected. Where the pavement began was the turn-off to Hatcher Creek Ranch, the road unmarked except by a cluster of realty signs.

"Mind if I take a little detour up here?" he asked Randy.

"This won't take long."

He turned down the gravel road running through a short, rolling stretch of wooded BLM land. He had not been in here since delivering Maggie Mae to the Haxbys. He slowed as three mule deer bounded up out of the brush along the road and climbed the hill on the opposite side. He waited until two stragglers joined them. The Hatcher Creek Ranch development started at an electronic security gate across the road. A sign warned that private property lay beyond, but the gate was propped open and he drove through. The grand design hinted by the entrance hadn't been carried out very far inside. A brown doublewide squatted next to a turquoise metal barn. A pickup with a snowplow was backed up to an empty corral. The green plastic sides of an above-ground swimming pool were almost drifted over.

"Where does Hatcher Creek run?" Randy asked.

"Nowhere," Leonard said. "Guess Hatcher Ranch wasn't a good enough name, so they promoted the ditch up to a creek."

A long roof was visible just beyond a row of trees. Except for the terra cotta tiles and leaded glass in the gabled windows, it might be a barn.

"That's a big one," said Randy.

"He was lucky. Sold off his development in time." Leonard turned down an unplowed street. *Bridle Pass*. "Hardly anyone's built since I was here last. This one's where we're goin'."

The Haxby house sat on a curved drive, evident under the untracked snow, leading to the three-car garage that presented one main flank of the house. The other half looked like giant garden gazebos shoved together to form a jumble of joining rooflines. Rough tusks of ice jutted from the lamb's tongue rainspouts.

"Looks like nobody's home," Randy said. "Or going to be."

A lockbox hung from the handle of the ornate front door. A piece of flashing flapped loose from one of the cornices. Two phone directories slumped on the steps—one splayed open out of its plastic bag. Leonard chewed his lip as the truck idled, half turned across the apron of the driveway.

"If we'd had her carcass, I think I would've left it on the porch," Randy said.

Leonard said nothing because he was tired of decisions that didn't matter anymore. He put the truck back in gear, letting the trailer wander wide over the yard's frozen crust.

The Jimmy

LEONARD RECOGNIZED THE TRUCK parked along his fence line before he saw the person who came with it. A cream, orange and gray Jimmy, a boxy, mid-70's shortbed that once sat on the featured corner at Dunham Motors. Its vintage could qualify it for collector plates and the paint job for hauling royalty in the Junction Tigers Homecoming parade, but knowing Dunham, the bodywork covered up a plenitude of shit just waiting to happen. Whoever bought it wanted attention more than transportation—the sight of it lifted his heart a little, he had to admit—and he wondered whether they were lost or broken down. At the gravel crunch under Leonard's tires, the figure turned, and through the trailing dust cloud that caught up with the truck strode the ghost of Amelia Earhart, found at last.

"Beautiful day," she said, "though I suppose you'd rather see some snow still on the ground." She indicated his pasture, dry but not ready to green up. "Your place?"

"So far."

The woman smiled. A fancy colored scarf and jacket on top, he noted, and jeans with boots for tromping around. "Meg Mogrin," she said. I'm with High Country Living."

"High Country Living." He tongued the words. "Can't

say I've heard of it, but I guess I'm doin' it."

Meg Mogrin smiled and spun back toward his fence. "This is a sweet little ranch."

Three words for all he had left in the world, and only one of them still seemed to fit. A few months ago, there were a dozen horses in the stubbly pasture, steam rising from their backs in the morning air. *Little* was still about right.

Meg Mogrin leaned right into his silence, as if it were an invitation. "Do I have this right?" She pulled a plat map from the seat of the truck and spread it on the hood, fingering his section. "I heard you might be interested in selling. I also heard you might tell me to go to hell."

He nodded. "Can't argue with your information either way." And where did she get it? There was plenty of land for sale in the area already, without much action as far as he could tell.

"So you're Leonard Self?"

"'Scuse my manners," he said. "I am. What's High Country Livin'?"

She handed him a card. Across the top it said: *Helping you create the lifestyle of your dreams.* "We match up people seeking high-value properties."

"Can't say I fit either end a that deal," he said.

"I've had some trouble reaching you," she said. "Don't you believe in telephones?"

"Oh, I *believe* in 'em, just got no *use* for 'em."

Her laugh was not a salesman-laugh-at-anything laugh, but of a woman enjoying herself. "I have a client who can't find what they're looking for on the market right now," she said. "Your property fits the profile. So will you show me around?"

She wasn't quite pushing, but showed no sign of giving up. Something was opening up in front of him that wasn't there a moment before, and he wanted to think about what it could mean. "Showin' you don't mean I want to sell, you understand."

"I understand perfectly," she said, swinging back into her Jimmy. "And looking doesn't mean anything, either."

He unhitched the gate and swung it open. As he considered the state the house was in, he half wished a man was following him down the drive. He took her around outside first, starting with the barn. The empty tack room was neater than the house and better smelling, with a malty mixture of horse, saddle-soaped leathers, wool and molasses-laced feed that would permeate the boards until grass grew up through their splinters, but he could see the infused air evoked nothing special in her. She moved briskly through the outbuildings like a woman retrieving her children from a china shop.

"What else can you show me?" she asked.

He walked her to the old cabin. After Junior left, it began to fill up with things he didn't want to store in the barn. He pushed open the door. She did not step inside.

"The buildings ain't much," he said.

"What's built isn't always what matters most about a place. You go back a long way here, don't you?"

"Yes and no. Depends who's countin'."

"Yeah," she said. Just one breath she made sound like a paragraph.

She seemed accustomed to taking quick stock of a place so as not to betray too much interest. He knew the house was not going to matter to her kind of buyer, but he had to bring her inside. As he understood from the horse business, Meg Mogrin had moved on to appraising the seller.

Stripped down, the house looked orderly enough as long as she didn't inspect the corners. She might not see the oilcloth was tacked to the pine table to prevent Stitches from pulling it off, a habit that appeared after Inetta died. The Tabasco bottle and the tin salt and pepper shakers were begrimed from his grasp, but no one else handled them. Dishes went from the drain board directly to their reemployment. The webby window glass was specked with spider castings, but intact, save for one cracked window in the bedroom sealed with caramelized cellophane tape. Around the sink, the linoleum floor had been worn to a scuffed underlayer so its marbled pattern resembled the gum-stuck underside of an old library table. Anyone in her business had to have come across worse.

She must have been looking for something she could admire in the sparse front room, pausing before two Brown & Bigelow litho prints stuck unframed to the wall. A chestnut-haired cowgirl in a pin-up pose pointed her smoking six guns at a placid Victorian lady with seal-brown braids thick as hangman's knots.

"These are vintage."

"My uncle saved 'em in a drawer."

"They still sum it up, though, don't they?"

"Sum what?"

"Never mind."

He set up two mugs—one plain and one from the LP gas company—and filled them from the percolator with what was now day-old Maxwell House Aluminum Roast.

Meg eyed the oily surface. "Any cream?" She looked without hope toward the refrigerator.

"Sorry."

She took a careful sip and set the mug down. "Land's an emotional investment. I've had people point guns at me for asking if they want to sell. Others hang on too long with the hope the world will change back in their favor. Those who say their land's purely a financial investment—they can end up being the most emotional. You strike me as more the patient type, interested at least in knowing your options."

"Patient don't mean I like where the world's goin', either."

"No, I guess not," she said. "I'd call that resigned."

"So far, this don't sound like much of a sales pitch."

"I thought I explained, we're not just about buying and selling land. I want to know more about your goals. We want clients to consider what's right for their lives. Some people, all they're looking for is their sale price. They don't anticipate... the costs."

"You don't last in the ranchin' business if you can't anticipate the costs, Miz Mogrin."

"It's Meg. And I didn't mean just the monetary costs."

"Me neither."

He walked her to her pickup. Meg had pulled some things out of him. He hadn't told her about the bills but how could he not have talked about Inetta? He wondered if she read the death notices before she came looking for old men's ranches.

"I have some ideas I want to work on," she said. "I'll be in touch, and you can tell me if any look like the right opportunity. No pressure."

"Didn't say..."

"You wanted to sell. I know. But you said enough. Get a life in mind first. That's my free advice on dealing with the old homestead."

"Night." He gave the tailgate a double-tap farewell as the V8 eased away, leaving behind the syrupy hint of a leaky gasket.

He thought about the visit longer than he should have. He told himself to remember that people like Meg Mogrin didn't represent people like Leonard Self—they used them.

In his business, he'd dealt with "lifestyle" people. They wore jeans and cowboy boots and bought trucks and often appeared laid-back and pleasant, but some had made their fortunes in unpleasant circumstances and were in a big hurry to relax. They were accustomed to money and reputation removing obstacles and were mystified to find it so difficult to stop a neighbor's dawn run with a tractor or to prevent the wind from blowing the smell of livestock in their direction. The lifestyle people weren't necessarily trying to drive the regular folks out. They just wanted the towns to move quicker and run a little less rough, with different food and better wine and more places to shop. They wanted solitary hikes with cell phone reception. They wanted culture—not the culture that was already here, but more like what they were used to in the city. They wanted to live in places where they could admire the views. In the process, the little mining towns turned into ski towns and the ski towns into lifestyle communities where the teachers and bartenders and hotel maids couldn't afford to live anymore. Grand Junction was too big to get taken over like that. But out on the edges, the land was turning over to the East Coasters, Texans, Californians and other people who wanted to live like the valley was someplace else.

The valley had its share of decent and generous families whose wealth came from selling groceries, healing people, making loans or building things. You'd never know it from their lifestyle because they didn't act any differently. The new wealth seemed to come from moving money around, dragging out court cases or turning more of life over to distractions. It wasn't crooked work, maybe, but it didn't strike him as particularly useful, either.

Leonard had once sold three horses to a ranch owned by a big-time fashion designer. The man actually sent a woman out with color samples that needed to match the horses before the sale went final. He left some ranch roads open so people could drive through and admire the scenery he'd laid out. The views of his livestock, meadows, fences and outbuildings *were* beautiful in a picture gallery sort of way, and his famous name on the landscape made you look at the snowcap on Mt. Sneffels and want to give him credit for it.

Leonard knew this: Meg Mogrin had not come by to tote up the value of his improvements or to judge the condition of the pasture. The ranch had been true to his and Inetta's life, but it lacked the sun-faded ruin to make it seem truly western to some eastern buyer's eye. She had something else in mind for the land and was probing for any sentimental nonsense that might jack up the price. Well, none of that left here. He had already let go of the ranch in his mind the moment he figured he could swap it for Inetta's cure. Now he was only leaving it behind to pay for her bills and his self-respect. If Meg could wrap up a deal and take this final load off, it would be fine with him. If not, he was sure the bill collectors could sort it out just fine.

Whoever ended up with it, a crew would appear one day to level the house, but first they might prowl for anything worth taking. They'd find it cleaned out except for that pair of pin-ups covering the demolition his fists had started on the worst night of his life.

Meg's pearl and orange Jimmy was filling up at the Loco Mart. When Leonard saw Vaughn Hobart at the pump, he pulled in behind. Unless she unloaded it cheap, it was hard to imagine Vaughn buying something like that.

"That truck still runnin' rough?"

Vaughn looked up in surprise. "Not something I worry about. It ain't mine."

"Seen it up my way a week or so back."

"Belongs to a realty woman. I'm doin' jobs for her company, settin' out the for-sale signs, mowin' lawns, pullin' voles outa swimmin' pools—that sorta thing. Beats gettin' up at three to deliver the damn paper." Vaughn tapped the nozzle on the fill tube and screwed down the cap. "So far, it's goin' good, kind of a steppin' stone to my original plan."

"What do you know about her? Why'd she be interested in my place?"

"Can't really talk about it." Vaughn removed the credit card receipt threading out of the pump, checked it and slipped it in his wallet. *Vaughn with a credit card?*

"Why not?" Leonard said.

"Perfessional discretion."

"What the hell does that mean?"

"Look what happened last time."

"What last time?"

"When Bryce and Pinky got fired."

"They got fired because they were stupid and got caught stealin' from their boss."

"Well, there you go. Meg's kinda tutorin' me on this real estate business and one of the things is perfessional discretion where you don't talk about certain shit."

"Vaughn, you're diggin' post holes, not sellin' condominiums. Jesus!"

"Why should that make any differ'nce?" Vaughn said.

Vaughn was right, and Leonard felt shamed for putting him down. "She's workin' with you, huh?"

"She says after I pass my six-month probation, I can pick up her clients at the airport."

"In that?"

"No, the Escalade. I gotta go. Take care." Vaughn clattered off, a white spume trickling from the tailpipe of Meg Mogrin's show truck.

Leonard pulled forward to the diesel pump and punched Pay Inside.

Trust Me

Two HAND-ADDRESSED LETTERS sifted out of the collection notices, insurance offers and oil change coupons accumulated over the week. One was from High Country Living, the corner of the envelope printed with a red ochre mesa ridged in gold. Fancy. Leonard tossed it unopened on the seat. There was also a card from Elliott. He opened it and saw he couldn't answer it. Elliott wanted to know about his plans for Inetta's ashes. He'd been so busy stiff-arming Elliott's offer to help, he'd forgotten about what he might owe him as Inetta's brother.

He sat awhile in the parking lot outside the trailer that served as the post office, letting his long-running obtuseness sink in. Inetta of course assumed Elliott would be part of it. Elliott did, too. But once Leonard had begun to shape his own plan for Artists Point, he'd left no room for anyone else. What he'd conceived as private act, a final pulling down of the shade, in this light felt sneaky and selfish. He wondered if he was wrong about what conventions should weigh on a man choosing to die. None, it had seemed to him, except not to leave a mess behind. Suicide—he preferred to think of it as his wrapping up—was self-centered by nature, and a man at the end of his string was bound to see himself at the focal point of it. Besides, it was his life that Inetta's death brought to a close, not

Elliott's. Now, neither one of them—Inetta gone and Elliott living higher than High Country Living—had any standing over what he was about to do.

He wondered if Meg Mogrin knew the difference between selling a property and a *place*. In town, the land underfoot was an afterthought, a rectangle just like the one next door. They had no view to speak of and could see in each other's windows but pretended they couldn't. Grew grass with city water they never had to think about. At his place, the view was the same it was a thousand years ago, and the stars weren't burned out of the night sky. When he drew from the ditch he tapped a water right a hundred years old. Whatever little he could trickle across his pasture seemed precious as blood. But maybe that didn't make the ground any more sacred than his uncle's hand-cut fence posts did. Maybe he was emotional about it after all.

No doubt people like Meg Mogrin and Elliott Ferrin could teach Leonard a thing or two about the world, but being born here didn't mean they could breeze back in and know this particular place. The truest things remained unspoken; they weren't in the damn brochure handed out to the newcomers. Native silence was a kind of power, and once you spoke the stranger's language, they had you. Once you opened up, anyone could come along and think they knew what you knew. What they could do. Where they could get ahead. How they could work around the rules or skip the costly lessons. Along comes this woman with some happy b.s. about getting his life in mind before he sells off his home place. She hires Vaughn and pumps him for information. Now she's sending letters. A little of this, a little of that. He could see it. Catch a fish by figuring out what the fish are biting.

A double knock came at the screen—knuckles rapping on the door and door tapping against the jamb. The screen mesh buzzed like a tambourine and the swinging hook added a little tick-tick-tick. Meg Mogrin stood on the stoop with a brown leather bag slung over her shoulder. "Okay, you win. No phone. You don't answer mail. I'm not even going to ask if you looked at my website."

He squinted through the screen at the yard. "Was hopin' to see the Escalade."

She frowned for a moment, tried to read him. "When I meet sellers, I take the truck. They want reassurance. My buyers are more interested in a comfortable ride."

"Seems kinda two-faced."

"I call it giving people what they want," she said, shifting the bag. "Can I come in? I'd set up out here, but you'd have to turn on the porch light."

"It's burnt out." He paused for a moment longer, then he pushed the screen ajar and she pulled it wide, drawing a protest from the rusty spring. She cleared a chair at the kitchen table, then waited for him to join her.

When he didn't, she said, "Okay. Did you read my letter?"

"Glanced at it."

"Good thing I meant for it to be a quick read. Have any questions?"

"I'm interested in why you showed up in the first place. Ain't used to strangers comin' around to offer me their services, unless it's for Easter Sunday."

She took a moment to answer. "For someone not interested in selling, you look half moved out already. Where's your livestock? You've got no mortgage and so far no liens on the property…"

She was tutoring Vaughn, all right. And what had Vaughn told her?

"You don't just drive around with a plat book lookin' for who's cleanin' up their yard. This place ain't exactly High Country Livin's style, and here you come after it. Maybe you think you smell a deal on a hardship case."

Looking dismayed, she reached toward him and said, "Let me back up. I meant to say this when we met before. It's got to be awful to have your wife's loss compounded by her medical bills, but surely you've considered this ranch is an asset that could help you out of the hole. My business isn't about exploiting anyone's hardship. It tends to sound like bull roar when I say it out loud, but my success comes from bringing together people to get what they both want. It's not curing cancer, but I can still help you, okay?"

Leonard nodded, waiting. She had one foot in sincere and one in slick.

"Then this is more to your question. There are too many listings that aren't priced to move in this market. Credit's getting tight. Development's dried up. I have to be creative or starve. I have to find sellers who can't wait and buyers who don't need to."

"And you think I can't wait."

She shook her head. "The fact is, your situation fits my client's situation and vice versa. I can help you both."

"Well, here's my situation. I owe a shitload and I don't care to know what happens to the ranch after me. None of it'll be good."

"Okay," she said. "What's your solution?"

"My business."

"Leonaarrrd…" she said, stretching toward him across the table. "You're not stuck. Give me a chance to show you."

Maybe he should've opened the damn letter after all. He crossed his arms and said, "All right."

She slid a map out of her bag, dug out a fat blue marker and drew around his property line. The map showed the adjoining sections, a few outlines of buildings, the drainage easements. His land as it existed in the assessor's files, the lawyer's office, the bank's portfolio.

"Two hundred sixty acres," she said, tapping the wedge representing his ranch. "That allows up to seven lots. For discussion, let's say you subdivide it yourself. You market them at one-twenty apiece, below the bottom end of what the Hatcher Creek lot owners are asking now. How many would you need to sell to pay off your bills? Two, three? But if that's what you're planning, you won't see that money anytime soon."

She winced sympathetically. "What else could you do, sell to other ranchers up here? Maybe that's as far as you got thinking about this."

"Maybe," he said.

"Neighbors wanting to expand." Meg rubbed the fat side of the marker around one corner of his land. "Donnie Barclay bought your other parcel across the road—suppose you already talked to him. Bureau of Land Management—no budget. Over here, Fokken the survivalist, right? No way. And back in here, the O'Neil Family Trust—not in the market. Who's left?"

She knew there was nobody. What was she setting him up for?

"You've got to talk to me. I need you to tell me what you want. It can't be just to pay your bills. What's the dream?"

He had spent the last months separating himself from the ranch and the house, acre by acre, horse by horse, item by item, memory by memory. He had prepared to let it all go because he was certain he had to. Each time in his life when he had things taken from him, he resolved to stay attached to less and less and now he was approaching perfect balance. She didn't know what she was asking.

"I won't tell you anything about me," he said, "without knowing who your client is."

"I can't disclose that. They have their own interest in privacy, but you don't have to worry. I can give you references. You can trust me."

What else would someone say right before they cheated you?

"Let me try this a different way." Meg reached again into her bag and found two plastic bottles of spring water labeled with the High Country Living logo. She set one on the table in front of him and cracked the seal on the other. "Too late for your coffee," she said. "Help yourself."

"My water's all right," he said.

She sighed, turned over the map and swept away the papers. "When something terrible happens in our lives, it can feel like our power of choice has been taken away. I had a sister who died young, and suddenly I went from older daughter to only child. I thought my life had to become worth two. It seemed my new job was to lift my parents' grief. I became a teacher. I married a nice man. I tried to be perfect in a very non-specific, non-troublesome way. I didn't choose any of it. Going with the flow, striving for perfection—those can seem like opposite choices, but they're both just lousy ways to surrender your life to another power."

Meg looked to Leonard for confirmation he was listening. "When our life turned out not to be so perfect, we separated and I moved back here while my husband and I tried to work things out. I didn't have a job. I was living with my parents again, sleeping in my sister's old room because my dad had taken over my bedroom for an office. It hadn't changed any, and I dug up a poem I'd found after she died. I thought at first she'd written it, but later I discovered she'd copied it from a Persian poet. Anyway, when I read it again, for whatever reason, the voice of this poet spoke to me through my sister's hand."

She unfolded a dollar bill. No, that was Ulysses S. Grant—a fifty, accordianed on itself until it was as thin as a pencil. She smoothed the bill and held it by the corners like she was about to read a proclamation.

> The breeze at dawn has secrets to tell you.
> Don't go back to sleep.
> You must ask for what you really want.
> Don't go back to sleep.
> People are going back and forth across the doorsill
> where the two worlds touch.
> The door is round and open.
> Don't go back to sleep.

Meg noted his quizzical expression. "He's writing about the thin boundary between the material and spiritual worlds, about seeking truth and love, about knowing why we're really here. Not having enough to live on was my great fear at the time, so I copied it onto what was a lot of money to me. Every time I looked in my purse, I had to choose—to spend it or keep going after something higher in my life."

He had heard many bullshitters in his life—salesmen who touched his shoulder and repeated his name; who asked questions about his health, his business and his family; who pretended to be interested in his point of view; who found connections, spurious and remote; who exuded success and offered to share it; who shared intimacies and invited them in return. He'd never had one read him a poem. Meg Mogrin probably knew Inetta was spiritual. Maybe she assumed the same about him.

Meg waited for a response, and when it didn't come, she

said, "Let me guess. You hate owing money and you'd hate selling even worse."

"Won't argue with that." It wasn't the whole story, but nothing ever was.

She opened a folder and slid it across the table. "Have you heard of the Conservation Easement Tax Credit?"

He knew a bit about conservation easements. Keeping the land agricultural was a good thing, but it bothered him to think of a dead man telling future generations what they couldn't do—even if he was the man. There were already too many rules and regulations laid on the land, and most of them favored those who didn't even use it. As for his situation, "Tax credits can't do much for a man with hardly no income and six hundred dollars in property taxes."

"You're lucky you live in Colorado, then, because you can sell your credit to a private party who is able to harvest the tax benefit."

"*Harvest the tax benefit*—sounds like farming the government."

"In a way. But the public gets wildlife habitat and views preserved for less than it would cost to buy the land. You get cash when you need it—even when land isn't selling—and then you can hold onto the ranch until you do decide to sell. If you don't like the tax angle, there are other scenarios. Your age works in your favor." She smiled just a little. "At least in the buyer's eyes."

She'd put together a deal that could bring him around three hundred thousand dollars. "Before you do this, you need a lawyer, a favorable appraisal, someone to manage the easement—and the right buyer. I've got them all."

The details became so much buzzing in his ears. He didn't want to know too much about how rich people got out of paying taxes, but he gathered some valuation of his property moved on another man's tax return, where the number got broken into smaller numbers, and those new numbers dispersed even further until nothing remained, not even what the man paid in the first place.

"So you're sayin' this ain't crooked." He didn't like paying the government, but he also couldn't abide the petty tax dodging he'd seen—cash wages unreported and bill of sale amounts written down.

"It's been abused," Meg said. "Inflated appraisals on land that didn't have much conservation value. They've cracked down, but this deal'll be okay."

"It'll take a while, I expect."

"A couple months or more. Do you need money sooner?"

"I was more thinkin' what if somethin' happens before the deal closes."

"Like what?"

"Like you said, I'm an old man."

"Do you have a will?"

He paused before he answered. "Only ones interested in my estate'll be collections people."

Meg reached across the table, and he thought she might take his hand if his arms weren't folded across his chest. "Then my recommendation would be not to die until this gets done," she said. "You might want to enjoy yourself for once."

"And what if I want to meet the big cheese?"

"I don't think so. He has people who handle these things."

"Like you."

"Like me. What are you worried about?"

How could he answer that? His plan had been to set himself loose from all obligations and attachments, but the ranch and his life with Inetta had seemed indivisible even at the end.

Taking money for it after she was gone felt profane. He saw Meg didn't expect him to answer. She slid her palm across the table, revealing the fifty, then pushed it off the edge with her finger so it dropped in his lap.

"What's this for?"

"Your pick. A little earnest money… or a reminder to ask for what you really want."

"Humpf." He folded it back along its creases. "Got reminders plenty."

"Don't we all," she answered. "But mostly of the wrong kind."

Dry Run

DEATH HAD BEEN ADMITTED into the room of his thoughts once Inetta sickened, and Leonard had more than a year to get comfortable with it, poke around its edges, let it tag along. He was not an impulsive man. Acting on the fly got people in trouble and he did not want trouble at Artists Point, but too much deliberation could undermine his resolve. He could face no longer being, but his last few minutes along the rim still had to be crossed and were best left theoretical for as long as possible. He donned the idea of his demise one sleeve at a time, slowly buttoned it up and wore it in his sleep. He allowed a plan to take shape in his mind, letting his methodical side consider when to arrive, where to park, how to distribute the ashes and which way to face, forward or back, as he went off. Each small decision worked out in advance reduced the chance he might be thrown off his plan.

Finally, a week before, he stood at the Artists Point overlook for a dry run and discovered his first mistake. He'd visualized the distance to the canyon floor from his accustomed waiting place along the road and had forgotten how many steps wound down to the point where he'd have to be. And instead of a sharply defined landing, the canyon bottom sloped away from the cliff face and was clotted with juniper. The drop was intimidating but not reassuring to a man seeking quick finality.

From a coffee can of sand and pea gravel brought to represent her remains, he cast some along the rim, noting how the grains scattered across the hard ground and wondering if this was what she wanted—to be crunching underfoot of tourists. He pitched handfuls over the edge to test the winds and confirmed Inetta would not fulfill her wish to float. Nor was there enough dust for him to fall wrapped in her cloud. He considered whether to hold her urn tight to his chest or to fling the remaining contents above his head when he stepped into the air. He went looking for a more extreme drop. He edged across the sloping rock of the upper rim south of the observation point, clinging to juniper limbs above where the cliff wall went concave. Inetta never scuttled over this ground this way, never focused on the abyss, even at the end. The shape of his loving gesture was getting lost. He needed to see the place the way she did—in a sweep of color and contrast, positive and negative. A place that could swallow them both whole.

Working his way back, Leonard heard tires roll to a stop above him. An engine shut off and ticked away its heat in the cooling air. Doors slammed. Laughter. Someone was coming down the steps to the overlook. He'd assumed sightseers would be off the road by dusk. Better come later next week. He ducked down beneath his hat brim and ascended quietly to the truck. He saw feet above him, then a flash of red that stopped his heart. It couldn't be, but there was no mistaking what they carried.

A voice: *Len?*

He had no breath to answer.

"It's Donnie. Donnie and Terri Barclay. What you doing out here tonight?"

"What're you up to yourself?" he said. And why the

hell did they have Inetta's quilt? The last he had seen it, she was wrapping it up in fancy paper before delivering it to the Barclay's house in town.

"You caught us," Donnie said. He had the quilt over one arm, the neck of a champagne bottle in one fist and a Maglite in the other. Terri carried a wicker basket.

Leonard should've known. Money was nothing to them. They paid all that for a damn picnic blanket. Inetta said they were happy with it. Maybe so, but how could they know the happiness it gave her? "I'll leave you to get on with it," he said, brushing past.

Terri put a hand on his arm. "How about you stay for just a bit?" She looked over at Donnie.

"We're gonna do a toast," Donnie said.

"Ain't much of a drinker."

"This won't be much of a drink."

"It's our anniversary," said Terri. "Thirty-five years."

"Congratulations." He tried to sound like he meant it. He and Inetta would've been thirty-seven together. Now, they were coming up on one year apart.

"Just have a sip," said Donnie. "Or raise a glass with us."

Terri took Leonard's elbow, gave him the basket to hold and turned him around. She walked him back down the steps to the flat ground left of the observation point and took two corners of the quilt from Donnie. They shook it out and spread it quail-side-up on the hard dirt.

Jesus. They probably didn't even remember where they got it. He felt the heat rising and wanted to leave before he said something unpleasant.

Terri patted the quilt next to her while Donnie untwisted the wire cage securing the champagne cork. "There's a story we want you to hear," she said, extending a plastic flute to Leonard.

"Donnie proposed to me on this spot. I knew something was up, because he'd never driven this far before pulling over to park."

Donnie let out a snort and the cork popped free. He guided the foaming bottle to the glass in Terri's hand, then to Leonard's. Leonard tried to hand it back to Donnie. There were only two glasses.

Donnie winked. "Don't worry about it. Me and Terri'll share."

"Anyway," Terri said, "Donnie had the thing planned out. It was a full moon, and I'd never been up here at night. He had the ring, some champagne…"

"Actually, it was Cold Duck," Donnie corrected. "Still, pretty classy. First time I ever had it. I was nervous about getting it open."

"So he brings me down to this spot for a little pre-proposal romancing and—I don't know, Donnie, what *were* you thinking?"

"Well, I didn't have it *all* planned out. I got her here and realized, until I asked her to marry me, we'd just be standing around, and then what afterwards? I wanted to be able to appreciate the moon and the stars."

"Et cetera," snickered Terri.

"Honest!" Donnie protested. "That, and she was dressed up. I was pretty sure Terri wasn't going to want to sit in the dirt."

"So he goes back up to the car and brings down this ratty camp blanket he had in the trunk."

"Best I could do."

"It was sweet. Anyway, our first anniversary came around, and Donnie says, let's go up to Artists Point again. So we did, and we brought the Cold Duck and the camp blanket and sat up here and thought back on how we'd been blessed."

"But the kids came and things, and we missed a year and then we gradually got out of the habit," Donnie said.

Terri nodded. "That's what it had become. You know, life gets filled up. You go along with it. You're not kids anymore. The ground's hard... And then I saw one of Inetta's quilts down at the Guild sale, what was it? Long time ago. It was already sold by then. It had a more or less conventional pattern, but it was like the pattern was about to explode. You know when you're watching someone come down the street and you make these snap judgments like 'old lady' or 'shoe salesman' or 'wino' and then they look you in the eye and you realize there's a real person in there? That was her quilt. It looked me in the eye, and I felt like I'd been stabbed in the heart!"

"She talked about it for two days," said Donnie.

Leonard thought of Inetta at night, her sketchbook, sewing in short little runs, the machine like a car starter: ruhr, ruhr, ruhr, trying, trying, trying.

Terri said, "I had to have something of hers, but I didn't know what. Donnie was not entirely on board with this obsession."

Donnie shrugged. "I didn't get what the deal was."

"You were a smart aleck. Inetta said she'd make something special for us. She asked if I had any old scraps of things that had meaning for me, and you said, *If she's so great, give her the camp blanket.*"

Terri turned to Leonard. "Our toast is going to go flat... I was furious with him. I thought, I'll show you. *We'll* show you. And when this came back to us, Donnie looked at me, he said..."

"I said, sonofabitch!"

She shook her head. "And *then* he said, *She brought it back to life.*"

Donnie took the glass from Terri's hand and raised it. "Inetta found something we had pushed down out of sight and out of mind. She took the quail that run through our yard and raised them up. She took this old blanket and said, why are you always looking for something new, Donnie? She showed me everything I care about in life is still right under my damn nose. She woke my ass up."

"Oh, Donnie, that's not a proper toast," said Terri.

"She woke my ass *up*," Donnie repeated. "We have not missed an anniversary here since, and we never will."

"Till death do us part," said Terri. She smiled at Leonard. "We thought you'd like that story."

The champagne warmed in his mouth, and when Leonard was finally able to open his throat, it trickled down like tears.

Scarecrow

LEONARD HAS GROWN USED TO the shocky burn of his damn prostate. The washboarded roads around the ranch provide a regular check-up, and there was never much in his day to keep him from pissing whenever and wherever he wanted. At the moment, he has to make it past the last stretch of lights illuminating Buffalo Run. He selects a break at the bottom of a long hill where a sagging sign announces a future development and a dirt track heads toward the river. He leaves the truck running, dismounts and selects the thirstiest-looking clump of bunch grass, which he waters down, to the mutual gratitude of man and plant. The weather's always been crazy but now it's getting strange. A cold snap last week froze the dog's water, and even in town it hit thirty-eight degrees. Last time a colder June day hit was 1984. Now it feels like eighty.

Something flickers in the corner of his eye. An erratic tumbling of black and white disappears with a buzz behind a clump of sagebrush. Finished, he steps further off the road toward the sound and scares up another burst. This time, he sees a raven trying to get aloft, its neck thrust through one handle of a white plastic shopping bag. Maybe it was scavenging some cast-off chicken bones; a light skeletal cargo shows through when the bag is backlit against the sky. **THANK YOU**, it says in bold red letters. **THANK YOU THANK YOU THANK YOU THANK YOU THANK YOU** HAVE A NICE DAY.

The bird tries to fly free of its clutch, but the bag serves as a drag chute that foils its effort, jerking it at odd angles as the open end catches the wind. The harder the raven flaps, the more the pouch billows and yanks it down.

He speaks low and soft, circling slowly and deliberately, trying to gentle it to him. "It's okay... It's okay." Horses would seek companionship from a man. But what does a wild bird see but threat? The raven thrashes away at his approach, the plastic thuddering like a kite reeled down from a gusty sky.

"Easy... Ea-sy."

Again the raven lands, falls, hard to tell which. It rests on the ground, heaving, its eye panicked and black. He gets near enough to see how the bird's long neck feathers catch the membrane and prevent it from sliding back over the head. Neither flight nor retreat can free it. A clever creature, but it can't escape this on its own.

He closes the distance slowly, but when he crosses some invisible threshold, the raven lurches, nearly cartwheeling before it gets in the air, one wing pointing straight up and the other beating against the tethering plastic. Working fiercely, it rises above his grasp, sinking lower as the distance widens, struggling to stay above the brushy snags. It banks sharply and dives out of sight.

"It's me or the coyotes, mister," he mutters.

He comes to a cut bank overlooking a gully. The bottom is a dry twist of sand, dotted with rocky runs and a tangle of deadwood swept up against a boulder. The raven sits dazed twenty feet below. He surveys up and down, looking for a forgiving path. He remembers the idling truck. The .32 is there. If he can't get close to the raven, it might be an option, but it wouldn't be an easy shot.

He's always measured animal lives as fractions of his, deserving respect but never sentimentality. The raven, representing neither companionship nor threat, food nor profit, lies outside his normal tables. Just one life out of many. The big bird stirs, one wing raking the rough-pebbled sand. Maybe its fate was carried in this shopping bag, just as Inetta's fate was to birth a runaway pancreas and his was to absorb whatever came at him until he walked it off the earth. He'd split fingers, broken ribs and flayed skin down to the gristle. A mare's unexpected kick was real, but the pain, he taught himself, was just a tardy signal to his brain, like the light arriving from a burned-out star. The trick was to take his mind to the moment past the injury and let pain ring all it wanted. He didn't accept the calls. But the other kind of pain sometimes slipped up behind him, quiet, a latecomer unseen at the back of a dark moviehouse. Instead of striking, it filled his mind with thoughts that slowly gained weight until his head sagged from his shoulders, and he barely had enough stuffing in him to remain upright, doing a scarecrow's job of it. Birds had it simple.

A wind has come up, or maybe he's finally noticing it. The raven walks in a tight, listless circle at the bottom of the wash, like a carnival pony on a tether. At some point, all creatures surrender, but he can't tell if the big bird is ready to submit to him. If it doesn't now, he's finished with this rescue.

He picks his way to a sharp incline of crumbling mudrock that spills into the wash. Not ideal for a man going stiff in the joints, but quicker than finding a more forgiving slope. A soft drift makes him think he can snowplow down. He steps over so the edges of his boots dig into the soil, then leans back into the hill and starts down, a dry little bow wave washing over his feet. He feels the ground harden to shale and he skids on pebbles that throw him off balance. His lead leg catches a rock as the rest of him proceeds downhill. He has just enough time to reach out his arm and think, *you dumb ass.*

How long has it been?

Lying still, he takes inventory. There's a thickening in his head rising upward from behind his right ear, as if his brain were a steak cooked only on one side. Dirt crusts in the corners of his mouth. His wrist throbs but doesn't feel broken. With the other hand he touches the back of his scalp and his fingers come back stained with a roux of blood and dust. *Can't die yet.* This seems funny to him, the way things do when they're too big to explain.

He sits upright, hugging his knees, making sure, feeling the pressure gauge throbbing in his head. Maybe he was out for only a few seconds. It felt like a few seconds. But the shadows seem farther on. He's lost his hat, a manure-spackled Resistol smudged nearly black on the brim and crown where he pushes it down against the wind. The raven is gone, too.

He spots the gouge marks where he tumbled and the hard rock ledge where he must have cracked his head. He rolls around to hands and knees and when he turns his head the earth stays on its gimbal. Vision clear. He rises carefully, ready for a dizzy spell, stands. Still steady.

Which way back up? He chooses downstream, away from the truck, where the ridgeline falls away. So much for his shortcut. He spies his hat, snagged in a clump of saltbush. He puts it on so the band rests just above the tender wedge of his scalp. At a hundred steps or so, a cascade of broken rock offers an easy staircase to the top.

He pauses there, looking once more for a sign of the raven. He caws out across the ravine—*rawk, rawk, krawk, rawk*—and waits for an answer. A gust tries to catch his hat and he presses down until it smarts. He works his way back through the scrub, picking a path around the ancient, fragile crusts that keep the desert soil anchored. Then there it is. The raven, a tree-tangled paratrooper, its chute speared by greasewood thorns.

The bird's obsidian eye, turned inward, no longer flits in panic. As it sips the air, the hackles concealing its nostrils rise and fall atop the black beak, its edges chipped and ragged. Horses blow and cows slobber, but this is the first time it occurs to him how birds breathe. The bird regards him, too. It could retreat a step into the bush or rise up to full strut, but it remains huddled. Resigned to whatever comes next. Death. What else would a bird expect?

It's okay, he whispers.

The raven is warmer than he expected, its bones barely distinguishable from the shafts of its feathers. In his fingers, the handle of the bag slips easily over the bird's head. He shakes out the bones, rolls the bag, ties it in a knot and stuffs it in his pocket. The raven takes two hops to clear itself of man and bush, looks back at Leonard as if to say, *what took you so long?* and then in three lazy beats lifts away.

One side of his neck is starting to stiffen as he makes his way back to the road, and walking the uneven ground in his boots accentuates the feeling that his entire skeleton is out of alignment. Better check his pupils when he gets back to the truck. He hears cars passing before he sees the pavement, and when he reaches it, he feels woozy all over again. Is this it? He checks the notch in the hill where he took after the bird, the flattened ground and the fallen sign. The right place, but where's the truck? Where's his goddamn truck?

And Inetta. *Sonofabitch!*

Hitch

WHAT TIME IS IT? The sun has dropped into a slot behind the cliffs, leaving the sky streaked with deep pinks and golds, while the road below seems to belong to a later hour. A deep, rhythmic thunder rumbles from far away. The Country Jam concert is miles from here, but what else could it be? His heart? He's alone at the bottom of a V in the road. No buildings in sight. It's a long way back up that steep hill to reach the nearest house, but no sense walking. The locals drive this two-lane. Someone will come by. Leonard half trots back and forth, watching for cars, checking the ground, as if his heightened agitation might make the truck rematerialize. He draws together what he knows. The truck, sitting in the open with its engine running and no one around, was just too big a temptation for some passing lowlife. It's probably headed toward Fruita, since that's the way it was pointed, and there's no sign of tracks turning around. There had to be at least two assholes involved. He gropes for evidence, trying to stay calm, pushing down the thing he knows for certain. *The pistol.* Oh, shit, they'll find his pistol. They'll cook up some scheme that makes sense only to idiots on drugs, and someone'll get hurt because he brought along a gun he should've sold long ago.

And the ashes. God damn! Does the urn look valuable? He

hopes it looks like something they can sell or give to their girl-friend and that they don't look inside and toss the contents out the window in their disappointment. Or out of spite. He feels himself shivering. It's not even cool out and his teeth are chattering. How could he slog through a whole damn year, get down to the last few miles, and then screw it up like this?

Sonofabitch! There's nothing to break, nothing to slug, nothing to do but roar into the gathering night. An airy, mocking version of it bounces back at him from the cliffs. His breath comes shallow and fast. He needs to calm down. It wouldn't matter if the thieves were twenty-five years old, six feet tall and three feet wide; his brain's still nineteen and ready for war. His whole life, he's tamped down anger—most every feeling—because you can't run a ranch that way. In the country, following your emotions leads to mistakes. You get bit when you get mad, whether by the mechanism you misjudged, by the enemy you created or by the poison anger puts in your belly. It does you no good, and yet right now, what's the alternative? He tries to think. Tries to put himself in the place of the thieves. Tries to reason through what a couple dumbasses will do with his truck. But thinking won't get him there. It won't speed up all that has to unfold at its own pace. To hell with the truck. He's already let it go. He needs Inetta's ashes and a way up to Artists Point. Tonight, like he promised.

Someone's coming down the long hill from the west. He steps across the road to meet the car. Stop, goddamn it. A Buick slows. Two shrunken old folks who can barely see over the dash swing wide once they see him clearly. He feels his chest expanding and the lump on his head throbs. *He needs to calm down.*

He crosses back to the pullout and bends over the scrabble, looking for clues, as if someone jumping out of another car and peeling off with his truck would leave a trail any different than the others who'd pulled over here to piss or fix a tire or see if they could get down to the river. Nothing. Nothing more than the usual roadside litter that attracted the raven—greasy paper and fast food cups, crushed plastic water bottles and cigarette packs. An empty Karkov vodka bottle. He picks it up with his finger inside the neck in case it turns out to be evidence, but the bottle is long dry inside, and how would fingerprints help him, anyway. He's got nothing. Nothing except the pressure building inside, his chest full of something other than oxygen.

Another car approaches, a grey Subaru Outback, a bicycle standing upright on a rooftop rack. Leonard lifts his hat to wave at the driver and feels the pulltab of blood-stuck hair peel away from his scalp. The Outback slows and the driver sets the flashers. A youngish man, late thirties, with his elbow slung out the window. He still wears his fingerless cycling gloves. The bicycle has the seat up high and handlebars down low, like those Leonard sees grinding up and flying down Monument Road. Takes a skinny man to stay bent in that position for long.

"Having some trouble?" the man says. His curly hair has been embossed by his helmet into a triple mohawk.

"A bit," says Leonard. "Got my truck stole. Now I'm in a pickle."

"I'm sorry. You reported it?"

"Got no way to call 'em." *Reported* sounds too neutral, too passive. He wants to track those losers down and then get up on the Monument and be done with his losses, not fill out paperwork about them.

"Here, use mine," says the man.

Leonard's seen cell phones before, but not one half-covered with rubber nubbins. "I just wanna call the cops, not type 'em a letter."

The man taps the keys on the BlackBerry, listens for a ring and hands it over. A dispatcher methodically takes Leonard's information, and for a moment, her official manner almost calms him. One step at a time, the facts, get it in the system. That's the way to solve this.

"Do you want to wait for an officer?" she asks.

He does not want to wait. Not a second longer. She asks him to hold. It's dawning on him again how hopeless the search will be. This is the Valley of White Pickups with all the oil field service rigs and work trucks that sit in the sun all day. His is a dually with a tail light out. That might be enough to get it pulled over, but the odds of it happening tonight are slim.

"Mr. Self?" The dispatcher is back on the line. "You're the owner of this vehicle?"

"Yep."

"And you last saw your vehicle about an hour ago?"

"Somethin' like that."

"This same vehicle has been in your possession over the last twenty-four hours?"

"I've been in it." What the hell was this?

"Is it possible, sir, someone you know might've taken it without your permission? Or you forgot where you parked it."

"I'm out in the middle of the boonies!"

"Well, sir, I'm trying to get the chronology straight."

What chronology? He thinks about hanging up but doesn't know how.

"Sir, do you have a number where we can reach you? Is this a good number?"

"Don't know. I guess."

"I'm going to give you the report number. You have something to write with?"

"Go ahead." He doesn't write it down. What would be the point?

Leonard returns the phone. The man says, "Don't you want to call your insurance company, too?"

He doesn't want to say his insurance has lapsed along with everything else. "Got bigger problems right now, and I don't even know what they all are."

"Okay, none of my business. Let me know if I can help. This's not a great night to get the cops excited about a stolen car"—he nods in the direction of Country Jam—"unless it has a baby strapped in a car seat. Shall we call them back?"

The man's trying to cheer him up. Leonard's beyond cheering.

"Hey, Leonard. My name's Joe. I can give you a ride home or something."

"How'd you know my name?"

"You gave it to the dispatcher. Are you okay? Why don't you climb in?"

Leonard doesn't move. Joe steps out of the Subaru. He looks ridiculous with his plastered hair, tight shirt covered with logos, those biker girdle shorts, and sandals with socks "It might take days for them to find your truck," Joe says. "You can't wait out here. Where do you live?"

Leonard's brain was moving so fast before. Now his thoughts feel caked with gumbo. "Need to find it tonight."

"You might be dehydrated. Here." Joe offers a nippled water bottle from the back seat. The water's too warm but Leonard drinks it down and it feels good. "It's no problem to take you somewhere. Or we can call someone. What do you think?"

What *does* he think? He'd whittled down complication and peeled himself away from people so he didn't have to make any more decisions. And now he's got no goddamn plan. Who the hell did he have left to involve in his mess? Leonard isn't going to ask Joe to haul him around looking for his truck. He can't call Winnie. Not his neighbors. Vaughn? That was almost funny. It was practically Vaughn's truck now. He can think of only one person who won't make things worse.

The High Country Living phone rings through to a recording that tells him to press one to leave a message, two if he needs immediate assistance. You could say he did. He presses two.

Vaughn Hobart must've moved up in the world.

"The hot calls roll over here when she's busy," Vaughn explains. "I'm on my way to a meetin'. What's goin' on?"

Was there any point? He'd never asked Vaughn for anything, never trusted him to follow through. He doesn't want to tell him about Inetta's ashes, and the idea of driving around the county in a droopy Crown Vic edges him closer to despair. But his real estate savior didn't answer, and who else has he got now—Vaughn or this Subaru-driving stranger in stretch pants?

Vaughn doesn't hesitate. "Where are you?"

Leonard arranges to meet Vaughn in Fruita, just a few miles away. The semi-utopian farm town on a corner of the Dinosaur Triangle had remained dry until well into the seventies. Now the mountain bikers living there are trying to make up for lost time. Joe takes him to a bustling pizza joint on a corner of the quiet main street and insists on waiting with him. Out front, kids on bikes practice standing on one wheel. Customers wait in line to order from a chalkboard menu, then cluster around wooden tabletops embedded with bicycle parts. Tattooed women serve up beer, pizza and salads at a constant clip and the doors are open front and back to coax through a little breeze. The pressed tin ceiling buzzes with the talk of happy young people who've brought the old place back to life. Far too cheerful a place for how he feels.

"You probably want to go home now," Leonard says. "I'm okay waitin'."

"No problem. I'm hungry, and I need to wash down the story I had to write this afternoon," Joe says, taking delivery of a Fat Tire over the counter and downing a long swallow before they reach a table. "You probably heard Rob Rydeen's getting ready to run for the state House."

"Heard his radio show long enough to turn it off. That's about it."

Joe leans forward, hard to tell whether it's so Leonard can hear him over the surrounding chatter or so no one else does. "I don't suppose that makes you a Democrat."

"I'm nothin'," Leonard says.

"Well, he's cooked up this event called Values of the Valley to celebrate how capitalism, moral correctness and constitutional principles are responsible for everything good around here. He's going to re-recognize every local conservative who's ever won an award for anything—and I mean anything. It's pretty transparent he's making an end around the party by flattering all these people in front of their friends. But can I write that? No. An intern could've taken the story straight from the press release, but the publisher wanted my byline on it. He's either trying to show how impartial the paper is or get me to quit."

"You're with the paper then," Leonard says.

"So far." Joe pulls from his pint. "I came up to your ranch once, I think. We never actually met. You wouldn't talk to me."

"I remember. Junior stayed with us a long time before that other stuff happened. Us talkin' about him didn't seem proper."

"It's fine—your choice," Joe says. "Personal things don't necessarily belong in the news, but I wonder if you'll talk to me now."

"About what?"

Joe signals for another beer. "I was thinking about Hardy Junior when I rode past Half Tunnel today. I'd say it was quite a coincidence to run into you, except I think about him every time I'm up there—and that's a lot of days."

"You just ride up and down it?" Leonard wasn't sure he wanted to get into this.

"When I don't have time for the full loop. It's worth it just to feel your heart hammer on the climb and then you get to look out over the valley as you swoop back down through the curves. You hug your line between the rock and the void and fly all the way home."

Leonard thinks how he's been driving Monument Road since before Joe was born. "I always felt like them curves just slowed me down."

"You can't get the same feeling in a car. If you rode a bike, your trip'd never get old."

"Hate to break the news, but if you hang around long enough, everything gets old."

Joe laughs, then turns serious. "On second thought, maybe I don't need you to talk to me about Hardy Crimmins. Maybe I'm the one who needs to talk." He extends the pizza platter toward Leonard, who declines. "Back then, I had this idea I was going to open people's eyes to the low-rent child abuse that seemed to be always going on here. I wasn't after him specifically, I just thought his case might help illuminate the issue. I'd dig into causes, discover whether it was really a widespread problem, uncover any other factors behind the accusations. Maybe change things for the better. The story on his arrest was just the first installment. The second was about the day Hardy went off Monument Road. I never wrote the third one."

Joe trades his empty glass for the full one and takes a quarter off the top.

"His death kind of kicked the stuffing out of me, and I didn't feel much like the enterprising journalist for a long time. See, I had him on the phone. I was talking to him right then on Monument Road. He was anguished about ruining his sister's life, but I didn't think he was suicidal. I was just trying to get him to pull over so it'd be safer to talk. I'll never know if that's why he drove up there or if something changed because I called."

Leonard is done with regrets. He doesn't want to think about the past. He'll be joining it soon enough.

"Can't help you on that."

Vaughn ambles in the door, canted, about to draw the cell phone holstered on his belt. Someone trails him, and it takes Leonard a moment to recognize Pinky Allred, beard shorn, face rosy—from scrubbing, it looked like, instead of booze.

"I was goin' to give you some shit, but now I see you, I think you need a hug." When Leonard doesn't laugh, Vaughn claps him on both shoulders. "Okay, what's this all about? I only know enough to be confused."

Leonard shrugs. He's not ready to give specifics. Not in front of a newsman who might happily chase a stolen cremation urn story. "I want to find them bastards tonight. Personal business."

"All right," Vaughn says. "You called the office; I thought it was the other. Let's narrow 'er down. How much fuel you got in it?"

"Not much," says Leonard. "Couple gallons." Enough to take him back up top for sure.

"They won't fill it with diesel at four sixty-seven, so they won't go far then, you think, Pinky?"

Pinky squinches his mouth to the side as if the question gave him a toothache. "I'd say they might strip it. Or go rob some place and ditch it."

Pinky should know. When Leonard pictured his truck thieves, Bryce Deaver and Pinky Allred came easily to mind.

"Let's hope for door number two," Vaughn says. "Then we'll have some help for sure. Otherwise, not with so much goin' on over Country Jam way. They got all the county deputies and the off-duties over there. Unless them fuckers run into a sobriety check, they're prob'ly good for a while."

Leonard says, "I ain't ridin' with a driver who's been drinkin'."

Pinky finds this hilarious. He slaps his thighs and bends over.

"Then you ain't been payin' attention," says Vaughn. "We skipped our AA meetin' to help your ass."

Joe looks all too interested in the action. Leonard gets up to break it off and Joe stands, too. Vaughn gapes at the revelation of Joe's Lycra cycling shorts. "He ain't comin' with us, is he? Only got room for three."

"I can fit you all in the Outback," Joe offers.

"You've done me favor enough, Joe. Don't want to impose no more."

Joe starts to protest and Vaughn jumps in. "How-ever," he says, "Joe could do *me* a big favor, as long as he's gonna stay and finish his pizza. I left the boss a message we was meetin' a client here—I kept your name out of it, Leonard—and it wouldn't surprise me if she decided to head on over. Now things've changed a bit, and I got her Jimmy. She don't like extra miles put on it." Vaughn winks at Leonard. "So we're takin' off now. You mind? Meg Mogrin. She dresses real good," he looks Joe over, "about your age, and she's held up pret-ty nice. Tell her I got everything under control."

Joe's still hoping for an invitation. "Why don't you just call her and tell her?"

Vaughn is already crab-walking Leonard toward the door. He speaks to Joe as if it were obvious. "'Cause I don't want to have to lie to her."

Leonard and Pinky shuffle for shotgun while Vaughn searches his pockets for the key. He motions for Pinky to take the middle. Pinky slides over and inclines his face toward Leonard, though his kicked-dog eyes don't make contact. "It's been a while. I done treatment—court mandated, but still. Takes a while to see things. Now Vaughn's kinda my sponsor."

"That right." Leonard has heard the reform and recovery lines from Vaughn too many times to be completely sold by this, but he needs the help right now and they are all he has. The day is ebbing and his promise to Inetta wasn't just some general affirmation. *A year to the day*, she had asked, and today was the day. Somehow, with all his preparations and his focus on getting himself through it, he lost the handle on that truth. Today isn't just the final day of his plan. *This is the day I lost her. Now I've lost her again.*

"You got anything you'd like to share with the group?" Vaughn says to Leonard.

Not now. Not in front of Pinky. "Why'd you bring Meg's Jimmy if she don't want you runnin' up the miles?"

"Same reason you took a ride from Mister Fancy Pants," says Vaughn. "My Crown Vic's temporarily indisposed."

Leonard would like to see Vaughn's expression when he learns his transportation shortcomings are going to end, but the secrets of this day are all bound up together, so he asks instead, "What's wrong with it now?"

"It don't like four-dollar gas," says Pinky, leaning into Leonard as Vaughn swats at him. From the whiff of him, the rest of Pinky's not as fresh-scrubbed as his face.

"You got anything on 'em?" Vaughn asks. "How they got there. Which way they mighta went."

"Truck was pointed west. Didn't see any sign they turned around."

"Well, maybe. Half the time what you see just confuses things, anyway, so let's go with what we know about assholes who steal cars."

Vaughn starts the pickup and scans the quiet side street before pulling away from the curb. "One is, they're lazy. Don't like to walk. Might just've took it for a short ride. Two is, most ain't too bright. I mean, why face a felony for somethin' that's risky to hang onto and hard to sell?" He looks over at Pinky. "So then what?"

"Three," Pinky says.

"Jesus, Pinky," says Vaughn, winking across at Leonard, "you got a short attention span. They take it where they can chop it. And three is, they don't take it to Buffalo Run. More, it's places like this." Vaughn steers the Jimmy toward a white F-350 in a sports bar parking lot. Right model, but the bumper sticker makes clear it's not Leonard's.

If you can read this
KISS MY ASS!

"I gotta get me one of them," Vaughn says.

I'm riding around with a posse of clowns. Leonard slouches against the door and thinks about hitting the handle right there.

Messenger

VAUGHN'S DESCRIPTION OF HIS BOSS serves well enough to identify the lithe woman in the grey silk suit who sweeps in the door. *Pret-ty nice.* She's not completely out of place in the pizza joint, but Meg scans the tables in the manner of someone come from somewhere more important, and—if he didn't know better—from somewhere in his past.

She follows his voice to the source. Her face conveys recognition but her eyes flicker over him and come away empty. It's not a big city, and she's in sales. She expects to know people who recognize her.

"How *are* you?" she says with practiced familiarity. "It's been—what, since…?" A professional holding him off, inviting him to fill in the gap while she searches for Vaughn and the chance to extricate herself.

"I've been trying to figure that out myself," he says. "Your man Vaughn asked me to watch for you in case you showed up."

"And?"

He realizes his instructions weren't that precise. "And to let you know they, uh, had to take off."

"Oh, sweet, so he sent a bicycle messenger."

He hopes she's joking. He remembers his helmet hair and makes a casual swipe to rearrange it.

"So who was with him? Vaughn said he was meeting a client here. You can appreciate that made me nervous."

Joe doesn't feel inclined to cover for Vaughn—especially since he doesn't know what he's covering—and he decides he doesn't want to lie to this woman, either. "Leonard Self. I found him standing along the road and brought him here. I didn't learn too much, except that his truck was stolen. He's a bit... taciturn."

Meg rolls her eyes. "So that was it. Did they say anything about being on the Monument? Was anyone else with Leonard?"

"Pinky was with Vaughn."

"*Pinky*? Vaughn has a girlfriend?"

"A guy. A protégé of Vaughn's, I guess."

"Vaughn's protégé. Okay, that's funny. And Vaughn's mine—my project. Was anyone else along?"

"No, but I was supposed to tell you he had everything under control."

"This is great. Nobody's answering their cells. It's not my idea of being under control. I suppose I should just trust him to do what he's doing. Thanks for waiting for me, at least."

She looks ready to leave. He wants her to stay, at least until he figures out what makes her presence so familiar and unsettling. Is it how she picked up on *taciturn* and *protégé*? Or is it just the second beer?

"I think I know you from somewhere," he ventures.

"My picture's in the real estate section all the time."

"No, way before now."

"This doesn't involve reincarnation, I hope. My past lives are kind of a blur."

Is it a brush off or just her sense of humor, he wonders. "I went to Junction. My name's Joe Samson. I'm a reporter for *The*

Clarion." Harmless, in other words.

"Not one of the port-a-potty Samsons!"

Great. Instead of recognizing his by-line, she associates his name with the big blue plastic suppositories.

"In college, the drunks used to knock them over," she says. "I remember thinking: so that's where they put the P in Samson."

"That's the first good one I've heard," he says. "So you grew up here, then? I don't remember any Mogrins."

"Oh, that's my married name—former. I kept it because it worked better for my job. In the old days, I was Margaret Vavoris."

Boneyard

THE FIRST LEG OF VAUGHN'S TOUR passes a refinery, a feedlot and several drilling supply yards that have nearly been emptied to outfit the current gas boom. Vaughn turns off the highway and follows a section road north into the flat farm country. He slows to a roll and peers toward a cluster of trailers and outbuildings set among a scraggle of Russian olives. A blue light flickers from one of the trailers. Vaughn turns the truck around in the middle of the road. "Looks like everybody's home and cozy tonight," he says.

Vaughn keeps up a commentary on the employment status, family arrangements, criminal histories and personality quirks residing in the houses he checks off his list of potential destinations for Leonard's truck. He lingers outside a yard that features an El Camino with a crumpled front hood parked on what should be the lawn. "I want that baby for my next ride. I keep waitin' for him to figure out he's never gonna fix it."

Leonard's not sure Vaughn will fix it, either. "How do you know all these people?"

Vaughn looks across Pinky at Leonard. "How you think? You live up where a man can't buy a drink or a cuppa coffee. Don't chase women. Worked mostly on your own and stayed outa jail. I should be askin' how come you know anybody at all."

They cruise up to a fenced-in storage yard with a pad-locked gate. Vaughn cuts the lights and stops the truck. "Look in the back, Pinky," he says. "Got some bolt cutters back there." He winks at Leonard. "Never know in this business when you'll need a set of bolt cutters."

"Which business is that?" Leonard says.

Two monstrous brown tanks bristling with bolts lie top-pled just inside the fence. Stacks of pipes, hoppers and rails. Pagodas of wooden pallets. A webbed conveyor belt detached from the rollers twists serpent-like through a sea of green thistles that will be a scribble of tumbleweeds by fall. A yellow and black CAUTION DOGS ON PREMISES sign rusts at the bullet holes.

Leonard suddenly remembers. "Shit, Vaughn, I had a pis-tol left in the glove box."

"Now you tell me. Well, get ready to run." He finds a short length of rebar and boomerangs it high over the fence. It hits something hard and dings a few metallic notes before going quiet. No dogs. No nothing.

They move up to the gate. There are no vehicles in view, though parts appear around a trailer and spill out of a crum-bling shed. Its siding has weathered to the bare boards and the roof has sloughed all but a few splinters of its wooden shakes. From the arrangement of the empty doorway and glassless windows, it must once have been a residence. Beyond the shed, towers of tire rims are stacked against the remains of an adobe wall that looks even older. The scene recalls the junk piles he saw at the C. Edwards establishment, a monument to fleeting abundance. Here the faltered machinery seems more sunken in place and the soil less likely to be reclaimed.

Rock-bottom old timers had chosen near-worthless fringeland like this—or been pushed into it—and for a while had taken pride in their ability to scrape together a life from almost nothing. They had counted on the land's difficulty to isolate them from the costs and corruption of civilization. But others followed, men with a knack for turning wilderness and wasteland into Zion, if only temporarily. This is where everything is headed, he thinks. It's right to get out now. It's okay to stop. There was once nothing here and how easily it would return to nothing.

Vaughn leans into the fence. His fingers, laced through the chain link, spread like talons. "No need for them nippers. Nobody home," he says. "This was my hot prospect."

"Somebody lives here?"

"I wouldn't say that. They still come here." He pulls back and turns square to Leonard. "So where the hell were you when they stole your truck?"

"Savin' a raven."

"Savin' a raven." Vaughn says this like he's filing it away for future reference. "I didn't know you'd gone all religious on us." Pinky, silent behind them until now, snorks at the joke.

"It was all tangled in a plastic bag." Leonard remembers the bag in his pocket and shows it to Vaughn, as if his story needs proving.

"*Thank you Thank you*," Vaugh reads. "Well, I hope he 'preciated it."

"Don't know if a bird knows the difference," Leonard says. "All it knows is bein' alive."

Vaughn considers this. "Yeah, how can you really 'preciate somethin' unless you know what it's like to do without?"

"I don't know if it works that way with dyin', but it sure does with pussy," says Pinky.

Vaughn shoots Pinky a look. "Hey-hey-hey, don't let's be talkin' about pussy. Leonard lost his missus last year. Have some damn respect."

"I wasn't talkin' about his wife," Pinky protests.

"Don't matter," Vaughn says.

Leonard moves away and waits by the Jimmy while Vaughn finishes setting Pinky straight. *Vaughn the sponsor.* What's Meg Mogrin done with him? He's only about half half-assed now.

The two men shuffle back. Pinky sets the bolt cutters in the back. The truck starts up like a throat clearing.

Leonard supposes he should be grateful for the company and on another night, he might've been. But tonight, while he's full of urgency and distress, they're killing time, babysitting him. Abner drove him and his sister around like this one Christmas Eve, craning his neck up at the miraculous sky over Glade Park, pretending to see a sleigh high among the stars, while the kids worked themselves into a frenzy of anticipation, Leonard frustrated and Emma bawling because she couldn't see it. When they returned, he found Santa had left him a tin plate popgun that shot a cork on a string. Quite a disappointment. Popguns were for town kids, and what was he going to shoot with it, anyway? He wanted a real gun.

Santa only brings toys, his father growled. *Be grateful he even found you.*

By the next fall, Leonard thought he'd figured out the Santa business and swore not to fall for that drive with Abner again. It was better to be honest.

So he tells them about Inetta's ashes, about his promise. Not the whole deal, of course. Just enough.

Samaritan

A COP ONCE EXPLAINED TO JOE how violence and death invested a place with an invisible spirit layer, and how over his years in law enforcement, his mind had overlaid the city with a ghost map of names and faces. He couldn't pass certain street corners and addresses without remembering gut-stuck fight victims, drunken crashes, children beaten by their mothers' boyfriends, frozen homeless men—the cases where he'd arrived too late. He had a hard time seeing the city the way other people did.

Joe thought he understood. The ravel of Monument Road had become that place for him, with milestones for moments he'd been caught unaware, afraid, ineffectual and mistaken, holding back too much or pushing too far. Helen marked Cold Shivers Point, of course, and tied him to Neulan's crimes. The ghost of Junior Crimmins guarded Half Tunnel near the west end. As he cycled between them, the road commanded all his senses, his blood and his breath. He came to know it in all conditions, felt he could sense any disturbance in its silent and ancient spirit. And always, he patrolled ready for another chance. A time when the man of words would be a ready man of action.

He imagined coming upon someone coiled on a ledge

like a diver, or perhaps a tremulous swimmer clinging for a moment before pushing into the deep end. Joe would glide smoothly to his side and hover, ignoring the depths, until the man submitted himself to Joe's sure and steady stroke. Or an anguished woman, eyes wild and wet, clothing torn, arms flailing as she hurtled toward the abyss. He would race after her and catch her at the last second and they would tumble together on the rock and he would comfort her with a long embrace. Or a despondent drunk, wavering on his perch, staring at the pinnacles like bottles on the back bar. Joe would take up the next stool. Let pass a neutral greeting. Share a joke:

God took three men to the top of a tall cliff and told them, because of the good lives they'd led, they'd be given one chance to leap off and enter heaven in any earthly form they desired.

The first man trotted toward the cliff's edge, jumped into the air and declared, "I want to be a falcon!" Instantly, he changed into a falcon and soared into heaven.

The second man ran to the edge, jumped into the air, cried, "Eagle," and instantly changed into an eagle that flew into heaven.

The third man sprinted forward and just as he reached the edge, he tripped on a rock and shouted, "Shit!"

A chuckle. Routine inquiries turn to deeper ones. Disappointments are shared. Tragedies revealed. And then, arms across shoulders, the two new compadres head back to the road.

But it never seemed to go like that except in the movies. Out here there was too much country and too few timely Samaritans. In the real world, hurting souls could easily place themselves on invisible cliffs in unreachable places—their intentions cloaked most of all from those closest to them. Helen's death was classified an accident but remained a mystery. No superman could arrive in time to stop Junior's plunge. Even the best defense, ongoing love and attention, too often proved not to be enough, and friends and family were left gasping the newly emptied air. Almost every week and sometimes more than once, the newspaper had to decide whether to acknowledge that someone else in the valley had found a doorway out.

Joe walks Meg past a beer-sign-illuminated crew blowing smoke haloes over a clutch of Harleys. Somehow a prickly pear cactus blossoms pink from a wine barrel planter studded with cigarette butts. She stops at her car and extracts her keys in a manner calculated to discourage extended talk. The curb will have to do for what he needs to say.

"Leonard and his wife were once foster parents for someone I was writing a story about years ago. I wanted to talk to him about what happened to the kid. He wasn't interested."

"I'm not surprised. He's had a tough year and this was an important day for him."

"Important? Beyond his truck getting stolen?"

"I don't talk about my clients' affairs. What happened to the boy?"

"He drove a van off the Monument. I was on the phone with him when he went over."

Meg turns her back toward the bikers. The Monument carves a distant line above them, visible against the darkened sky. "On purpose?"

"Yes."

"I gather you knew my sister."

She was making the transition easy for him. "I did, a bit. I liked Helen. And I'm so sorry about what happened. I was a kid then, wrapped up in myself, and I didn't think I was close enough to reach out to your family. And then time passed and it seemed too late to say anything without reopening the pain."

"It's okay. It's never too late. But I stopped looking for sympathy cards a long time ago."

"There's more, though, and I feel like I should say it. About Helen and Neulan Kornhauer."

"You don't need to tiptoe. I'm used to it." She says it evenly, but she braces herself against the car door. "He's a thrilling story. I mean, Ted Bundy only passed through town once. Neulan, the psychotic choirmaster, dwelt among us. By getting mixed up with him, Helen's life was reduced to one short sentence—the one about how she died. Period. If you knew her, you know she was more than that."

He's taken the trail to this exposure and now can't decide whether to edge over it facing the wall or the abyss.

"She was," he says. "She carried this spark that always seemed ready to explode whatever was around her. Her ferocity attracted me and intimidated me both. I assumed it was the same for Neulan."

"Do you think he killed her?"

He's unready for her directness. "I think he was culpable."

She frowns. "You *are* a word man, aren't you?"

"Look, I'm trying to confess here. It's hard. I didn't know exactly what happened on Cold Shivers with Neulan, but I thought my experience with Helen somehow reflected a universal truth. I defended him at the time because of what I believed about the two of them—she was the risk-taker, he was just a nerd. I thought if I did the right thing, it would lead to the right result. But I couldn't see all the way inside Neulan."

"No one could. So you and I and a busload of church people couldn't save her. How do you protect someone who's so fearless? Lock her up? Make her afraid?"

"But what if my story freed Neulan to go on to harm other women? He could still be at it somewhere."

Meg squeezes her hands together hard, as if her right side is trying to get the left to submit. "You don't know that, Joe. And even if he were out there, what would you do this time? We had our chances. More than once."

"You?"

"Neulan Kornhauer called me." She says it as if Edgar Allen Poe wrote the line. "Right before he disappeared. I actually met him at Cold Shivers—with my ex along—I'm not nuts. He seemed anxious to assure me he hadn't harmed Helen."

"He told me he could never kill anyone, because murderers burn in hell."

"We can hope," she says grimly. "I'm dealing with my own stuff now. Helen's murder, suicide, fatal accident, whichever you want to call it, forced me to see how indifferent the world is and how little I actually control—about this much…" She opens her arms to the width of her shoulders. "And sometimes, not even that."

He resists the impulse to step closer. "I think we need an exorcism."

"What?"

"Or voodoo. Drive Neulan out for good. Create a little circle of hell for him right here. So he doesn't still hang over us. We want to remember Helen, but here we are, still stuck on Neulan Kornhauer."

"When I asked Neulan to meet me, I told him it was so we could exorcise Cold Shivers."

"Did it work?"

"I just don't go there."

Joe can't tell if she's troubled by his suggestion, but he plunges ahead, pulling a free newspaper from a street rack, and starts ripping away, shaping a head and shoulders out of a four-page section, producing eight arms and four torsos. "Pretty crude. I wanted to give the full string-bean body effect, but let's agree it's him. Got a match?"

"You want to burn it right here on the street?"

"Him. His evil spirit. His entire suffocating story. As an offering to Helen."

Meg shakes her head and loosens a smile. "I don't smoke, but I know who does."

A big man with a biker braid growls something and the rest of his group turns to watch Meg's approach. She steps confidently into their circle and gestures toward Joe. Whatever she says is worth a good laugh—and a butane lighter.

"Good job. What was so funny?"

"I told them you were getting cold."

"Seriously?"

"You're the one in the spandex. The big guy wanted my phone number for it."

"And you gave it to him?"

"I gave him Vaughn's. I'm pissed he's not answering my calls."

Joe holds the effigy toward her so its arms flutter in the breeze. "Go ahead. Light it. Do you know any spells?"

"I thought you were the exorcist," she says.

"My only qualification is ex-altar boy, but I can think of one thing that fits."

"Go for it."

"Grant us the serenity to accept the things we cannot change; the courage to change the things we can; and the wisdom to know the difference."

Meg's hands, fisted in prayer, slowly relax. "It sounds so simple when you say it like that." She holds the lighter to the effigy's arm. The flame catches and licks up one side, spreading through the layers. Joe holds on as long as he can, then drops Newspaper Neulan in the street. The burning figures slowly curl away from each other. Arms separate and send up black puffs that turn to thin white exhalations as their fire dies. Soft grey ash scoots across the pavement and disappears. One body, another, until the final one flickers in surrender.

Meg stares through the spot on the ground where the darkness last sealed itself. Joe had meant this ceremony to be light, to reduce Neulan to a cartoon, down to nothing, but her mood seems heavier now. She raises her eyes to him. "This wasn't quite right for me. But thanks for trying."

The group in front of the bar has watched in silence, but now a voice booms from the blue and red glow: "Sweetheart, you need some *wood* if you want to start a *fire*." A ripple of laughter, then the riders begin to mount their bikes. Screaming ignitions awaken a metallic bullfrog chorus.

"Look at our friends over there," Meg says, "riding on the last vapors of the dinosaurs. You think they care the fire's about to go out? They feel like kings. I can't look back *or* forward without seeing the end. Maybe it's my sister. Maybe it's this valley. How can we look around us and believe God put us at the center of creation? All of humankind's just a morning mist that's mistaken itself for the ocean!"

Joe feels suddenly exposed in his cycling attire, inadequate to the moment, but he takes the chance. He opens his arms toward Meg—shoulder-wide—and says, "All the more reason for us drops to stick together."

"I'm not Helen," she says and steps in just long enough for him to know she will not be back.

Amends

LEONARD HAD LEFT THE RANCH with a mental list of his few remaining steps. Take the last handful of bone chips out of the blue pot. Set it safe on a flat stone before climbing over the rail. Face east and push away hard as you let go. Open your hand quickly and flick up the ashes. Hold silent to the bottom.

Some piss poor plan it turned out to be.

He no longer scans every driveway and parking lot. No one does. The cab is close with the sour smell of warmed-over sweat. Vaughn's phone goes off and he smothers it without looking at the call. Leonard leans against the door, his temple pressed to the cooled window glass. Driving around created an illusion of progress for all of them, but somewhere in the meandering Leonard lost his anticipation, then his patience and eventually his impatience, leaving only sub-thoughts dark around the edges. Exhausted, he could succumb to the drowse tugging at him, except for Pinky's jiggling right leg filling the cab with his pent-up anxiety. Leonard's chest throbs with a noxious fullness, which feels more radioactive than alive. He might as well be in a space capsule with no room to move and no way home. If he stepped outside he'd expire with the one breath left in him, a frozen husk floating forever.

It had once seemed important to clarify for himself he

was not planning a suicide; he'd simply picked his day to die—a day that joined him with Inetta once more in the purest way possible, with a promise fulfilled, at the time requested, in the place that mattered most. He couldn't suddenly undo this and flow the other direction. This all was decided long ago. He thought now of his old man going through his final day. What were his preparations? There was no one to ask and none to tell. Leonard had always imagined him bursting out wild and angry in the moment, but maybe he came to it quiet and methodical. Leonard can see now how his father might have thought he had to resolve every earthly obligation.

Vaughn has endured the silence for as long as he can stand it. "You know, we don't have to continue this shit if you've had enough. I get makin' a promise. I do. But what's another day or two? A week, if it takes that? She'd cut you some slack. She always did."

"What do you know about it?" Leonard's tone is fierce, meant to cut this off.

Vaughn steers through a trailer park, hardly look-ing around, easing over the speed bumps, gathering himself. Finally, he says, "Inetta didn't have much use for me, but I seen enough of her to know you were one lucky sonofabitch. I ain't sayin' you didn't deserve some luck, but goddamn, Len, you got to have her before you lost 'er! I never got within a mile of a chance with a woman like that. A woman who damn near car-ries you and lets you think you're doin' all the work? A woman who fits all your knobs and your moodiness and your dumb shititude? A woman who just goes about her business without expectin' you to help fold the doilies and go to church every Sunday? I can't imagine what that's like, but if I had it, I know I'd hate like hell to lose it.

"Don't take this wrong, but once I found a nice pair of

gloves in a café booth. Real soft, with little holes for your knuckles and a snap across the back. I shoulda turned 'em in, but they fit me perfect and so I kept 'em. Made me feel like a rich man. One day, I lost the left. Dropped it somewhere. Half a pair ain't much use, but I never could toss it. Kept the right one, hopin' it would bring back the other, I guess. It killed me to have it, too, 'cause it reminded me how sweet it was when I had 'em both.

"Here's what I do see about this. Some things won't never come back no matter how long you hang on. Most men find 'em a new woman quick as they can. I ain't tellin' you what to do here, I'm just observin'. I shoulda said some of this before, but I ain't too good with this sensitive shit, and I figured you'd just go all crotchety and silent on me anyhow. Kinda like now. So, I never said much the times I come by when she was sick and after. Didn't feel I had the standin'. Didn't seem you were ready to hear it. Anyway, I'm sorry I wasn't a better friend on it."

Sorry. Leonard tries to remember when Vaughn did come by. Was Vaughn there early when he was still so numb he might have missed if the President himself dropped in? Did he get lost among the waves of church people? Was he in there somewhere with the stragglers? He was a talker and he would have stood out amid the quiet tidying by the ladies from the seniors fellowship, the quilting group and the book club, as they calibrated his transition from bereavement to self-sufficiency. Did Vaughn drop off groceries? Slip in and do chores? Leonard remembered the earnest young couple in training to be missionaries who showed up with a "Grieving God's Way" pamphlet and then continued to call, as if he'd signed up to be their practice heathen. A visit from Vaughn in there would have been a true relief. But his friend was right. They would not have had a talk like this. These were words saved for later, and not just anyone would dare to say them even now.

Leonard looks past Pinky and his stuttering leg. Vaughn's eyes are fixed on the street, his body turned a quarter off the wheel as if he's about to jump out the door himself. Leonard says, "Sorry, too. I shoulda called you an ambulance that day. I thought you were just fakin'."

Vaughn turns Leonard's way, against the twist of his torso. He blinks twice before he says, "It's all right. I think I was born to be a little crooked. *We will not regret the past nor wish to shut the door on it.* That's from the Big Book."

Pinky nods. "You can't regret shit. Remember—but not regret."

"I know you two're tryin' to make it better," Leonard says, "but there ain't no better for what I got."

The pizza place is dark. Some motorcycles burble away from a bar, flowing through the traffic circle around the little square, spinning off toward the lights leading to the freeway. A woman hugs her chest to the back of the last rider. Black top, bare legs and cowboy boots. What was her name? All Leonard can think of is *Wanted.*

"Guess we're done," Leonard says. "No need to take me back up tonight. Just drop me across to the Super 8, and I'll check with the police tomorrow." Like hell. He has no money and no idea what he'll do next.

"You could stay with us. More the merrier, huh, Pinky?"

"You and Bryce don't have that place anymore?"

The question stops Pinky's bouncing leg. "Me'n Bryce're on differnt pages these days."

"Yeah, Bryce's page is the Game and Fish shit list," Vaughn says.

"He got caught peddlin' trophy elk last summer," Pink says. "Just the racks. Poachin' *and* leavin' the meat. He deserved it."

"Pinky's been workin' on his Steps, Len," Vaughn says, but it's clear the line is directed at Pinky.

Leonard isn't interested in listening to their recovery talk. Any kind of talk makes him tired now, but even worse is the too-closeness of people wanting to be helpful with that *surrender to a higher power* shit. At least have the honesty to call it giving up.

"I still got a ways to go," Pinky says.

He looks over to Vaughn, who shrugs and says, "Up to you."

Pinky's leg starts working the invisible treadle again. "It was all Bryce's idea. I shouldn'ta went along."

"What was Bryce's idea—the elk?" Leonard says.

"You know."

"He don't know, I told you," says Vaughn.

"So what're we talkin' about?" says Leonard.

Pinky's leg bobs faster. His shoulders slump and his head drops. "Burnin' your stable."

The stable. It takes him a moment. The stable's long gone to ashes, buried and left behind with the rest of the ranch. The stable burning. He runs it back: the confusion in the dark, the ice in the tank, the rumble of the fire and the pitch of the horses' cries, the smell—how the smoke was not one thing but a nightmare scent commingling cedar and rubber and hay and horseflesh, the sweet jumbled with the hellish. And Junior on his knees, tongue-tangled, soot-faced, his red-rimmed eyes drooping on stalks of tears. Guilty, the boy cried. Guilty, they all thought.

So there was another version: Bryce and Pinky sneaking through the dark to the stable. Throwing something up against the back wall, lighting it, moving off to watch it burn. Surprised to see Junior burst out with one of the horses. Leonard running around in his long johns. Them pretending to help with the fire so they could see his shock up close. And afterward, how they must've celebrated. No chance of getting caught after the boy's confession.

If Pinky's after absolution, Leonard thinks, he and Bryce should've applied long ago, and not to him. Redemption was always Inetta's department. Now it's too late for amends. Too late for everyone, but especially for Junior. The poor kid always got hind tit, bottom rung, last picked, back of the line, short straw.

"Stop the truck!" Leonard growls.

"Come on, Len…" Vaughn says.

All his life he's burned with a slow fuse, and look where it got him. "Stop it right now!"

Pinky leans his head back. "I want to…"

"Stop the goddamn truck!"

Vaughn hits the brakes. Pinky lurches forward to catch himself on the dash. Leonard hits the door with his shoulder and half spins to the roadside. He steps into an alkali flat tamped down by semis taking a break from the interstate. "Get out here."

"I ain't gonna fight you," Pinky says.

"He'd hurt you, Len."

"Now!" Leonard takes a step back and thrusts a finger to the ground before him. "I ain't gonna fight. I want you to hear a thing or two."

Pinky leaves the cab warily, like an old man lowering himself into a hot bath. Canopy lights from the nearby Shell station glow behind him so Leonard can barely make out his face in the fleeting dusk.

"So you want to make amends for the stable. You ever hear of Hardy Crimmins, Junior? Not his old man. The boy. That night after you and Bryce come around, he was down on his knees beggin' me to forgive him. For burnin' my stable. Maybe that's where you oughta be."

Pinky lowers one knee to the ground, ready to fend off the charge he still fears may be coming.

"All right, that's a good start, but this ain't no marriage proposal."

Pinky drops the other knee.

"Okay. Now go ahead and say you're sorry. You didn't mean it. It was a accident. Bryce made you do it. Whatever it is you have to say to me."

Pinky turns his palms forward in supplication. "Maybe this ain't the best time…"

"Well, you be sure to get back to me when it's more goddamn convenient! Meantime, I want to help you think about what you two done. Look down. Whatta you see?"

"The ground, I guess."

Leonard scuffs the hard soil in front of Pinky. "Feel of it. What is it?"

"Warm?"

Leonard kicks harder and sends up a spray of grit.

"Dirt, sand. I dunno, dust?" Pinky says.

"That's right. Little grains and pieces of you don't even know what. Junior was only twelve years old then and already he's gone to dust.

"You and Bryce with your damn sneaky-ass revenge might as well've burned him up along with them three horses that never did nothin' against you. And whatever you thought, I didn't do nothin' either. Worst I did against you was make Bryce drive home in his undies. You screwed up your lives all by your own selves. You're sorry but you don't even know what for.

"So this boy takes the blame for your crime. He did one little wrong smokin' in the stable, and so he thought he done the big one, too, and he faced up to it. He didn't lie, he didn't weasel, he was scared shitless, and still he was ready to take what come to 'im."

Leonard turns his back on Pinky and walks a slow circle. "And you know what happened when he begged me on his knees? I was so goddamn disgusted, I couldn't say a word. A man should be able to forgive a twelve-year-old boy. Instead, I cut 'im loose. Never saw 'im again. Never saw 'im again except for a picture in the paper—and when he was just some little bits of bone and dust. So, yeah, it's good to say you're sorry for the things you did, but the hardest amends are the sorries for what you didn't do."

Leonard returns to stand over Pinky. "Here's the deal. You can't make nothin' up to me. I'm past it. The stable's long gone. The boy's dead. You can't make it up to Junior. You and me didn't mean to let 'im go down the drain, but we both of us had a hand in it. He thought he burned my stable because of you, and he thought he could never be forgiven because of me. So here's what we're gonna do about this amends business."

Leonard leans on Pinky's shoulder and eases himself down to his knees. He pulls out his empty wallet. It's two pieces of cheap cowhide laced together, but supple from the attention of a man who knows how to keep leather working, worn to a near ebony on the flank side and a sunburst pattern where his fingers fish for it in his pocket. He spreads it flat across his palm and displays to Pinky the tooling on its two halves. Two words, all caps: LEN, it says on the darkened side, and DAD on the other.

"This come like a letter from a dead man, too damn late. But we ain't. We're still here. We're gonna go find us the woman who brought me this and tell 'er her brother didn't burn the stable. That's it. That's the best we can do."

"I wish I'd catch on to the lesson better the first time they teach it," Pinky says. "Fuck the motel. You come back with us." He offers his arm and Leonard pulls himself up against the younger man.

Back in the truck, Vaughn taps Pinky's knee and says, *Now, that wasn't so bad, was it?* The knee's answer is stillness.

"She's calling," Vaughn says. "Again. Shit."

He takes Meg's call this time, stepping out of the truck and circling with his head down. He appears to be having two conversations—one that makes him smile and one that makes him scowl and rub the back of this head. When he returns, his face is serious.

"They found your truck."

"Where?"

"Where we're goin'—Dinosaur Hill. Cops called Joe's phone lookin' for you."

Dinosaur Hill, where a century before a paleontologist discovered a great trove of dinosaur bones he sent to a museum back east. Now it's a scree-covered park with an interpretive trail that loops back to the old dinosaur mine. They cross the river and head up the road toward the Monument.

"Did she say how it was?" Leonard can't bring himself to ask about the ashes.

"I think it's okay. They used it to hold up Jack-a-Lope Liquors and must've had their own wheels stashed up there in the parking lot."

A police cruiser blocks the entrance and another one is

pulled further in, its headlights casting a glow from behind a darkened hump of earth. The truck must be in there somewhere.

"This here's the owner," says Vaughn to an officer.

The cop pulls out his flashlight and checks Leonard's ID. "Registration for the vehicle?"

Under a whiskey bottle left at Vaughn's back step. Leonard shakes his head.

"Can you verify your whereabouts earlier this evening, Mr. Self? It's something we have to check."

"I didn't rob no liquor store."

"I understand, sir, but vehicles used in the commission of a crime sometimes have a way of being reported stolen when they weren't. And yours, well, we've had several calls about this truck today."

"What calls?"

The officer flips back a few pages in a notebook. "Post office downtown. Rocket Park. Another one from a private residence concerned about the driver's mental state. She didn't give a name, but the vehicle could've been yours. Do any of these sound familiar?"

The dog nazi. The lady with the kids. Winnie. Why were all these women tracking him? "Spilled a gal's drink out on I Road. Anybody call you about that?"

The cop looks at him quizzically and Vaughn steers Leonard away a few steps. "He's had a rough day. Can he get his truck?"

"Well, it was used in the hold-up and we're still getting the evidence from it. Do you need it tonight?"

"He lives way up on Glade Park," says Vaughn. "It's all the wheels he's got."

"We can work it out, then. Come on with me." The officer heads up the drive.

"Was there a urn in the front?" Leonard asks.

"Excuse me?"

"A urn. A blue clay pot."

"Let's ask Officer Hostetter. She's doing the forensics."

A compact woman with short blonde hair and latex gloves is wiping down a door handle with a swab on a long stick. As they approach, she keeps her concentration, dropping her sample into a plastic bag and sealing it before she looks up.

"This is Mr. Self, the owner. He wants to know if he can get his truck tonight."

Officer Hostetter looks Leonard over, then to the other cop. "I think we're almost good here," she says, "but I'd like to get a DNA sample from you, sir, if I may. You don't have to consent, but your DNA is already in these pouches, along with the bad guys'. It all goes to the CBI lab, and once it's there, into the criminal database. It's so we can sort you out, for your protection. We don't like to put innocent people in there who don't belong."

DNA. Leonard didn't know what the letters stood for and he barely understood what it was. Something in his bones, his genes, a sort of chemical fingerprint that separated him from the rapists and murderers and connected him all the way back to the cavemen. A necklace packed tight with beads of information on human life, but not like your regular life, which was mostly the string. What difference did it make if they had it? What difference on earth if they didn't? He'd said he and Pinky were going to go talk to Junior's sister. Did he mean it? That was before he had his truck back...

"Can I look inside?"

She nods, indicating the open door. "It's a very quick procedure, sir. I just swipe the inside of your cheek with one of these and we're done."

The dome light illuminates the cab and he peers across the driver's seat to the opposite corner where he'd left Inetta's urn. It's dark on the floorboard but the yellow streak in the glaze picks up the light. The stopper is still tight.

"I'm very sorry, sir," says Officer Hostetter. "I had to look inside the container, but the contents seem to be in place. You can check for damage and let us know if there's anything missing. Looks like they cleaned out your job box in the back. You can file a report. And the keys. We've looked around and haven't found them. I hope you brought a spare set."

Vaughn sees Leonard sag, nudges him, extends a key.

"Nice of you to offer, but I shouldn't take the Jimmy," Leonard says.

Vaughn holds up the key near the tip of Leonard's nose. "I couldn't figure what the hell this was doin' on my stoop," he says. "Then you called, and I thought it was some scheme—signin' your truck over and then reportin' it stolen—but that ain't you. Still don't get it, so feel free to clue me in some day. Right now, though, I'm in a heap of shit with Meg, and you're gonna get me out. Remember that perfessional discretion I told you about? I think I gotta go back on it."

No Next

Inetta had said she'd be watching. Well, if she was, she was going to see him laugh. She was going to hear his voice echo off the red cliffs of the Monument. She was going to stand by while he opened wide and let this lady cop take some of his saliva and seal it in a pouch. He was innocent enough. He didn't know where his DNA would go and didn't care. It could dry up and blow away with the rest of him, a particle of dust collected someday by a spaceship come to figure out how the hell anything had once lived in this inhospitable place. Right now, he didn't care about any of it but getting up to Artists Point.

Inetta had said to him: *Why should you care whether the Creator made the whole universe or just nudged one atom that rolled and rolled into this big old complicated ball? Either way, God's work. It's still a miracle.*

She had always said he wouldn't know a miracle if it bit him in the behind.

The valley he's leaving used to be a sea, now dry as a brick with a scatter of dinosaur bones. He's climbing a thousand acres of sand dunes turned to stone. Fremont people vanished. Utes banished. Cattle trails overgrown. CCC camps passing out of memory. The Fruita Dugway abandoned. Winking antenna masts on the Black Ridge await their turn. Below him the citrine glow of the city, weeping the earth's energy through a million shining wounds. Layer upon layer of time lifted before him, more than he can fathom, as he crawls up the face of the Monument with his little bucket of bone.

You shouldn't always look for the end of things, Inetta would say right now, and she'd have a point.

"Well, here we are." Leonard says it aloud. To himself. To Inetta. He stops short of the stubby sign, his front tire bumping against the red sandstone curb. He shuts off his truck, leaving the window down. A familiar bouquet loiters around a mixed clump of sage, juniper and piñon. He looks across canyon and valley, to where the oceanic sky meets the long earthen reef of the Grand Mesa. Below him, the prow of Artists Point. Both blunt and colorless now, merging into the deepening darkness.

How often he had been here, restless, patrolling the boundaries past the barricades while Inetta shot her Kodak—before she switched to a sketchbook, which extended his wait even longer. He killed time, kicking stones off the edge, hooting after echoes, stretching and yawning and twirling his hat. He sat in the truck fingering dust out of the dashboard louvers and listening to the station that played Hank Williams, George Jones and the Stanley Brothers. Used to. Now it played preachers nonstop.

It's a short walk down to the overlook, where a waist-high fence runs along the point. Painted a fleshy tone to match the sandstone, its top rail has been worn to silver. As he descends the stretched Z of the stone staircase, he recalls how Inetta went down these same steps as if on a wedding march, slowly, her sketchbook husbanded under her arm. Later, as he fussed above, she climbed back to him, radiant, all his again. His impatience always dissolved in that moment, and he knew he would return with her the next time she asked.

And now here he is with and without her. This time it's his turn to take the steps slowly, reverently, bringing his right foot flush with his left before descending to the next, the way he'd always planned it. He tries once more to grasp her intent, the reason she wanted him here. What was her plan?

"You're out kind of late, cowboy."

The words come up behind him, smile-sharpened, and slip between his ribs. He turns but doesn't see anyone. He knows the voice, though.

"I kept looking for your invitation."

"Got behind on my mail," Leonard says.

"Opening it, too, I bet."

Sarcasm doesn't bother him when it's the truth. "Sent you somethin' just today, though it might have some postage due on it."

"That's sweet of you," says Elliott. "I'll look forward to it."

Inetta's brother sits on a shelf where a spreading juniper found a fault in the rock and made the most of it. The last few times Leonard saw him, Elliott dressed like a lawyer down to the shiny loafers. Tonight, he wears running shoes, a broad-brimmed hat and the kind of jeans that come from the store looking half worn out. His peach-colored dress shirt, though, is starched and pressed.

"Help me up, will you?" Elliott says, reaching toward Leonard. "I got stiff sitting here. What time is it, anyway? My phone's dead from roaming in this dead zone and whenever I wear a watch in this town, I just end up frustrated."

Elliott's are numbers hands—the hands of a man whose

work smoothes the way with dinners, telephone calls and favors.

"I'm really glad to see you." Elliott wraps Leonard in a side hug. "Thank God I packed something to read. And then there was the floor show."

"What floor show?"

"A gentleman on a motorcycle brought his lady friend up here. They seemed to appreciate the view from the railing. Anyway, I meant to catch you at the ranch. I was supposed to hitch a ride on Rai's jet with Amanda—Mrs. W number three—but she decided to go to Palm Desert instead of Aspen. You probably don't know this, but it's not that easy booking commercial into here at the last minute."

Elliott is smiling now like he enjoyed the challenge and Leonard wonders if he smiled for the boss's wife when she changed her plans.

"Vaughn told me when you missed me, you all figured you could just hook up with me here," Leonard says. "I wasn't meanin' to cut you out. Thought I was sparin' you. Didn't think you knew."

Elliott takes a grip on his shoulder, hands no longer so soft. "Of course I knew. Inetta told me. That's how things are supposed to work in families. And I knew you'd do what she asked—to the letter and the day. We both knew. I just didn't expect this would turn out to be a midnight matinee."

"Me, either. My truck got stole on the way. Some boys robbed a liquor store drive-up with it."

"Oh, God, I really don't miss this country," Elliott says. "But otherwise things are okay? At the ranch it looks like you've been busy."

"Cleanin' up a few loose ends."

"Loose ends! The house was stripped down to the walls.

The barn's so clean it looks like you're ready to open for summer stock."

"Wouldn't know what that is. Sold off the livestock."

Elliott makes a time-out signal. "Joke. Summer stock's a kind of theater. My sister was good at reading your slants and silences. I'm not. Answer the question like I'm an idiot child. Are things okay up there?"

"I got a offer on the table."

"Yes... And..."

"This woman come along and said she had a buyer. Not a buyer, exactly—a tax deal. I started the paperwork."

"Planning to show it to anyone? An attorney? Maybe your brother-in-law, the business guy?"

Leonard shrugs.

Elliott steps in closer. "What's this?" He touches Leonard's shoulder near his collar. "You're a mess. It looks like blood."

"I s'pose. Cracked my head."

"Did you think to maybe wash it? You've got blood on your hat, too." Elliott takes a bottle of water from the gym bag. "Put your head down."

Leonard bends over and feels the still-cool water run over his scalp, around his ear, down his neck and over his cheekbones to the ground.

"Better?" Elliott says, dropping the empty bottle next to the bag. A golden mesa ridged in ochre. High Country Living.

"Looks like Vaughn set you up pretty good."

"It was nice of him."

"And how did you two hook up again?"

"Pure luck. He was dropping someone at the airport. He recognized me from the funeral. Look, I tried to call. I had no choice but to just show up. I'm here because of Inetta, but mostly I came for you."

Leonard shifts his weight. "Coulda been more appreciative when you offered to help out."

"That's not what I'm talking about. You have people who love you. Someone's made you an offer and now it looks like you're ready to take it and move on with life."

"Looks like."

"You have to decide what you really want." Elliott has succeeded in business by veiling his thoughts and dampening his emotions. Maybe Elliott's mask is now turned toward him.

"Figure you know more about that than I do."

"What do you mean?"

"Someone else said that same exact thing to me almost," Leonard says. "You know a Meg Mogrin?"

Elliott pauses. "I do."

"And so you already know about the deal you been quizzin' me on."

Elliott answers at a whisper. "I was hoping to convince you to take it…"

"Ain't that kind of a roundabout way to do it?"

"Very. But you may recall my straightforward offers didn't get too far. I thought I had to work around your pride if I was going to be any help at all."

"So you're the secret client she was talkin' about. Didn't realize you had that kind of money."

"The money's Rai's. I put together some ideas and brought them to him. He signed off because there was something in it for him and because he adores me—more than the boss really should. He doesn't need more land but he can use the Colorado tax credit. I found Meg and she seemed sharp enough to handle the front end and keep me out of it. Otherwise, I was afraid you'd just see it as your brother-in-law stepping on your affairs."

"You're right, I would." He'd thought doing everything himself would be simpler, but now he sees the pattern. Inetta, of course. Elliott and Rai Winterzee. Meg Mogrin and the Persian poet. Vaughn, Winnie and the police. Donnie Barclay and Terri. Even Pinky and the reporter. Only one missing is the Lone Ranger. "It woulda been a lot simpler if I'd said yes to you in the first place."

"Well, if you're ready to start listening to me now, I have a suggestion."

"Okay."

"Let's not do this in the dark." It's not too dark to see the bright bead in Elliott's eye. "Don't mean to take over—just that I've done way too many of these."

Leonard thinks back to his dry run, how he'd put no ritual to it. How casting the gravel from the can had reminded him of scattering chicken scratch.

He feels he has to say it. "She said her and Jesus'd be watchin' today."

"I'm sure Jesus can see in the dark just fine, but I was thinking about us. We could say something tonight for Inetta and then come back in the morning."

Another thing he hadn't planned. The only poetic lines he can recall are *Ashes to ashes, dust to dust* and *Don't go back to sleep*. Maybe this was why people held onto their Bibles, for the times that drove them beyond their own words.

"Don't know if this is right," he begins. "You were with us there at the start, Elliott, and I'm sure Inetta's glad to see you here now. I am, too. She used to get on me when I'd gripe about the way somethin' turned out. She'd say, *You don't even know how a computer works—how can you pretend to know how God works?* Her point was, if we can't fit our pea brains around God's intentions in the world, that's man fallin' short. Well, then I've surely fallen, because I don't understand why the most God-lovin' woman on earth had to die before me. She loved her Bible and all, but this was her holiest place. She'd come out here to throw her arms around creation like it was all the proof she needed. May her soul rest here in peace. I loved her more than anything I can say."

Elliott nods. "She was right." He cocks his head for moment, lets the silence lap around them. "You are right. This is what God wants us to see. Peace and quiet is what he really sounds like. Someone always wants to fill it up for you. With cathedrals and mosques. With prayers and incantations and hallelujahs. Inetta understood. She didn't bother talking us heathens into God. She just tried to draw us into the big picture.

"I've got to say this, Len. My hometown thought a faggot deserved whatever happened to him. My parents were sure I was going to hell. I thought I might as well go. Somehow my sister came away from the same town and the same church filled with love and compassion. She saved my life. But she didn't do it alone. You came along and got her out of there, and then you both let me see what love was really like."

He opens his arms toward Leonard. "You took me in like a brother. I thought you knew and you accepted me for what I was. I thought that was so amazing—a hick like you!—and then later I realized you were totally clueless in those days... but it's all good now. You gave me exactly what I needed at the time, and you gave it to her, too."

No side hug this time. Leonard enters the orbit of Elliott's embrace.

"Guess I'm your ride," Leonard says.

"I guess you are."

"Which hotel you at?"

"Uh-uh," Elliott says. "The ranch."

"You sure? You saw the place."

"It's been a long time since I got to sleep in a barn."

Listening to Elliott read is almost like hearing Inetta's voice again. The windows are down for the breeze and Leonard drives slowly. The urn secures the stack of letters in Elliott's lap and his sister's words hover in the dome-lit space of the cab, drawing husband and brother together. Though he knew she wrote to Elliott often, Leonard never gave much thought to what she might be saying—never considered how he would figure in her letters beyond news of broken ribs and late nights in the foaling shed—yet there he was:

> We've had a bad week here. The stable caught fire Tuesday night and three horses killed, the stable a total loss. Our foster boy, Junior, fell asleep with a cigarette.
>
> Len had to tell the truth about what happened. (You know how he is.) Will make it right with the owners somehow, but this means we're out of the boarding business for good, I'm sure.
>
> I am worried about Len. He's taking it hard. He always acts like nothing bothers him, but I can tell this goes deep. Sometimes he gets these black spells and thinks there's no hope for anything. Isn't it something a man so steady and true can't take heart from the good he puts in the world? I try to remind him what he has accomplished, how he has persevered to give us a good life. We have been so blessed, and this is just a bump in the road.
>
> *Love, Sis*

Sis. He had always tried to be the same person to every-one, reliable and unsurprising—yes, steady. But this wife-woman-sister-friend who always spoke to him in one voice was someone a little different to Elliott, as she may have been to everyone who knew her. Being consistent and staying within bounds was his idea of integrity. He was not wrong about that, but he saw his boundaries were too small. Inetta's path through life seemed so modest and indistinct, too, scarcely more than a game trail, yet it connected with other trails that stretched across the valley and then on and on. Elliott and Larry. The quilting circles, the classes, the potters shop. Shower of Blessings Holiness Temple, Reverend Peasely and the Bible study group. Winnie and the rest of the book club. The ones who bought her eggs at the door or her quilts in town. The Barclays. The women who came out to groom and ride their horses. Junior and Shannon. The doctors and nurses. Ted from the hospice. The visitors who filled the house when he was so dazed he could hardly see. All the people he had dodged, ignored or fled, she connected him to and maybe they saw him anyway, illuminated in her unwavering light. The way she knew him.

It's shorter to the ranch from the west via the back gravel cutoff, but he stays on Monument Road all the way to the main fork at the east end. He's out here later than he's ever been, and it's worth it to rise along the shoulder of No Thoroughfare Canyon and swoop down upon a sleeping Glade Park. Solitary yard lights spread below him. In the dark from a distance, it's hard to tell which belong to the old places and which to the newcomers. He can't see it, but he can smell the sweetness. Someone's started haying.

He runs through the day's leftover business. Explaining to Vaughn about the truck. Picking up the dog and apologizing to Winnie. He'll have to sign some papers with Meg Mogrin he doesn't care to read. A taillight needs a bulb and over the front step, too. He should tell the police about his missing gun. He'll have to locate Shannon Crimmins and let her hear the truth about Junior. Him and Pinky. Somewhere at the ranch is a shorthand tablet with a few blank pages left in it. He'll have to start himself a new list.

It's dark once they get past Fokken's place, the stars more like advertisements for light than useful illumination, but Leonard knows both sides and every foot of road ahead. The fence posts are straight and the wire snug. The culvert where the creek sneaks under the road is clear on both ends. And at the top of the rise, the headlights will catch the free compact disk from America Online he stuck to a post to mark his driveway.

He'd started this day without the words he needed to corner his thoughts. Knowing a thing and saying it was the difference between fixing something yourself and describing how to do it. The difference between feeling love in your heart and sounding like a damn greeting card. Most of the day, he'd tried not to think on it, but now he finally can say where he'd gone off track. Love was the doing not the undoing. It was the going not the stopping. It was the remembering not the forgetting. The earth, not the heavens. The being, not the been.

Leonard stops the truck and reaches across to stay Elliott from jumping down. *Hang on*, he says, and then he gets out to open the gate.

CHARLIE QUIMBY

Charlie Quimby's writing life has always crossed divides. A playwright turned critic. A protest songwriter who marketed for a defense contractor. A blogger who covers tax policy and the realities of homelessness. He's made other people sound good in the *Harvard Business Review* and at the NFL Hall of Fame. Splitting time between Minneapolis and his native Colorado inspired this novel.

www.CharlieQuimby.com

TORREY HOUSE PRESS

The economy is a wholly owned subsidiary of the environment, not the other way around.
—Senator Gaylord Nelson, founder of Earth Day

Headquartered in Salt Lake City and Torrey, Utah, Torrey House Press is an independent book publisher of fiction and nonfiction about the environment, people, cultures, and resource management issues relating to America's wild places. Torrey House Press endeavors to increase appreciation for the importance of natural landscape through the power of pen and story. Through the *2% to the West* program, Torrey House Press donates two percent of sales to not-for-profit environmental organizations and funds a scholarship for up-and-coming writers at colleges throughout the West.

Visit **www.torreyhouse.com** for our thought-provoking discussion guides, author interviews, and more.

Forthcoming from Torrey House Press

My So-Called Ruined Life
by Melanie Bishop (January 2014)
Having lost her parents to murder and the judicial system, Tate McCoy tries to take control of her seventeenth summer.

Wild Rides and Wildflowers: Philosophy and Botany with Bikes
by Scott Abbott and Sam Rushforth (March 2014)
Two guys on bikes offer often humorous, sometimes poignant insights into the male psyche, botany, philosophy, and true friendship.

Available now from Torrey House Press

Facing the Change: Personal Encounters with Global Warming
Edited by Steven Pavlos Holmes
Through personal and vivid encounters with climate change, this diverse array of writers inspires readers toward awareness and action.

A Bushel's Worth: An Ecobiography
by Kayann Short
Rooted where the Rocky Mountains meet the prairie, Short's love story of land celebrates our connection to soil and each other.

Evolved: Chronicles of a Pleistocene Mind
by Maximilian Werner
Werner explores how our Pleistocene instincts inform our everyday decisions and behaviors in this modern-day Walden.

The Legend's Daughter
by David Kranes
These fast-paced stories set in contemporary Idaho explore intricate dynamics between fathers and sons, unlikely friends, people and place.

Grind
by Mark Maynard
The gritty realism of Hemingway joins the irreverence of Edward Abbey in these linked short stories set in and around Reno, Nevada.

The Ordinary Truth
by Jana Richman
Today's western water wars and one family's secrets divide three generations of women as urban and rural values collide.

Recapture
by Erica Olsen
This captivating short story collection explores canyons, gulches, and vast plains of memory along with colorful landscapes of the West.

Tributary
by Barbara K. Richardson
A courageous young woman flees polygamy in 1860s Utah, but finds herself drawn back to the landscapes that shaped her.

The Scholar of Moab
by Steven L. Peck
Philosophy meets satire, poetry, cosmology, and absurdity in this tragicomic brew of magical realism and rural Mormon Utah.

The Plume Hunter
by Renée Thompson
Love and lives are lost amid conflict over killing wild birds for women's hats in Oregon and California in the late nineteenth century.

Crooked Creek
by Maximilian Werner
Blood Meridian finds *A Farewell to Arms* in this short and beautiful novel set in 1890s Utah.